Antonio's Wife

Antonio's Wife

a novel by Jacqueline DeJohn

ReganBooks
An Imprint of HarperCollins *Publishers*

Photographs on pages xii, 4, and 426 © by Hulton Archive/Getty Images. Photograph on page 214 © by J. S. Johnston/The New-York Historical Society.

HarperCollins books may be purchased for educational, business, or sales promotional use. For information please write: Special Markets Department, HarperCollins Publishers Inc., 10 East 53rd Street, New York, NY 10022.

FIRST EDITION

Designed by Diane Hobbing of Snap_Haus Graphics
with Stephanie Goralnick

Printed on acid-free paper

Library of Congress Cataloging-in-Publication Data
DeJohn, Jacqueline.
    Antonio's wife : a novel / Jacqueline DeJohn.— 1st ed.
        p. cm.
    ISBN 0-06-055800-8 (acid-free paper)
    1. Abandoned children—Fiction. 2. New York (N.Y.)—Fiction. 3. Married women—Fiction. 4. Women singers—Fiction. 5. Birthmothers—Fiction. 6. Opera—Fiction. I. Title.
PS3604.E37A84 2004
813'.54—dc21

2003047205

04 05 06 07 08 BVG/RRD 10 9 8 7 6 5 4 3 2 1

For my great-grandmother Anna and my

grandmother Filomina,

whose lives inspired this tale.

And

for my parents, John and Josephine,

whose love compelled me to tell it.

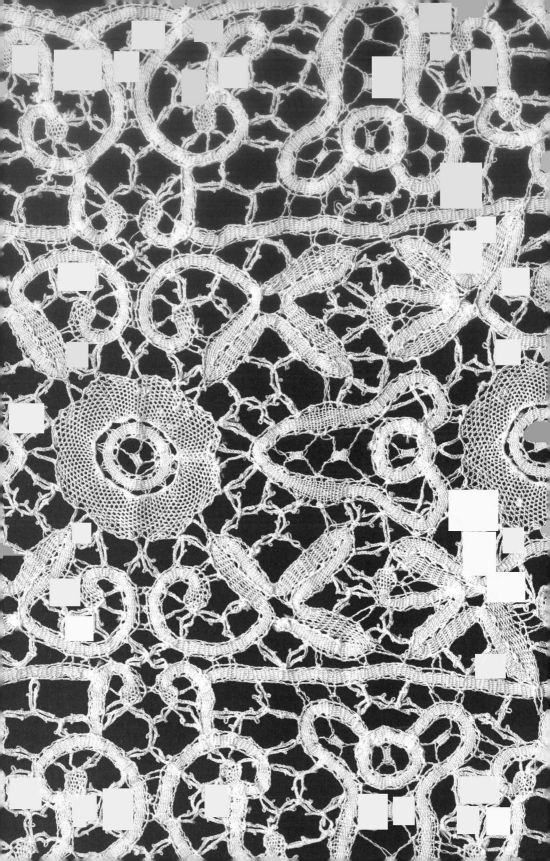

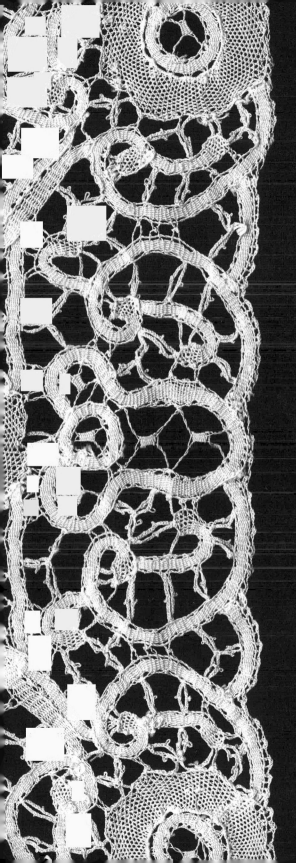

Contents

Acklnowledgments

*T*HERE ARE MANY PEOPLE who contribute knowingly or unknowingly to a novelist's work. Good minestrone isn't made without adding a lot of ingredients to the pot and letting them lovingly simmer.

Over the years, many unwitting influences added to the broth: teachers, friends, strangers, lovers, novelists, and filmmakers. Everyone and everything was thrown in to intermingle and enrich *Antonio's Wife*. If you find yourself bobbing among the unmentioned and you are reading this, I thank you in my heart, if not on the printed page, for your encouragement, respect, and the spice you've added.

Destino's hand stirred the pot over the years. I can best trace its efforts on my behalf by expressing my gratitude: first to the Onondaga Public Library in Syracuse, New York. There, as an adolescent, I idled away summer days, sitting in a window seat at its Hazard Branch, reading and dreaming of someday becoming a writer.

When I returned, many years later, to that same branch to work on *Antonio's Wife,* the library staff lent me their overwhelming encouragement and support. Many thanks to Nazaree White, Walter Noiseauz, Janice Rathburn, Celeste Moore, Rose Zeppetello, Becky Bernas, and Zita Colagiovanni. Special thanks to head librarian, now retired, Karen Pitoniak and to Patricia Gottschall for reading early drafts of my work. As the first person to read and then reread *Antonio's Wife,* Patricia provided insightful comments that were rich stew bones for my broth.

In Italy, Signora Rose Rossi, head librarian of the Neapolitan section of La Biblioteca Nazionale di Napoli, miraculously opened her doors for me in September 2001, when they were firmly locked for renovation. The information, friendship, and espresso she and her staff provided were priceless. Thanks also to the Teatro San Carlo in Napoli for allowing me to do research and for giving me a backstage tour. In Rocca San Felice I thank Signor Lucio DiVito for his many kindnesses, including translating and deciphering family genealogy. *Tutti amici, grazie tanto!*

In Sicily my good friend Signora Connie DiBella opened her heart and home to me, then introduced me to Victoria Granof, who led me to Amye Dwyer. Connie and Victoria led me to my publisher, Judith Regan.

Judith was the publisher *destino* picked and Aliza Fogelson became my editor. What can I say about Aliza? She has been a tireless champion for *Antonio's Wife*. It was Aliza who saw its early merits and it was her patience, knowledge, and editing skills that helped me refine and enrich the story until it became *brodo forte* containing what I hope is the perfect balance of meat and spice. Thank you, Aliza, for your complete faith in my ability and your gentle seasoning. I will always be grateful.

I also offer my sincere thanks to Fordham University's Mitch Rabinowitz and its computer lab, as well as those who read and gave me comments about the early drafts: Linda Frasier, Ann Guerrini, Gina Kuriakose, Tara Cappello, Kevin Moloney, and Cheryl Strear. And to Evan Marshall, Rosemary Carroll, Martin Landey, Mort Janklow, Michael J. Walsh, and other professionals at the top of their fields, thank you for your time and effort. Most of you scarcely knew me; your generosity kept me on *destino*'s path.

Finally, if you, the reader are moved to write or create . . . trust that you have all the ingredients you need to start your own minestrone. I promise spice will be provided along the way and *destino* will do the rest.

Prologue

FEBRUARY 9, 1950

Naples, Italy

THE BOBBINS

ℰVENING IS CREEPING UP THE HILL—
side toward my balcony; I feel the air growing cool, but the rays of sun are still warm on my hands as I work the bobbins and place the pins. Listen. Can you hear the sea wind rustle the leaves of the twisted olive trees on the hill? Do you hear them laughing . . . whispering . . . *"la figlia di put-tana, la figlia di puttana,"* the daughter of the whore? No? Perhaps you can hear them calling "Antonio's wife . . . Antonio's wife". . . .

Those were names I answered to long ago, but they're gone now . . . just memories, part of a story I like to tell about who I used to be, before I was reborn. There, look! See how beautiful the Bay of Naples is? It clutches at the dancing skirts of the Mediterranean like a jealous lover. And on the far side, on the beach at Mergellina, the fishermen are still mending their nets just as they did the day I departed for America.

Come. Come closer, pull your chair up next to mine. Would you like to learn about the lace or hear about the mysterious events that brought me back to life? I can tell you now that everything is over and done, all the threads snipped, and the lace lifted from the pillow. I can explain why the strands had to be twisted and tied in such an intricate design. What the mystics would term *destino* is just a stubborn thread worked into an elaborate piece of lace, of which we are all but a small part.

It's odd, but even though I learned to work lace over fifty years ago and understand some of the threads' comings and goings, I'm still a novice when I look at the complexity of the Master's work. It seems we are conscious of the patterns in His majestic design only in the moments when we're closest to the earth and stars, when we lay down our petty struggles and are swept up in something greater, like nature . . . childbirth . . . death. Sometimes, if we're lucky, our pattern is whispered to us by the saints when we knead the bread, hang the wash, or turn the record over. But we come closest to seeing a repeating motif or recognizing familiar threads moving through time just before we drift off to sleep. As we give up our struggle and fall into sleep, the tangle of bobbins is lifted and for an instant the pricking of the pattern is clear. . . .

My life was a tangled web before *destino* led me to the opera house. That was where I was reborn and found my way in the weeks after I met the diva. In those days I wasn't myself . . . no—not the woman you see before you. I was another. I did my best in those days to pass through life without causing a ripple, without making a sound. I left no trace, for I was no one and wished to stay hidden, like the pricked pattern fastened to the lacemaker's pillow. . . .

Part I

NOVEMBER 6, 1908

New York City

THE THREADS

Chapter One

THE SOPRANO PLAYING TOSCA threw out her arm and showed the knife she'd been hiding in the folds of her skirt. The blade glittered wickedly in the stage lights, the music reached a crescendo, then, unexpectedly, she jammed the pearl-handled knife she'd been holding into her own chest.

"No, no, no!" she shouted in heavily accented English. "I would rather kill myself than submit!"

She gripped the villain Scarpia's jacket as she struggled in a death throe. The baritone's massive body lurched forward as she sank to her knees. A tremor passed through her body, her grip lost its power, and she fell backward onto the ornate Persian carpet, dead.

Everyone watching gasped. Tosca wasn't supposed to kill herself; she was supposed to stab the evil Scarpia, who had just demanded sex in return for her lover's safety.

The Manhattan Opera House was filled with invited guests and press who'd come to watch the final dress rehearsal. They buzzed as they scrambled for their libretti. The opera was new to many, perhaps they'd missed something.

In the wings the cast and crew edged forward. Everything had been proceeding smoothly and the production was sure to be a huge success; now this. . . .

"Hey, Franco," a stagehand high above in the flies called to his friend. "She's at it again!"

The men were preparing the flats and backdrops for the next scene, the battlements of the Castle Sant'Angelo.

"The *Times* reporter's out front too!" Franco said, shaking his head as he gazed down on the prone soprano. "What the hell's wrong now?"

"It's the knife. It's too small. Besides, she hates that baritone, Bonzinni. Hammerstein should have sacked him months ago. His tempo's always off. Mark my words, she won't go on until they give in."

"How are they going to get out of this? Tosca's dead!"

"Ya got me."

They watched in grim amusement as everyone checked his libretto.

"Yes," everyone whispered, poking a finger, "it's right here!"

At this point in the music, Tosca was supposed to have turned, flashed the knife for all to see, and stabbed Scarpia in the chest. "This is the kiss of Tosca!" she was supposed to have cried as she thrust the knife. They read on. Mortally wounded, Scarpia was supposed to have fallen to his knees . . . unable to call for help as the blood rose in his throat . . . Tosca was supposed to stand over him, goading him to die . . . until finally he choked to death on his own blood! Wonderfully dramatic Puccini, but this . . . what was this all about?

The baritone playing Scarpia was as startled as everyone else. He'd never, in the many times he'd played the rapacious villain, had a Tosca turn the knife on herself and commit suicide. Not even that terrible performance in Palermo when he'd been so foully out of tune the audience had hissed, thrown fruit, and finally howled, "If she doesn't kill you, we will!"

He stood over her, clutching the safe-conduct papers he'd just pretended to sign, his mind as congealed as cold pasta. He was the one who should have been dead on the floor. The last forty minutes of the opera belonged to Tosca and Cavaradossi. What was he to do? He looked to the conductor for help, but the conductor was glaring at Tosca.

He repeated his line and his acting gesture, hoping somehow to dispel this moment and bring Tosca back to life. When nothing happened, he clutched his chest melodramatically, staggered back and forth, then dropped to the floor next to Tosca, dead. He didn't care what they did; at least he was out of the dilemma.

Open-mouthed, everyone turned to the conductor. All that was left to finish the opera off in complete disaster was for Tosca's lover to break out of prison and throw himself onto the pile.

"Signorina!" the conductor coaxed with vexation, tapping his baton on the lectern. "*Basta,* signorina, enough . . . *basta!*"

After a moment the figure of the soprano stirred.

"I—I—I cannot—go—on—" she began, hammering her heels into the floor like a five-year-old, her volume increasing with each kick, "with this—this—this—madhouse! *Questo è un casino!*" she finished, shouting like a street vendor.

She jumped up and flung the small prop knife she'd been clutching as though it defiled her hand. All eyes watched the knife skid across the floorboards, its retractable blade aiming for the harpist's head. He ducked. It crashed discordantly into the strings and fell harmlessly to the floor.

"You, signore, I see," she said, whirling toward the conductor, "still think you can bamboozle me!"

Complete silence fell over the opera house. All eyes were now on the conductor.

"Do something!" the eyes implored him. "She's ruining the production!"

No one dared move. The star soprano stomped to the stage footlights, impatiently pulling the train of her gown. Her hot eyes skewered the frail, white-haired conductor, who stood with his slender baton still raised.

"In case you do not remember," she said in a measured voice laden with sarcasm, "the person you are trying to bamboozle is not a chorus girl being given her first solo. She is Francesca Frascatti!"

She stamped her foot for additional emphasis. The conductor gripped his baton with both hands, remembering the invited guests and press. The baton bent under the strain like a bow about to give flight to an arrow. After all he'd gone through in the past week with this Medusa from *Napoli,* he felt like pummeling her to jelly or throwing her headfirst down a well.

"Signorina Frascatti, we know who you are. You do not need to remind us. We all have great respect for you and your experience, but we have discussed this point many times. Many times! Why the knife must be small, unobtrusive. . . . I must remind you, now, *per favore,* that this is an invited dress rehearsal! We are to open tomorrow night!"

"You are shouting at me?" Francesca inquired, very aware of the public and press waiting in the plush velvet seats.

"No, no, signorina, I do not shout, I only ask," the conductor whispered, trying his best to be genial, but his fury leaked out as though poured into a sieve. "As one Italian to another, I implore you. Tosca must—"

"I only ask! I only? I? Who is 'I'? Some piddling *peasante* who worked his way up to conductor from second violin? I sang Tosca at San Carlo two seasons ago with the maestro himself."

The conductor knew it was his move. All eyes watched him expectantly. Outside of giving in again he didn't see a way out. He hated giving in. He knew he was right. Why must she challenge him at every juncture? He looked at her, standing rigidly before him, and thought, How can someone so talented, so beautiful, so . . . so . . . delicious be so thoroughly odious?

Francesca Frascatti at thirty-six was in top form and voice, at the pinnacle of the opera world. Under the spotlight her upswept hair, crowned with a twinkling tiara, had turned to curling tongues of chestnut fire. Sparks leaped from her espresso eyes. The golden lighting and artfully applied stage makeup dramatized her straight Roman nose, slanted almond-shaped eyes, and full-cut lips. Donatello could not have painted a lovelier angel.

"I performed this opera throughout Europe to standing ovations!"

"Signorina, we do not question—" the conductor tried to catch her.

"Nineteen curtain calls in *Milano,* twenty-two in *Venezia,* thirty-six in *Napoli!* Every performance sold out. I was deluged with flowers! Deluged! They stacked them in the alley after they overflowed the dressing room and flooded the lobby. The people tossed jewels stripped from their bodies. Students unharnessed my horses and dragged my carriage through the streets singing arias—"

"*Si, si! Si calmi*, signorina, your voice, *stai attenta!*" the conductor soothed. "Do not harm your voice—"

"Men followed me in the streets. Women tinted their hair to match my shade. I couldn't go out in public without a veil. I had proposals of marriage from two counts, a grand duke, and the Prince of Monrovia. Now you, a second-class violin, presume to ask me to compromise myself? To ruin my reputation? To prostitute myself to fulfill your fantasy of how Tosca dispatches the evil Scarpia?"

"But signorina—"

"No, no, and no!" she cried, throwing her arms out as though pushing down the pillars of Samson's fabled temple. "*Disgraziato!* You tried to trick me."

Suddenly she clutched her throat with both hands as though she'd heard something snap. This was not a good sign and the conductor knew it. If she'd injured her voice, it would be fatal and he would be blamed.

Out of the corner of his eye he saw Oscar Hammerstein, the owner-manager of the opera house, hovering in the wings.

Hammerstein had taken off his signature top hat and was wiping sweat from his forehead. The removal of the hat was serious; the man was dangerous bareheaded. He glared at the conductor meaningfully. "Take care of the situation immediately!" the look said. "Don't make me come out on stage to do it for you."

Those assembled knew that success depended on the "golden voice," "the voice of the century," the voice that Oscar Hammerstein had imported from Naples for the sum of three thousand dollars a performance. It was the highest amount in history. Higher than Patti, Calvé, Melba, Caruso, higher than anyone. . . .

The lowly chorus members received twelve dollars and fifty cents a week. They didn't matter. They could be replaced, but "the voice of the century" . . . who would pay them if she injured her voice and canceled her performances? Who would pay their rent and feed their children? Certainly not the conductor. The chorus turned and glared at him in unison.

"Let the poor woman alone. Can't you see you are torturing her?" their eyes snapped.

She immediately felt the switch in allegiance and met their fierce gaze. "Help me!" her moist eyes pleaded.

Her breasts, thrust forward like twin crème caramels in her Empire gown, were quivering. Her hands fell away from her throat, her mouth worked silently, forming words the cast and audience members could not imagine. The air was charged as in the moments before a fierce thunderstorm.

What was she trying to say?

Ringed fingers flashed as she reached toward them beseechingly. The assembly gasped as she teetered toward the conductor and the very edge of the stage. For an instant she stood upon the lip. They feared she might faint and fall headlong into the orchestra. The conductor thrust out his baton in alarm. A hard-hearted cellist moved his cherished instrument out of harm's way.

Then, as swiftly as a gust of wind heralding a hurricane, she changed course, opting for a gut-wrenching scream over a passive faint. It filled the house, bounced off the walls, and reverberated like a Chinese gong in close quarters.

Wave after wave of angry tone buffeted the galleries. The hair on the heads of those assembled stood on end. What a voice, they thought in unison, what breath control! No wonder Hammerstein pays her three thousand dollars a performance. Could that note she's holding possibly be a C above high C?

This unnerving howl had not subsided a moment before a spate of thick Italian dialect followed. This was not the precise, poetic Italian of classical opera, no; this was the harsh language of the gutter, learned in the streets of Naples.

"*Testa di cazzo! Imbecille! Questo buffone è un grand asino, un cetriolo*"—Head of a prick! Imbecile! This big clown is a huge ass, a cucumber—she ranted to the gods and those present.

She leaped over the prone baritone, whirling upstage like a dervish. She flung prop pieces, turned over chairs, pulled down curtains, and lobbed lit candelabras. Hot wax and curses flew in all directions.

"Bring down the curtain," Hammerstein shouted. "Bring it down immediately, I tell you!"

The curtain rushed down on Bonzinni, who had to be pulled from its folds. He limped dramatically from the stage, supported by stagehands, as the soprano continued her wild harangue.

"What's happening?" the supernumeraries whispered. "What's wrong?"

These youngsters were playing their first parts as church attendants, choirboys, and soldiers and were shocked by such an abusive display of emotion, but the old-timers shook their heads ruefully. They'd seen behavior like this before and acknowledged it among themselves with a wink and a chuckle as they dodged flying set pieces.

This wasn't a Donatello angel whom Hammerstein had hired for eight performances of Puccini's *Tosca*. No. This was a full-blown demon, a bitch goddess, a whore of Satan, the worst kind of evil . . . a prima donna of the first order. This was a diva! A *diva assoluta!*

Hammerstein ordered the orchestra to play interlude music. Then he followed after her as she stalked off the stage.

Cesca sped toward her dressing room. When she reached the steel stairs she removed her shoes, lifted her hem, and tiptoed the rest of the way. She threw open the door, surprising Alice, her American dresser, who was going through her belongings.

"What are you doing?" Cesca demanded.

The pasty-faced blonde whirled, shoving the private papers back into the diva's leather case.

"I'm looking for a . . . a . . ." Alice cast around desperately for an idea.

"No, no, I know . . . you look for a needle and thread!" Cesca said as sweetly as burned sugar.

Her pet ocelot, Lucifer, tethered by a long chain to the far wall, grumbled at her tone. He knew, even if the dresser didn't, that his mistress's mood was dangerous. She'd suspected for days that Alice was going through her personal belongings and eavesdropping on private conversations. Now she'd caught her with sticky fingers.

"Yes," Alice replied, shamelessly stealing the idea, "that's it exactly . . . a needle and thread, Miss Fraskooti." She mangled the name like tin in a punch press. "I wanted to fix . . . my . . . my skirt. I caught it on a nail backstage."

She showed her hem, which had been pulled down. "No great stretch of imagination necessary," Cesca thought—her dresser was always slovenly in appearance.

"You won't find a needle in my desk drawer or in my portfolio."

"I'm sorry, miss. I thought—"

"Never mind what you thought! You can easily get a needle and thread in the costume shop."

Lucifer jumped to his feet, startled by Cesca's tone and a sudden sharp rap on the door. Hammerstein thrust his head in. Alice dropped a curtsy in his direction and darted into the clothes closet.

"Signorina Frascatti, the audience is in turmoil. You must come back to the stage!"

"I must?" She turned to Hammerstein in a fury, clutching a shoe over her head like a cudgel. Lucifer jumped onto the chaise longue, straining his chain. "You are ordering me?"

"I'd never order you, signorina," he replied genially, keeping his eyes on the snarling cat and remembering the conductor's bad judgment. "Are you . . . feeling . . . ill? Is it your voice?"

"*Si, è vero!*" she sobbed. "It's my voice!"

She staggered to the chaise longue as the shoes fell from her hands. Lucifer jumped down, playful once again. He recognized the change and knew the real danger was past. He stretched out and began pleasantly gnawing one of the discarded shoes.

"Alice, a blanket! Two blankets! I feel ill. Signore, my throat . . . my nerves . . . I cannot go on. Call the doctor . . . call a priest . . . there's no way . . . no way I can go back on that stage."

Chapter Two

～❀◌

MINA DIPPED HER FINGERS into the icy holy water, touched her forehead with the sign of the cross, and genuflected. The familiar scent of frankincense enveloped her as she dropped her coin into the donation box and lit a candle. She focused her mind on the flickering flame, one desperate petition sent to *Gesù* in a host of many. Which request would He find worthy of reply? For a moment the nagging knot of sin that had sat in her viscera since she'd arrived in America uncoiled slightly.

She hurried up the aisle past the sprinkling of contrite parishioners mumbling over their rosary beads. In this strange church she was safe from prying eyes, but her conscience would demand she confess these stolen moments before returning to work at the opera house. She glanced at the vaulted ceiling trimmed in marble and gold leaf before slipping into the confessional. Her little church downtown didn't have such rich adornments. She pulled the curtain closed behind and knelt to pray: Please let this uptown priest have a different answer.

As she waited for the priest to slide the screened window open and hear her confession, she silently reviewed her sins. Again she wondered if *Gesù* was punishing her for her past life. If only I could take it all back, she thought. But why would He arrange a marriage and then punish me for accepting a fresh start? If only she hadn't died, I wouldn't have—

The door clacked open, startling her.

"Forgive me, Father, for I have sinned," she murmured. "It's been two days since my last confession."

She rushed through her normal recital of venial sins, then hesitated.

"There's something more, my child, before I grant absolution?"

"Yes, Father. I—I've done something terrible. I'm not sure what to do about it."

"Something terrible? A mortal sin?"

She thought it over. None of the others had called it a mortal sin.

"I don't know, Father. It's gotten so complicated. I only wanted to make a fresh start, but I've had to tell so many lies."

"What was the first lie? Tell me about that." His voice was soft, encouraging.

"I had to lie so I could marry Antonio, but I've been keeping a secret . . . a secret about myself from everyone. It's making my life unbearable. I want to confess, to get it out in the open, but you see, if I tell anyone I'll put my life at risk, not because Antonio will beat me, but because . . ."

She hesitated again. She knew he was sworn to secrecy, but she hated this part, having to explain why, telling intimate details about her past life to a stranger. She knew he was supposed to be God's representative on earth, but priests never felt like God to her. They were always impatient when she asked for guidance. She didn't think *Gesù* would be impatient.

"Would *Gesù* punish me for lying? Would he make my husband beat me?"

"Our Lord never punishes. He—"

She gave an involuntary laugh as the fire and brimstone of Sodom and Gomorra crossed her mind. "What about Job?" she asked. "He was a just man. He didn't lie, and I—"

"Those were trials Job suffered. It was our Lord's way of testing his faith. There's a difference between a test and a punishment."

"So you think He might be testing me? What does our Lord say about husbands beating wives? Is it a test? Father, I'm afraid . . . he gets so violent; I don't know what to do. I want to run away, before something bad happens."

"You're Catholic, married in the church?"

"Yes, but I wasn't supposed to marry him. Father, how am I to know what *Gesù* intended me to do?" She whispered, "I thought He was speaking to me, giving me a sign, but I think I misunderstood. I think *Gesù* didn't mean for me to make this marriage. If only my papers were in order, I would leave him."

"Leave him?" the priest sounded astounded. "Marriage is a sacrament. The Lord is present in your union. You can't abandon it because your relationship is difficult. If you left your marriage you'd be abandoning the Lord. It would put your immortal soul at risk."

"Yes, yes, I know all that. But what's really important . . . what I really want to know is—"

He cut her off, with the same admonishments her parish priest and all the other priests she'd visited over the last few months had given. They were all shocked that she would consider leaving her marriage. They harped on submission and obedience. She should be a good wife, she should find a way to please her husband, she should do penance. . . . On and on they went. It was all her fault.

She'd always listened patiently in the past, hoping for some crumb of advice she might use to save herself, but today she didn't have the time. What did priests know of marriage, anyway? What did they know of *Gesù*'s will? She wondered if they knew anything at all or if they memorized everything from books the same way she'd memorized her catechism.

"You must ask our Lord to—"

"Are you saying *Gesù* doesn't care if my husband kills me? I must accept my fate?"

"My child, your tone is aggressive. Remember, a wife should be meek; perhaps this tone is why your husband . . ."

Aggressive? She'd like to show him aggressive. She'd like to act like Antonio, tear off the window grill and shake him till his nose bled. She was sick of priestly platitudes. She was tired of being meek and mild. The meek didn't inherit anything but pain. She decided she'd better get back to work before she said something to this uptown priest that she'd have to confess downtown.

"I understand, Father," she said, getting up from the kneeler and rubbing her sore knee bones. "Thank you for your advice. I've got to go back to work now."

"My child, it's your immortal soul I'm talking about. You must try harder. Think of our Holy Mother's pain as you say your rosary today. . . ."

She didn't stay to listen to the rest of his useless advice, but exited quickly as he gave penance and granted absolution to an empty confessional.

It was frantic in the costume shop of the Manhattan Opera House when she arrived. The pedal sewing machines made a racket as seams were eased and hems were altered. The women shouted over the noise, ripping and stitching, making last-minute adjustments after the final dress rehearsal. She eased into the mayhem feeling dizzy and weak after descending the narrow stairs. The air was thick with spicy Neapolitan dialect, snipped basting threads, and the latest gossip.

"—the set almost burned down. Thank God, Claudio doused it—"

"They rushed him to the hospital and he—"

"—her lover, Dante! Didn't you know? He's having an affair with—"

"She's impossible, that woman is a—"

"—monster!"

"—a devil, demanding more money. I heard—"

As she struggled to unbutton her coat, they reveled in the gossip like sparrows in a birdbath. It broke the monotony of their humble lives to dip into the world of the rich and famous and splash around for a while.

Mina loved her place in the shop and the women she'd come to know over the last six months. Like her, they were poor, culled from Lower East Side sweatshops to concoct from simple cloth, rhinestones, and lace the glittering world of make believe and dreams . . . the world of grand opera.

Gingerly Mina pulled her injured left arm out of her coat sleeve and shook off the rain. She hung the coat on a peg and retied her kerchief as a sling. Inside the faded silk bandage she tucked a small brown package she'd taken from her coat pocket.

"What's happened?" she finally asked, smoothing back the loose hairs that tickled her lips.

She only half listened to their replies as she scanned the room for Simonetta, the costume mistress, who had sent her on an errand. She took her tape measure and sharp scissors on their black cord out of her sewing drawer and put them around her neck.

"She finished the performance?" Mina asked.

The women assured her that the diva had, but not before disappearing into her dressing room for a half hour, causing a scandal the newspapers were certain to report.

"Oh, the newspapers, yes, a terrible problem," she said as gravely as she could manage.

They expected her to be shocked so she acted the part, but she knew that most of what happened with singers was nonsense. The opera house and daily scandal sheets used such incidents to create excitement and lure the naive public. They paid their nickel and greedily devoured news of their favorite stars. They followed their antics, dissected their love lives, copied their fashions, and flocked to their performances. She knew that gossip titillated, filled the seats, and allowed her to keep her post, but she didn't care about any of it.

It belonged to the world above, the world of make-believe and privilege. Her world was in the basement, compassed by cloth and thread, long hours and hard facts. Her colleagues longed to be part of the glamorous world of opera, but she preferred to stick to reality behind the scenes. She happily did what was demanded and concentrated on her job. In between stitches she practiced English with her closest friend, Lilli, so that she might improve her future. She was learning fast, but was too embarrassed to speak more than a word or two. She knew that if she studied hard and saved her pennies diligently, she might build herself a real future.

Lilli was currently the center of attention, acting out the prima donna's temper tantrum as seen from the wings.

"You're talking about the *new* soprano, Signora Frascatti?" Mina asked.

The women hooted.

"You'd better not let her hear you call her signora!" one of the women said.

"Yes! She's signo . . . *rina*"—Lilli snickered, batting her eyelashes and twirling coquettishly with a length of ribbon tied under her chin—"even at her age . . . with all the lovers she's had!"

Everyone laughed at Lilli's imitation of the diva.

"Have you seen her lover, Dante?" Lilli demanded.

"So manly, he's—"

"So handsome!"

"Do you know, I hear he's twenty years younger than she—"

"Twenty years . . . He'll wear her out like a piece of soap!"

The women giggled at the wild rumors, discussing in vivid detail the imagined sex life of Francesca Frascatti as they sewed. Mina laughed when the others laughed, but conversations about sex always made her uneasy. Lilli teased that she was a prude, but she knew she wasn't. She just couldn't understand how the women could get so excited about an act that was embarrassing and painful.

When Simonetta entered the room carrying a jumble of trim, Mina was secretly relieved. Now she had a reason to escape the conversation.

"Backstage! I'm telling you," Lilli whispered, "I saw them together, with these eyes!"

Lilli had moved on to describe the backstage tryst she'd witnessed between the lover and the diva's dresser, giving all the juicy details. Mina kept her eyes on the harried costume mistress.

"What's wrong with Simonetta?" Mina whispered when Lilli paused.

"The conductor and Bonzinni aren't pleased with Scarpia's costume," Lilli replied with disgust.

The women shook their heads and clicked their tongues.

"Where's the designer?" Mina asked.

"Drunk. He stuck Simonetta with it again. Doesn't want the blame." Lilli shrugged and happily returned to her story.

Mina felt sorry for the old woman. The others thought her a testy slave driver and avoided her, but Mina knew that under her crusty exterior was a tender heart. At sixty-eight, Simonetta was simply worn out by the frantic demands of narcissism. Designers would breeze in with sketches and expect her to make their exotic ideas work. Tenors and sopranos were never satisfied, her staff preferred gossip to sewing, and she was always overwhelmed with too few solutions and too little time.

Mina did her best to shift some of the pressure to her own shoulders, for she'd come to respect and love the costume mistress. Simonetta had saved her from the sweatshops, and she knew she'd never be able to repay her kindness.

When she'd first arrived in the country the only job available was in a Russian shop, sewing pants for twelve hours a day. Each night, exhausted after her shift, she'd carried the heavy unfinished work home balanced on her head. On the way she'd peddled her handmade lace from store to store.

One evening in a tiny notion shop on Mott Street, she'd overheard Simonetta complaining about her duties at the opera house. Mina had wound up her courage and asked for work, but the old woman had barked that she had enough drones to do the cutting and stitching. Later, when Mina had produced a length of elegant lace to show the owner, an opening had miraculously appeared.

The very next day she'd started working directly under Simonetta and the designers. It hadn't taken long for Mina's enthusiasm and artistry to win Simonetta's respect. Soon she was helping with more than lace and trim.

Mina picked up Tosca's folded shawl from the back of her chair. She was almost certain she was supposed to attach the fringe she'd been sent to purchase. Time was short, but then so was Simonetta's temper.

"Signora Simonetta?" she called across the racket, waving the paper packet.

Simonetta didn't raise her head. She was arranging medals and trim on the cutting table as though involved in a life-or-death chess match. Mina crossed the room to her side.

"Signora? *Mi scusi,* but the shawl for the first act? I've purchased the fringe. Did you want me to add it?"

"Why are you bothering me, Mina? Can't you see I'm busy?" Simonetta gestured as though flicking away flies.

"Yes, Signora. May I help you in some way?"

"This jacket, *disgraziata,* will be the death of me. It must be made more grand, but I'm not to change it."

"I don't understand."

"*Eccola!* You're not alone. Change it, but don't change it. That's the demand. It must be more . . . impressive, in a vulgar way. I suggested a change of color—red, perhaps—but no, it must be black. How am I to make vulgar with black?"

Mina laid the package on the table and studied the jacket. The satin shawl in her hand was heavily embroidered with thread. Her finger traced the flowered pattern as her mind tried solutions.

"In my village we had a pompous mayor who overdressed on feast days, with fringed sashes that hung past his knees. He looked foolish, but it made him feel distinguished." She laid the shawl at an angle across the jacket. "This peach satin is embroidered with identical thread, making it elegant, but perhaps a contrasting color with heavy golden fringe?"

Simonetta looked at Mina for a moment, annoyed. Sashes . . . fringe . . . maybe. But no, it wasn't grand enough.

"Or . . ." Mina had a sudden idea; hesitantly she took a piece of chalk from the box on the table. "*Permesso?*"

Simonetta nodded. Mina swiftly sketched ornate scrolls on the folded cuff.

"We could embroider thread here and on the lapels. Maybe red?"

Simonetta looked irritated. Embroidered scrollwork on a man's jacket—ridiculous. But as she watched the pattern emerge she became excited. "No, no, not red, gold! It's perfect! We won't need medals." Simonetta pushed the clutter aside. "Help me trace out a pattern. We'll get the twins to do the work. Do you think they can finish by tomorrow night's performance?"

"Of course, signora."

Simonetta sighed in relief and patted Mina's cheek. "You're a treasure, Mina."

Mina blushed with pleasure. "The shawl, signora, what would you like me to do with it?"

"Ah yes, the shawl. The new soprano insists the shawl needs emphasis . . . whatever that means." They laughed now that the cloud had passed. "Take it to her and see if the rosebud fringe I sent you to purchase will suit. Otherwise I don't know what to suggest."

"Take it to her?"

"Yes, Mina. *Subito!*" Simonetta turned aside.

"But signora, surely you would be—"

"You're as capable as I. You cannot remain so timid. This is not Italy, where we were under the landowner's thumb. Take it to her immediately."

Mina was uneasy being ordered above. Opera people were degenerates—that's what Antonio had said when she'd told him about the job offer. He'd shouted and pounded his fist on the table, insisting she wouldn't be safe at the opera house. She'd thought him foolish and had a difficult time convincing him she'd only be working among women. He'd allowed it because of the increase in pay, but she'd quickly discovered he was right.

Her first day she'd gotten lost backstage trying to find the workshop. The men had leered and made crude jokes. When she'd finally asked for directions, a workman had pressed her against some curtains in the wings and fondled her breasts while the others laughed. She'd been able to push him away, but since that day she'd refused to venture backstage or talk to anyone but the women in the shop.

"Ask for assistance if you lose your way. And hurry back. I need your help with the embroidery pattern."

She climbed the stairs, clutching the shawl over her breasts, alert for danger. She hurried through the wings, behind the gilded set pieces and canvas flats, dodging wooden braces and wires to reach the opposite side of the building without incident. She stopped a woman going out the stage door and got directions, then she banged down a spiral flight of steel stairs. The diva's dressing room waited at the end of the hallway.

She went swiftly to the door and raised her hand to knock, then put it down. What if the diva was having a sexual encounter? Lilli said Signor Hammerstein had purchased a silk chaise longue for that very purpose. And what about the savage leopard the diva kept as a pet? She'd heard it ate beefsteaks fetched from Delmonico's restaurant. What if the diva and her lover were naked . . . or the leopard attacked her . . . oh, she'd heard so many terrible stories—

It's only gossip, she told herself, nonsense to sell tickets. There's nothing to be afraid of in that dressing room. Don't be a child! She whispered a prayer of protection to *Sant'Anna* and raised her hand to knock.

Chapter Three

*T*EN CURTAIN CALLS and a cozy press conference after her temper tantrum, the diva was back in her dressing room. "That was the worst dress rehearsal I ever had!"

She wiped the last of the cleansing cream from her face and threw the soiled cloth to the floor. Alice attempted a soothing shoulder massage but only succeeded in bobbing the diva's head around like a cork on a stormy sea.

"Just loosen the bones and give me my robe. *Ho freddo adesso! Tutti i giorni fa freddo in questa camera.* Every day it's cold! Cold is no good for the voice!"

The light in the diva's eyes danced like drops of water in a hot skillet. She was always angry about something, but Alice couldn't figure out why. The diva didn't speak English well, and all that Italian made her task impossible. Alice constantly got her facts wrong and gave imprecise information.

"Now, now, Signorina Frascatti," Hammerstein cooed, "everyone knows a bad dress rehearsal promises a successful premiere."

He sat on the piano bench overpronouncing English in his thick German accent as though practicing an elocution exercise, while Alice loosened the corset lacing.

"Alice!" the diva exclaimed, pulling away as though tortured. "Your hands are like *gelato!*"

"I'm sorry, Miss Fraskooti," Alice said, shoving her hands into her armpits. "I try to keep them warm, but—"

"It turned out beautifully. I spoke with the reporter from the *Times*. He thought your voice magnificent and your jump from the castle breathtaking."

"*Si, si,* breathtaking, exactly right. I need two more mattresses. Thick. I almost broke my neck. And if I do . . . well, you can sing Tosca, but I don't think you'll fit in the costumes."

"Absolutely, signorina." He made a mental note. "It was a wonderful piece of luck, your knowing the reporter from the *Times*."

"From *Napoli, si.* An old friend. He understands that arrogant Milanese's trick!"

"You were doing beautifully until you got to the knife," he said with false compassion. He puffed on his cigar, surrounding them in a cloud of blue smoke.

"You were doing beautifully? Of course I was beautiful! I was splendid! I'm always splendid! But you're blaming me for this fiasco? This incompetence? This stupidity!" She waved her hand at the smoke and made a little cough. "Your cigar, signore, bad for the voice," she said, politely holding out a large crystal ashtray.

He broke the hot ash from the tip and stuck the stub between his teeth. "Well, I mean, the conductor's request was—"

"Stupidity!"

"Here's your robe," Alice said, looping the folds of sheer burnt-orange silk and satin over Cesca's outstretched arms.

"He insulted me with a fruit knife!"

"How do you mean insulted? Signorina, don't you see the irony of a small fruit knife?"

"Irony? Your irony is idiotic! A fruit knife cannot kill a great villain like Scarpia. *Madonna mia!* Is there no bread in New York?" Her eyes questioned Alice, then Hammerstein in turn. "That baritone is as big as a rhinoceros. You want the audience to believe Tosca kills that horror with a puny fruit knife? Ridiculous!"

"I agree, signorina—" Hammerstein said, looking at his watch.

"And after we all agreed on a large knife, he tries to trick me by putting out that ridiculous dart. In front of the press! Trick me? Francesca Frascatti!"

Alice removed the fire screen and poked the logs. Cesca brushed out her hair. She tried to catch Hammerstein's eye in the mirror, but he seemed fascinated by the little charms attached to his watch chain. She cleared her throat once, then did so repeatedly until he looked at her with concern.

She mouthed the words "Get rid of Alice" and jerked her head in the dresser's direction. He looked at her stupidly.

"What?" he mouthed back.

"Get rid of her," she repeated silently, jabbing a finger at the dresser's back and gesturing at the door.

"Oh!" he said suddenly. "Alice . . . could you get me a . . . a . . . I need you to go up and check on a . . . a . . ." The dresser looked at him expectantly, still trying to poke the ashes to life.

"I want to speak to Signorina Frascatti about a . . . a . . . Oh, for God's sake," he said, coming up short, "just get out and leave us alone."

Alice shot a suspicious look at the diva, but she was arranging her hair and humming the same dreadful tune she often repeated when she was content. "Miss Fraskooti," she said at the door, "I'd like to go home now, if you don't need me. I'll be back tomorrow, two hours before curtain."

"*Vai a casa? Si, perfetto! Va bene, domani. Va via. Ciao!*"

Alice stared.

"Go home?" Cesca asked, pausing after each word as though speaking to a very stupid child, "Yes, perfect! That's fine. See you tomorrow. You can go now. Good-bye!"

Alice exited swiftly. Cesca waited a moment, putting her index finger to her lips.

"Signor Hammerstein," she began loudly as she carefully crept to the door, "that baritone, Bonzinni, is making me—"

She whipped the door open to reveal Alice crouching, like a kangaroo, with her hat in both hands.

"Did you drop something, *cara?*"

"Ah, yes, miss," she said, jumping to her feet, her face red. "M-m-my hat!"

She waved it in Cesca's face for emphasis, then hurried down the hall, pinning it to her wispy blond hair without a backward glance.

"Ha!" Cesca trumpeted as she slammed the door. "Hammerstein, I want you to get rid of that dresser immediately."

They continued in Italian.

"She isn't performing well?" he asked, stroking his waxed Van Dyke and thinking of Alice's plump thighs.

Only two weeks before, he'd given her an office job as a favor to a friend. In return, she'd shown her gratitude with several brief but very pleasant late-night encounters in the set shop. During their last meeting, she'd expressed a desire to work as a dresser, so he'd placed her with Francesca.

"She hasn't been a dresser long, but . . . Why do you want to get rid of her?"

"Because she's stupid, she doesn't speak Italian, and she's fucking my fiancé!"

"What?" He almost swallowed his cigar.

"You're shocked that she's fucking him or that I state it so frankly? Which, dear friend?"

"Well, I—I—"

"Look, Oscar—I may call you Oscar, may I not?"

He nodded his head vigorously.

"Very well, Oscar, you're a man, eh? All right, you understand these things. Some women are this way. Like some men, they can't help themselves. It becomes a nasty habit, you understand?"

He swallowed hard, but she didn't wait for his answer.

"This isn't the first time Alice has done something such as this, right, Oscar?"

He fiddled with his watch fob again, his eyes averted. She could see by his manner that the information she'd received was correct. He'd been with the girl, and Alice had been spying. She continued with a smile. "Nor is it the first time for Dante," she added casually.

He looked up, tomfoolery sparkling in his eyes.

"Why I put up with Dante is my business," she said, shaking her hairbrush at him. "I don't choose to discuss it."

"No one's asking, signorina. I would—"

"But . . . I will not put up with my nerves being stretched like a thrice-turned mandolin string. I didn't become *diva assoluta* without pain and struggle. I made myself . . . like Adam, up from the dirt, so I'm not afraid to fight. I speak the truth, plainly. No, what distresses me is, I must suffer the ministrations of this . . . this . . . stupid girl with a voice like a tin fork on china, who has icicles for hands, breath like moldy onions, and the *coglioni* to be screwing my worthless fiancé!"

She ended by stamping her foot and glaring at him. Lucifer remained bored.

"Well, of course, Signorina Frascatti, she's dismissed," Hammerstein huffed. His vanity was smarting from Alice's easy virtue. What had his friend set him up with? A common prostitute? Not the first time indeed!

"Don't terminate the girl. After all, I'm not heartless. Find her another position, wherever you like, but I don't want her near me in the present or future."

Future? He stopped fuming and started counting ticket receipts. It had taken every connection and manipulation he could muster to obtain this appearance. If he could win her and form an alliance, he'd break his competitor Gatti-Casazza and the Metropolitan. He'd reign supreme! Perhaps she'd agree to extend her engagement. He'd do anything to obtain an extension. Oh, the money he'd make if she agreed.

"I'll release her as you say," he blustered, visions of greenbacks twirling in his head. "She'll never work in another opera house in America"—his cold cigar carved circles in the air—"or on the continent. Why, she'll never get another—"

"No, no, no, Oscar, you're not listening. I don't want her released."

Francesca put her hand on his chest appealingly. Not want her released? He stopped, startled, and stepped back, a little surprised by the intimacy of her gesture and the sweetness of her tone.

"She's young," she said, leaning into him, her lips brushing his ear.

"But she's insulted you, Signorina Frascatti. Your fiancé—"

"Oscar, Oscar, you must call me Cesca. We're getting to know one another after all these rehearsals and meetings, eh?" She cocked an eyebrow at him, amused.

"Very well, Ces . . . ca," he said, remembering the box office receipts. "I'm shocked, shocked by Alice's behavior. I apologize for her insulting lack of morals." Trying for a conspiratorial tone, but sounding stiff, he added, "It certainly doesn't represent the accepted moral standard of the Manhattan Opera Company or—"

"Relax a little, Oscar. We're cosmopolitan, after all, sophisticated members of the opera world," she said with a little laugh. "Besides, it's not as insulting as the fruit knife. She keeps Dante occupied. If you fire her, it'll take him several weeks to find a replacement. He'll exhaust me, you know? And my performance will suffer . . . you wouldn't want my performance to suffer, eh?"

She led him to the chaise longue and drew him down next to her, head to head, arms entwined. The spotted cat curled at her feet, watching her with twinkling eyes.

"I must save myself for my art. Mustn't I, Oscar?"

"Of course you're right . . . Cesca."

"Oscar, I want you to tell her it's because she doesn't speak Italian. Only that. Don't mention the indiscretion. I don't want Dante to know that I . . ." She hesitated like a shy schoolgirl.

He looked confused for a moment, then caught on. "Ah, yes, I understand completely."

"Get me a sweet Italian girl. Inexperienced, young, a quick learner who's hungry for a good position. There must be someone in this opera house who can handle the little job."

She saw that Oscar had a pleasant glazed look, for she'd purposely let the front of her robe slip open to reveal a small, firm breast tipped with a peachy erect nipple. Rumor suggested he'd enjoyed many relationships with his prima donnas. She thought a little flesh might make him malleable. "Get me someone with warm, dry hands."

"It can be arranged," he replied as though the air had been punched out of his lungs.

"Remember, don't speak of this or release Alice. Perhaps I can coax my best friend, Errico Caruso, to give a performance. You know, only his closest friends and family call him *Err*-ico. Perhaps you'll call him *Err*-ico soon!" She flipped her hair back over her shoulder and her lips brushed his ear as she whispered, "Or maybe my dear Tetrazinni will give you better terms on her contract, eh? All things are possible, Oscar. Especially now that you have my help with that tired old lion, the Metropolitan." She chuckled.

Caruso? Tetrazinni? His brain was dancing with joy. "A new dresser . . . yes, yes . . ." he said, staring breathlessly into her dark eyes and thinking of ink on crisp hundred-dollar bills.

"Let Dante have his little romp, but not in my dressing room, eh? Later you can bring her back to her former position, under . . . anyone you like."

The door opened.

"Signor Dante!" Hammerstein practically shouted, jumping to his feet. "We were just talking about you." He dropped Cesca's hand as though stung by a scorpion.

"Indeed?" Dante said stiffly, removing his gloves. "I seem to be the topic of a very pleasant conversation."

"Oh, no, signore . . . I mean yes, it's very pleasant, but it's not—"

"*Cara,*" Dante said, his eyes upon her open robe, "you're entertaining! Perhaps I should come back."

Hammerstein followed Dante's gaze and instantly recalled what he'd heard. Dante was a notoriously jealous, hot-tempered Roman who had shot an overly ambitious admirer of Cesca's in Paris, or was it Vienna? It was only a flesh wound, but the ensuing scandal had been great box office. He, however, saw no percentage in being shot for publicity's sake.

"We were just discussing the need for a new—"

"Knife!" Cesca finished as she retied her wrapper.

"Yes, yes, that's it exactly." He rushed to the door. "I'll go now and obtain the breast—bread—knife and the—"

"Yes, Oscar, *subito,* eh? Tomorrow's the premiere."

"If you'll excuse me," Oscar said, tipping his hat. "I've so much to do." He exited abruptly, careening into a young woman waiting outside the door with Cesca's first act shawl.

"Oscar!" she called, her voice imperious. "Who's that woman you've crushed? Ask her to come in, and you stay here too."

Dante smiled and moved behind the chaise to watch the melodrama unfold. Cesca was a master of manipulation; he pushed aside her chiffon wrapper and bent to kiss her neck.

"Come in, young lady. Signorina Frascatti would like to see you."

Hammerstein ushered the slight young woman forward. She was about five feet five with dark brown hair parted in the middle and braided into heavy loops that rested on the back of her neck. Dante thought her face unusually attractive, graced with almond-shaped brown eyes that she shyly cast down when he caught her glance.

"Leave the door open," Cesca ordered. "It's always so hot in here."

Leaving the door open had the desired effect. Those passing in the hall slowed their progress, hoping to enjoy a glimpse of the inner world of the *diva assoluta.*

"Ah, my new Italian dresser!" Cesca trilled in English for all ears to hear.

"Cesca," Hammerstein said startled, "I thought you—"

"You're Italian?" she asked.

Mina nodded.

"You come from the costume shop?"

"Yes, signo . . . *rina,*" Mina finished, remembering Lilli's warning, but barely understanding the English. "I've brought you some fringe," she added in Italian.

Her hands shook as she showed the shawl and the rosebud edging.

"*Perfetto!*" Cesca cooed. "It will be ready tomorrow evening?"

Mina nodded.

"What's your name?"

"I . . . Antonio's wife." She dropped a curtsy, her eyes never leaving the carpet.

"Antonio's wife . . . she doesn't have a name of her own," Dante mocked gently.

"*Stai zitto,* Dante. Where are you from?" Cesca asked, studying Mina's face.

"*Napoli,* from . . . ah, I come here . . . Salerno—" Mina's English was swallowed up by fear.

"Ah, a Neapolitan Signo . . . *ra!*" Cesca laughed. "And such a young one!"

She was from the nearby hills with that dialect. Still in her teens . . . obviously frightened . . . wearing a mended olive work dress, forgotten straight pins threaded into the bosom . . . around her neck a tape measure and scissors . . . plain gold earrings . . . calloused hands . . . broken nails.

Cesca felt the wind of the bay gust over her. She could smell the streets of Naples, where she'd started at sixteen, the fresh *zeppoli* frying, the smoky charcoal braziers, the sea smells, the sewage, cheap perfume, and hoarse groans under the arches. . . . The complications of this life are too much to handle when you're so young, she thought, even without having to deal with a diva.

"A wounded bird, Cesca?" Dante whispered, his eyes on the makeshift sling holding the girl's left arm. "What happened to your wing, little one?" he asked in Italian.

"I pulled my shoulder getting onto a trolley car," she replied softly, refusing to look up. "It's almost healed."

Here's someone I might trust, Cesca thought. I don't need to rely on Oscar. Besides, he set me up with a spy. Who knows if he'll find another? There seemed to be no artifice to the girl's manner; she was as mild and earnest as a prayer.

"Come, give me your hand."

The girl hesitated, her eyes on the powerful animal at her feet. Lucifer stretched his neck toward her, sniffing the air. His silky whiskers quivered.

"Lucifer's a big baby," Cesca said. "He won't hurt you."

For reassurance Cesca held his leash. The girl came bravely forward, her gaze on the ocelot. Lucifer rubbed against the girl's legs, seeking affection. Her hand trembled, but it was warm and dry.

"Do you know about me?" she asked.

When Mina lifted her eyes they fell upon the man rubbing the diva's shoulders. He was roughly handsome, tall yet robust, with softly curled caramel hair and a square jaw. When he smiled she noticed a faint scar bisecting his upper lip. His sea-green eyes were spangled with gold and his gaze struck her heart like a sharp stone. A giddy attraction swept over her, melting her spine. She blinked. His power frightened her.

"I know you're playing Tosca," she replied, switching her attention to the diva.

He must be the lover, she thought, her heart racing, The one Lilli said she caught backstage with the dresser. Suddenly she felt as though they were alone in the room. Her breathing went shallow. His hands were on the diva's shoulders, but it felt as though he were caressing her own flesh. She felt his lips brush against her neck . . . a chill traveled up her spine . . . she remembered Lilli's crude account of the backstage encounter.

She tried not to meet his gaze, but couldn't resist. When her eyes met his, he promised a whole tabloid of naughty pleasures. Her wildest fantasies would be fulfilled, if she would only give him a chance. . . .

"But you've heard things?" the diva demanded, pressing her fingers.

Mina pulled her hand back and covered her neck where she'd felt the lover's hot kisses press. The flesh beneath her corset tingled with a mixture of embarrassment and longing. Her saliva felt as thick as glue. She wanted to speak, but her tongue wouldn't move. Was this what the women meant when they laughed and teased about sexual longing?

"She's shocked by us, Dante. She's heard I'm a monster! A devil!"

They all laughed, staring as though she were a sideshow oddity. She bit the inside of her lip and tried to find a safe place to fix her eyes. Anywhere, she thought, anywhere but his eyes! Intimate details came to her mind. Lilli's descriptions . . . the chaise longue . . . sweaty bodies entwined . . . explicit descriptions of tongues and breasts . . . the women's encounters with husbands and lovers. . . . The images swept over her, making her feel she might faint.

Unable to avoid the pull of his energy, she glanced back. "Let me touch you," the lover's eyes whispered, "let me undress you . . . give you pleasure . . . fulfillment . . . kisses tinged with honey . . . embraces of angel's wings . . . joy on a bed of silk. . . ." It crossed her mind that she might risk her life for a touch of his lips.

This stranger created feelings in her body she'd never felt. She closed her eyes, shutting him out, and drew her breath back slowly, like a silken cord. She had to get out of the room; she had to get away from him. If she didn't, she wasn't sure what she might do, what she might say. Quickly, quickly, get out and never come back.

"Answer the Signorina," Hammerstein insisted.

"Yes, yes," she blurted out hoarsely, because the air had become as heavy as one of her pressing irons. "I've heard disgusting things about you!" She'd used the word *infamia* and a shocked silence followed.

"Do you know who you're speaking to?" Hammerstein demanded. "Signorina, I apologize for this crude peasant." He yanked her behind him. "She's a fool. I'll personally find you a proper dresser who—"

But the diva cut him off, ranting in English while the cat snarled and jerked his leash. As she stood behind Hammerstein, Mina's heart was pounding. How had she lost control of her tongue? The Signorina was furious. Mina didn't understand the English but assumed the Signorina was ordering her dismissal. Hammerstein shoved her out into the deserted hall and ordered her to send Simonetta immediately to his office.

She berated herself as she ran to the dressing room. Why hadn't she lied? A lie had readied itself in her mind, but the lover's gaze had pulled the truth from her lips.

"He wants you immediately," she whispered to Simonetta. "Something's wrong."

"Is it the fringe?"

She shook her head. "They asked if I'd heard gossip about the Signorina."

"What did you tell them?"

"I said . . . yes," she said, holding her hand over her racing heart. "I said I'd heard disgraceful, disgusting things—"

"*Gesù, Maria!*"

Simonetta couldn't imagine what had made Mina say something so foolish. She left instantly, trembling as much as Mina, for she'd never been summoned by the owner. Someone's head was about to be lopped off.

Mina worked nervously on the tracings. The women watched her out of the corners of their eyes. Though they were sympathetic, many were also secretly pleased. Mina had lightened the workload since she'd come to the shop, but she'd also shown them up. Her hard work and cleverness made them feel lazy and dull. They suspected she was about to get the sack. She'd be forced back to the sweater's. Sixty cents a day.

Mina pulled her rosary from her pocket and wrapped it around her left hand, whispering prayers as she worked.

"*Sant'Anna*, please intercede. I beg of you, don't let me lose my place. I know I said the wrong thing and I'm not worthy of your aid. . . ."

After a long quarter hour, Simonetta returned. When Mina saw Simonetta's face, a cold sickness seeped into her stomach. Why was it that when you thought everything was going well and you felt safe, bad things happened?

"I'm to dismiss you," Simonetta said.

"Dismiss?" The blood drained from her veins. "Signora, I didn't want to speak . . . they demanded it. If I've made an error or displeased, let me go to them and explain."

"No, there's nothing to explain. It's been decided. You're dismissed this minute."

Mina squeezed her thumbs in her fists and tried not to cry as Simonetta rang the brass bell on her desk. The women stopped working and turned toward them with guilty smiles of excitement on their faces. More gossip! Oh, *Sant'Anna,* Mina thought, not only am I to lose my job, but I'm to lose it in front of everyone.

"Ladies! Mina's no longer to work in this shop. She's being dismissed, because she's been"—Simonetta paused for effect—"promoted to first dresser! You'll report to Signorina Frascatti at five o'clock tomorrow evening, and you'll be her personal dresser for her stay at the opera house."

"Dresser?" she asked, confused.

The workroom was silent with shock, then a scattering of applause. Lilli's face radiated joy, but a few others were wooden and cold.

"*Brava,* Mina!" Lilli shouted. "*Complimenti!*"

Mina was flushed with embarrassment as the women came forward to offer congratulations. *Struffoli,* a homemade honey cake stuck together in little pieces, appeared.

"I was taking it to my sister's, but this calls for a celebration."

"Signora?" Lilli asked. "May I make espresso?"

"Of course! We must celebrate!" Simonetta said.

The room buzzed with questions. Mina clutched the worktable, her knees weak. They expected her to work with that horrible woman, the one who'd been terrorizing the opera house? The one everyone said was the devil, a whore, impossible to please? And the Lover . . . the one with eyes that touched you from across the room and saw inside your soul? It wasn't possible. She couldn't do it. She'd refuse. Surely they couldn't force her to work for that woman . . . and . . . and associate with that man. That man . . . who took her breath away.

"I've lost her because she has dry hands!" Simonetta announced. "Yes, that's precisely why I lost you and why she now has you, because of your hands."

Mina caught hold of Simonetta and pulled her close. "Help me, Simonetta. I can't work for her. I've no experience."

Simonetta was too distracted by the excitement of the moment to hear the terror in Mina's voice. "She wants the driest, warmest hands in the shop. I should have given you something to sweat about when I sent you to her, eh? Oh, well," Simonetta sighed, "you can always come to visit. Perhaps you won't mind doing a little lace work for us between acts."

"Signora, please," she pleaded. "I can't go back there." The fiery fingers of the lover were stroking her flesh again, but this time they reached beneath her petticoats. "They're horrible people," she whispered, remembering all she'd heard. "Degenerates. I can't work for them. I'd— I'd rather go back to the sweater's."

"Don't be silly, Mina," Simonetta said as she hugged her warmly. "You're getting a raise of seven dollars a week. The Signorina insisted on it."

Seven dollars! With seven dollars a week, and what she'd already saved, she could escape the predicament she was in. She began to tremble violently. What was she to do? She'd have to work for the diva, the money was too much to turn down, but that man—she'd have to stay away from that man. Once again she pressed her palm against her throat where his lips had brushed. "I know nothing of being a dresser," Mina murmured.

Simonetta slipped an arm around her waist to keep her steady. "You'll learn," she said. "And unfortunately, if you learn well, you'll never come back to my shop. You'll make a very good living up above. I'm happy for you, Mina."

The women tore the *struffoli* apart and offered her advice about her new position, the diva's lover, and the best ways to handle a monster like Signorina Frascatti. As each woman embraced her, they covered her with honey and envy.

Chapter Four

WHEN OSCAR LEFT with Antonio's wife, the mood in the dressing room changed abruptly. Dante waited a moment, then checked the hallway to find it empty and silent. "They've gone," he said as he closed the door. "We gave them a good show."

All traces of his gigolo demeanor vanished. Cesca's arrogant attitude melted into anxiety.

"You've brought the men?" she asked.

"Yes, they're out of sight in an alcove at the end of the corridor."

"They've uncovered something?" she asked, pacing nervously.

He nodded and went out. A moment later he returned with three men wearing bowlers and overcoats. "Go in, gentlemen, and make yourselves comfortable."

The men entered the room, nodded politely as they removed their hats, and arranged themselves in front of the grand piano. Dante sat on the chaise next to Cesca and took her hand. "Before we get started, tell us what happened with Hammerstein," Dante said.

"The charade's set."

"He believed you?"

"Yes, he swallowed the bait whole. I'm certain he sees me as the stereotypical prima donna. Fire and ice. After my little performance on stage this afternoon the newspapers will be full of my temperament. I asked our friend at the *Times* to help us with the illusion."

"And Alice?"

"The reason for her release is your supposed affair. He himself has been with the girl, so he was easy to convince."

"How about the rest?"

"As you saw, I have an Italian dresser, chosen randomly. If need be, I'll keep changing dressers until we're satisfied."

"Excellent! Now we can concentrate on our mission. *Cara,* this is the man who's been supplying our information, Inspector Bevilacqua. Our friend Petrosino sent him and his men to us. They're formerly with the New York City Police Department and are very discreet."

A smartly dressed man stepped forward.

"How do you do, Inspector Bevilacqua?" She stood up and offered her hand.

The flash of a diamond in his pinkie ring momentarily caught her eye.

"Such an interesting ring," she said, turning his hand over to study the figure. "I love unusual jewelry." His ring was heavy with bright gold and intricately carved. A beautifully faceted diamond sat in the open mouth of a Medusa's head and the snakes of hair entwined to form the band. "I had hoped Signor Petrosino would join us," she said, releasing his hand.

"He works in disguise, signorina. None of us know his identity. It's necessary to protect him from members of the Black Hand who wish to see him dead."

"You've never met the man you work for?" she asked, surprised.

"He gives orders through intermediaries. He's never far away."

"I see." She examined each man in turn, wondering if they could be trusted. "Well," she finally said, "I've asked you to come because I wish to hear the news with my own ears."

Dante noticed that the formality of the meeting seemed to steady her.

"These two gentlemen, as well as others, will be working with me on the case," Bevilacqua said. "Vincenzo Manzaro and Giuseppe Colombo." The men stepped forward and nodded when Bevilacqua named them.

"May I say that it's a great pleasure to meet you, Signorina Frascatti," said the fat, swarthy man with the mustache introduced as Giuseppe Colombo. "I'm a great admirer of your singing."

"You've heard me sing?"

"On the gramophone. I have the recording you did with Signor Caruso."

"Oh, yes, the gramophone, I'd forgotten." She was suddenly nervous again. She gave Dante a worried look.

"I promise you, *cara,* we can trust Bevilacqua and his men. Please sit down, gentlemen."

"Dante has explained to you why we must be cautious?" she asked, her brow creased. "The man we're dealing with will stop at nothing to defeat me. We believe he planted a dresser in my employ as a spy. He's vastly wealthy, and unfortunately, money will corrupt the most honest of souls."

"I can vouch as completely for my men as I do for myself," Bevilacqua promised. "Although we'll use a larger team of men, only we three will have all the details. And yes, signorina, you're correct. Your dresser, Alice, is a former prostitute employed by the Pinkerton Agency to spy on you."

Cesca sat down abruptly. She watched Bevilacqua draw a small leather-bound notebook and pen from his inside chest pocket, then her gaze fixed on the other men perched on her new silk-covered slipper chairs. Dante paced.

"We're in the process of checking the shipping ledgers and marriage licenses for the past two years," Bevilacqua said.

"Two years!"

"As a precaution. You don't have an exact date and we want to be certain. Records can be misplaced. I'm afraid we haven't yet located a Maria Grazia Muscillo or Maria Grazia Checci. We're cross-referencing for the village you gave us. Again, so far we've found nothing."

She felt crushed by the news. "I was so hoping it was good—"

"Wait, *cara*," Dante said, taking her hand, "there's more."

"We're investigating the gentleman who placed Alice," Bevilacqua said, checking his notes, "a Don Emilio Lampone. He arrived at the Plaza Hotel last night."

"Oh, Dante! I knew he'd come."

"Easy, Cesca. We have the best investigators. Emilio was forced to hire Pinkertons because we got to Petrosino first," Dante said. "So far we're ahead of him."

"He's traveling with a young Frenchwoman, a ballet dancer. He's supposedly here on business for his vineyard."

"If he's here for other reasons we'll soon uncover them," Dante reassured her.

"We've already placed one of our men inside the opera house so you'll be secure."

"My life's in your hands, Inspector."

"Now, Bevilacqua, the rest of the news," Dante coached.

"Signorina, we don't want you to give too much importance to this news . . . but one of the clues Signor Dante gave us may have yielded fruit, though it's a long shot. We believe that yesterday afternoon we spotted the earrings he spoke of in the Essex Street Market."

"The earrings?" she asked, shocked. "I never thought . . . How can you be sure?"

"They're not sure at this point," Dante interjected.

"Even though the earrings described are very distinctive, my man didn't get a clear view. We're in the process of checking on the identity of the woman wearing them." Once again he glanced down at his notes. "She's about five feet five inches, dark hair, appears to be the right age, and must be living in the tenements near Mulberry as you suspected."

"She's all right? I mean, she appears to be in good health?"

"Oh, yes, signorina, she was very robust," Colombo offered quickly.

"Unfortunately," Bevilacqua said, glaring at Colombo, "we lost her in the crowd on Grand Street."

"That was my fault, signorina," Colombo said with shame in his eyes. "A horse slipped on the wet cobbles. I was just next to him. It was a nasty break; they had to shoot him."

"I apologize for Colombo. He has a soft spot for animals. In the commotion she got away."

"*Dio!*" she cried, gripping Dante's hand. "So close." There were tears in her eyes.

"Don't worry, Signorina Frascatti, I got a good look at her," Colombo said. "I know the general direction she was headed. She'll return in the next few days. Everyone needs to eat."

"Besides," Bevilacqua interjected quickly, taking back command, "we may flush out her identity from the shipping or marriage records in the meantime."

"But Emilio's arrived!" she said. "He must know *Tosca*'s only a cover. Why else would he plant a spy? We don't have much time to find her! Madame Zavoya mentioned the earrings, do you remember? But she also mentioned danger. And blood."

"Madame Zavoya?" Bevilacqua asked, his pen poised. His ring twinkled.

"A psychic Cesca met on the ship coming over," Dante offered.

"I see," he said with a hint of disinterest as he scribbled the name. "We'll return to the market, scour Mulberry Street, and then . . ."

His voice droned on, but her mind was journeying back across the sea to reexamine the crossing and her encounter with Madame Zavoya. She was sifting her memory for any clue that might give her the answer before the enemy could discover it. What was it the woman had said about the earrings? Could it be, as ridiculous as it seemed, that the Russian woman was right?

Chapter Five

MINA PULLED AN INSIDE STRAW from her broom. If she used the upper portion, which had been tied tightly to the handle, it would be clean. The baking sponge cake filled the one-room apartment with its nutty aroma. She opened the door of the wood stove and inserted the straw. It came out clean; not a crumb stuck to the bristle.

Pleased, she removed the cake and set it on the windowsill to cool. Through the gritty windowpane she saw the junk-strewn fire escapes and frozen clotheslines of her neighbors. A feeble sifting of snow had collected on the worn stone ledge. It was the first snow of the season. Antonio was working on Pike Street. She hoped he'd gotten her message. She would need to hurry if she wanted to get everything finished in time.

Next she checked her stew. Chunks of veal, fresh mushrooms, onions, and peppers simmered in a light broth. She poured wine from the stoneware jug at the bottom of the cupboard into a glass tumbler and added it to the mixture. Not too much—the homemade dandelion wine could make the stew bitter if she added too much. She tasted the sauce. Perfect! She sighed; just the bread left to finish, but she was so tired.

At the rickety table, where the loaves were proofing in their tins, she sat and rested her chin on the palm of her hand. She stared fixedly at the torn black edge of the rose-covered linoleum and let her anxious heart revisit yesterday's events.

Once again fate had intervened. This was a last chance to set things right and win Antonio away from . . . from his other distractions. This new position and raise would make him realize how valuable she was. He couldn't deny that now, and he'd stop treating her so thoughtlessly. Then, when she told him about the baby . . . he'd be so happy.

She wasn't positive yet, but she guessed her dizziness and exhaustion might be a sign of pregnancy. She knew a child would win his heart. Didn't every man want a child, a son to carry his name? A family will make him stay at home . . . he'll treat you with love and tenderness . . . he'll stop his wicked brutal ways. He won't stop, she told her jabbering mind, nothing will make him stop! You're the wrong woman for him, you should never have agreed to marry him, what were you thinking. . . . She pushed aside her useless thoughts. If he didn't stop, what then? She thought of the money she was now making. If she added it to the money she'd saved, she could get away.

Suddenly energized, she got up and, using her right arm and hip, pulled the heavy, worn dresser aside. Ever since her wedding night she'd been putting away pennies, nickels, and dimes beneath the floorboards. She removed the extra slab of linoleum that hid the hole in the floor, and pounded her fist on the boards. Once, before using this precaution, she'd put in her hand and brushed against something soft and muscular.

She peered inside cautiously and drew out her bank. Sitting on the floor with her legs tucked under her, she took it apart. It was made from a bean can inverted inside a coffee tin and wrapped tightly with rags. She knew the rats had sharp teeth, but they couldn't reverse the cans in the hole and gnaw into her savings. If she kept checking, her future would remain safe.

She loved stacking the coins like the turrets of ancient castles. Each addition proved she was making progress. She had twenty-three dollars and eighteen cents. Compared to what she needed, it wasn't a lot, but now she would build faster. Seven dollars a week! Oh, *San't Anna,* please continue to help me, she prayed. If you help me I can get away from this awful place . . . maybe even buy a little house in Brook-a-lyn.

A place for flowers, vegetables . . . and a baby. A baby needs a decent place to grow up, with no rats to gnaw off its fingers and toes. She'd heard horrible stories about rats in the tenements. No child of mine will be placed in that kind of danger, she thought as she placed her hand on her belly. She smiled, thinking that no one but *Gesù* and *Sant'Anna* knew what might be happening inside her body. No one—

"Antonio's wife!" Teresa Santo called up the air shaft. "Peppina's back. Your husband wasn't at the work site."

Mina quickly wrapped her stash and replaced it in the hole. She shoved the dresser back and checked the room. Everything was in order.

"Antonio's wife? I know you're there, I can smell the cake you're baking."

"I'm here, Teresa," she called, rushing to the window.

"What are you doing home? Have you lost your job?"

She pushed up the sash. On the table the glass of wine was more than half full. She'd poured too much again. Antonio would be angry. Well, she thought, he can't be angry today. Today I have wonderful news to tell him. The wine is not wasted if it's drunk in celebration.

"Answer me! Have you lost your job?" Teresa shouted, letting the whole tenement in on their conversation.

"No, no, Teresa. I haven't lost my job. I have something wonderful to tell you."

"So tell me."

"Not this way. Come up. I'm putting the bread in and can't come down."

She took the glass and raised it to the statues in the corner. "To my new job and . . . my baby!" She drank the wine in one gulp the way she'd seen Antonio do. The liquid burned her throat and brought tears to her eyes. "Holy Mother of the Virgin," she croaked as she poured water from the pitcher. "I don't know how men stand the taste of this stuff. It's like drinking a fire."

She wiped the glass clean on her apron and filled it with water for Teresa. Then, using her strong right hand, she loaded the six loaves of bread into the oven, using her left forearm to steady the tins. She sharpened her paring knife on the leather strap and tested it with her thumb. Humming contentedly, she peeled peaches for the cake and listened for Teresa's tread on the stairs.

A few minutes later, groaning like a wooden ship on a rough sea, Teresa puffed into the room.

"A chair, I have to sit down. *Gesù Cristo,* but those steps are steep."

Teresa threw her two hundred and eighty pounds onto the chair and wiped her face on her flowered apron. She grasped the customary glass of water, required after the one-story climb, and gulped it down. Mina refilled the glass.

"Well, what's this wondrous news I must kill myself climbing Mount Vesuvius to hear?"

"Will you have some fruit?" Mina asked, pushing the bowl of peaches toward her friend with shy pride.

"I don't need . . . Peaches! Out of season?" Teresa whistled through her broken teeth. "*Mamma mia!* This must be big news."

Mina was self-conscious, but pleased by her friend's reaction. Teresa took a ripe peach and smelled it appreciatively. "Last night I—" Mina began as she pitted the peaches.

"No, no, don't tell me," Teresa said as she bit into the peach, juice running down her chin. "You're pregnant. That's why you have peaches, a craving. You're foolish! You think he'll change now with the baby coming? Ha, you've been careless, he'll be angry, and you'll really be trapped. What'll you do now to—?"

"Dear friend," Mina said, "that's not my news." She loved Teresa like a mother, but now she wouldn't tell her about the possibility. Not after Teresa had said she'd "been careless"—as though becoming pregnant were in her control. "But it's something almost as wondrous," she said, wiping her hands. "I have been—"

"Not pregnant? Hmm . . . Wondrous news? Let me see. . . ."

Mina waited politely for Teresa to offer another guess. She knew well this guessing game Teresa liked to play. It usually took twenty minutes to tell a two-minute tale.

"Antonio has left you! No, you've found a lover . . . and are going to run away."

Mina thought suddenly of the lover's sea-green eyes. "Would mortal sin be wondrous news?" she asked harshly, doing her best to keep the memory of last night's erotic dreams from surfacing again.

"Not so bad for you!" Teresa laughed, but seeing Mina's discomfort she stopped. "Men! Who needs them?" she continued, changing tacks. "We only need them to make the babies, and they're not so good at that. Too much trying! They huff and puff and wear you out. Then, after they are dry, they strut like roosters, as though they did it alone. We should discard them after they make the children, just like we throw out the husks from corn. They're a worthless lot."

"Some men are good."

Teresa laughed. "What are they good for, tell me? They're children finding fault with everything. They force us to be their mothers, then they chase other women, who they make their whores. They come home drunk, cursing and punching, demanding sex, and we're supposed . . ."

While Teresa continued, Mina thought about the "poor man's pastime." In the close tenements the sounds of it filled the night air like bullfrogs croaking in a swamp. She knew the others heard Antonio too. She'd often pulled the rough sheet over her head in shame while her husband lay snoring, but now she realized Teresa had *also* heard the beatings. "We mustn't become like them, Teresa. We must keep looking for the good. Besides, after we ate the corn in the old country we made soft cushions from those dry husks."

"That's true!" Teresa said. "Not such a bad idea, put them where they could do some good, under our asses." She shifted her buttocks from side to side on the hard wooden chair and laughed heartily at her joke, but her laughter turned to gasps when she accidentally sucked the peach pit she'd been chewing into her throat. Mina struck her sharply between the shoulder blades, and Teresa spit the pit onto the floor. There was a serious silence while Teresa wiped her mouth and hands on her apron.

"Are you all right?"

Teresa nodded, staring at Mina. She rubbed her throat; it was sore where the pit had lodged. Mina's quick thinking had saved her life. Mina shrugged off Teresa's thanks and retrieved the pit from the floor.

"Well, Antonio's wife, what is it? Tell me. A relative is coming? You got some money—?"

"Yes, it is money," she said.

"Mother of God!" Teresa shouted, jumping to her feet. "It's the numbers—you hit the numbers!" She swung Mina around. "You can leave this rathole! What were the numbers? Did you have a dream? How much—?"

"Sssh! No, no, not the numbers . . . or so much money."

"But it's money?" Teresa asked. Mina nodded as she closed the window. "Tell me! You are killing me!" Teresa exclaimed as she sat back down, watching Mina closely for clues.

"I am trying to tell you. Please be a little patient. Last night when I came back to the shop after—"

"The costume shop? It has something to do with the opera. Let me see—"

"Yes, the opera. Please, Teresa, let me tell it by myself. I'm so nervous; maybe we should have a little more wine. It burns going down, but I feel lighter now and not so nervous."

She went to the cupboard with Teresa's glass.

"Wine? You're drinking Antonio's beloved wine? Alone? *Gesù Cristo,* but the news must be special!"

Mina poured a healthy glass for herself and a little for Teresa, then sat at the table. While the two women sipped the wine, Mina told Teresa how she'd been given the promotion. When Mina finished, the glasses were empty and Teresa's eyes were filled with surprise.

"Seven dollars a week! *Madonna!* For that kind of money, perhaps you'll be singing for her," Teresa laughed.

"I helped Simonetta finish and came home after midnight. I must be back for this evening's performance."

Teresa regarded her thoughtfully. "Today's payday. Antonio will come home and wonder where you are."

"That's why I sent Peppina down to the site, but you said she—"

Teresa folded her arms stiffly across her breasts. "I'm sorry, Mina, I won't let Peppina go to that saloon. Three short blocks from the waterfront, that saloon is no place for a young girl."

Mina paced. "I'll have to go myself," she said, nervously rubbing the gold cross she wore around her neck between her fingers. It wasn't the women's bodies that had often been found bobbing in the shadow of the Brooklyn Bridge that frightened her.

"Don't do it. When he comes looking," Teresa said, "I'll tell him where you are."

"No!" Braced by the alcohol, she was determined not to lose this chance. "He wouldn't like a neighbor to tell him this news. It's better if I go." Mina's hands were shaking when she took the glasses to the sink. She didn't dare to look at Teresa. "He won't be angry," she said, trying to be cheerful. "This is good news. A large raise—"

"If you go to that bar you're bound to see"—Teresa hesitated uncomfortably—"something you shouldn't."

"Oh, Teresa, you don't believe gossip."

"Keep your raise a secret. Put the money aside—"

"It wouldn't work. He hates the opera people. He says they're perverts. If I tell him about the money he might let me work at night. I must go convince him."

Teresa looked meaningfully at Mina's sling. "Last time it was bad."

"But this is a raise. He'll be happy. We're saving for a—"

"Don't tell him!" Teresa said, slamming her hand flat on the table. "He'll steal it. Mina, you've got to get away. I told you about that Sicilian woman. . . ." There were tears in Teresa's eyes that conveyed the unspoken anguish of Mina's plight. Mina put an arm around her friend's shoulder and gently stroked her back.

"It'll be all right, Teresa, don't worry. *Sant'Anna*'s helping me. Things are going to be fine now. In a few months—"

Teresa jumped to her feet, startling Mina. "What's that burning smell?" Teresa asked.

"The bread! *Madonna!*" Mina ran to the oven and threw open the door. With her weak arm she struggled to get the tins out quickly. All six loaves were hopelessly scorched.

"*Maledizione!*" Teresa hissed, crossing herself superstitiously and kissing her bunched fingers. "Burned bread. Mina, it's a bad omen!"

Chapter Six

*T*HE EARTH WAS AS UNYIELDING as a cherry pit, but Antonio DiGianni slammed his pickax into the six-foot-deep ditch on the corner of Pike and East Broadway and cleaved the clay into clods as easily as if the earth had been tenderly drenched in summer rain.

A battered group of workers stood above him, on rough mounds of earth, shifting from foot to foot to keep their feet from freezing. They leaned on their tools, cupping hand-rolled cigarettes in their calloused palms, and turned their faces into the damp wind blowing off the East River, just five blocks south, to watch their *paesano,* Tonio, tirelessly heave the pickax.

He was dressed against the cold like the other men: in a union suit and wool flannel shirt with a moth-eaten merino vest layered on top and dirt-encrusted trousers tucked into battered boots. His jacket hung on a support post, for it interfered with his movements and slowed him down. He wore a mossy green cap to keep his hair out of his eyes and had tied a greasy bandanna around his neck to keep the sweat he hated so much from running down his back.

With each swing of the pickax, he was dusted in fine bits of earth. His breath puffed out like smoke from the stack of a steam locomotive and the men watched in envy as he chugged along, breaching the earth like some crazed, windup digging machine.

To the men, Tonio was a Titan capable of feats no other dare attempt. He was the oldest, the leader. They admired his zeal in a ditch, his skill with his fists, and his earthy charm with women. Most of them were still in their teens and had only been in the country a few months. He was their template of success and they wished in their hearts to be like him or at least to be liked by him. All the men in the group wished it but one: Mario Catanzaro.

Mario stood apart from the men, his lanky body leaning against a post. There was a sprinkle of dark stubble across his chin and hollow cheeks. His gray eyes were hooded as he observed the scene and drew on his clay pipe. He was the quiet one in the group. Solid and determined. The one the men went to for advice and an occasional loan. The one studying English at night by kerosene lamp and the one who wanted more from life than a snoot full of beer at the end of the day or a flop with a whore at the end of the week. Mario saved his money. He kept to himself.

He wasn't physically strong like Tonio, but he was shrewd and dangerous with a grape knife. Awake or asleep he kept the curved blade strapped to his right calf. In an instant he could snap it open, take a wicked bite of flesh, and end a confrontation. That was how he'd met Tonio, aboard ship, their first night in steerage. Tonio had gotten into an altercation and had defended himself admirably with his fists, but when his opponent pulled a knife, Mario had intervened.

His ability to coolly deal in violence had won Tonio's respect. For Mario's part, he'd thought Tonio a hothead, but he'd always believed his friend's heart was good. For four and a half years the two had been closer than brothers, but today, as he watched him work, a hazy suspicion was crystallizing.

Mario was thinking his assessment might have been wrong. Perhaps what Biaggio and the men hinted at was true—that Tonio wasn't a friend, and that his heart was as black and corroded as the sewage pipes they were repairing. If what he now suspected turned out to be true,

Mario would gladly sink his knife into his best friend's heart with as much force as Tonio threw the pickax into the solid earth.

"*Madonna puttana!* The Madonna's a whore!" Tonio cursed in familiar Neapolitan dialect. "Let me see your balls now that I've done the work for you. Give me your hand, Mario."

Mario grasped his wrist and pulled him from the trench. Tonio wiped the sweat from his forehead with the back of his arm, smearing his face with dirt, then he looked the group over with a smirk. "Go on, Sale, get down there. Let me see your skinny ass sweat."

Salvatore, a tender fourteen-year-old, and Salvatore's cousin, Paolo, jumped into the trench. The men called them *Sale* and *Pepe,* salt and pepper, as much for their initials as for their habit of always doing things together. They began to break up and shovel out the clods of earth.

"It took me, one man, less than twenty minutes to break up the soil. Let me see how fast you two women can shovel out my work. Mario, time them on your watch," Tonio said as he strutted over to the community cache of beer pails.

Mario felt the men's eyes on him as he took out his prized gold watch. It was a present from his former bride-to-be, a girl from the old country, from the mountains near *Napoli*. As the second hand swept the face and he counted the minutes, his thoughts turned back to a year earlier.

America wasn't the golden dream Mario had hoped for, but at least he was getting more than bread for his labor. When he wasn't working or studying he was dreaming. Dreaming and saving for his own business, because being a day laborer simply traded one tyrant for another. He knew it would take time and planning, and he was willing to make the necessary sacrifices; but after four years he was lonely.

Though the days had flashed by, the nights had lagged and troubled him. He'd kept company with the men, going to the bars, playing cards, and going through the motions at the dance halls his friends dragged him to, but the women he met there weren't to his taste. Not that he was a saint—he sewed an occasional wild oat—but the encounters left him irritated, not pacified.

Sex wasn't the answer to his need. He'd tried courting a few women from Mulberry Street, but those women seemed more interested in spending his pay than in getting to know him. He wanted a woman he could respect and who strove to exceed expectations as he did. Finally, disgusted by scant return on his attempts, he'd given up his search for intimacy.

It was Tonio who'd renewed Mario's interest and given him hope. He'd told him a story about an exceptional girl he knew from his village, Rocco San Felice. The last time he'd seen her she had been thirteen, but he'd heard she was still unmarried. She was feisty and virtuous, but no man in the village would marry her because she was illegitimate and tainted with the same hot blood as her mother.

Mario laughed at such ignorance. It wasn't her fault she'd been born out of wedlock. Her own character or lack of it was the only issue. Tonio swore the girl was beautiful, strong, and independent, and because Mario understood how it felt to be a spoon among forks, he was moved by her plight. He'd written to the village priest, explaining his desire to make a match, and he was overjoyed when the priest wrote back, asking him to send passage money.

It took several months to conclude all the details, and during the final days of the transaction he began to have second thoughts. His friend Tonio wasn't the best judge of character. Perhaps he was making a mistake. But the day Mina stepped from the darkness of the shed on Ellis Island to meet him he'd fallen in love. She was all that he'd hoped for: a spring lamb among goats.

"I need some beer. Pass a growler over," Tonio ordered Mario. Mario registered Tonio's demand and handed him a beer pail, but his brain continued to churn images.

Before the wedding Mario had arranged for Mina to stay with their friend Biaggio's two sisters. Her first night in America he'd dressed up in his only suit and brought bread, wine, chocolates, and a box of pastries over to Biaggio's sister's house for dinner. He was so nervous and excited he stuttered and knocked his wineglass over, soaking the cloth. His fiancée was shy and a bit fearful, refusing to meet his eyes, but he considered her behavior natural. It would take time for her to trust him.

The third night he brought wine and pastries and loosened his tie. He followed every movement as she helped prepare dinner. She was so graceful and lovely; he couldn't believe his good fortune. When the women began snapping beans for dinner he pitched in. They teased him about women's work and he joked back, trying to put his future wife at ease, but she was still shy. When her fingers found the same bean he'd picked from the colander, their eyes finally met.

"*Mi scusi,* Signor Catanzaro," she said, not letting go.

"Mario. My name is Mario, Signorina Rossi."

Her crimson lips parted in a smile, showing even white teeth. "Friends call me . . . Filomina. Mina, if you prefer."

Her face colored, but her dark eyes twinkled as she took the bean from him and "accidentally" brushed his palm with her fingers.

"Signorina Mina," he'd said, savoring the sound of her name on his tongue and her touch on his skin.

He was floating with joy in the overheated kitchen. Everything was going to work out, he was certain of it. The love was there submerged in her eyes and in her voice; she would learn to care for him, and in time, passion for him would rise to the surface. He'd been in paradise that night until Tonio had come to join them for dinner. Then he noticed her eyes turned away from him. They would never return.

A few days later Tonio claimed he'd been struck with "blood fever" that night and had immediately fallen in love. Only true love, he claimed, could turn his allegiance to ash and turn Mina's heart toward another flame. Tonio insisted it had to be *destino*'s plan, a plan that could not be denied. Tonio begged him to allow Mina to decide.

Mario tamped down the anguish he felt and asked her to choose.

"It's true. I love Signor Antonio," she said. "I've known him since I was a child, and though you're kind, you're a stranger to me, signore. I appreciate your paying my passage here, but if I must choose . . ."

His white-knuckled hands were jammed in his pockets when she chose Tonio, and for friendship's sake, Mario had accepted what everyone called "*destino*'s plan."

Since that day he'd kept busy and buried his anger. He told himself he was happy for his friend, but at night he tossed and turned, dreaming of Mina and the life that should have been his. The visions ate away his heart and corroded his spirit like acid. He had always been the one who'd never had more than a glass of wine with dinner, but now in order to keep his feelings in check he drank in secret. He could have accepted fate's cruel torture if only Tonio had settled down with Mina, but Tonio was still carrying on with his Irish whore, Kathleen Shaunessey.

"Hey, *Sale,* you better shovel faster," Tonio mocked, "your sand's running out." He gestured to the men to bang on their shovels to distract the diggers, then set himself behind the two and began shoveling the dirt back into the ditch.

"You're throwing more dirt on Sale than out of the trench, Pepe," one of the men called down to the harried pair.

"Hey, Sale, you using a teaspoon or a shovel?" another jeered.

The men hammered and shouted encouragement to cover the noise of the dirt falling back faster than the two could throw it up and out. It was all part of the *fratelli di sangue,* brotherhood of blood, an important test for *paesani* who wanted to fit in. This group of Neapolitans was having a good laugh at the expense of the two greenhorns. After a few minutes Tonio threw down his shovel and upended a beer can.

"This growler's dry as a virgin's cunt!" he shouted, glaring at the group. "I sweat my balls off digging a hole up Satan's ass and there's not even two swallows of beer to wet my whistle when I'm done."

He stomped over to the other cans, finding they too had been emptied. Grasping the handle of the last growler in his scarred fist, he savagely beat dents into the container until, in a fury, he flung the battered can skyward like a rocket.

All gaiety stopped. Sale and Pepe in the ditch had the excuse of their digging, but those on the sidelines turned away and began urgently moving earth from one of the many piles to a wheelbarrow. No one wanted to deal with Tonio in a temper.

"Which one of you *finocchi* finished the beer? Huh?" he demanded, his face distorted by anger. "Tell me, queers! Which one of you did it?"

"We sent Sean for more beer. The Cocked Hat's only a few blocks from here," Biaggio said evenly.

"I don't give a fuck how close the Cocked Hat is. Where's the respect? The respect for a *paesano,* huh? Who's the *bastardo* who finished off the growler?" He slammed his foot down on one of the tin cans, crushing it like a peanut shell.

"Take it easy, Tonio! We can get more beer," Biaggio said.

"*Stai zitto*, Biaggio!" Tonio yelled, his face purple. "*Gesù Cristo,* you men stop jerking off and answer me!"

Mario watched the men scurrying around like ants and pitied them. Only last night they'd watched Tonio viciously beat a vodka-soaked Polack to a pulp in the back of his mistress's bar. His fury had been so hot,

Mario and Biaggio had been forced to pry him off. Then Tonio had turned on Biaggio, and only Mario's cool reasoning and the threat of his knife had checked his madness. It was clear the others would never have enough guts to stand up to him. "I drank the last of the beer," Mario said.

Tonio whirled to face Mario's impassive stare. The men looked up quickly, a charge of electricity in the air. Was it going to happen? After six months of tension, was the dam about to be breached? Mario's face was open and friendly, but his tone was hard as paving stone. Yes, the men thought, the buried insult had finally surfaced. Flint was about to be struck.

"You? You don't drink," Tonio laughed. He clapped Mario on the shoulder and turned back to the group. Their eyes darted away.

"I did today," Mario insisted. "I finished the last drop while I watched you sweating blood in the ditch."

Tonio turned back, aware of the challenging tone in Mario's voice. What was going through his friend's mind, to challenge him this way in front of the men? Mario was no match for him with his fists. Why, it was laughable; Mario had the punch of a poet. His challenge was insanity! He must be joking.

"Why do you protect them?" Tonio asked under his breath.

"Because you're the kind of animal men fear."

"They should fear me! The stupid asses drank the growlers dry!"

"No. I drank the growler dry," Mario said, gripping his shovel for strength. "I, Mario Catanzaro, do not care if your spit is dust or your throat is as parched as the rocks of Sardinia."

Tonio's instincts hurled him forward, yet everything else seemed to slow down. He cast aside the empty growler as Mario's shovel toppled to the ground. Mario planted his feet and put up his left arm in anticipation of Tonio's punch. From the corner of his eye Tonio saw the men drop their tools and form a ragged circle. He focused his attention on Mario. Mario's face was set, his eyes were deadly. All the men were watching. The air felt as heavy as a wheelbarrow of wet cement.

Tonio's brain signaled caution; Mario could outmaneuver him with his knife. He wondered what was in his friend's mind. He knew the men had been ribbing Mario, telling him things to get him riled up and trying to get him to lose his temper. Everyone said Mario was too easygoing. "Watch out," they teased, "one day the volcano will shoot rocks to the moon!"

But it had to be a joke. Mario didn't have a mean bone in his body. Why, he'd handed his fiancée over without a second thought. He was like a brother. He couldn't be serious. This was a poor attempt by Mario to show he too could let off steam. After a long moment Tonio began to laugh. What a fool Mario was! To insult him, the leader of the group, the toughest middleweight boxer on the Lower East Side. He actually thought he was going to take on Antonio DiGianni? It was insanity!

"He does not care!" he said, turning to the others, who stood frozen in place. "Did you hear him? I can be as dry as the rocks of Sardinia!"

The men stared at him, confused.

"Ha, ha, very funny!" Tonio shouted. "He's learning to curse like the rest of you cucumbers!"

They glanced at one another. They knew Mario wasn't joking, but they laughed with Tonio to dispel the awful tension.

"Who's been teaching you? You've finally learned to swear like a man! Well, if you drank the beer, you must have needed it. I'm glad you had your fill." Tonio picked up the shovel at Mario's feet and threw it into a mound of soil like a javelin, then went to fetch his jacket from the post. Mario stood with his fists ready, staring at Tonio's back. He couldn't believe Tonio was laughing off his insult and walking away. His hand reached toward his right calf as he stepped forward.

Biaggio stepped between.

"Where's that little potato peeler?" Tonio growled. "Biaggio, didn't you say you sent that *bastardo* Sean for more beer? And something to eat?"

"Yeah, I sent him to the Cocked Hat an hour ago," Biaggio said, grabbing Mario's wrist and blocking him from Tonio's view. "I don't know where he could be."

"I was saying—" Mario started.

"*Stai zitto!*" Biaggio said under his breath, drawing a flat hand across his throat in a cutting motion.

Tonio remained oblivious.

"It's almost time to be knocking off for lunch anyway," Tonio said. "Let's go to the Hat. Kathleen's got the five-cent lunch set up by now. I'll buy a round."

The men cheered. "What's the celebration?" Biaggio asked.

"I netted a fine purse off that Polack last night," Tonio said in a jubilant tone. "And my friend Mario finally curses like a man. *Andiamo!*" He tossed his jacket over his shoulder and started off down the cobbled street, leaving the others to clean up. Mario's knife was in his hand and he would have followed, but Biaggio stood in his path.

"Why did you do that, Biaggio?" Mario asked through his teeth.

"Because I'm a real friend to you and he's a madman. You're behaving like a stupid woman. Do you want to end up smashed?" he asked, pushing the crushed tin at his feet with the toe of his boot. "In jail? There's a place for everything. Let's go get some lunch."

"I don't want his lunch," Mario said, pulling away.

"Ah, but you'll eat his lunch just the same. You've been smart, Mario, to stay friendly. There's plenty of time and many ways to settle old debts."

Chapter Seven

*W*HILE CESCA WAS APPEARING in Rome, before arranging the engagement at the Manhattan Opera House, she'd received startling news. An envelope had arrived addressed with the spiky, urgent script she knew and loved so well. Sister Anselm, Cesca's first voice teacher and the cook at the convent where she'd been raised, had written that the trail she'd been following for the last two years now led to America: "Your talent will shine brilliantly in New York and you will achieve all we have been seeking these years in your training."

Cesca had understood the code. Within a day, certain of the eager greed of Oscar Hammerstein, she'd booked passage with Dante on a ship out of Naples. She'd cabled Hammerstein from port, and confirmation of her "limited engagement" had come the next day on board. He'd offered her eight performances of *Tosca* over a two-week period and she'd hoped it would give her enough time to search the city without arousing suspicion.

Nervous and impatient to arrive, she'd paced the decks from early morning to well past midnight. The third day of the journey Dante, who had been passing his time playing cards in the salon, finessed an interesting tidbit of gossip. It concerned a Russian woman traveling with them in first class who was making a stir. The woman, rumored to be part of the extended royal family, was a famous mirror gazer, a visionary, who could see relatives of the living and the dead in a polished bronze mirror. The mirror was carried under lock and key and had supposedly belonged to a fifteenth-century Hungarian sorceress of ill repute. It had been passed down from mother to daughter, along with the ability to see the unknowable.

He suggested, jokingly, that the woman might help them, and was dumbfounded when Cesca actually sought an appointment. The woman, who never left her stateroom, refused through intermediaries. She was on holiday, and no amount of money, flattery, or maneuvering would induce her to give a reading. In addition, she was booked solidly in America. "Perhaps," she offered, "on my return from San Francisco?"

Assured by several passengers that Madame Zavoya was a genuinely gifted psychic capable of giving her the information she required, Cesca came up with a scheme. Through the captain of the ship she offered an evening of music for Zavoya and her friends in return for a reading. An evening of Italian arias and folk tunes was dearer to Zavoya than gold, and an appointment was set for the very next day.

Once the agreement had been reached Cesca didn't know what to think. She'd never had her palm or tarot cards read and didn't believe in any of the supernatural nonsense that currently gripped the intelligentsia. She remembered well the superstitions that had infected her little village, as well as her strict Catholic upbringing. The darkly veiled nuns had forbidden any dabbling in the occult. Dark deeds, the unknown, gypsies, and spirits were Satan's tools.

The next day when she sat down at a table in the darkened stateroom of Madame Zavoya, she was trembling like a twelve-year-old before a reprimand. She was instructed by Madame's assistant to loosen any tight-fitting garments, to clear her mind, to breathe deeply and rhythmically, and to concentrate on her question. Madame Zavoya would do the rest. The assistant lit candles and dimmed the gaslights further. All was still, dark, impenetrable. Cesca heard the sound of soft sulfur flaring and then smelled the sweet, thick scent of incense.

The Russian came to the table. A large, amorphous figure in dark, flowing clothes, her face was covered by sheer silk scarves. When she rested her bejeweled hands on the black cloth Cesca saw bright red-varnished nails tipping pudgy hands. The assistant wafted several sticks of incense over her, sending forth a cloud of smoke. Then they were alone.

"Don't be afraid. There's really nothing supernatural about this process. It's simply a means of focusing the mind."

Madame Zavoya's voice was deep and melodious. She stretched her arm across the small table and tapped Cesca's forehead between the eyebrows three times. "Focus your question here, in the third eye."

"I want to know—"

"No. Do not tell me. Concentrate on your question. Focus it as though it were a ray of pure sunlight shining from your soul." She removed her veils and arranged her flowing garments. Zavoya was a plump, pleasant-looking woman of middle age. "You will see that the spirit is more powerful than the mind can ever imagine," she said with a mischievous smile.

She lifted the purple velvet cover off a shining gold circle of light lying on the table before her and sat with her eyes closed in deep concentration for what seemed a lifetime. Cesca grew calm, a bit bored, and then impatient. The incense was cloying, she felt shut up, trapped. She stifled a nervous giggle. It crossed her mind to get up and leave, the whole thing seemed so ridiculous.

"There," Madame Zavoya said in awe, waving her hand over the surface of the mirror, "there . . . do you see it?"

"See what?" Cesca asked, startled by Zavoya's sudden question in the stillness of the darkened room.

"Concentrate on your question, force the ray of knowing into the heart of the mirror. Do it, do it now!"

Cesca stared at the mirror for a few moments, with her question focused like a spotlight, and then glanced away. The room felt charged with energy. It reminded her of opening night, standing behind the curtains while the orchestra played the last notes of the overture. Zavoya's eyes were still closed. She began emitting a low humming sound, like a little swarm of bees near a hive.

This is ridiculous, Cesca thought, annoyed with her own stupidity in promising a night of music in return for a bit of cheap theatrics. She was about to get up when she glanced back at the mirror, which seemed darker, as though clouded over by steam.

"The earrings . . . I see the bright stone earrings," Zavoya hummed in her singsong voice.

The hairs on Cesca's arms stood up. "Who told you about the earrings?" Cesca demanded, feeling cold.

"I see them glitter. First on one and then another. Threads and air . . . spider's webs. She does not seek that which has been lost. Death has closed that path. I see suffering . . . danger, darkness, and fear."

"What danger?"

"Those stones are dear to her . . . dear to her like . . . a mother's love. It is a mother's love that will save her."

"I don't understand you. Where are the earrings? Who has them? Where is she?" Cesca demanded.

"There is trouble . . . grave trouble. And blood . . . blood as dark as the stones on her ears."

"Where can I find this woman?"

"She is . . . with you. Oh, I feel pain . . . pain. . . ." Zavoya writhed in pain, putting her hand on her side and twisting her body, her face creased with intensity of feeling. "There are three . . . three . . . knives . . . a curved blade . . . amber glass, and pearl. Jealousy and revenge . . . jealousy and lust . . . jealousy and greed . . . threads that bind . . . knives that cut. Across the sea, a child is lost. . . . Ahead of you . . . yes, it is all ahead of you. Find without looking. Look without knowing. It is kismet."

"Kismet?"

"Fate."

The mirror flashed with light.

"Be careful, there is sorrow and tears . . . and in a web . . . death. That is all."

The assistant was back, helping Madame Zavoya to her feet. Cesca stared at the polished disk of bronze. What kind of tricks were these? Who had informed her about the earrings? Not Dante—he didn't know, for she'd forgotten to tell him.

"Wait, I don't understand. Madame Zavoya?"

The attendant covered the mirror and ushered Madame out of the sitting room still waving her incense. Cesca stood up.

"But what am I to do? Where am I to look?" She followed Zavoya to her dressing room and wedged her foot in the closing door. "Madame, please—"

Zavoya turned her distant gaze upon Cesca one last time. "Do not look back. The past is gone. You will be found. And she . . . It is kismet! That is all."

Zavoya slipped away into her bedroom, melting into a haze of smoke, as the door closed in Cesca's face.

BACK in her dressing room, the vision before Cesca's eyes faded like the smoke of the incense. She found herself holding her hairbrush and staring stupidly at her own image reflected in the mirror. Her anxious eyes were as dark and deep as mountain pools. Her skin looked chalky. She wrapped her arms around her body for warmth. The men had gone. She was alone and chilled to the marrow.

That damn Alice hadn't banked the fire properly and it had gone out. Well, tomorrow there would be a new dresser to tend the fire, and if *Gesù* willed, her answer would come soon enough. Kismet. *Destino.* She began to dress. "Do not look . . ." Madame Zavoya had said. "You will be found."

Chapter Eight

AFTER TERESA LEFT, Mina set up her wash-tub. Using only her right arm, she clenched her teeth and bore the pain of several trips up the two flights of stairs from the communal water faucet. She topped off the bath with boiling water from the stove, then stripped, stepped in, and scrubbed. She soaped her hair and rinsed it with vinegar to make it shine, then arranged the thick braids into intricate loops. Crouching naked next to the bed, she pulled out the wicker trunk Mario had helped Antonio carry to the room.

She took what she needed and was about to shove the trunk back, when she stopped to lift the sleeve of the white wedding gown from its tissue. She brushed it tenderly against her face as the faint scent of dried lavender floated up. For an instant she was a child again and her grandmother's eyes were shining in the lamplight as she crossed the bobbins back and forth, teaching her to make lace. The satin was cool and soothing against her skin; it reminded her of her dead mother's hands.

She winced remembering how Biaggio's jealous sisters had tricked her out of wearing the gown and delicate veil. A "modern American suit and hat will make Antonio proud," they had said. "He loves everything American. You don't want to be *cafone.*" The suit had instead made him doubt her purity and had earned her a black eye. She sighed. She should have realized the sisters wanted Antonio for themselves. She'd have to save the beautiful gown for a daughter. She tucked the sleeve gently into the tissue and pushed the trunk back.

It seemed to take forever to put on her corset and roll up her stockings. Her right hand was trembling with fatigue by the time she slipped on her Sunday dress. Frugally she dabbed perfume on her throat and fastened her plain gold earrings. She smiled nervously at the white-faced woman she saw in her mirror and critically assessed her appearance. The sling stood out conspicuously against her dark dress.

Her shoulder was almost healed, just a little sore in the joint, and she would need both hands tonight. She unfastened the scarf, extended her arm, and flexed her fingers, reassuring herself that her arm was strong. She placed the cloth on her bureau and knelt. *Gesù* hadn't been too helpful lately so she'd decided her petitions should go to holy women who might better understand her problems.

"*Sant'Anna, Madonna,* help me," she murmured, beseeching the statues in the corner. "I cannot lose this chance."

She locked the door and headed down the steps, determined to find her husband and get his permission before she took the trolley uptown.

At the Cocked Hat Kathleen had just finished setting out the "free lunch" in the back room. On the buffet table she'd placed a pot of cabbage with a few bits of corned beef, a large jar of dill pickles, several crusty loaves of day-old bread, a pot of butter, cold baked beans, some sliced cheese, and half a baked ham.

The men in the front room had been waiting patiently while she finished up, smoking stogies or spitting tobacco juice into dented spittoons on the sawdusted floor. They eyed each other's glasses jealously, knowing their pints would allow them to partake in the bounty only if their glasses were more than half full by the time she rang the bell and opened the ladies' entrance. The longer she took to set up, the closer they'd come to having to buy another pint.

"That's it, boyos!" she said, swiping grimy palms across her stained apron. She slipped the lock and rang the bell sharply. In with the cold came a stream of ragged working girls and children who'd been waiting impatiently outside the door.

"Come on in and warm yerselves. The lunch is out. Hey! You there, scrape yer feet. This ain't no shanty!"

They squeezed through the door and hurried to the bar to pay the tariff and get their pint. Then they headed for the food and the potbellied stove to cop a seat as close as possible to the coal fire.

A few scraggly children rushed forward with growlers, weaving and pushing to be first in line. Through the archway she saw one of the ruffians slyly stealing a piece of ham.

"I see ya, Sean Catagan. Put my ham back where it belongs or I bat yer brains to butter, ya little hooligan."

Sean slipped the slab of ham out of his pocket and patted it back in place on the china platter. He dare not ignore Kathleen Shaunessey, who had been known to bloody a grown man's nose or blacken a ditchdigger's eye with her tough, ready fists. Even though he was paying to fill beer cans, it didn't entitle him to a taste of her table.

"Get yer lazy bum over here and give me a hand with pints and growlers and I might give ya a bit of lunch. Hurry it up before I change my mind. Take it easy now, lads, there's plenty for everyone."

Sean rushed to help. The other children eyed him enviously, their own hunger-pinched stomachs groaning with the same intensity his belly felt.

"Good afternoon, Mrs. Shaunessey. A pint of ale if you please," the first woman in line said, pushing her nickel across the counter with two stiff fingers.

Her tongue wet her cracked lips in anticipation as she watched Kathleen pull the first ale. To the woman's consternation the glass was more than half filled with foam.

"Don't worry," Kathleen said, laughing at the woman's expression, "I know my business." To Sean's surprise she dumped the foam and ale into his growler and said, "Pull her another and make sure there's not but a splash of foam." She handed Sean the glass and watched him pull off a perfect pint.

"Thank you kindly, Mrs. Shaunessey!" the woman said, clutching the full glass to her breasts.

Sean cocked an eyebrow at this rare occurrence, but kept pulling while she tallied the coins. The line was long and her mood became more jovial with each nickel dropped in the till. Since she'd begun the "free lunch" the saloon was filled day and night with working stiffs.

Sean stood at his post while she set about refilling the cabbage pot and dumping the scraps, whistling under her breath and swinging her skirts. He'd never known her to be so free with food and ale, and he was wary of the gay mood that lay upon her. Something was up with the devil himself if a tune from Kathleen was hanging in the daytime air. "Yer feeling fine today, Mrs. Shaunessey!"

"What's it to ya, Mr. Catagan? I suppose yer lord and master, Mr. Antonio, sent ya to fill his growlers and run yer bum back to the work site." She elbowed her way to the buffet, threw together a sandwich of ham and cheese, smeared on a bit of mustard, then wrapped the whole in a napkin. "Get yerself some grub, then take this and those growlers back to his lordship." Sean rushed to fill his bowl and have a seat on the floor.

It was true; Kathleen *was* feeling very generous. For wasn't it only last night that she'd gotten another tidy purse from a fistfight held in her back room for the amusement of the local toughs, and wasn't there more to come?

After paying off the dazed opponent she'd stuffed two wads of greasy greenbacks into her stocking tops. In addition, she'd won an extra fist of cash by betting on the winner, her lover, Tonio. With two rolls of hard cash rubbing together between her thighs and the third one between her breasts the sensation was better than the stroke of a stiff cock. Her spirits were soaring.

* * *

TWO blocks from the East River Mina got off the trolley car. The smell of seawater and sewage and the cry of the gulls that swooped down to feed on the rotting garbage around the piers reminded her of the Bay of Naples. As she crossed the trolley tracks she took steady, slow breaths to settle her stomach and keep from vomiting.

She was desperate to avoid a confrontation with Antonio, but it would be too great an insult to his manhood to have a neighbor tell him his wife had changed jobs. She had to get his permission. Teresa had told her to look for an ancient cobbler's shop that was on the corner of Cherry Street a few buildings from the saloon. As she hurried along the narrow street, searching for the cobbler, she thought over the six months of her marriage.

Two weeks after their wedding Antonio had announced he would start working double shifts, six days a week. He'd start early and finish late in order to earn enough to save for a house away from the tenements. Of course, he'd need to relax a little with cards and a drink or two, so he'd bunk with Mario as he had before the wedding. He'd thrown the lodgers out of his old place on Mulberry so she had her own place to stay and he'd promised she'd see him every day when she brought his lunch.

One day a week he'd come home for the night and collect her pay so that every penny they earned was saved. "We can make it in America," he'd said. "Hard work and separation are small sacrifices to make for our children." After seeing the decaying apartments everyone lived in, Mina had quickly agreed to the plan, but she felt lonely and isolated. Each day as she left the apartment to take his lunch to the work site or to go shopping in the market, she wondered at his reasoning when her neighbors drew aside as she passed, whispering.

It didn't take long for Biaggio's sisters to snipe about another woman, a black-haired Irish saloon keeper who'd been involved with Antonio before her marriage. "He's in love with her," they'd said, "and will never break it off." She'd been upset by their catty remarks but had hidden her feelings until she could run back home to demand that Teresa tell her the truth.

"Of course there were other women," Teresa had said. "What kind of man stays alone for five years? But he's married to you now and working hard for a house. Forget those evil gossips. Jealous tongues always find something to say."

So Mina had taken Teresa's advice. She'd ignored Biaggio's sisters and the strange women's stares, but a feeling that something was going on behind her back with another woman dogged her days. At night she'd toss and turn thinking over his explanations: he stayed away for the sake of work and their future, he was exhausted from heaving a pickax and only needed a place to flop, it would only be a year at most they'd have to sacrifice like this, then they'd be together and have everything. . . .

He'd told her that if she had need of him she was to send a messenger to get him. On no condition was a decent woman, especially his wife, to come into the saloon and boardinghouse where he spent his off hours. Her knees wobbled when she caught sight of the swinging sign, a three-cornered hat on a ground of green, but she forced herself forward. After all, she wasn't doing anything against his orders. She wasn't going inside.

At the back entrance she put her hand up to shade the grimy glass and peered inside. She didn't see Antonio in the crowd of people drinking and eating in the back room, but there was an archway leading to another room. Perhaps he was in there.

She grasped the doorknob, thinking she should just go in and speak with him like a normal human being, but even though she wanted to open the door she couldn't make her hand turn the knob. She knew Antonio's anger too well. She put her hand down and balled it into a first, her soul rebelling at the injustice of the situation. She'd have to wait like a dog in the street for her master.

It wasn't fair that she had to obey his wishes over her own needs, but even in America it was her duty as his wife. She pushed her fury down and stood off to the side, hoping a woman would come along. She didn't dare approach a man to send inside. If she didn't find a woman quickly she'd be late for her new job.

While she was anxiously watching the street, the door of the ladies' entrance swung open and a woman with long black hair stepped out. The woman carried a heavy garbage can to the curb and dumped the contents into the gutter. She hadn't noticed Mina standing against the wall, and Mina wondered if this was the black-haired woman, the one Biaggio's sisters had gossiped about, the one they said was having an affair with her husband. She wanted a better view and edged forward cautiously, jealousy and curiosity mixing in equal parts.

What did this woman have to do with Antonio? Was she the reason he didn't come home at night? Were they really having an affair? She decided to find out. "*Mi scusi!*"

The woman whirled, looking startled. "For the love of Christ, ya scared the piss outta me!"

Mina didn't understand the words, but the tone was angry. The woman was attractive in an overblown, obvious way. Her eyes were clear blue and cold. Around her face she'd pinned back her curly hair, but in back thick strands snaked to her waist and fell over a plunging neckline that showed ample breasts.

"Antonio DiGianni?" Mina tried. Then in Italian she added, "I need to speak with him."

The woman recognized her, for her face moved from fear to haughtiness. "He ain't here."

The woman didn't speak Italian. How was it possible that she was involved with her husband if she didn't understand his language?

"Antonio?" she asked again, pointing inside the bar and gesturing that she wanted him to come out.

"Not here!" The woman shook her head. She waved her hand as though dismissing a child and started back inside, her pail swaying. Mina tried to push past her to look inside the open door, but the woman turned and blocked her way. Her face was angry.

"No! This is my bar and you ain't welcome. Get going!" the woman shouted, giving her a shove. "Go on, get outta here."

Caught off balance, Mina stumbled off the curb and into the gutter as the woman slammed back inside.

Chapter Nine

～❦～

HERE YOU ARE, you little prick!" Tonio said, coming into the back room of the Cocked Hat. "Sitting on your ass, stuffing your mug while we freeze our *coglioni* off at the site! Where's the beer Biaggio sent you for, eh?"

Sean jumped to his feet, but Kathleen waved him down.

"Leave him be. I needed his help today with the free lunch. Jimmy's got the afternoon off." She embraced him roughly, kissing him square on the mouth. "For the love of Pete, what are ya doing here at this hour?"

He pushed her toward the bar. "I came for my end," he announced to the men, grabbing her ass, "and maybe a piece of yours."

She swatted his hands away while he laughed at his joke and the annoyance he'd sparked from her eyes. "What the hell's wrong with ya, ya dumb wop? We agreed to split it tonight after closing." Suddenly aware of the lump the wad of cash made in her dress, she swept around the end of the bar and shoved the roll further down in her corset. "Yer wife was just here, looking for ya, but I sent her packing. She—"

"Can it!" he snapped, peeling off his jacket. "Tell me later, get me some beer. We're celebrating last night's fight."

Kathleen glared at him, doubly mad, first for ordering her around in front of the men and second for shutting her down. It had to be big news for his wife to come snooping around, but he was going to make her wait. It was clear the subject was closed.

"Give the men drinks," Tonio ordered. "I promised them lunch."

"Lunch? And who's going to be paying for their drinks?" Kathleen demanded, a snarl in her voice.

"I am. Out of your winnings," Tonio said coldly. "I earned every penny myself. I spend it any way I like."

"Why, ya Neapolitan ape! Share and share alike, ya said. We're supposed to be partners. Fifty-fifty. Ya don't get the whole payday, and ya'll pay for drinks out of yer end of the money."

"I gave them the show. The sweat came from my hide. I won and you're paying." He banged his fist on the bar and stared her down.

It was true, Tonio had given a good show, but he would've decked the bum in the first round and bored everyone. She'd managed and maneuvered him to create the necessary drama, then chose the perfect moment for him to knock out his pathetic foe. And she'd set the admission. He'd thought two bits was plenty, but she'd held firm at fifty cents. She had to bear the risk alone of being blown in—an illegal fight could take her liquor license or even the bar itself.

"Men," Tonio called, "help yourself to the eats."

They emptied her pots and jars faster than chickens pecking corn. She could do nothing but clamp her jaw and pour out the beers Tonio demanded. Here it was all over again, a man telling her how to run her business, a man ordering her around, a man taking all the credit.

Well, he might get away with it today, but she wasn't going to let Tonio DiGianni take Jack Shaunessey's place riding her like a pack animal. She glared at him, watching him strut, a shine of new brass about him that she'd provided, and thought bitterly that she'd returned to the same spot she'd been struggling so hard to escape.

She'd married Jack Shaunessey, the owner of the Cocked Hat and a whale of an Irishman, from Galway, two days off the ship. Her hope had been that his "weak heart" would quit on him in the sack, but the bastard had held on for seven years. After the first week she knew she'd made a bad bargain, for the bar was hard work and Jack wasn't an easy man.

He'd played her like he played his fiddle—fast and hard—and left her a passel of gambling debts and a hidden second mortgage. She'd been able to tuck a bit by, but drunk as he was, Jack had a sharp eye and a tight fist when it wasn't him spending. She wasn't able to save much.

If it hadn't been for the lien on the two-room bar she'd have been within a few hundred dollars of her goal, but after paying off his markers she didn't have enough left to buy a stale beer joint. With this new venture and side bets she might bankroll her dream: a posh bar and restaurant above Fourteenth Street that she had her eye on.

"Kathleen, another beer," Tonio shouted from a front room table as he shoveled his food.

A hot retort readied itself on her lips, but she caught herself. It wouldn't do to lose her temper. No, he was her only ticket at the moment. Besides, her hold on him was easy to maintain, if she was smart.

She slid out from behind the bar, carrying several pint glasses of ale, and set them on his table.

"Here ya are, Tonio, darlin'," she said, smiling down at him invitingly. She settled herself on his lap, spreading her skirt and sliding her hand down behind her to seize her target.

"*Madonna!*"

The men looked up from their food.

"Hush, ya dumb guinea," she whispered, leaning back, "do ya want everyone to know?"

She massaged him slowly as he joked with his cronies. They ignored her antics as they gobbled their food and scraped their bowls with dry bread. She saw Tonio's hand tremble as he lifted his glass. She smiled, knowing she'd be the one to give orders now.

He tried to get his free hand under her skirts, but she squirmed away, giving a rollicking laugh to one of Biaggio's jokes while sliding her buttocks back and forth on his thighs. His hands gripped her shoulders as he pressed his lips against her ear.

"Let's go in the pantry," he growled sotto voce.

"What?" she purred, leaning back. "What did ya say, Tonio? I can't hear ya." She closed her eyes, enjoying his hot, desperate breath on her neck. He was a cornered mouse under her paw. Should she gut him with her claws or let him play?

The crash of a chair hitting the floor snapped her eyes open. Mario stood across the table, ash-faced, staring at someone over her shoulder.

"Signora!" Mario said, concern plain in his voice. "Do you need help?"

The men at the table stopped eating, startled. Kathleen saw their eyes dart between Tonio and whomever stood behind him. So that's the way of it, she thought. I gave the bitch the heave-ho, but she didn't leave. She slipped her arm around Tonio's neck and swiveled in his lap to look over his shoulder.

"I need to speak with you, Antonio, it's important." The voice was soft, but his wife's eyes were hard. Kathleen didn't understand the Italian, but there was a steely current of resolve in the tone that was bound to make it a good show. She hung on Tonio's neck, giddy with excitement as he buttoned his pants under cover of her skirts.

"I think this little snippet must be yer wife," Kathleen giggled, stroking his hair. "She seems a bit upset, darlin'. Why don't ya see what she wants?"

"Mind yer own business," he shouted. Then in Italian he snarled, "*Gesù Cristo!* I told you never to come down here."

The whole room went quiet. No one moved. Mina's heart had dumped its icy blood into her bowels when she saw the woman on Antonio's lap. The gossips were right! He must be having an affair, for the black-haired woman was nuzzled against her husband's neck with a look of triumph on her face. Mina felt like a pincushion pierced by everyone's probing eyes. If I don't change my face, she thought, they'll never know my shame. I'll keep my face still and no one will suspect how much this hurts.

She took a step back, trying to calm herself. Antonio pulled the woman's arm from around his neck and stood up. The self-satisfied look on the woman's face vanished as she slipped off his lap and lurched forward, trying to keep herself from hitting the floor. So he's cruel to his mistress too, Mina thought. He hasn't singled me out for harsh treatment.

He came at her with a raised fist, but she didn't cower. She couldn't believe he'd strike her in front of everyone. Suddenly, Mario stepped in front of Antonio, shielding her. He took her gently by the arm and led her toward the back room, away from the gawking crowd.

"You need to step outside to talk, Signora DiGianni. A saloon is no place for a lady. Come away from the confusion," he said softly.

They passed quickly thorough the back room. As they went out the door she glanced back over her shoulder. The woman was laughing and pawing her husband while the men smirked and whispered behind their hands. What a fool she'd been all these months believing Antonio's lies. Everyone had tried to tell her he was having an affair.

Outside everything seemed too real, too sharply focused, too bright . . . she felt sick. She pulled away from Mario, her stomach lurching, and vomited into the gutter. She was so ashamed . . . so stupid. Tears filled her eyes as Mario offered her his folded handkerchief.

"You mustn't believe everything you see, Signora DiGianni. A saloon's not the real world. People do things after they've had a few drinks they'd never do elsewhere."

She took his handkerchief and wiped her mouth. "That woman?"

"She owns the bar," Mario replied. "She's very friendly with the men, very bold, it's necessary for her business." Mario looked at her encouragingly and smiled. She could see he felt sorry for her and that he was ashamed of her husband's behavior. It was strange. She'd been afraid of

Mario when she met him. He'd seemed cloudy and dark, perhaps because he'd been unsure of himself. She wasn't certain of the reason.
She'd interpreted his insecurity as sinister and threatening, while foolishly overlooking Antonio's self-assurance. She'd allowed Antonio to
charm her with honeyed words, so sure she was being led to the right
choice, but now Mario's character was as clear as the oil from a first
pressing of olives.

"It's all show," Mario said. "You mustn't worry about her. Those kind
of women behave . . . Well, I mean . . . she isn't like you."

"Is she having . . . ? Is Antonio . . . ?"

Mario glanced at his feet and jiggled the change in his pocket. She
knew the truth; he didn't have to say it. It was there in the set of his jaw,
the tension in his shoulders, and the sadness of his eyes. Oh, how she
hated Antonio. If she could smash his face to little bits this second it
wouldn't give her enough satisfaction. She was trapped in a nightmare,
and if it weren't for Mario's reassuring presence she would tear her hair
and rend her face in anguish. Snow fell silently, cold and wet like the
tears that streaked down her cheeks.

"Don't cry, Signora DiGianni. She isn't worth your tears."

"Signor Catanzaro, I know my husband is—"

The back door banged against the wall. She stepped behind Mario
out of Antonio's reach and tried to compose herself as best she could. It
wouldn't do to air her dirty laundry here on the sidewalk.

"I came to tell you I got a promotion at work," she said with a quaver
in her voice. "I'm going to be working at night now."

She bit her lip and clutched Mario's hanky in her fist, trying to stiffen
her spine.

"I'll decide what you're going to do," Antonio said. "You're—"

Mario cut in, slapping Tonio on the back. "That's great news!"

He slipped his arm around Tonio's shoulder and took out his pipe. He
would need to turn the situation around. It was clear Tonio was dead set
against his wife's promotion. Mario leaned against Tonio's shoulder. He
bent to tap his pipe against his boot and loosen the burned tobacco.
"What kind of promotion is it, Tonio? It must be big if she came all this
way to tell you."

Mina saw Mario wink and blessed him in her heart for his diplomacy.
She answered as though Antonio had asked the question.

"I'm going to be a dresser, if you permit it. For one of the opera singers. She . . . she asked for me personally and—"

"No!" Tonio snapped. "I don't—"

"Personally! Do you hear that?" Mario asked. "She asked for your wife personally. That must mean a raise in pay too."

Mina stepped forward boldly. She had to win him over now or lose the job. "Yes. I'll be getting *a lot* more money."

"I don't know, Tonio," Mario said, sounding uncertain. "The men'll be pissed as hell when they hear a woman's making more money than them and bringing it home to you."

Antonio shook his head and looked sour. "At night? No decent woman—"

"Hey! I'm out of pipe tobacco," Mario said, fumbling in his pocket. "You got some?"

"Sure, sure," Tonio said, pulling his pouch from his jacket pocket and handing it to Mario.

"Thanks," Mario said, filling his pipe. "How much of a raise is she getting?"

"S . . . everal dollars." Mina said, catching herself in time. "It'll be four extra dollars a week."

"Four dollars! *Gesù!*" Mario whistled. "What a treasure you married!"

"We . . . you can save for the house much faster," Mina added.

Mario nudged Antonio in the ribs. "You lucky bastard!" he whispered. "Four dollars a week! It's more than most men make."

Mario handed Antonio back the tobacco pouch and scratched a match against the sole of his boot. He drew on his pipe and chuckled.

Antonio's expression changed when the amount of the raise sank into his consciousness. He turned on Mina in disbelief. "Four dollars?" he demanded. "You're getting four dollars! On top of what you're already making?"

"Yes, *eight-fifty* all together." She watched him turn it over as he rubbed his chin. It made her sick to think that the money she'd planned to put in her bank would now go into his pockets to spend on his whore. Well, at least she'd held back three dollars for herself.

"This blend's smooth, Tonio. Thanks," Mario said.

She watched her husband stuff the pouch Mario handed him back into his coat pocket. He didn't seem irritated anymore. Mario's ploy had worked. Antonio had calmed down because of the money and the respect Mario had offered. She softened her voice and tried to be her most submissive. "I don't want to keep you from your work, Antonio. I know you're busy. Is it all right if I go now? I don't want to be late and lose this chance."

Mario pulled Antonio to the side. "You're smart to let her try it tonight," he whispered. "When she comes home you can always say no if you don't like the setup."

Antonio shifted his weight, put his hands in his pockets, and adjusted them insolently on his hips. He reminded Mina of a schoolyard bully. Finally he grumbled, "I'll be waiting for you tonight. You bring home your pay and tell me the details, then I'll decide if you can keep the job. Go on, get going before you screw it up."

Mario saw the gratitude in her eyes as she nodded good-bye. He watched her hurry down the street and was sorry for her predicament. He'd never deny his wife an opportunity to better herself. It pleased him that he'd helped her keep the promotion, but she was going to have a difficult time dealing with Tonio. He wasn't going to like her making more money than he did. His ego was too big for that.

"You're smart, Tonio. She's a hard worker," Mario said, doing his best to grease the wheels. "She'll make you a fortune if you play her right."

"Yeah," he said, moving back inside the bar. "Four dollars extra! *Gesù!* Why, she makes the same wage we do, and we work double shifts."

Back inside, Tonio took his place at the table and finished his meal. The men eyed one another, but didn't dare ask what had transpired. After a few minutes Kathleen brought him another ale and returned to her place on his lap. "What'd yer wife want?"

"Shut yer yap and mind yer business."

She watched him sop his bread in his dish and stuff his mug. Direct questioning wasn't going to get her anywhere, so she started in again, joking and stroking. In a matter of minutes he was back to his old self and the tension was gone from the group, but she noticed that Mario kept his eyes on his plate. His mood was dark and he finished up quickly.

"Let's go in the pantry," Kathleen murmured, slipping her hand down the front of Tonio's pants. "I need to talk to you about the upcoming match."

He didn't gasp this time, but she felt him twitch with anticipation.

"Mario, you and Biaggio take the men back to the site," Tonio said, standing up and grabbing his cap from the table. "I need to talk to Kathleen."

"Sure, no problem," Mario said, impassively getting to his feet. "*Andiamo!*"

Kathleen detected resentment under Mario's facade before he turned away. She'd seen it simmering there ever since Tonio had taken away his mail-order bride. The rest of the men were leering at the cap clutched in front of Tonio's pants.

"Go on, I'll see you in a few minutes," Tonio said, pulling Kathleen away.

Kathleen waved merrily to the men. Her laughter faded as she trailed Tonio to the pantry.

Once inside with the door latched Tonio wasted no time. He hoisted her onto the counter, crashing pots and kettles out of the way.

"Knock it off, ya dirty bum," she said tartly, pushing him away. "Ya'll need to tell me what yer wife wanted if ya want a go at me."

He shoved her skirts up, but she held him off with her foot.

"She's got a new job working at night," he snapped, pushing her foot aside.

"Perfect, it'll keep her occupied." She laughed as his coarse tongue licked her throat, and put her leg around his waist. "So why'd she come around?"

He pulled her hair and shook her pins loose. They rained down on the tin counter like dry peas and her dark hair flowed around them like a curtain.

"To ask permission."

"She asked ya for permission? That'll be the day I'd let ya get yer hooks into my business."

He'd never taken his marriage vows seriously; Tonio knew where his bread was buttered. The marriage had simply been a way for him to make some easy money and follow his stupid dago customs. Let his wife do the dirty work and bear the children. She'd have the best of Tonio to herself.

Kathleen dismissed his pathetic wife from her mind as a flood of lust washed over her, mixing with the scent of lye soap and stale beer. She buried her nose in his hair, savoring the smell of oil of roses he used to dress his dark curls, and unbuttoned the front of his pants. She loved the heavy smell of sweat that always enveloped him. Here was a virile young man to do her justice, not some doddering old fool who needed to be led by the hand.

Just the musky scent of him in a room could make her wet with anticipation. She popped her breasts out of her low-cut dress and he set on them hungrily as though they were one of her "free lunches" and he a Bowery bum.

She gasped in dizzy pleasure as he bit and sucked and she tried desperately to draw a deep breath against her tight stays. Her hands were working him, stoking the fire of his lust, until in a white-hot haze, her eyes half shut, her head thrown back, she guided him to her. She braced herself on the counter as he drove sharply into her again and again, pushing herself forward eagerly, wrapping her legs around him and hammering her heels into his buttocks with each rough thrust.

"Give it to me, darlin'," she crooned, arching backward with her eyes closed. "Give me all of it! Give me . . . every . . . inch!"

This was no longer a game she was playing for control; no, she was rolling and sliding, ass over teacup. Whatever might happen to the two of them, she knew they would rise or fall together. That had been clear since their first meeting, when they had taken one look at each other and a white-hot arc of lust had fused them.

Jack had suspected they were lovers, but no one had had the guts to tell him that while he was rolling in pain upstairs, with the cancer eating away his pancreas, they were doing it right below—on the counter of the locked pantry or standing up in the barrom after closing, unable to understand more than two words spoken, for Tonio was fresh off the boat.

They were well matched sexually, sweating and sparring in a violent parody of lovemaking that was rough and satisfying and exactly what she required to reach her climax. She'd never had a kind hand upon her in her life, and Tonio's savage passion seemed normal and right. They went blow for blow.

One night, shortly after they'd met and mated, he'd slapped her around in a drunken temper. She'd waited patiently with her split lip and black eye until he'd passed out from drink, then she'd beaten him with a wooden table leg. Tonio had wound up at the hospital with a split skull, two cracked ribs, and a new respect for Kathleen Shaunessey.

After that, he'd behaved himself with her, but he was always spoiling for a fight. It wasn't a big leap for her to think of profiting from his temper. Boxing was a manly sport and the coppers didn't see any harm in raising a few dollars for the "widows and orphans fund." They'd sat down as partners and figured the cost—how much to pay the rummies and what cut was needed for her friends at the police department. They'd even worked out an agreement with the Black Hand for protection.

Soon he'd be getting bigger and better fights. She didn't mind the outlay of cash, for you never got something for nothing, and if watered whiskey, stale ale, "free lunches," fistfights, and gambling put an extra penny in her pocket and made her the owner of the saloon she was desperate for, she'd run the risk. Becoming a lady in silk was her only real passion.

I'll be leading the life by thirty, she told herself as she pounded against his hips. Wearing silk and satin . . . oh, yeah. Silk, just like silk . . . by the time . . . I reach thirty. Thirty . . . thirty . . . thirty . . .

She pushed hard against him as the counter screeched with each thrust. And it would all be because of her . . . one . . . bit of luck . . . in life . . . meeting her match in Tonio. Yeah, if it all worked out as planned, the back room of the bar would be a gold . . . mine. . . .

"Oh, Tonio, Tonio, does it feel good? Does it?" Kathleen moaned, sucking his tongue deep into her mouth and pulling his hair. "Tell me, Tonio, tell me, how good . . . how good?"

He was hammering against her like a blacksmith at the anvil, red hot and molten. "*Carogna,*" he spit out in Italian. "You bitch," he groaned, pulling her off the counter and shoving her against the locked door. "*Lo voi!* You want it, you bitch! You want it? *Eccola, eccola,* here it is . . . here . . . take it!" he grunted over and over as he came. "*Carogna di puttana.* You fucking . . . bitch of a whore."

They were both giddy, sucking air into spent lungs, their hearts thumping. They clung together covered in sweat and shared grime. Kathleen dug her forearms into Tonio's shoulders for support, her muscles twitching. He set her back on the counter, laughing and trembling with relief, his hands resting on her thighs.

"Oh, that was good," she sighed.

"Good. Yes, very good." He touched something foreign between her thighs and drew back his hand. "*Ma, che cazzo fa?*" Tonio asked, taking a damp roll of cash from between her legs. "What's this?"

"Oh, the money," she laughed. "I forgot all about it, I put it in the top of my stockings for safekeeping." She twisted the front of her long hair up and worked in a couple of pins from the counter. "Well, we gave the money a good fuck too! There's another roll just like it in my other stocking."

Tonio looked down at the two rolls of cash. "You divided the money?"

"Of course I divided it. They're both the same. An equal split left or right, take yer pick."

"You cheat me?"

"Cheat ya! Why ya stupid ass wop bastard!" she said, shoving him away sharply with her foot. "I oughta crack yer skull. We're partners, ain't we? Fifty-fifty? Why would I cheat ya?"

"Because you're a lying cunt. You want that bar more than you want me."

"Darlin', ya wouldn't love me if ya thought I could be taken advantage of," she said, sliding off the counter and arranging her hose. "But it's all there just the same. Count it, ya prick."

"I can't come back tonight," he said after he'd finished the count and stuffed one roll into his pants pocket.

"Whaddaya mean? I got some fancy guy coming round. We're supposed to plan the next match and have a bit of sport."

"What do you call what we just had?"

"I call that a short pint!" she said, flaring up and putting her hands on her hips. "So yer wife got herself a new job and ya ain't coming back. Ya got some nerve coming in here and having a go with me."

He didn't say anything; just put his hand in his pocket. "I almost forgot," he said. He pulled a crumpled bit of paper out and gave it to her.

"What's this?" she asked suspiciously.

"Something for making the match."

"Why . . . Mr. Antonio," she said, staring down at the intricately worked seed pearl and cut red stone earrings that glittered in her hand. "I can't believe my eyes."

In five years he'd never given her a gift. The anger drained out of her as she slid her hand into his still open trousers and kissed his mouth. "Why, darlin', that's the sweetest—"

"I've got things to do," he muttered, pushing her hand away and buttoning his fly.

She looked at the earrings in her palm. "It's that virgin bride of years, ain't it? That's why yer giving me cheap jewels. Mamma's boy! She's got yer balls tied up with butcher's twine, ya go running whenever she pulls the string!"

"Shut yer trap. I told you, I got things to do." He pushed his hair back and pulled on his cap. Shouldering his way through the door, he entered the back room with his old swagger.

"Well, I won't put up with it, ya hear?" she shouted, tearing after him. "Ya won't be having paydays in the back of my bar, me taking the risks while yer spending yer time free and easy in that bitch's bed." She remembered that he'd taken both wads of cash from her stocking tops. "Wha'd ya do with my cut? Give it back to me, ya thieving wop."

She grabbed the back of his jacket and yanked him around, facing off with him, fists up. "Ya think because ya give me a lousy pair of earrings that I'm gonna let ya go back to fucking her, huh? For a frigging bunch of cheap stones?" She threw the packet at him. It bounced off his chest and fell to the floor. "Nothing's gonna make me stand for that!"

"This," he said with a grin, shoving the second roll of wet cash between her breasts, "will make you take it and beg me for more."

She made a swipe at him, but he dodged her and went out, banging the door behind him. She threw the door open and stepped into the street after him, pushing a passerby out of her way. "Ya better be back here tomorrow," she yelled after him. "Do ya hear me? Money or no money!"

He carried on walking and the wind brought back a whistled tune to her ears.

Free and easy. Just like every man she'd ever known once they'd had their fill. Who had control of the situation now? She stepped back inside and watched through the glass until he turned the corner. Her heart jerked uncomfortably. He was going to spend the night with his wife, and she was alone.

She looked down at the earrings in the sawdust, then bent to gently pick them up. They lay cool in her palm while the jealousy was a searing piece of peat in her throat. The red glass and tiny pearl earrings were the tenderest thing he'd done for her.

She went to the mirror at the end of the bar and slipped the long curved wires into her pierced ears. They were heavy, pulling her lobes down, and backed with what appeared to be gold but obviously had to be brass. Intricately worked, they had a three-dimensional design and the seed pearls formed a letter *K,* or was it an *L*? She couldn't make it out.

Where on God's green earth did he get these pieces of junk? she thought, looking at the dangling earrings that almost touched her collarbones. Men have such terrible taste. She shook her head from side to side and the heavy stones glittered. Well, it was his first present, and that made them dear, gaudy or no.

Chapter Ten

MINA GRIPPED THE RAILING of the station steps, carefully placing her feet as she descended from the platform of the elevated uptown train, afraid of slipping in the wet snow. As she picked her way through the press of people her mind was turning over the encounter at the saloon. She was certain someone had given her the *mal'occhio*, for her life was plunging wildly into chaos. Perhaps it was that dark-haired woman who'd put the evil eye on her, but did the woman know how? Did they have the *mal'occhio* wherever she came from?

Well, of course they did, it was the same all over the world if someone wished you evil. Oh, God, she thought. It's true! Antonio *is* having an affair. She stopped abruptly and pressed her knuckles against her lips, trying to think straight. Someone bumped her from behind, and she heard the mumbled apology but didn't acknowledge it. She didn't see anything around her, only the eyes of the black-haired woman from the saloon with the look she'd always hated. The look that said she was worthless, a worthless, dirty whore.

Her eyes filled with tears as she trudged on. Why? Why was He doing this to her? It wasn't fair. Her old life was over. She'd promised to change. She'd paid her penance; she wasn't the same woman now. Why wouldn't He forgive her? Why wouldn't He let her be happy? Hadn't He led her to this place? This marriage?

She remembered how loving Antonio had acted those first two weeks. He was handsome and charming just as she'd been told. She'd realized almost immediately that he was purposely trying to steal her from Mario, but no one suspected that it suited her purpose to marry him. Only God knew why she wanted to marry Antonio DiGianni. God had listened to her prayers and had helped her win him. Now He was turning His face away.

She'd done her best to be a good wife, but Tonio's affair wouldn't allow him to see her value. Oh, that woman! That strumpet! That whore! The way she flaunted herself, she was no better than a common streetwalker. Mina dug her nails into her palms and reminded herself she should be Christian. Doesn't *Gesù* say to forgive? You know how it feels to be called a whore, she told herself. But she didn't want to forgive. She wanted to uproot every black hair on that Jezebel's head and feed her body to the dogs. It was that woman's fault her marriage was failing.

That sly piece had clung to Antonio even after she knew he'd gotten married. Mina had seen the look in her eye at the saloon; his mistress meant to take her husband. To do her evil. If it hadn't been for her holding on, things would have worked out perfectly. What was she going to do? How could she continue in this intolerable situation? She'd have to find a way to get rid of the mistress, then Antonio would become loving again.

She tore at the problem with every step she took. She'd have to win Antonio back. This promotion was the first step. He'd respect her now. Didn't Mario say she was a treasure? And if what she was hoping was true and she turned out to be pregnant, he'd turn away from that awful woman and come home to his family. Oh, she hoped she had a son in her belly. If she gave him a son, he'd turn his back on his whore and never wander.

Mario had been so kind and helpful. She would never have had this chance if it hadn't been for his interference. Why had she been so foolish and denied his proposal? He would never treat her with such contempt.

By the time she reached the stage door she had an excruciating head-ache. When she tried to pull the door open her wounded shoulder re-belled. She switched to her right, but realized that that arm was trembling from the toll of the day's activity. How would she perform her duties with two weak arms? Oh, *Sant'Anna,* help me, I'm so afraid, she prayed.

Bangs and shouts buffeted her as she slipped past the knot of musi-cians smoking cigarettes on the stair. The backstage area was a dark carnival of activity scented with fresh paint and sawdust. Screeching backdrops were being hoisted into place on rusted pulleys, and every-where she looked ropes were strung and secured. The ropes reminded her of a ship's rigging, and the men scurrying past with furniture, stat-ues, and candelabras to dress the set seemed like raiding pirates.

She watched the workmen anxiously and did her best to slip by un-noticed. The last thing she needed was to encounter another brute. What would happen once the Signorina discovered she knew nothing about being a dresser? If she failed, she'd most likely be put out of the opera house and lose everything. She thought about appealing to Simonetta. She might be able to salvage her old job and tell Antonio the Signorina had changed her mind. She turned toward the stairs leading to the costume shop and almost started down them, but she couldn't give up the chance.

If she did well, with just one stone she'd win Antonio *and* have the money she needed to buy her little house. Her emotions swung between hope and doubt as she gazed up into the flies where the men adjusted lights and flats on the catwalks. It made her knees melt to see them so high above and so fearless. She needed to be fearless too, to stiffen her spine like a taut rope.

She felt the sick apprehension in the pit of her stomach turning to ex-citement as she started down the spiral stair. Surely this new job wasn't more complicated than learning a new pattern of lace. How difficult could it be to care for costumes and help someone dress? She could learn—she wasn't stupid, as Biaggio's sisters implied. She would over-come the *mal'occhio* and pass this test of Job.

At the end of the corridor the dressing room door stood open, wait-ing. A profusion of flowers spilled out. Orchids and violets tumbled from mossy baskets, multihued roses filled tall vases, and ornate arrangements of lilies, carnations, daisies, and irises were scattered among gaily wrapped packages and pyramids of fruit in cellophane paper. What an abundance of riches lay ahead if only she had courage!

"No, no . . . later," she heard the Signorina say with irritation. "Come back in an hour. I promise some photos for your paper after I do my hair and dress. Yes, yes, in an hour. I can see you then for a few minutes."

Two men with inked slips in their hatbands hurried down the hall and brushed past her. She stopped on the threshold to peek inside. The Signorina was standing in the middle of the room, still wearing her coat and scarf, holding two small dogs while a Western Union man, all shiny brass buttons, delivered a stack of cables. The white dogs snarled and yapped. He tipped his hat and winked at Mina on his way out.

"Thank God you're here!" The Signorina set the dogs down and pulled the scarf from her rag-tied hair. "Take these two barbarians and give them some water. They're driving me mad!"

She waved toward the pantry. Mina hesitated, her confidence and hope suddenly fleeing. "Signorina—"

"Everything for the animals is there. I left Lucifer at home so you won't need to bother with him. After, you must hack through this jungle. I can't close the door to keep the riffraff out!"

"No, no, Signorina Frascatti"—the words spilled like meal from a torn sack—"I came because—you know I injured m-my arm, my hand is weak. I'm so sorry, but it won't work properly and the other is just as bad. I was hoping—I came to tell you—" She squeezed her eyes shut in sudden terror, feeling dizzy and sure she would faint. "I'll—I'll find you a replacement immediately. You'll need someone with two hands to help you tonight." She steadied herself against the doorjamb.

"You're resigning? Ridiculous! Why, you've only just arrived! We will fetch some ice for the injury."

"Please don't bother. I did it a week ago." Mina bit down on her lip to keep the tears from welling in her eyes. How can I be so weak? she thought. I'm giving up without even trying.

The Signorina took off her coat. "You have one hand, yes? That other dresser had none. She had blocks of ice for hands. You'll be perfect. I don't need a replacement. Dante, stop stuffing yourself with grapes and do something useful. Run, get me some ice."

In her anxiety to explain, Mina hadn't noticed the man who'd caused her so much discomfort the night before, leaning on the piano eating grapes. Here was the other reason her doubts compelled her to make an immediate escape. The lover smiled at her mischievously while he crushed the ripe fruit between his teeth.

When he looked at her she felt a flash of heat rush through her body as intense and quick as the bright powder used to illuminate her wedding photo. A strong, twisting sensation started between her legs and prickled into her stomach. It was uncomfortably intimate, yet strangely pleasant. She couldn't have felt more naked if she'd just stepped from the washtub.

"I don't believe you were formally introduced to Signor Dante the other night. Signora Di—"

"Filomina DiGianni!" the lover supplied as he leaped over the flowers. "Dante Romano, at your service." He lifted her hand and kissed her knuckles. She yanked her hand back, but it was too late. His touch scorched her body like an overstoked furnace and turned her brain to charcoal. Every thought she'd had evaporated. She dropped her eyes to study the carpet.

Cesca noted her new dresser's reaction. "Stop, Dante, you are embarrassing her," she said in English. "Go get the ice."

"Ice will not help the injury if she did it last week."

It was clear her dresser didn't understand English well. "Get ice for my champagne, *caro,*" she said in Italian. Then in English, for the long ears in the corridor she added, "Run along, pant like you do after all the beautiful young women in *Roma . . . Parigi . . .* New York. This little one is not for you."

Using her dresser as a shield, Dante fleshed out the scene by playfully casting grapes at Cesca.

"*Cara,* you know those rumors, well . . . they're not . . . true! And where . . . am I . . . supposed to find . . . ice . . . and champagne . . . now?"

"Use that brilliant Italian mind of yours," she said, swatting the missiles aside and stamping her foot in feigned annoyance. "Alice has hot blood. Surely she would know where there is ice."

His pelting with grapes continued.

"*Fermati!*" she shouted, throwing her silver hairbrush across the room. Her dresser jumped in fright as it crashed into the fancy dressing screen. Cesca continued her harangue in English for the entertainment of the onlookers. "I said stop! Go get me some ice!"

Dante spun her dresser around. "Welcome to *l' inferno!*" he whispered loudly. "You're about to enter the eighth circle of hell! Use these as ammunition to save yourself."

He dumped his grapes into the startled dresser's hands and hurried out the door.

"*Mi dispiace,* I'm sorry," she said, slamming the door and reverting to Italian. "Dante sometimes has difficulty understanding English."

Mina considered the sticky mass of grapes. What should she say? What should she do? She watched the Signorina closely for a clue, but the Signorina seemed unconcerned with her plight and was busy opening telegrams. "Hang your coat and come here. I want a closer look at your injury," the Signorina ordered.

Mina's fingers quivered uncontrollably when she extended her arm. She gasped when she lifted it above her waist.

"How did you do this?"

"I tried to carry too much water from the basement. I was stubborn and wouldn't rest on the way."

"Carrying water? You sound like a wretch from *Les Miserables!*" Cesca laughed merrily at her joke, but regretted the flippancy when she saw the hurt in her new dresser's eyes. She had long roots in poverty herself. Who was she to laugh at this unfortunate child? She riffled through her telegrams, annoyed with herself. Carrying water? That wasn't what she remembered the girl saying last night. She'd said she did it getting on a trolley car. There was obviously more to the situation than she wished to confess. Or was it that she'd hired another spy? She considered her new dresser closely.

Mina wore a horrid, limp, eggplant-colored dress, too short in the skirt, but carefully mended and edged in elegant lace. Around her shoulders, in the festive style of Italian peasants, she wore a colorful cloth shawl crisscrossed over her breast and tucked into her waistband. Her dark hair was swept back with cheap metal and fake stone ornaments, her boots were split and scuffed, but a pure soul shone from her dark eyes.

"That lace is beautiful. Did you get it from the costume shop?" Cesca asked.

"No. I made it." Her dresser touched the lace at her throat self-consciously.

"You're a lace maker? How interesting! Where did you learn?"

Her dresser glanced away. "Ah . . . in the mountains . . . near Naples."

"Oh, yes, I remember, near Salerno, wasn't it?" Her dresser nodded, but didn't meet her eyes. "You can help me open these cables. You won't have to lift anything heavy, I assure you. Tomorrow or the day after, your arm will be better."

Mina hesitated, her heart vexed by her predicament. "It's not just my arm. You see, my husband doesn't want me to work with . . . at night."

"Nonsense! He won't refuse if I give you another raise." The Signorina winked and took the parcel of cables to her dressing table.

"Another . . . oh, but you've already been too generous."

"Don't tell me you're turning down money?"

"No. I need as much money—I mean I—" Mina clamped her lips shut. She was so nervous she didn't know what she was saying. The Signorina looked at her curiously. She must think I'm greedy, Mina thought. "That is, I meant to say, I'm saving for a house. But I'm afraid I . . . I won't please you." The fear she'd felt earlier returned to engulf her like a tidal wave. "Oh, signorina! I don't know what to do, what to say. I don't how to be a dresser."

There it was. The truth was out. She put her head down to keep from showing her shame. Whatever happened now was in *Sant'Anna*'s hands. Please persuade her to let me try, she prayed. She's a good woman. She can help me win back my husband. I just need this little chance.

"Come, sit!" the Signorina ordered. "I give the orders and you must obey me instantly. I'm like Caesar in the field. No matter what arguments you make I won't send you back to Rome. Pull that chair over here."

Mina took a shaky breath and sat down.

"Being a dresser's nothing. I'll teach you all you need to know."

A little sob of relief escaped her throat as the Signorina pulled an elegantly embroidered handkerchief from her drawer and pressed it into her hand. On one of the corners of the linen handkerchief Mina saw two entwined Fs stitched in satin thread.

"Keep the handkerchief—a lady never knows when she'll need one," the Signorina soothed. "Don't worry!" she said, clicking her tongue. "You'll see how quickly you learn."

The hanky lay in Mina's hand unused as the tears dropped into her lap. She couldn't help herself. She hadn't expected understanding. She'd expected the diva to fly into a rage and scream for a replacement.

"We are *compaesane,* you know?" the Signorina said. "Country-women." Her voice was gentle, solicitous.

"I do not think my people know yours, but you're very kind, signorina."

"No, not so kind. I'm too self-interested to be kind."

The Signorina took the handkerchief, blotted Mina's tears, and pushed the damp cloth into Mina's sleeve. She brushed aside the loose hairs surrounding her face. The gesture made Mina feel like a pampered child.

"Who are your people?" the Signorina asked, taking Mina's face in her hands. She traced Mina's bone structure with her eyes. "Everyone in the mountains is related. Tell me about yourself, tell me everything."

"I'm no one, just a girl from *Nap*—from the mountains near *Napoli.*"

"And I am not? Don't let these rich trappings fool you. I came from a small village not so different from yours. I dug in the dirt with my hands and trod the earth with bare feet. I worked and slept in my only dress. I went hungry. I'm the same"—she spread her hands and made a little pirouette—"only time and the accountrements have changed."

The Signorina's eyes twinkled with humor and warmth, but Mina didn't believe that this woman who had everything would understand what had made her sell her soul for a bad marriage in a strange land.

"I tell you what," the Signorina said, clapping her hands like a gleeful child, "we'll trade histories. It'll help to pass the time that drags between arias. I'll tell you how I became the famous Francesca Frascatti, diva, devil, monster! And you'll tell me how you became a lace maker and came to this opera house."

"No, I couldn't. I mean, I have nothing to—"

The Signorina put her hand up. "It's a requirement, a duty. If you're to work for me I must know who you are. It's a question of trust . . . respect."

Mina knew the Signorina meant what she said, and a sudden panic rose in her throat. She couldn't tell anyone who she was. It was a secret she couldn't share. Unaware of her panic, the Signorina shifted articles on her dressing table, making room for flowers.

"Last night you said you knew about me," the Signorina began. Mina's hand trembled as she passed the Signorina a vase of roses. She glimpsed her own image in the mirror and saw a flush of pink creeping up her throat as deeply hued as the buds in the vase.

"You said, if I remember correctly, you've heard I'm 'infamous'!"

"I was wrong to say it, forgive me. It's only gossip and I know how false gossip can be."

"No, no, you were right to say it. That's exactly why I decided to hire you. I require honesty. I'm tired of lies and half-truths and all the pretense that has been my life."

The Signorina held up an arrangement of delicate orchids, turning them to and fro. "They're beautiful, aren't they? Rich, exotic, delicate, spun on thin air and decay. I tell you honestly, Mina, these orchids are much like my life. They look beautiful, but they're a product of degradation."

We have that much in common, Mina thought, my life is also spun on degradation. Degradation and a tangled web of lies. Every crossing of the bobbins, every new knot tied is a degradation taking me further from my true self. I'm trapped by an intricate pattern of lies that even He can't tease apart.

She had a sudden desire to unburden herself. Why not get it all out in the open? Would this woman understand? Should she risk telling her anything about her life? Perhaps, she reasoned, I can trim just enough of the worst parts . . . and substitute others. I could tell her the stories from the ship; they might ease her sorrow. There seemed to be so much loneliness and disappointment hiding under the Signorina's bright performance. If I'm careful I can share a little and she'll never know—

"What do you say? Shall we trade life histories?"

"I promise to tell you what I can," Mina said carefully.

"I'm a nosy woman . . . it's my nature. I sometimes ask very personal questions, really none of my business, but"—she laughed and shrugged her shoulders, forgetting her grim mood—"if you do not want to answer you must say, 'That's too personal,' and I'll not press you. Do you understand?"

Mina nodded.

"*Perfetto!* Now, I'll be first. Let's see . . . Should I start with my tail or horns? I'll start with my horns. The convent . . . Oh, yes," she mocked when she saw the surprise in Mina's eyes. "The devil you are to work for came from a convent. Raised and trained by nuns. Touch iron! No one would believe I almost became one myself."

Chapter Eleven

OVER THE COURSE of the next three hours, while Mina learned how to arrange flowers, care for the dogs, and press the costumes to the diva's satisfaction, the Signorina shared bits and pieces of her life. The men from the newspaper returned. They waited in the hall while the diva applied makeup and taught Mina how to clean the sponges and brushes. Mina worried about the waiting men, but the Signorina laughed and proclaimed, "Divas must not be too accommodating or they get little respect and less publicity."

When she was satisfied with Mina's work, she ordered her to open the door and received the reporters with a flourish. They conducted their interview as she untied her hair, arranged it, and finally pinned a tiara into it. Then the Signorina beckoned Mina behind the dressing screen to help her into her second act costume, and while the Signorina went up to the stage to have pictures taken, Mina took the dogs for a walk.

The Signorina was at the piano warming up her voice and Mina was arranging items in the small pantry when Signor Dante returned. Mina was surprised at how handsome he looked dressed in a tuxedo with a black silk cravat and diamond stickpin. He was a perfect magazine fashion plate. He juggled a floral bouquet, a bucket of ice with champagne, and several glasses. Mina took the bottle and glasses, and he gallantly presented the flowers to the Signorina. Then he opened the champagne and poured out three glasses.

The Signorina said she needed champagne before each performance to purify her voice. They both insisted that Mina have a stem of wine with them for luck. They clicked glasses and made toasts. It was her first taste of French wine. The bubbles made her sneeze. Signor Dante refilled her glass twice; she tried to refuse, but the Signorina insisted. Soon she was floating like one of the bubbles rising through the sweet gold-tinged liquid, she was so happy.

Then there was a startling rap on the door. "Five minutes!" a voice on the other side called.

It was time to go up on stage.

Mina stood in the dark wings holding different items needed for the performance: the rosebud-edged shawl, a large bunch of silk lilies, and a hand mirror. They were waiting for Tosca's entrance. Mina tried to appear confident, but she could feel the sweat creeping down from her armpits. It was her turn to tell a story.

"You know," Mina whispered tensely, "my *Mammina* used to sing 'O *Marenariello*,' just like you. Let's see, I would have been . . . thirteen when she died. I hadn't seen her in five years."

The Signorina leaned toward the action on stage, like her pet ocelot watching a stranger, every muscle of her body engaged. She wasn't listening to Mina's story, thank God. For the moment she'd been forgotten.

"Where is Giacomo? He's going to be late for his entrance," the Signorina said to herself.

"Who?" Mina asked.

"Ah, there he is!" The Signorina sighed with relief and made a little wave of her gloved hand to the man playing the sacristan on the opposite side of the stage. He saluted her with a smile. "How does my hair look?" the Signorina asked Mina.

"Beautiful, signorina, you look—"

"Sssh! *Silenzio* backstage," the Signorina reproved.

Mina felt as if she'd broken all ten commandments with just four words. Obviously, rules for divas were different.

"All right, the mirror, hold it up."

Mina jerked the mirror up with her left hand. The Signorina put on her hat.

"Hold it steady."

Mina pressed her arm against her chest with her right hand for support. Her shoulder throbbed. She'd already had several mishaps. First, her hand had trembled so violently she'd dropped a vase of flowers, soaking an expensive carpet, then she'd scorched the hem of the cape used in the third act, and finally, the Signorina had to finish her own hair during the interview.

The sacristan knelt to pray as bells chimed and Tosca's lover, Cavaradossi, entered and uncovered a painting he was working on. The sacristan inquiried why the artist hadn't eaten his lunch, packed in a wicker basket. He was portly in his priestly grab, which underscored his concern about wasted food.

Singing about food reminded Mina that Antonio was at home waiting. She hoped he enjoyed her special supper; perhaps he'd be in a good mood when she arrived. Perhaps this very night there would be a wonderful change in her life. She'd win her husband away from his mistress and prove she was worthy of love. If only . . .

"Up, Mina, up! I can't see! *Stai attenta!* Careful! Have you got Saint Vitus' dance? Hold it steady. Watch out, you're crushing the lilies! Up . . . no, no, a little lower."

As Mina angled the mirror back and forth the Signorina struggled to get a view and tie her chin ribbon.

"Quickly, the flowers!" Mina shoved the lilies in the Signorina's direction. "That's my cue! The shawl!"

Mina fumbled, the cloth dropped. She scrambled to pick it up, but stepped on it.

"Mario? Mario?" the Signorina sang, then to Mina she whispered, "No, no, what are you doing?" The Signorina yanked hard on the shawl, knocking Mina off balance. Mina clung to the curtains to keep from falling down and loosened her grip on the mirror.

"Where are you, Mario?" Tosca sang, calling to her lover Cavaradossi. "Put it on one shoulder, I am distracted, angry. I drag it in!"

Frantic to make her entrance, the Signorina whipped the shawl out of Mina's hand. It caught the edge of the mirror and sent it crashing to the floor. To Mina's untrained ears it sounded like a cannon being fired as it splintered into a hundred sparkling shards.

"*Gesù Cristo!* What a *casino!*" the Signorina snapped as she swirled away.

The audience burst into wild applause as the diva made her entrance. Mina stood behind, at the edge of the lit stage, stunned. *Dio*, she thought, now I'm truly finished. She wanted to slink away and never return, but she dropped to her knees and began collecting the pieces. Now she only had to wait for the dreadful experience to be over. Two more acts and then certain dismissal.

"Seven years' bad luck, eh, little dove?"

Mina whirled, thrusting out a shard of the broken mirror defensively.

"Careful! It's only me," Dante said, seizing her wrist.

"Oh, signore, you frightened me!"

"You already have one injured hand, you don't want to cut the other," he said, gently taking the glass from her. "I can do that. Let me help you." He crouched to help, but a bored stagehand waved them both away with his broom. Dante wondered why she'd reacted so drastically. The raw fear he'd seen in her eyes when she turned reminded him of the rabbits he'd caught in snares as a boy.

"Let the gentleman clean up," Dante said, leading Mina to the side of the stage.

"I'm afraid I'm not much help to the Signorina."

"Cesca doesn't want help," he said with amusement. "She wants control. She directs. Then if something should go wrong she can complain it was done incorrectly. That way *she* never makes a mistake. I'm afraid it's very much her disposition. You'll suffer from her temperament."

"I think she's very kind."

"Ah, I see you already love her. She has that effect on people . . . when she wants. And if she loves in return she'll feed you ambrosia and you'll grow fat with devotion, but if you're an enemy, be careful, Lucrezia Borgia was simply sugaring your tea."

"Lucrezia Borgia?"

"A terrible villainess. She used poison rings and intrigues in . . . Never mind, let's go back to the dressing room. She'll be onstage for a while."

"I shouldn't wait here?"

"No, no, there's a break between acts and she'll change costumes. Come, I know her routine, I'll show you."

In the dressing room Dante took up a book of poetry and threw himself onto the chaise longue. The dogs jumped up to join him. He tried to read, but he found himself going over the same lines again and again. He was anxious for the pieces of his case to come together. It had been almost two years, and although this bit of detecting was challenging, and he'd enjoyed his time with Cesca, he was tired of playing a role. He'd need a strong dose of honesty after his masquerade. He gave up his book and surreptitiously watched Mina as she went about her duties.

She seemed a charming, sweet young woman and he wondered if she was as artless and transparent as she seemed or if, like the other dresser, she was hiding something. He'd ordered a perfunctory check on her background, but it would take a day or two to get back a report. He didn't think it would turn up much.

She was fussing with the pots of makeup and brushes on the dressing table, unaware of him, and the glare from the electric lights around the makeup mirror illuminated the little wisps of hair that had come loose from her braids. They showed golden around her head. He found himself thinking that they were like . . . like a spider's web glittering with morning dew. And like the web she seems fragile, but I'll bet she's strong.

The tender feelings he thought he'd left behind in his youth swelled within him. Yes, spiders' webs strung with jewels of dew . . . For the first time in years he let himself be carried back to the outskirts of Rome and his beloved solitary morning tramps through the wild fields surrounding his family's estate. He could hear the crack of the brush underfoot, the sound of birds calling in the trees.

He was a boy again, before his father's death, before the bitterness of his mother's remarriage had poisoned his life and cast him out. He was discovering the delicate webs stretched between the limbs, sparkling in the rising sun. Gifts from the gods, left hanging, like Jason's fleece. Yes, he thought, this woman is beautiful in simple ways, like the small birds and field flowers I loved to paint, or like the dew that sits gently on the threads of the invisible workers in the wild.

The angle of the light revealed a small indentation splitting the tip of her nose that was oddly endearing, and her upper lip was formed with peaked edges he found tantalizingly erotic. He'd love to paint her delicate face. Her skin was as white as one of the camellia buds in the vase she awkwardly arranged. It pleased him that the same hand that had colored the roses arching over the vases on the dressing table had tinted her cheekbones. She was natural, touched only by God's brush.

So different, he thought, from the women I've known in Europe—limp noodles, boiled and sauced for society's taste. Like actresses upon the stage, the young women he'd squired about had been coached and instructed in every move, their actions and ideas chosen to please and entrap. They'd bored him with their staged feelings and calculated replies. They were as false as Cesca in her role of diva. He wondered what it might be like to kiss Mina, though he knew she was a pious married woman.

He'd seen a rosary in her hand earlier and knew it was now tucked in her apron pocket, but it wasn't the beads that had signaled her devotion to her vows. She was her husband's wife. Antonio? Yes, she'd said, "I'm Antonio's wife" when she introduced herself. As though it were her only identity. Honor, obey . . . till death do us part . . . not just words . . . immutable laws . . . a unique woman. Did her husband know what a rare gift he'd been given?

"Do you like America?" he asked, suddenly putting a stop to his rampant musings.

She didn't turn to face him, but continued arranging the table.

"It's different than I expected."

"In what way different?" he asked, coming to stand behind her.

"Everyone here speaks English, for one thing."

He heard a touch of annoyance in her voice, but didn't heed it. "Yes, but you've solved that problem beautifully. You work among your countrymen." She moved away and took Cesca's second act costume from the dressing screen where it had been hanging. She began laying out the matching pieces. "It must be difficult to come so far to start a new life," he persisted, following her.

"Not so difficult when you have no choice. A woman must go where she can eat."

Once again she moved away, and once again he followed her.

"Surely a lovely young lady like you would never starve."

He saw her body stiffen. He'd only wished to pay her a compliment, but it came off sounding like an insult. "I beg your pardon, Signora. I didn't mean to imply . . . I only meant, you certainly could have made a good match in Italy. If . . . if you wanted to, that is. Please forgive my foolish words."

In the silence that followed he felt acutely uncomfortable. It surprised him. He hadn't cared before what people thought. It had actually amused him that others thought him a wealthy woman's faithless paramour, but in Mina's presence his role was embarrassing. He wished he could explain that he too understood hard work and slim prospects. Unfortunately, he had to keep silent to guard Cesca's secret. He went back to the chaise longue and his book feeling like a fool.

Mina's first thought had been, He's like all the others. Other men in Italy had made sexual advances to satisfy their lust and "help her out." They'd all thought that because she was poor and had few options, she'd never object, but she'd run away and chosen marriage to a stranger over that kind of life. She was respectable now: How dare he suggest that she, a married woman, might be open to his advances?

But then he began to blush and stammer, apologizing and begging her forgiveness like a true gentleman. Perhaps, she thought, he simply misspoke. It was an improper conversation, but he was trying to be friendly, not lecherous. She gave him the benefit of the doubt and hummed the tune she'd picked up from the Signorina, pretending to be confident, but as she fussed with her chores she noticed her hands were shaking.

Whenever she was near Signor Dante a strange heat percolated through her body and she couldn't quite catch her breath. The women had warned her he was dangerous—a seducer and libertine who'd try to charm his way under her petticoats—but she didn't believe the gossip. After all, the Signorina was kind, not a monster like the others had said. Outside of what he had just said, Signor Dante had done nothing to make her think him promiscuous. The women in the shop were bored gossips, embroidering terrible tales. Why, at this very minute they were probably gossiping about her—

Suddenly a vivid picture flashed in her mind.

The book Signor Dante was reading lay tossed on the carpet. She saw herself on the chaise longue, her clothing disheveled, his body entwined with hers. They were kissing as one of his hands lifted her petticoats and crept over her dark stocking tops. His other hand was pressing against the fabric of her breast . . . the long fingers stirring her submerged emotions. . . .

"The fire is dying," she blurted out. She rushed to remove the screen and work the fire, hoping to stop the intimate twisting she felt and the sudden illicit image. With her weak hand she took up the poker and tried to arrange the logs. As she prodded them one slipped from the pile and rolled onto the carpet. "*Dio!*" she cried.

The dogs hopped down and began yapping as she jabbed and kicked the glowing log onto the tiles. Unnoticed, her hem brushed among the embers. Dante threw his book down. It tumbled onto the carpet as he rushed to her rescue with fire tongs.

"Signore, please, you will get yourself filthy," she protested weakly. "It's supposed to be my job."

"This is nothing. Your shoulder's still weak. I can do this little chore for you," he said, lifting the log back into the fire with a smile. "I used to tend the fire at our home in the country."

He turned swiftly back to take the poker from her and found himself standing much too close. She was gripping the iron like Tristan's sword. It was all that stood between them. Dante saw it tremble.

"You're tired. Let me finish," he said. He reached for the poker, but found her hand. She held on for a moment, her eyes locked with his, until she suddenly let go and jumped back. The poker clattered to the tiles.

"Oh! Excuse me, signore, I—" she said as she bent down.

He scrambled to pick it up and knocked her head. She almost fell, but he grabbed her forearms and kept her steady. His eyes were watering from the strength of the impact. "I'm sorry. Are you all right?"

"Yes, yes, I am all right." She laughed nervously, rubbing her forehead.

Dante retrieved the tool, thinking the jolt had certainly knocked any romantic urges he'd felt out of him. As he rose he glimpsed a fiery scallop creeping up her taffeta dress. Her hem must have brushed the hot embers. He saw a blue flame flare; in a moment her whole skirt would be a torch. Instinctively he shoved her back and fell on top of her trying to smother the flames.

Mina was startled when he knocked her back onto the carpet. She couldn't imagine what was happening. She couldn't see his face, but felt his hands pulling her skirts. The shop's gossip immediately came to mind. "Be careful, he's lecherous, he'll try to get under your petticoats." Her heart hammered in fright; he *was* like all the rest. "No, no! Stop! Please! Help me! Someone help me!" She lashed out at him and the dogs howled and snapped, adding to the confusion.

"Hold still! Don't fight!" he insisted.

She kicked him, trying to get him off her legs, but he grabbed her ankles and shoved her back roughly. Back and forth she rocked, trying to sit up and get out from under him, but he'd pinned her legs by sitting on them and she was paralyzed. She sat up and beat on his back.

"Fire!" he shouted over the barking dogs. "Signora, your dress is on fire."

Her heart was thumping like a pageant drum when he tipped a vase of roses onto her skirt. The shock of the cold water penetrated her terror and she helped him beat out the remaining embers. She lay in a twisted heap as he crouched next to her, his fancy white shirt flecked with bits of charred taffeta.

"Are you all right?" he asked, shaken by the harsh rush of adrenaline. "Your legs aren't burned, are they?" He tried to push up her skirt to check her legs.

"Please, I can check my legs myself," she said, pushing his hands away.

"Pardon me," he said, embarrassed by her tone. "Let me help you up."

She scanned her skirt in the long mirror. Her white slip was singed in spots and showed starkly through a wide breach in the taffeta to the waistband. If Signor Dante hadn't acted quickly she most certainly would have been severely burned. "Thank you, Signore," Mina said quietly. "Thank you so much for saving me. In one day I have managed to b-break a valuable antique mirror, set myself on fire, and attack you. I— I'm so . . . so . . ." She began to tremble violently. She swayed, then her legs went out from under her and she plopped to the floor.

All her ardent hopes vanished before her eyes. She was such a fool! She'd made a mess of her chance tonight, including mentally accusing Signor Dante of attempted rape when he was only trying to save her. How could she be so silly as to think an elegant gentleman like Signor Dante would stoop to make love to a peasant girl? She'd never get out of the mess she was in. She was too foolish, too pathetic. Raw sobs of disgrace broke from her throat.

"A dress can be replaced, a mirror is nothing," Dante said, crouching to face her once again. "There's no harm done. You're not hurt, are you?" He wanted to check to be sure she was only sobbing with shame and relief, but he didn't dare. One of the dogs licked soot from her fingers. Her face was white, her eyes glazed.

"Little dove? Little dove, can you hear me?" he asked, pushing the dog aside and taking her hand.

Mina didn't feel his hand on hers or hear his voice. She was far away, staring at the burned tins of bread from that morning. *Maledizione!* It had been an omen, just as Teresa had predicted. She hadn't been watching the signs. She'd been too proud. *Sant'Anna* had tried to warn her with the bread, but she'd been too thrilled with her promotion and too caught up in her plans for the future. Now she'd never win love and respect. After the Signorina saw the mess she'd made of everything she'd be returned to the private hell reserved for women of her kind.

Chapter Twelve

*I*T WAS ALMOST TWO O'CLOCK when Mina arrived home, exhausted but jubilant. After all the rank confusion and amateur abilities she'd displayed, the Signorina had simply excused them as "opening night jitters." She'd congratulated Mina on making it through the premier performance with her, "*à la flambé!*" and invited her to join the gala opening night party. Though it was late, Mina felt she couldn't refuse.

Wearing a dress borrowed from the costume shop, she'd stood, arms entwined with the Signorina and Signor Dante, drinking toasts with the wealthy patrons and the cast until they had willfully smashed their glasses. What a glorious, confusing night it had been. The Signorina had wanted her to take the dress she was wearing home, but she'd insisted on changing back, and Signor Dante had kindly taken her out to a cab.

She sighed happily as she took her key out of her purse and pushed the entry door open. Everyone had been so nice. Perhaps her luck was changing. She smiled, remembering how Signor Dante had laughed at her insult to his integrity. He'd thought it all a grand joke and had even made a special toast in her honor when she—

"Where have you been?"

An iron hand gripped her forearm and Mina leaped back against the wall, alarmed. She saw a familiar silhouette in the doorway against the moonlit street and smelled sour liquor.

"Oh! Antonio, you frightened me! I was at the opera."

"Till this hour?" he asked, yanking her inside.

"I was invited to celebrate after the performance."

"Celebrate? Celebrate what?"

"The new job. The one I came to see you about."

"The man who had his hands all over you at the opera house, he's part of this new job?"

He shoved her forward and she tripped. She instinctively threw her hands out to catch herself on the marble stair, but he jerked her up, painfully pinching her biceps. She climbed swiftly, trying to keep him from wrenching her shoulder again. Oh, Lord, she thought, he must have come uptown and seen me with Signor Dante.

"He was just seeing me safely to a cab."

He sniffed her. "You've been drinking?"

"A little champagne," Mina said, purposely ignoring the pain and keeping her voice light and bright.

"Champagne! Where did you drink champagne? Who were you with?" he asked threateningly. "Tell me! Tell me quickly."

"I was with Signorina Frascatti, after the opera, as I said."

"And that man?"

"Her fiancé. It was late. He wanted to make sure I was safe."

She disengaged his hand from her arm, doing her best not to show fear as she unlocked the door. How dare he accuse her? Hadn't she caught him only a few hours before with his mistress? Now he hoped to accuse her of infidelity and distract attention away from his own misdeeds.

Inside, the kerosene lamp had been lit and cast a small circle of light. His stone jug of dandelion wine sat on the table next to an empty glass. He'd been drinking; she'd have to tread carefully. In the shadowy light she could see him watching her out of the corners of his eyes as she took off her coat.

"Who's this Signorina Frascatti?"

"The opera's prima donna."

Antonio's pale blue eyes darkened with rage. "You expect me to believe you've been drinking champagne with a prima donna? You've been fucking around with that man I saw you with, haven't you?"

"Like you've been fucking around with that black-haired woman?" she snapped.

The retort was out before she could stop it. She never answered him back when he was drinking; it was too dangerous, but she was reckless with indignation.

"Shut up!" he shouted, stumbling toward her. "You don't question me, I do as I please."

She backed away and put the table between them. "Tell me the truth, Antonio. I know you're having an affair with that woman."

"You're crazy. She's that way with all the men. I can't stop the way she acts."

"You didn't look like you wanted to stop her."

He grabbed her purse off the table and took out her pay envelope. He ripped it open and counted the contents. "You said you got a raise, where is it? Let me see this promotion."

"Answer me! Is she the reason you only come home on payday?"

"Where's the extra money?" he shouted, darting forward and catching her arm. "I want to see it."

She tried to pull away, but he twisted her arm painfully. "Stop! You're hurting me," Mina said.

He jammed the purse into her stomach, knocking her breath out. "Hurry up," he insisted. "Let me see your new job."

She clutched her purse and backed away. "I don't have the money, I won't get—"

"You lying bitch!"

The slap cracked like a dry branch as it glanced off her temple. Pinpricks of light danced before her eyes. The next breath she took felt damp, as though she had just surfaced through water. She stumbled back into a chair and tried to catch herself. The lamp wobbled dangerously.

"Please, the oil lamp," she cried. *Sant'Anna,* please don't let him start a fire, she prayed. She fumbled for the chair to support her, but they both thudded to the floor. He kicked the chair away and reached for her, but she scrambled toward the bed. If she could get under it he might become frustrated and leave her alone. The tactic had worked once before, but as she edged under the springs she felt him grab her foot.

She curled into a ball, locking her hands behind her head and covering her face with her arms as he pulled her across the linoleum. It was the only way to protect herself from some of his fury. She heard him bump the dresser, knocking it against the wall. Glass shattered. She smelled the sweet fragrance she loved so much and knew it was her only perfume bottle. While this pleasant scent filled her senses, her husband pummeled her back and head.

"I told you! Never come to the saloon! You want to act like a whore, I'll treat you like a whore." She felt the golden wedding band that she'd so happily placed on his finger six months before banging against her ribs as he cursed and punched. *"Figlia di puttana!* Don't ever question me!"

The pain seared through her, but she was silent, only gasping when he struck a particularly mean blow. She wanted to fight back, but didn't dare. The one time she'd tried, he'd beaten her so badly she hadn't been able to get out of bed for two days. He twisted his hand into her hair and pulled her up from the floor, jerking her around the room and slamming her into furniture.

In between blows she heard a rhythmic banging. Teresa must be hitting the ceiling with her broom handle. It wouldn't help; neighbors had never stopped him in the past. He would beat her until the rage in his belly was spent. He was intent on his task; only the crash of furniture and an occasional grunt of effort punctuated the silence.

Finally he stopped hitting her and dragged her to the bed.

"No, no, please!" she pleaded frantically. "You don't have to do this. . . . I want to make you happy."

"Shut up, you slut," he shouted. "You're going to spread your legs for me, like you spread them for all the men. I know you and your mother from the village, you filthy whore."

He threw her onto the bed and climbed on top of her: pinning her down, tearing at her clothing and hair, biting and mauling her breasts. He crushed her lips against her teeth in a savage imitation of passion, groaning with satisfaction. She tasted blood and wondered if he was this way with his mistress. How did she stand it? Mina was sick with shame, for she knew the whole tenement could hear him through the air shaft.

As he jammed himself into her over and over she turned her head aside, concentrating on the smell of the spilled perfume. It swept away the stale sweat of his body and transported her out of the wretched body her soul was trapped in. The scent reminded her of bright cut flowers. Flowers that, in the spring, filled the stalls in the streets of Naples . . . streets narrow and winding that led out of the city . . . to the city . . . to the countryside . . . to the cemetery . . . and a grave.

She ignored him and struggled to feel the late summer sun on her back. She could see a bouquet in her hand . . . and taste sugared *zeppoli* on her tongue . . . a cool breeze was blowing from dark clouds off the bay of Naples . . . soon there would be a crash and fat stinging drops of rain . . . a summer squall . . . only a summer squall . . . it would pass. . . .

This wasn't supposed to be her on the bed, being vilely attacked. No, he should have married another. She tried to envision the other girl, but she was far away . . . rocking on the sea . . . rocking and running . . . running across the rocky field toward her *Mammina*. In the distance she could see the two women laughing, *Mammina* and her daughter . . . how happy they were, swinging clasped hands as they walked down the country lane in Rocca San Felice. . . .

She pushed desperately forward to smell the flowers they both carried. She wanted to catch them . . . to watch them dance . . . and help them pick wildflowers . . . She wanted her mother to be alive. She ran after them, but she couldn't catch her breath in the hot summer sun. She couldn't catch her breath . . . couldn't smell the flowers anymore. . . .

The body being brutalized on the bed didn't belong to that girl on the path. The soul that had taken this identity was slipping away. Going . . . where was it going? It was hurrying after *Mammina*. Stop! she cried, trying desperately to catch them.

"Stop! Stop!"

How strange it was that the stubborn thread holding her soul aloft over the bed and the blue summer sky refused to break and set her free.

T H E light was just beginning to creep through the patched window when she eased out from under the weight of his body. Her husband lay on his face, mouth open, snoring loudly, with his pants down around his ankles and his boots on. The disgust and loathing she felt for him overwhelmed her and it flashed through her mind to put a knife in his back.

Unconsciously she moved to the table and silently pulled the drawer open. Her hand drew out a bread knife and she studied the blade. I can end my torment if I act quickly, she reasoned. He's asleep, he can't stop me. "Do it!" her anger urged. "He deserves to die. He's an evil man . . ."

She put the knife down on the table. Her hands were shaking. She clasped them tightly against her chest, appalled by what she was thinking. Antonio *was* a vicious man, but God would punish him. She wanted the beatings to stop, yes, but she couldn't take his life. Only God could do that. She needed to find another way.

Her bodice was torn down the middle. She pulled off the sleeves and unfastened her burned skirt and petticoat. Wearily she stepped out of them, every movement scorching her flesh like a hot iron. She crouched over the basin, using what was left of her torn undergarments to wash. Above her rolled stockings the insides of her thighs were bruised purple and she was sticky with blood and semen.

She dipped the fabric into the cool water and washed as best she could. The blood on the cloth saddened her—she must not be pregnant after all. Another woman would have been pleased to think she wasn't carrying such an awful man's child. But she wanted a child. A child would give her a reason to live.

She dumped the foul water and poured some fresh to wash her face. In the mirror over her dresser she saw a cut on her temple and bruises on her neck. She took the mirror to the window and gingerly examined the cut in the rising light. It was deep and ran into her hairline, crusted over with blood. She could clean it, but it was going to look bad in daylight.

She tried smoothing her hair, but her scalp hurt too much to use the comb. Knots of hair, pulled out by the roots, came free in her hands. She piled her hair up, wincing at the pain caused by lifting her arms. When she scraped her sore scalp with a hairpin she sobbed with frustration and self-pity, but she stopped herself. Tears changed nothing. She'd learned that lesson long ago in Italy when she'd lost her mother. When she was forced to struggle on alone. She could cry her heart out and nothing would change. She'd have to ignore the pain, concentrate on what she needed to do to stay alive, and make some kind of plan for the future.

She pulled on fresh underclothing and her only decent dress, the faded olive work dress. She'd have more freedom of movement than in the taffeta. She would wrap a scarf around her throat and arrange her hair in a style that covered her temples. Perhaps she should cut some bangs. She would tackle that problem after Antonio left for work.

She cut thick slabs of salami, hard cheese, and bread for two sandwiches and wrapped them in a clean cloth with trembling hands. What should she do? The situation was becoming intolerable. One day, if she didn't get away, he was sure to kill her. She'd tried to be patient and wait for God to reveal His plan, but it didn't seem to be working. She had to leave him. She thought of her little stash beneath the floorboards. There was enough to get away, but where could she go?

None of her friends, not Teresa or Simonetta or Lilli, could take her in. They were struggling too. They couldn't crowd in another soul, especially one with a violent husband attached. She wouldn't shame herself or them by asking. She could go to the church . . . but hadn't the priest rebuked her? He would say it was her duty as a Catholic wife to submit, and then he'd send her home. The police? They wouldn't lift a finger.

Teresa said that two years ago a Sicilian woman living on Elizabeth Street had gotten her skull crushed. The police had done nothing; the husband had happily remarried.

There was something called the "rule of thumb." The law it was based on gave a husband the right to beat his wife as long as he didn't use a stick thicker than his own thumb. If he killed her with the stick, well, that was the law. A woman was like a table or a dog; she was her husband's property.

Even in Italy it was so. Didn't the Bible proclaim it? Wasn't a man free to beat his wife to death if he wanted, free to rape her if he willed? She could do nothing to stop him. She was his slave and had no protection; for if she killed him, even to save her own life, she could end up in jail to answer for her crime, and God would see her as a sinner.

Gesù, Sant'Anna, help me. I want to make my marriage work, but I need your help. Make him leave that woman and stop drinking. Touch his heart so he won't be angry. If you help me, I'll find a way to stay with him, but if not, I'll be forced to break my vows. I know I swore before you, "in sickness and in health, for better or worse." But if I don't get away, one night he will surely kill me, and if I should get pregnant, a beating might kill my child.

She paced. How could she change him back to the loving man he'd been before their wedding? She'd been given a chance for a new life and she must do her best to hold on to it. She had to get rid of the mistress, but how? She started on breakfast, making her plans for the coming weeks. Yesterday she'd been stupid in her jealousy and fear. She'd told him about her raise and later made him angry by confronting him about the woman. At least she'd been wise enough to keep part of the money secret.

She would continue to put money aside as she'd planned. If she couldn't win him back from his mistress, she'd leave. Leave? Her heart leaped at the thought of packing a bag and running away. She didn't want to sin, but the idea of being free of his cruelty lightened her soul.

What was it Teresa had said? "Get a lawyer . . . leave him." Where would she find a lawyer? She didn't speak English and was barely educated. *Gesù!* She wasn't even a citizen. And there were serious problems with her papers. She'd be suspect if she went to a lawyer and he examined her papers too closely. She could be arrested or deported back to Naples. But was jail or deportation worse than death?

Oh, *Sant'Anna,* she prayed, help me. I know I am unworthy, a sinner and a liar, nothing for you to bother about, but please, please, help me. I can't do it alone. She waited a moment before cracking the eggs, her eyes closed, her face turned up toward heaven where *Gesù* and the saints looked down. She waited for a sign, an answer, something that would tell her that her choice was a good one.

The clock ticked in the stillness, a bird chirped, but *Gesù* and *Sant'Anna* were silent as they always were.

Chapter Thirteen

"**E**NCORE! BRAVA! FRASCATTI!**" the rapturous crowd shouted, demanding her presence. "Francesca, *brava!"*

Only moments before, a defiant Tosca had discovered her lover dead, killed by Scarpia's treachery, and his men had driven her to the parapet. "Scarpia, we meet before God!" she'd vowed. Then she'd leaped over the ramparts of the Castle Sant'Angelo to a crushing death on the stones below. For the first time in her career, Cesca had handled the twenty-foot drop onto a stack of down and cotton stuffed mattresses poorly, landing on her stomach. She was gasping, painfully doubled over, when Mina and a stagehand helped her up.

"Are you all right, Signorina?" Mina asked.

"I—I—" After a moment, ashamed of her amateur landing, she replied, "*Non c' è male,* not bad."

Mina reattached Cesca's ornate paste tiara, which had torn loose, and Cesca rushed through the warren of flats and supporting timbers to take her curtain call. She joined sweaty hands with Cavaradossi and Scarpia and, as the stagehands pulled back the heavy curtain, stepped forward into a tidal wave of sound.

Sweeping into a deep curtsy with her back straight, her chin high, she threw kisses as the crowd pelted her with flowers, but instead of feeling triumphant she feared she might vomit. That hadn't occurred since her first performance in Naples twenty years before. Her eyes swept the diamond horseshoe, box seats reserved for the wealthiest patrons, and she was suddenly aware of the reason for her discomfort. Emilio was in the audience.

All night the second gilt box to the left had pumped a stream of malice toward her, as if someone was trying to make her feel small and worthless. As long as she'd had the task of singing and acting she'd been unafraid of the coming confrontation, but now even this wild tribute wasn't enough to take away the shame he'd once made her feel. For an instant the stage disappeared and she was fifteen, lying naked in a vineyard, caught in a passionate embrace with the *padrone*'s son.

The crowd's worshipful approval took the edge off her nausea for a moment. She was no longer a helpless peasant in Emilio's employ nor a struggling mandolin player singing for a few lira in Naples. No, she was *diva assoluta* with the world at her feet. Emilio and his scorn could go to hell! She turned to face him, but the chairs stood empty. Emilio and his party had gone.

"*Basta!*" she shouted as the curtain closed again. "Enough! It's enough for tonight."

"But they're calling for us," Bonzinni responded, pulling her forward. He hadn't had this many curtain calls since he was forty pounds slimmer and twenty-five years younger.

"I said, enough!" She threw down her flowers and grabbed the stagehand's arm. The curtain jerked to a halt. The cast and crew muttered among themselves, annoyed by their short-shrifted glory. "Let us not be greedy, *amici*. Seven curtain calls! We mustn't appear desperate."

She whirled away with Mina holding the train of her gown. Her heels made a racket as she hurried down the stair. When she stopped to catch her breath, Mina blotted the sweat from her face. She heard a woman's high-pitched giggle float down the corridor, followed by a familiar bass tone. It was Emilio in her dressing room.

"Is something wrong, signorina?" Mina asked.

"A devil from my past has come to torment me, but I shall beat him back to hell."

Mina suddenly looked as frightened as she felt. Cesca smiled to reassure her and dried her palms against her gown. Then she took several of the largest floral tributes from Mina. "I'll take these. Go before me as we do every night. Put a smile on your face. Be merry. We are happy . . . triumphant . . . nothing is troubling us. Hurry, go ahead."

Mina opened the door and Cesca entered like a goddess.

"Signor Lampone, how kind of you to come," she said, passing the flowers back to Mina and graciously putting out her hand. "Your lilies arrived just before the curtain."

Caught in midsentence, Emilio was forced to take her extended hand. In the present company he could do no less. He hesitated only a moment before he courteously bent to kiss it, but she saw he did not miss her refusal to address him as Don.

"It is delightful to see you again, Signorina Frascatti."

"And you, signor."

"I have been asking after Lucifer. He's not traveling with you?"

The group murmured cautiously at his remark. "Lucifer?" Emilio's paramour asked, eyebrows arched in surprise.

"My pet ocelot. He's not a fan of Puccini, he prefers Mozart; so he's at home."

Everyone laughed. "How absolutely delightful," the blond girl said in French. "A leopard that likes Mozart."

"My niece, Solange," Emilio introduced her.

"*Enchantée!*" Solange said, making a small curtsy.

"*Charmante*, mademoiselle. Such a young 'niece,' Signor Lampone," Cesca said, wagging a finger at him mockingly. "Naughty, naughty!"

Cesca radiated charm as she shook hands with Emilio's friends. They congratulated her effusively.

"You were superb," Solange chirped.

"In the nine years since the maestro created *Tosca* I have not heard better," Emilio said.

"High praise indeed! For I know you heard it performed in Rome only last year with the maestro himself," Cesca replied.

"Is that how long it has been? It seems longer." Emilio reflexively touched his right biceps where her bullet had pierced it.

She saw his unconscious gesture and turned away, a smile of pleasure on her lips. "I assure you, I remember it like yesterday, one short year ago."

Emilio inspected the flower-packed dressing room. She noticed that when his eyes landed on Mina, patiently waiting in the corner to help her undress, he smirked and bowed.

"I see you've made some exquisite changes in your dressing room," Emilio said.

"Yes! This screen is so bohemian! Don't you think so, Emilio?" Solange enthused. She was clearly irritated, and Cesca thought she was doing her best to draw Emilio's attention away from her beautiful young dresser.

"That screen cost a fortune! The Signo—*Cesca,*" Oscar said, puffing up with self-importance, "insisted we spruce up the room. New paint, silk upholstered chairs, Persian—"

"Oscar, the room was in tatters," Emilio said. "What better way to spend my donations than on something beautiful?" Everyone followed his gaze as it pointedly returned to Mina.

Cesca was pleased. Let him stew, she thought. I've replaced your little spy and now you're out in the cold. "It's true, we artists do not work well in a sinister atmosphere," she said, holding out her arm for Mina to remove her bracelets, but giving Emilio a meaningful look. "It makes one feel almost . . . fettered."

The group murmured a polite agreement.

"Signor Dante has been kind enough to offer champagne, but I thought perhaps we might have a late supper at Delmonico's," Emilio said to Cesca. "I'd be very pleased if you and your fiancé . . . and Oscar, of course, would be so kind as to join us."

"My opera duties force me to decline this evening," Oscar said. "Another time perhaps."

"We'd be delighted," Dante said, crossing to Cesca. "*Tesoro,* my treasure, are you feeling up to dinner?" She acknowledged with a wink that it was as he'd suspected, Emilio would be fishing for information. She kissed Dante sensually as he twined his arms around her waist and gazed lovingly into her eyes. "We usually dine at home after a performance," Dante said, kissing her wrist and continuing up her arm, "alone."

"I'm always ravenous after a performance," she said, acting the coquette, "but of course, signor, it would be our pleasure, tonight, to dine with you."

"Perfect!" Emilio said. "Solange was hoping to chat with you."

"I'm so thrilled to finally meet you. I've heard so much gos—I mean, I've heard a great deal about you," Solange stammered with embarrassment.

Cesca laughed at the faux pas and played the libertine. "I must strip naked and wash. Excuse me, ladies and gentlemen. Unless, of course, you'd like another performance?"

"We'll go on ahead to Del's and take a table. *Che vi diamo, signori,*" Emilio said as he swept his party from the room.

THE ride uptown was tense. Cesca was sure Emilio's arrogance indicated he knew more than they'd suspected. Dante reminded her that Emilio delighted in mental dueling.

"Whatever he has planned, we can turn aside his épée and get our own information, if we thrust and parry adroitly," he said as he concentrated on his driving.

"He's too bold," Cesca said. "He was staring directly at Mina when he mentioned 'changes.' "

"*Cara,* the 'changes' he referred to *were* your new dresser. That's his game. But he's been in that dressing room before, he's given money to the opera house, for God's sake, he's a friend of Oscar's, so he *implies* that the changes are in the decor. If you were to confront him outright, he would say, 'I'm referring to the paint, the furniture, the chaise.' Then he'd tighten like the skin on a grape."

"But does he know we're aware he planted a spy?"

"He had one informant, I'm sure he has other—"

"Oh, God, I hate all this," Cesca said fretfully.

"None of it's important. He can't know for sure. Remember, no matter how he baits you tonight, you must not step into his trap. Don't give him a scrap of information. He's planning something, you can be sure of that, and we must discover what."

"He won't win, even if . . . even if I must go to jail." Cesca clutched her evening purse.

"*Cara,* you didn't bring a pistol tonight? Did you?"

"Don't be a fool," she said, trying to laugh off his question.

"You're planning to shoot Don Emilio Lampone in Delmonico's? In

front of everyone? Perfect! He'll be dead, you'll be in jail, and I'll be free
to go home."

She looked at him with fire in her eyes. "Someone has to stop him."

"Use your brain tonight, not bullets." He pulled the automobile to the
curb and turned off the engine. They argued in front of the restaurant
for ten minutes. Then, exasperated, he threw up his hands and gave in.

THE suspect handbag rested next to him on her chair. The dinner
service had been swift, the food excellent, and although the conversation
had been tense, Dante saw no hint of trouble. As the dessert order was
being taken and the coffee service was being laid, Solange chatted gaily
with Cesca. He made small talk with Emilio. Then the mood at the table
changed subtly.

"Will Tosca be your only performance, signorina?" Emilio asked, addressing her directly for the first time. "Or will you create another character this season?"

"Hammerstein's very pleased with his profits. He's begged me to stay
on and I've consented to do another opera."

"Oh, I hope it's *La Traviata*! I love that opera!" Solange said, leaning
across the table toward Cesca.

"Ah, yes, the timeless story of a woman out of her class," Emilio
sniped, intending the double meaning for Cesca. "You'll play Violetta,
the jaded courtesan, of course."

"No, I'm to play Madama Butterfly. The innocent young woman
cheated of true love."

"Such a wonderful story," Solange said. "Poor Butterfly has a child,
but the lovers are separated, and her child—"

"Is taken from her," Emilio said, a glint of ice in his eye. "Yes, Solange,
I am very familiar with the plot. You know, I never thought of it until this
evening, but isn't it ironic that a man named Pinkerton crosses an ocean
to take the child from her mother?" He laughed.

"Ironic?" Solange asked. "No, Emilio, I find your humor sad."

"In the end the mother is so heartbroken by the turn of events she is
forced to commit suicide," Emilio said.

Dante thought the part about Pinkerton crossing the ocean a little
ham-handed, but everyone got the point. Cesca's cup clattered in its

saucer as she put it down. Dante knew she was internally fuming at Emilio's veiled threat. He brushed aside an imaginary crumb from his lips and settled his napkin on his lap. His hand secretly moved to cover Cesca's purse.

"The premiere in Rome was an absolute horror," Solange said obtusely. "A wind from the wings picked up poor Rosina's kimono, puffing it out, and the crowd howled that she was pregnant with Toscanini's child. You know, of course, they had a secret liaison?"

"Yes," Cesca said dryly, looking at Emilio. "A cabal wishing to smash the maestro's masterpiece was sent to the theater to stir up trouble. They thought they could destroy him, but their evil plotting did not succeed."

"Our hero triumphed in the end. Didn't he, my love?" Dante said, catching her hand as it inched toward her purse. "The cabal that wished to ruin him was unsuccessful in their attempt."

Dante lifted her hand and kissed the inside of her wrist. He gave her a stern look, then pinned her hand to the damask cloth. The waiter placed a tall glass of strawberries and cream in front of Solange. She rattled her spoon in excitement and puckered her lips.

"Mascagni told Puccini, 'Your opera has fallen, but it will rise again,' " Solange said. "Like a phoenix, Mascagni knew it would rise from its ashes. It was his destiny."

"You know," Cesca said, biting her words as if pruning a rose bush, "I keep hearing this word *destiny . . . destiny . . . destiny—*"

With a flourish the waiter delivered Cesca's dessert, a crisp meringue swan swimming in a pool of custard cream and berries. Dante saw the pastry chef peek from the service door to gauge her reaction. Even in her present state of enmity she did not ignore the kindness. She paused and blew him a kiss of appreciation. Beaming, he ducked back inside the kitchen. The conversation stopped long enough to allow the waiter to pour more coffee.

"Destiny is the will of God," Emilio said. "Even you, Signorina Frascatti, do not have the power to change it."

"You think so?" Cesca asked challengingly as Dante squeezed her hand in warning. "*Madama Butterfly* was written after an agonizing struggle. Giacomo did not pluck it from the air, a gift from God delivered whole. He sweated blood over it, shaping and polishing . . . he created it with his desire . . . his determination and his wits! Fate, Signor

Lampone, is our doing, not God's. If we are disappointed in our life we must blame ourselves, ask ourselves what role we may have played in our downfall."

"Here, here!" Dante mocked, trying to slow her down, but she ignored him.

"It may take stealing or whoring, bullets or murder, but our lives are ultimately shaped by our own hands, and I, for one, will take up whatever weapon necessary to stop those who would bar my way and tell me I must be satisfied with 'the will of God.' "

There was an uncomfortable silence at the table. Cesca's swan trembled on its lake of cream. Dante chuckled and reached for the sugar bowl. "As you can see," Dante said, "Cesca feels very strongly about fate. You mustn't cross her in that regard, not if you value your life."

Emilio seemed pleased by Cesca's show of temper. He'd gotten under her skin and was obviously planning to be more of an irritant in the future.

"I offer an olive branch this evening, Signorina Frascatti," he said smoothly. "I tell you frankly, I wish you every success in your opera career. I harbor no grudge for what happened outside Rome. I do not wish unbridled rancor to interfere with my future plans. Rome is no reason for revenge."

"There is to be revenge?" Dante asked with interest. He raised his espresso cup and smiled mildly at Emilio.

"In life, as in opera, there is always revenge," Emilio said.

"I thought we were talking about destiny," Solange interrupted.

"Eat your strawberries, *ma petite*," Emilio said, patting her hand, "and hush!"

Solange pulled her hand away exasperated. "Emilio thinks I am a fool because I'm blond and enthusiastic. You, signorina, are a prima donna, and I have appeared as a dancer in over twenty operas, but of course Emilio's the opera expert at the table . . . aren't you, *uncle?*"

Emilio helped himself to some fruit and cheese, ignoring Solange's temper. "Almost, *niece*. But to continue, let us suppose, say, that we are Puccini, writing our own opera."

"All right," Cesca said, "let us suppose."

Emilio warmed to his task, offering a slice of apple to Cesca on the point of his knife. She looked at the sharp blade extended to her from across the table. Here it comes, she thought, just as Dante predicted. The first thrust. She shook her head, indicating her swan. Emilio removed the slice of apple from the knife's tip and chewed thoroughly. As he spoke he used his carving to accent his scenario.

"A child is born to a nobleman by a low, deceitful woman. This woman, a servant, convinces her lover, over his father's objections, that the child she is carrying is his, and they run off to the city. There she rises to a position of prominence in the music world by whoring."

"Whoring!" Dante laughed. "She rises only through whoring! What a talented young woman! I wish you had her talents, *tesoro*—you'd have saved yourself a lot of struggle and given me quite a bit more pleasure."

Solange giggled.

"As I was saying, she uses her body and her guile to turn the young man against his father."

"So the familial relationship wasn't strong?" Dante asked, as though very interested. "Otherwise the whore couldn't separate the father and son so easily."

Emilio gave Dante a caustic look, then continued. "The father tries everything but is unable to break through the wall of lies surrounding his son. Eventually he learns his son has died in poverty and neglect. But this woman's evil is not finished. Using her fame and fortune she now tries to keep the child born of that union from his rightful blood."

The background babble seemed to roar in Cesca's ears as Emilio stared into her eyes challengingly. How dare he call her evil? How dare he use the words "rightful blood?" He was the one who had refused to compromise, to make peace. For a moment everyone sat stiffly waiting for her reaction.

"This is the first act?" Dante asked, breaking the tension.

"It is," Emilio replied. "Now in the second act, don't you think this duplicity must be repaid?"

"It was the grandfather who chose to deny the child's legitimacy," Cesca said in a low, intense voice.

"He didn't trust the virtue of the woman," Dante said. "Or the blood line."

"Be careful," Solange said, scraping the bottom of her glass. "Your opera might end like the one where the hunchback mistakenly kills his own daughter. Things like that happen when revenge gets the better of you." Solange tapped Emilio on the hand with her spoon for emphasis. He pulled his hand back, annoyed.

"Operatically speaking," Dante said, leaning across the damask, "if your opera were taken to its logical conclusion, what would be the second act and the climax?"

"After searching for the child, the grandfather discovers she was given up for adoption and has traveled to another land. He finds her and solemnly promises the mother her daughter will have everything"—he put his his hand over his breast—"including the name and respectability the mother tried so brazenly to steal for herself. There will be servants and wealth, an education, and eventually a perfect marriage. Happiness unending."

"You're suggesting a happy ending? At what price?" Cesca asked in surprise.

"The grandfather will demand some kind of justice," Dante suggested to Cesca, wagging his index finger in her face for emphasis. "The scales must balance!"

Emilio dipped his head in agreement. "The mother has to abdicate," Emilio said coolly, discarding the spent apple core. "Justice demands she lose her child, just as the father lost his son. The mother's character will have no further chance to taint the child." Emilio sipped his aperitif, apparently pleased by his scenario.

Dante was amused. He leaned back in his chair applauding in mockery. "What a wonderfully egocentric plot," Dante said. "The grandfather as innocent victim."

Solange tapped her spoon against her empty glass.

"Do you remember that tragic opera, Emilio? I was in it when we met . . . you liked it so much. What is it called?" She paused. "There's a court jester and a duke . . . the jester's daughter ends up by a river bank in a sack?" Solange looked at each person at the table inquisitively.

Cesca knew Emilio was no jester. He'd threatened to take Maria Grazia once before in Rome. He'd never admit his culpability. He wished to blame her so he could shield himself from the part he'd played in his son's death, he, who had been the maker of his own unhappiness. How she pitied him.

"Oh!" Solange cried. "What's the name of that damn opera?"

"Rigoletto?" Dante asked politely.

He knows Maria Grazia's in America, Cesca thought. He knows I've followed her here and he's planning on taking her from me. If he can, he will make certain I never see my daughter again. Evil man, I will not allow it! Cesca grabbed her purse.

"Yes! That's it!" Solange cried. *"Rigoletto!"*

"My love," Dante said as he quickly slipped his arm around her shoulders and gripped her tightly against him, "in *Rigoletto,* if I remember correctly, doesn't the father ultimately destroy *himself* with his stubborn desire for revenge?"

She tried to shake off Dante's interference and fumbled in her purse to find only powder, change, keys, and a handkerchief. Seething, she then tried to locate her gun in his coat pockets, but he held her fast. She felt him brush his lips against her neck in what she knew he hoped passed for an amorous exchange. "Don't take the bait," he whispered against her ear as he held her wrist.

"Yes, yes, now I remember," Solange said. "He pays an assassin to deliver the body of his enemy to him, but the jester's been cursed by his own pride. The plan backfires, and in the sack he finds his only child, dead."

"Shut up, Solange!" Emilio snapped. "We are not discussing *Rigoletto.*"

"Stop, *tesoro,* we're in public," Dante chided as he pulled her other hand from his pocket. "You must save your amorous behavior for after dinner." He put a spoon in her hand. "You haven't touched your swan," he said. "And it's certain to melt in all this hot air."

Cesca's meringue swan bobbled as she shot to her feet. She was about to launch into a stinging rebuke, but the room went suddenly and profoundly quiet.

Her attention was forced away from Emilio, across a sea of disapproving white faces, to fix on the entrance to the dining room. A tall, well-built black man stood at the door. The shock wave hadn't been caused by his blackness or his fame as a serious contender for the heavyweight championship, but by the beautiful white woman on his arm.

Jack Johnson and his white companion stood at the entrance to the main dining room with pleasant, set looks on their faces, but Cesca could see their eyes were stony. In cosmopolitan New York City it was still taboo for whites and blacks to mix, and even at Delmonico's, in a cultured milieu, prejudice stalked them.

It only took a moment for Cesca to react.

"Jack! Jack Johnson!" Now all the goggling heads snapped in her direction. She smiled and waved her hand. "Won't you please come join us for dinner?" she asked in English, as clearly as possible for the benefit of the packed dining room.

There were gasps. The maître d', stiff in outrage at her exhibited bad manners, was immediately at her side. He pulled the table she was struggling with out, so she could sweep around it and stride across the room to the boxer's side.

"Cesca!" Johnson embraced her with genuine warmth, then turned to the woman at his side. "My dear, this is Francesca Frascatti, a friend from London. And this is beautiful Etta Duryea, my future wife." They exchanged greetings as though speaking in a private parlor as all of Delmonico's gaped. "I'd heard you were in town. Appearing at the Metropolitan?" Jack's face radiated warmth.

"No, I appear in *Tosca* at the Manhattan Opera House. But I don't suppose you'll buy a ticket. You see," she said, smiling at Etta, "Jack once told me that opera reminded him of a squalling cat forced to fight a howling dog over a supper only one would finish."

"Cesca's pretty good at fisticuffs herself. It's good to see you after London."

"And you," she said, guiding them toward the lounge. As they entered the lounge, it too went silent. Behind them the dining room erupted in chatter. A wiry, mustachioed man with a foot on the bar rail stared, his mouth open.

"What are you looking at?" Cesca asked evenly. He closed his mouth and turned away, unable to match her fierce stare. "I congratulate you on your success in finally arranging a championship bout! You will join us?"

"We'll eat someplace else," the dark giant said slowly with his Texas twang. "I guess, at this time, there's no table available. Reservations, you know?"

Cesca knew reservations at Delmonico's were unheard of; even Mrs. Astor waited for a table.

"Nonsense, they'll find two chairs and you'll dine with me."

"Cesca, I know you're a heavyweight in this crowd and you probably can produce those chairs, but we're not in the mood to fight. We just want a little supper. I'd rather not bother tonight."

"In that case you and your charming fiancée must come to call. I have Mondays free. Do you still remember how to play *Tre Sette?*" He nodded. "Then you'll come play with Caruso and me. After I beat Errico, he gets even by making mountains of pasta he knows I cannot resist. You'll both come, yes?"

"It will be our pleasure," Etta said.

They exchanged good-byes and Cesca made her way back to the table, where they finished their desserts and coffees without further incident and said their good-byes at the coat check.

"Was the woman a . . . a . . . professional?" Solange asked Dante in a disgusted whisper. "Who was that man?"

"An intelligent, kind, and incredibly powerful man!" Cesca said, slipping into her wrap. "He's an uncompromising gentleman and a great athlete who's going to be the next heavyweight champion of the world."

"He may be the next champion, but to come into this company with, with . . . that woman . . ." Solange said.

"That woman happens to be his fiancée. Fiancées are not paid for their company, like . . . some people, mademoiselle."

Solange's face reddened as she took Emilio's arm. Cesca and Dante stepped to the curb.

"Don't you think any of us guessed you're a paid companion?" Cesca asked. Solange lost her smile. Cesca's laugh boomed on the silent street. "I've been a paid companion, mademoiselle, it's no tragedy, it's only a means to an end. Live life by your own rules. Use those who would use you. That's my motto! The motto of whoring." She turned to Emilio. "I've no time for hypocrites, as you well know, signor."

"Goodnight, mademoiselle," Dante said as he handed Solange up into the waiting hack. He slammed the door and smiled carelessly at Emilio. As the carriage pulled away he called, "I know you'll continue to work on your opera. I'll be waiting to see how your second act resolves."

Chapter Fourteen

~ℚ♭~

*T*HE LITTLE WHITE-TIPPED TAILS
on Cesca's mink muff swayed in the sharp wind as she left the stylish
dressmaker's shop on Dante's arm. Even though the weather had turned
and the day was sunny, the wind was cold. Dante helped her into the auto
and settled the lap rug snugly about her legs.

It had been a week since the premiere. The critics had been ecstatic,
praising her voice, her acting, and her beauty. She was the toast of the
city. The newspapers carried daily articles showing her at society gather-
ings and outings. She'd received offers to appear in San Francisco,
Chicago, and other cities for fabulous sums of money, but she couldn't
take pleasure in conquering her fifth continent.

She'd suffered through a long week of foreboding, waiting for
Inspector Bevilacqua to once again find the woman with the earrings.
She was especially anxious now that Emilio had boldly admitted he was
in New York to take Maria Grazia if she was found. His Pinkertons were
exerting pressure and offering money for information. Would she be able
to outmaneuver him and find her daughter in time?

At any moment news might arrive to prove that the sighting in the
market was a dead end. Her apprehension was intense. It followed her
to bed and gave her nightmares, and even though she acted gay and
carefree, beneath the facade her nerves were as frayed as a violinist's
horsehair bow after a violent passage. Respite came only during performances and while sharing stories with her new dresser.

She liked Mina and found that the little she shared about her past indicated a difficult life, reminiscent of her own in Naples. She was struck
by the many similarities between them and saw Mina as a timid version
of herself. Involvement in her dresser's life had taken her mind off her
own troubles and she'd decided to aid her, if she could.

"Money and power are delicious, Dante! Even on short notice, they
modified everything as stipulated. The measurements came from the
costume mistress, so they are sure to fit. Cash always provides the necessary incentive."

"Yes, as they say, 'Money talks in America.' " Dante slammed the door of the Pierce-Arrow and sprinted back to the shop owner who stood shivering on the stair. She handed him several long boxes that he placed in the boot and then he climbed inside the auto and directed it up Sixth Avenue.

"The dresses you ordered for yourself will be delivered to the house and—" Dante said.

"Yes, fine, who cares? What news did you obtain while I was being fitted?"

"Inspector Bevilacqua saw the earrings again in the market and traced the woman to a saloon downtown."

"Where is this saloon?" She was ready to drive there immediately and confront the woman.

"On Cherry Street, close to the river and not far from Little Italy where we've been searching. They've been holding illegal prizefights in the back room. It'll give us a perfect cover to go down and identify the owner of the earrings."

"You're going with them?"

"Of course. I've been perfecting a disguise. I'll be a boxer, and Giuseppe Colombo will be my trainer."

"You a boxer? Ridiculous!"

Annoyed, Dante jerked the steering wheel to cut around a delivery truck. "Bevilacqua caught one of Emilio's Pinkertons shadowing him. He's afraid Emilio might have gotten some information."

She was suddenly frightened. "But I—I—"

"It's all right. Bevilacqua told me he's been feeding the man false information. I'm afraid Emilio's second act will suffer." He chuckled at his own joke and lay on the horn. "Get out of the way, you fool!" he shouted, sticking his head out the window.

"I'm coming with you."

"What? Absolutely not! You're too well known, you'll be recognized."

"Do you think you're the only one who's able to apply nose putty and crepe hair? I too can disguise myself. I assure you I'll be unrecognizable."

"No, it's too dangerous. I'll drop you off at the house and go alone."

"Who's paying your salary? I'll decide what's too dangerous."

He sounded the horn and swerved through the tangle of carriages and automobiles in the intersection. "Why did you hire me if you are planning to do all the detective work yourself?"

"You need me. You don't know what Maria looks like. You'll need an expert's advice."

"You haven't seen her since she was a child."

"Don't puff out your chest and get cross," she said, softening her tone at Dante's obvious annoyance. She put a hand on his arm. "Don't you realize I see Maria in every young girl her age? I can't sit home and wait. If it's her, I want to be there. We're so close I must see for myself."

"Even if you put our plan in jeopardy?"

"I promise, if you think I can be recognized after I've disguised myself, I won't go. Agreed?"

"You're a stubborn ox."

"Good, it's settled then. Let's hurry to the theater. I want to enjoy our surprise before the performance."

After Dante parked and unloaded the auto, Cesca stopped to speak with Hammerstein in his office.

Dante went ahead alone, carrying most of the boxes and a nosegay of yellow and bright pink snapdragons. He stopped unnoticed on the threshold of the dressing room to watch Mina. Once again he was taken by surprise at her artless beauty.

She was deeply absorbed in scoring the bottoms of Cesca's shoes with a knife and didn't notice him. Still wearing the same dress she'd worn every day for the past week, only the fringe of curls around her delicate face was different. He drew a deep breath, savoring the image. Try as he might, he couldn't crush his attraction to Mina.

Most of the time he was able to keep his mind occupied. In the mornings he searched the immigration records. There were hundreds of ships' manifests to go through, and without a correct name or date it was taking longer than anticipated. In the afternoons, he checked in with the men he'd posted at the Essex Street Market and those assigned to Little Italy. There was always something to do, but it didn't seem to be enough.

So he'd given himself the additional task of personally scouring Mulberry Street where the Neapolitan immigrants settled. Every afternoon he applied disguises and prowled the streets, the shops, and the marketplaces. He was sure Maria Grazia would gravitate to her countrymen and he'd find her among the carts and stalls, but he had to admit that in the back of his mind he also knew it was Mina's neighborhood.

During his forays she remained on the periphery of his thoughts, for he might bump into her and he told himself to be prepared. He knew he could throw the operation into danger if he was exposed, but he wouldn't give up his risky forays. Awake or asleep, his thoughts turned obsessively to Mina.

Until he'd met her, women had been minor distractions, idle fancies. He'd never allowed a woman to enter his inner sanctuary. He enjoyed his studies and his solitude too much to allow women to sully that holy ground, but now his free nights were an annoyance. The watercolors that used to soothe and captivate him were irritating, and he didn't have the patience to work with the tiny parts and gears of his watches and locks.

He anxiously waited for performance nights so he could return to the opera house. He told himself he needed to maintain the cover story of being the diva's lover, but in his heart he knew the truth. It was an excuse to sit beside her as she ironed or did lace work. Like a schoolboy with a first crush, he indulged himself shamelessly and set about drawing her out.

She was stiff and shy about being alone with him at first, but he started by talking of his own life and interests. He told her how his step-father had favored his younger brother, how they'd argued, and how he'd been disowned and forced to make his own way. He didn't admit to being a detective, but he talked enthusiastically about advancements in crime detection. He shared his poems with her and asked for her perspective. It wasn't long before she began to relax and share some of her own life.

Just as he'd expected, she was charming and unspoiled. Her heart brimmed with simple pleasures and honest observations about the world. Yes, he thought, looking at her from the threshold of the dressing room, she's as tender as buds of crocus pushing up through the soft earth and just as sweet.

"Here you are, little dove," he said, offering her the flowers wrapped in paper with a mock bow.

She jumped with fright at the sound of his voice. "Oh, you're here!" Then she laughed at her fear and took the flowers from his hand.

She'd just been wondering where he might be. Whenever he was near, time passed so pleasantly. He made her feel like a carefree child, a playmate. He was teasing and tender, causing her to forget her troubles. Antonio and her marriage seemed far away when she was sitting or talking with him. He was so different from her husband, who was stiff and formal whenever he wasn't drunk and angry.

The few men she'd known in Italy, and now in America, never talked of twilight in the fields. They never asked for her viewpoint or insisted on knowing her feelings—not even Mario, who was gentle and kind, spoke to her of the profound secrets stored in his heart. Signor Dante's behavior confused her. She'd never known anyone like him, and she had to admit she thought of him more than she should.

Through him she was beginning to see a new world. Now when she walked through the streets her eyes picked out details she'd never noticed before. She listened to others with different ears. There was another life hidden under the obvious, the everyday. When she was with him she felt shaky, like a new colt. Questions and urges percolated under her skin and she wanted fresh answers. When he wasn't present she wished him near. Well, she told herself, she missed sharing ideas . . . seeing another way of looking at life.

She got up and impulsively matched his playful bow with a curtsy, then began looking for a vase. The room was crammed with blossoms; the cold weather had not stopped the deluge.

"These are summer flowers. It's snowing. Wherever did you get these?" Her twinkling eyes held puzzlement.

"There are greenhouses . . . warm rooms made of glass where gardeners trick flowers, like these, into thinking it's summer."

"They trick flowers? All year long?"

He chuckled at her surprise and nodded. "It's only one of many modern miracles available to us now."

She sighed. The rich didn't have the problems of the poor. How different his life was from hers. No wonder he saw things differently. Rich people never go hungry or have to do things they hate to stay alive, she thought as she searched for a container to hold the snapdragons.

"You mustn't think me a rogue," he said as he set the boxes on the piano. "Cesca helped me pick them out for you." He tossed his topcoat and hat onto a chair.

"They're for me?" She turned away to delight in the flowers alone. No one had ever given her flowers, not even Mario when he was courting her. She bent to sniff the puffy yellow and pink bouquet in her hand. "Oh, they're lovely, Signor Dante, thank you! Thank you very much."

She suddenly felt the heat of his body against her back.

"They don't have much fragrance, though they're pretty"—his voice was barely audible and his breath caressed her neck—"yet not so pretty as you."

She loved the smell of his spicy cologne mixed with spent tobacco. Something, probably his hand, brushed her elbow. At his touch she drew a sharp breath. She crossed quickly to the pantry. "The flowers are very nice, Signor Dante."

"You needn't be so formal," he said, following her. "We're friends, aren't we? You must call me Dante and I'll call you Mina, if you'll give me your permission."

"Thank you, *signore*," she said firmly, turning to face him, "but I must speak in a more formal manner. I'm a married woman working for the Signorina and you're the Signorina's fiancé."

She saw sudden embarrassment on his face. It pained her to hurt him, but she needed to put distance between them. Why, just a moment before, she'd almost been longing to see him and now she was as happy and excited as a child at a feast day celebration, all because of a nosegay.

"Well, yes," Dante said, "that's, ah, true. I suppose you could say I'm her . . . however—"

"I know you're only being kind, but people gossip terribly."

"A good answer, Mina!" the Signorina said, sweeping into the room carrying more boxes, which she dumped on the piano. "I see Dante is starting in on you."

"Ah, Cesca, you're so jealous, I'm only trying to be friendly."

"I can see."

"She thinks I'm trying to seduce her with snapdragons," he laughed. He sat down, a flush of color on his cheeks from being caught flirting.

"They're a gift from the both of us, Mina, but you're right to be wary of Dante. He loves to look, which I encourage, for the world is filled with beautiful things, but sometimes he likes to touch." She removed her gloves and swatted him meaningfully with them. "Don't you, Casanova? Didn't we discuss this?"

"Cesca, I was only—"

"I know what you were *only* . . . and I want it stopped immediately. Do what you like with the others," she whispered caustically. "Leave my dresser alone." She tossed her gloves into his lap.

"Cesca, you must stop treating me like a child." He flung the gloves back. They dropped to the floor like dead birds.

"Then you must stop acting like one."

Mina came between them and bent to retrieve the gloves. Perhaps, she thought, there is some truth to the gossip. They're acting like jealous lovers. The Signorina removed her wrapper and hat. Mina took them to hang up. "Your arm is much better," the Signorina said, nodding pleasantly.

"It's been a week, signorina."

"Has it been so long?" the Signorina asked.

"I was working on your shoes for the second act and realized I didn't have any pain left. I scratched them up so you won't slip again." She showed Cesca the soles of the satin slippers as the diva impassively poked the curls of her hair into place at the mirror.

"You were hysterically funny, Cesca, lying sprawled out like that in front of the evil Scarpia, with your dress up over your head. It looked like the invitation to copulation you'd been so vehemently repulsing. It's a wonder the audience stopped laughing. Perhaps Giacomo should rewrite *Tosca* as a comedy. Something along the lines of *Lysistrata*!" Signor Dante laughed himself into a coughing fit. Mina hurried to get him some water. He choked it down, still chortling.

"Ignore him, Mina, he's a fool and a tiresome one at that," the Signorina said, calmly ordering and stacking her boxes and parcels. She looked Signor Dante over critically.

"Don't you have anything else to occupy your time? You said you were going to visit with your friends, what were their names? The two musicians . . . Colombo and Bevilacqua? Don't you need to get some things together for this evening? Do Mina and me the courtesy of leaving. We want to talk."

"As you wish, my little harlot." He picked up his hat and coat and paused in the doorway. "You two tell more tales than Aesop. I expect to find them collected one day, in a fine leather-bound edition." He tipped his hat and closed the door.

"Sometimes I find him amusing, but the rest of the time he gives me a headache," the Signorina confided as she cut the strings on her packages with her ornate sewing scissors.

Mina missed Signor Dante's presence already. "He's wonderful, signorina, you're very lucky."

"Do you like him, Mina?"

"He's so different . . . from the men I've known. He knows about everything."

"Yes, isn't it tiring?"

"I think it's wonderful, I learn so much every time we speak. He says things my heart only dreams of confessing. He's very sympathetic. He'll make you a wonderful husband."

"Oh, I'll never marry Dante. He's not my type!" The Signorina laughed like a schoolgirl. Mina was shocked. "But he's your type, isn't he?" the Signorina teased.

Mina concentrated on wrapping the cut strings around her fingers. "I . . . I could never capture such a man. I am not beautiful or intelligent enough. I have nothing to offer him. I'm only an ignorant country girl. He . . . he needs a woman to challenge him . . . his mind. He likes to think, explore. You know? Besides, I'm a married woman, signorina."

"Oh, that. That's easily fixed."

Mina's heart seemed to skip a beat. "How would I fix that?"

"Simple. A divorce."

"But how does one get a divorce?"

"You get an attorney. I'll give you the name of one here in New York if you like."

Here was the very information she'd been seeking, but she was afraid to take it. Hadn't she promised God she'd try to get rid of the mistress?

"I . . . I could never get a divorce. The church doesn't allow it."

"Surely you don't believe in a God that would damn you to hell for making a mistake? Here, I'll write his name down for you. He's excellent! I used him to go over my opera contract. He's a first generation American, but he speaks Italian fluently. His office isn't far from here." The Signorina took a pen and wrote the name on a piece of her stationery, then tucked the folded paper into Mina's apron pocket. "At least now if you want, you can inquire."

"But signorina—"

"I'm so bored with you calling me signorina," she cried, throwing down her pen. "We're friends, aren't we? Won't you call me Cesca?"

"If I call you Cesca, I must call Signor Dante—"

"Ah, yes. Well, don't pay attention to him, Mina, and he'll tire of his amorous behavior. I know I needn't tell you he's mostly talk. Did he tell you he's a duke?"

"Yes, but I know better than to believe him."

"Oh, but he would have become duke if his father hadn't died. His family gave him lovely manners and a wonderful sense of humor, but he gets bored so easily. He's too educated for his own good. He amuses himself with flirtations. It's only when some foolish girl takes his overtures seriously that he has trouble. Like all men, he's interested in pretty women like you."

The Signorina patted her cheek. Mina was embarrassed by the compliment. She didn't feel pretty and didn't believe Signor Dante was interested in her. The Signorina took her hand. "Do you like your work with me?"

"I love it." Mina's eyes became moist as she returned the Signorina's firm grip on her fingers.

"You're happy with us?"

"Oh, yes, signorina. Very happy."

"Good. I—we want . . . so much to help. Well, I feel as though we are becoming friends."

Mina shifted uncomfortably. It was true they'd been amusing themselves by telling each other stories and the Signorina had been very kind, but she didn't feel they were friends. Friends implied equals. Though Mina laughed and did her best to fit into their world, she felt naked and foolish most of the time. Friendship would never bridge the chasm of class. As much as she wanted to be like the Signorina and capture Signor Dante's affection, she knew she was only a common girl who had been inexplicably blessed with a lira's worth of luck.

"Yes, we are getting to know each other," she said tactfully.

Cesca noted the starch in Mina's tone and changed her tactics. "Excellent! Then would you be willing to give me your opinion? I'm surrounded by so many sycophants that I never know if they're telling me the truth or only saying what they think I want to hear."

"Syco . . . sycophants?"

"Hangers-on—you know, people who are nice or pretend to be because of my money, my fame."

"Syco-phants, oh, yes, of course."

The Signorina took the top off one of the boxes and lifted the tissue.

"I bought some dresses and I'm not used to American fashion. You know the tastes of the city. It's not so formal here as it is in Europe; I don't want to be overdressed. Tell me which ones you like and when you think I should wear them."

She pulled a violet dress with a high-boned neck of lace from the first box. The pigeon-breasted top had tiny pleats with iris buds tucked into the folds. It was finished with dark purple ribbons.

"It's lovely!" Most of the dresses Mina had worked on in the costume shop were rude creations, built only for stage use. They were hastily sewn, made with stiff fabrics and cheap trim. This dress was French silk, hand sewn and decorated with handmade flowers and lace. Her eyes followed the delicate lace pattern enviously. She'd never seen such a beautiful confection up close.

"Where would I wear it?" the Signorina asked.

"To luncheon or to appear in public, like when you go to one of those women's meetings."

The next box held a thigh-length, russet wool jacket with inserts of striped taffeta and a matching skirt. On the cuffs were tiny embroidered leaves and it had a low-scooped neck with a curved collar. It was finished with elegant gold and pearl acorn buttons. The sleeves of the buttercup waist, made to be worn beneath, were narrow with removable cuffs.

"It's a day suit, for work or business. I might wear something like this—if I were you—for rehearsal or to meet with Signor Hammerstein."

"What about this blue one? Do you like the lace? I know you're a lace maker, I hope the quality's good." She carelessly passed the box to Mina, watching her face for a reaction.

"It's the most beautiful of the three. It's also for daytime, simple and elegant, but you see here, this is bobbin lace. It's difficult to make and the patterns are passed from mother to daughter. It comes from Belgium now, but it used to be made in many villages in Italy."

The look on Mina's face told all. Dante had said the blue dress was a perfect combination and Mina wouldn't be able to resist.

"I don't know," Cesca said. "The blue dress is so different from what I'm used to. We're about the same size. Try it on for me, so I can see it on someone else. I'm not sure I want to keep it."

"But you must keep it. The others are very pretty, but this dress is special. The lace is unique and the workmanship very fine."

Cesca watched as Mina examined the tiny stitches and ran her hands lovingly over the fabric. "Try it on, Mina." She waved in Mina's direction as though exhausted. "I can't decide."

Mina ducked behind the dressing screen and removed her dress. The rustle of the new fabric and the smell of the acrid indigo dye were a delight. She'd never put on anything so fine. As she slipped into the bodice she thought how the color reminded her of the Mediterranean Sea in the summer months. The lace on the sleeves and neck was like the fluffy clouds that sometimes scuttled across the sky.

"Is it not beautiful, signorina?" she asked as she stepped out from behind the screen.

"Very beautiful," Cesca said, looking at Mina's radiant face.

Mina made a little pirouette and ducked her head to look in the mirror. Why, in this dress I almost look like a lady, she thought, holding up the boned neck to get an idea of what it would look like fastened in back.

"The dress suits you very well, Mina, but I don't think it's my style at all. It must be returned."

The Signorina's face was sour.

"With your hair, the color would be perfect, signorina."

"No, no, now that you have it on I can see it's too youthful for me."

"Too youthful? Really?" Mina peered in the mirror, thinking the dress perfection. How could the Signorina think—?

"Oh, dear!" the Signorina cried.

"What's the matter? Is something wrong?"

"Damn it! I just realized the dressmaker purchased the fabric at my request and cut it to my measurements. I can't return it. How stupid of me! I'll never wear such an immature style; everyone will laugh. The great Signorina Frascatti trying to be a coquette!"

"You're still very young. You could—"

"No, no, it's impossible! It's bad enough I call myself signorina . . . the dress is for a twenty-year-old. I'll not be made a clown." She stamped her foot, suddenly every inch a diva. "Dante would never stop teasing, no, no, no! Such a shame to waste it, to store it in a closet . . . or . . . wait a minute, I have an idea. You'll keep the dress."

"Oh, no, Signorina Frascatti, I couldn't keep your dress, you—"

"Why not? It fits you perfectly."

"I . . . well, even if I gave you a few dollars a week, I couldn't afford—"

"Don't be ridiculous! I don't want money. The money's already wasted. Why should the dress be thrown in the trash when it looks so pretty on you? It'll be a gift. You burned your other dress in my service."

"But you've already given me so much."

"You're faithful and honest. You deserve a reward. The dress is yours."

"But—"

"I'll not listen to another word!"

In less than a week Mina had learned to read the diva's tone. The battle was lost. She turned back to the mirror and examined herself in the glass. What luck she was having! The Signorina was right: it fit her perfectly, and the color was—

"Oh, *Gesù!* I had the dressmaker purchase accessories, including shoes and a bag, to match—and a beautiful merino wool coat to go on top. Well, you'll have to keep everything. And I won't take no for an answer. I just can't abide waste, and I refuse to listen to Dante tell me he told me so!"

Mina started to protest, but the Signorina silenced her. "I expect to see you wearing the dress and coat to work and not save it for a special occasion. And take the petticoat we decided was too full for the second act costume. The skirt needs some fullness. Pack up quickly now, we need to get ready for the performance."

Cesca was grinning with delight as she undressed and slipped into her robe. She had a ready excuse for the other dresses Mina had admired. In a few days she would tell her the dresses had been worn in society and couldn't be worn a second time. Mina must do her the favor of taking them off her hands. What good was all her money if she couldn't indulge herself by making someone happy?

For the first time in years, she felt truly human and alive. This was better than creating a new role, better than receiving excellent notices, better than taking a new lover . . . well, perhaps not that good. Cesca started to remove her street makeup and watched Mina order the boxes. She thought she saw something dark, a shadow perhaps, at the base of Mina's neck where the collar lay unfastened. She squinted into the mirror trying to make it out.

At the back of Mina's neck were elliptical bruises, fading purple and yellow, fanned out like fingers. And on the inside of her lower left arm four dark spots, a fifth spot on the forearm, showed the vestiges of a mean grip. In her excitement Mina had forgotten that her neck and arms would be exposed in the new dress. Cesca realized with startling finality that Mina was being beaten.

"When did you meet your husband?" Cesca asked as casually as she could manage.

Mina tied Cesca's hair back and poured water so she could wash her face.

"Before, ah . . . New York." She paused. "After she died. I mean before . . . my *Mammina* died."

"Your mother's dead?" Cesca stopped washing. "You told me your mother sent you here."

Mina shifted from foot to foot, handed her a towel, and coughed lightly. She wouldn't meet her eyes. "No, no. I said my mamma sent me here."

"Is this something you would rather not talk about?"

She could see fear hiding behind the smile on her Mina's face. What was going on? Was she lying? Had Emilio succeeded in planting another spy? She toweled herself dry and began powdering her throat. Then she suddenly stopped and swiveled in her chair. She met Mina's eyes, searching for deception.

"What do you mean? Your mamma sent you, but your *Mammina* is dead?"

"Well, you see, my real mother—*Mammina*—she died when I was thirteen. I . . . I was adopted."

Mina sounded stiff and uncomfortable, but her behavior made sense. Adoption in Italy was a shameful secret. So that was the reason she was acting so strangely.

"Adopted . . . I see . . ." Cesca said with interest. "Go on, tell me quickly, you met him before your *Mammina* died."

Mina glanced around, hoping to find an excuse to escape her task, but there was no way out this time. She'd tried for the past week to encourage the Signorina to talk. It had been easy to sidetrack her, the Signorina had so many stories, but now it was her turn. If she wanted to keep her job she'd have to tell the Signorina something. Mina only wished to remain a cipher, but she was trapped. The Signorina was waiting.

"Yes," Mina said, beginning her story. "I was cutting wheat in the fields with . . . Mamma Rosa. . . ."

Chapter Fifteen

~๏๏

$\mathcal{M}$AMMA ROSA AND THE GIRL
worked as a team, their heads down and their eyes on the wheat. That is
the normal way to work. One person cuts, the other gathers and ties, and
sometimes a third will load the sheaves into a cart. They noticed the cool
air first, not the overcast sky. The weather moved in from the south, dark
clouds stacking up like wheat in a cart, obscuring the late autumn sun.

The girl had been swinging the scythe, and Rosa had been tying the
sheaves with the others. They had been working all day, except for a
small break for cheese and bread. Now, with the threat of rain, the
workers hurriedly stacked the sheaves into the carts and pulled the
tarp down.

"*Vieni!*" Rosa called, balancing the last bundle on her head. "Hurry,
we must go before we get drenched."

"I'm coming, Mamma. I just want to finish my row." There were only
a few meters of wheat between her and a perfect job. She hated to leave
the small swath uncut.

"Forget the row, you'll have another tomorrow."

"Please, Mamma, I'll finish quickly. The storm is still approaching."

"Hurry, you'll have to walk back, I can't send the wagon back for you."

"Just to the end of the row, I promise."

"I don't want you wet and sick."

Rosa was pulled aboard and the cart lumbered off. It was only a short
walk. There was ample time for her daughter to get back before the
storm broke.

The girl was swinging the scythe so intently she didn't hear the boys
joking as they came up the path. If she had, she surely would have hidden in the wheat, but she did not notice them until they arrived at the
stone wall.

There were five: the twins, Claudio and Carmelo, fourteen; their
cousin Beppe, who was a bit simpleminded; Gaetano, the village bully;
and Domenico, who had been studying for the priesthood until he'd
been caught in the sacristy tapping the holy wine. They were a bad lot,

drunk and on their way home from the local fair where they had been causing trouble.

"Hey, look who's cutting wheat—the disgrace."

"*La figlia di puttana,*" Claudio mocked.

"Hey, *bastarda,* don't you know there's a storm coming?" Domenico asked.

"Where are your father and mother? Didn't they teach you to get out of the rain?"

"Haven't you heard?" Beppe said. "She doesn't have a father."

"No father? Did she crawl out of a squash blossom?" Domenico joked.

She cut methodically, shutting them out. They'd been taunting her for years because she was illegitimate. At first she'd tried to reason with them and understand their cruelty. Then had come tears of shame. Finally hatred and hard fists. But getting into fights and giving bloody noses hadn't stopped the villagers' thoughts and actions.

"Perhaps she's deaf!"

"Hey, are you deaf, *puttana?*"

"Oh, leave the whore alone. Haven't you heard?" Carmelo asked. "Her father's a *padrone.* He'll come and get her one day if he has room for all his bastards in one house."

Gaetano braced his hands against the stone wall and ran his eyes over the girl as she bent to tie the sheaf. Her skirt was pinned up, in the manner of all field workers, to keep it from getting soiled. In the dying light her thin underskirt allowed the shadow of her shapely legs to show through. Her strong young body pressing against the cheap cotton fabric of her petticoat excited him.

"You're not bad looking for a *bastarda.* One of the devil's spawn. Your mamma must have been one red hot pepper!" Gaetano said as he jumped the wall and approached her. "Maybe you're like your mamma, eh? Blood of her blood. Maybe you'd like to have a little fun."

Gaetano turned to gesture his meaning to the other boys. He pulled his hands toward his thrusting hips and moaned obscenely. They laughed.

"Get her, Gaetano. Show her who's boss."

Laughing with the rest, confident of their support, he turned to find her holding the scythe in a defensive stance.

"Oh, so you want to play hard to get!" he laughed. "That's okay, I like that, it makes me hotter when I have to work for my pleasure."

Gaetano circled her slowly, like a wrestler looking for a hold. Each feint he made she matched. He made several attempts to grab her swirling skirts, but missed. When she stumbled over a rut in her wooden shoes and almost fell, he moved in quickly, trying to catch her leg. She swung the scythe, brushing his chest.

"Be careful, Gaetano, she swings that scythe like a gladiator. She'll draw blood if she can," Claudio warned fearfully.

"It's I who will draw the first blood," he said, anger mixing with his lust. She'd almost cut him. No woman was going to show him up, especially in front of his friends. He'd fix her good when he got hold of her. "After I'm finished you can have your turn, boys. Come on," he taunted, "come on, daughter of a whore, be nice or no one will ever have you."

This time she rushed in, struck him on the arm, and sliced through his shirt.

"Ah!" Gaetano screamed in pain and fear. "She's cut me!"

His bold actions were forgotten as the red stream soaked his linen shirt. He retreated toward the wall, falling in the wheat. He crawled backward, watching her incredulously. The others jumped the wall and rushed to help him.

"*Carogna!* She's a bitch!" he shouted, glaring at the shallow cut on his arm. He stooped to pick up a stone. "What is it the Bible says about whores?" he asked.

"It says to stone them," Carmelo said.

"No," Domenico corrected. "That's for adulteresses."

No one seemed to care about the distinction as they gathered stones from the road.

"You whore of a whore. We'll make you pay for Gaetano's arm!"

They began flinging stones in her direction, not seriously at first, but then with more relish when a few found their mark and whet their taste for evil. She backed away to dodge the stones, but they cut her off and circled her.

"You cowards!" she shouted. "You call yourselves Christians? You quote the Bible but come filled with wine to a field and test your manhood on a helpless girl? You're not men! You're not even worms worthy of contempt. I spit on you. I spit on your children"—she spit on the ground for emphasis. "Your children will be less than bastards with worms and cowards for fathers."

The sharp stones hit faster and harder. Good marksmen, they aimed for her face and head, trying to harm her and silence her forever.

She felt dizzy and stumbled into the still uncut wheat to hide. One wooden shoe pulled loose. They followed her, throwing handfuls of stones. Tripping over a rut, she lost her other shoe and twisted her ankle. She cried out in pain for the first time.

As she crashed to the ground, they pelted her body. She could hear the stones thud as they bit into her flesh. Surely she would be dead soon. She was praying for help, but waiting for oblivion.

"You there, what are you doing?" she heard a man's voice shout. "Leave her alone! Are you crazy? Stop, I tell you!"

"*Gesù Maria!*" Domenico exclaimed.

She pushed the matted wheat aside and saw Domenico drop his stone. He backed away openmouthed as the stranger rushed in. The man grabbed a hank of Carmelo's hair and rammed a fist into his face. There was a sickening crack of bone, then blood poured from Carmelo's nose. Claudio turned in panic to desert his twin and smashed into a terrified Beppe. Her tormentors had obviously lost their nerve.

Only Gaetano remained unfazed. His three friends ran as though Satan himself poked a pitchfork into their buttocks while he stood his ground.

"This is none of your business, DiGianni," he said.

She feared for the stranger named DiGianni, for he was smaller than Gaetano.

"I make it my business when innocent women are attacked."

"Oh, she's not so innocent, I assure you. She comes from a long line of whores."

The man didn't wait for more insults. He released Carmelo's hair and kicked him aside, then threw himself on Gaetano and fought savagely.

With the pain of each blow the stranger appeared to grow calmer and more precise while Gaetano's pain made him wild and careless. Several blows to Gaetano's soft belly cut off his wind and then a stunning jolt to his head sent him crashing to the ground. The two men rolled in the wheat with the stranger's fury mounting. It flowed into his arms, suffusing him, until vengeance sparked from his eyes like lightning bolts.

As they struggled, each seeking a better hold, the stranger's hand found her wooden shoe. He slipped his hand inside and slammed it into

Gaetano's head. The impact knocked Gaetano unconscious. She felt a thrill of satisfaction when the stranger climbed on top of Gaetano: now he would pay for the malicious things he'd said and the evil he'd tried to do.

She'd been forced to bear the shame of her mother's crime her whole life. God had sent this stranger to deliver her, and the vicious taunts would finally be answered with proper punishment. The stranger choked Gaetano with one hand while he beat him with the other. Over and over he hit Gaetano in the head with her wooden shoe. Yes! she thought. Yes! Punish him, make him suffer as I have suffered.

After a moment the skin on Gaetano's forehead split open and blood seeped into the indentations over his closed eyes, making crimson puddles. Each time the stranger struck, bloody drops flew off her shoe and spattered her where she stood watching. In between the whacks of her shoe she heard a dull crack and saw Gaetano's nose and cheek collapse. On and on the stranger went as Gaetano's hair became matted in blood and his face turned to raw meat.

"Stop, stop, signore!" she cried, overcome by the gruesome sight. "It's enough!"

She wanted revenge, but this prolonged torture was too intense for her to bear. The stranger's eyes were glazed and set like a piece of pottery. He couldn't hear her cries. "For the love of our Holy Mother! Stop! You're killing him." She caught his arm and tried unsuccessfully to pull him off. "Signore, I beg you, stop. For my sake, stop!"

He struck her in the chest trying to force her away, but she wouldn't budge. She struggled with him a few moments before he realized she wasn't the enemy. He was panting when she pulled him up. He stared right through her—almost, she thought, as if at someone he hates, someone who isn't standing in this field. She pried her bloody shoe from his fingers.

"He'd have raped or killed you," the stranger said as he returned from somewhere far away.

"He didn't kill me," she said. "I'm not disgraced."

"He wouldn't have been kind enough to pull me off you."

"I'm not kind, signore. God is his ultimate judge, not you or I."

Thunder cracked overhead and rain hit them in fat drops. Using her apron she tied the last two sheaves together and tried to lift them onto her head, but the bundle was too heavy for her shaky arms to lift.

"Get the scythe," he ordered. "I'll carry the wheat." Balancing the bundle gracefully on his head, he climbed back over the wall and bent to retrieve his pack. She watched, startled by his skillful performance. Who was he? Where had he come from? He was no more than seventeen, handsome and strong. Why hadn't she seen him in the village?

"Hurry, let's go before we get soaked," he shouted.

"What about him?" she asked, indicating Gaetano, who was slowly coming back to consciousness in the downpour. "We shouldn't leave him."

"He won't drown. Leave him to your God and the rain, signorina!"

Chapter Sixteen

DANTE CHECKED HIS WATCH. It was almost twelve—well over an hour since Mina had finished her duties and gone. Cesca was adjusting her disguise one last time in front of the mirror, powdering down the sheen of her nose putty. She smiled broadly at him, revealing stained teeth.

She'd darkened her front teeth with charcoal, altered her nose slightly, and thickened her eyebrows. A brown wig had been ratted and soiled to hide her red hair, and as she adjusted it he saw that she'd removed her nail polish carelessly and rubbed soot into the creases of her hands and fingertips, then washed to leave an ingrained look. To look like a tart she'd applied a little too much face powder, rubbed rose rouge high on her cheeks, and added bright red lipstick. Her worn clothing and shoes were streaked with grease and doused with coal ash in all the right places. Finally, she'd brushed her clothing down and tidied herself up to give the impression of someone doing her best to be respectable. She'd done a fine job of transforming herself from diva to drone.

"You look great, let's go," Dante said. He beckoned her into the hall and she followed him up the stairs. As they began to cross the stage behind the set, Dante caught hold of Cesca and held her back. Two men on the opposite side of the flats were struggling with an awkward piece of furniture. Petrosino's man inside the opera house had engineered a chore to keep Emilio's spy distracted while he and Cesca slipped out tonight.

"Don't ask me," Petrosino's man said. "It's got to go to the carpentry shop for repairs. Last-minute orders from Hammerstein. Hey! Be careful, watch that brace. Don't drop it!"

Dante heard them crash into something. The man's a decent actor, he thought, at least he keeps things lively. When the men started down the stairs, grunting with exertion, Dante grabbed Cesca's hand and led her through the fire exit to a waiting hack.

The cab took a circuitous route to the Lower East Side. Down Fifth Avenue to Washington Square Park, over to the Bowery, across Grand Street to Clinton, and then back along the river. The hack pulled up in the shadow of the massive new bridge that was being erected over the East River.

There wasn't a hint of wind, and the lazy wet snow coated every object. Layer upon layer built up to plop off the branches of the sickly trees, crisscrossed wires, and sodden trash heaps. On the pavement it liquefied, giving a slick reflective surface to everything the streetlights touched. Cesca felt chilled through, but it wasn't from the weather. They traversed the last few blocks on foot.

"You're sure this is the place?" Cesca asked, pulling her skirt up from the filthy pavement with distaste as she stepped over the litter.

"It's just up the street on the corner—you'll see," Dante said.

"This waterfront is worse than Naples where I first started singing."

Dante heard the loathing in her voice as she took in the cardboard and tin shanties surrounded by piles of trash and ash cans. Ragged children and adults huddled under overhangs or in doorways, staring out at them with dead eyes as they passed. The creatures didn't even bother to beg.

"I wanted to save her from this."

"You did what you thought was right, Cesca," he said, putting an arm around her shoulder and pulling her close. "Concentrate on the present, save the *mea culpa* for later."

"You look ridiculous in that outfit," she mocked. "Even your shoes have holes in them."

"You don't look better. Where did you find that wig and ragged coat? It looks like something from *La Bohème*."

"I ransacked the costume shop. Tonight I'll play Mimi to your Rodolfo." She laughed, but Dante felt the hand holding his arm tremble.

"You're more a hussy like Musetta than a shy Mimi," he said, patting her hand reassuringly.

"Oh, Dante, to be so close. I'm counting on you to get me through."

"Just play your role. I'll do the rest."

He heard her take a deep breath before he pulled her inside the saloon. It was noisy and dimly lit, jammed with grubby men and a smattering of cheap-looking women swilling beers and whiskeys. In the corner, a knot of people argued over a dart game, and at several tables around the periphery men played cards. He pulled her along by the sleeve as he forced his way through the throng toward the archway.

"I'll get us something to drink," he shouted.

She grabbed his arm and pressed her lips to his ear. "Where is she? I don't see her."

"Be patient. Keep an eye out for Colombo. He'll be acting as my trainer and the promoter of the match. He came ahead to meet her. What do you want to drink?"

"Get me anything you think will suit. And hurry back."

While Dante fetched their drinks, she pushed toward the archway and scanned the front room. It had a patched low tin ceiling with broken wooden slats poking through. She kept away from the walls because the plaster fell off in nasty crumbs if she leaned against it. Dante waited for their drinks beneath a beer advertisement styled after Manet's *Olympia*. A long mirror dotted with age spots hung behind the bar, throwing back the images of the tired patrons. She almost didn't recognize her own reflection, but Dante was a different story.

He'd darkened his hair with boot blacking, added a mustache and a scar, but he'd been raised with nannies and valets. That kind of finishing didn't tarnish so easily. Although he matched her attire and was doing his best to pass for a dull knife among greasy spoons, he came back through the crowd with their pints of ale looking more like a duke than a drudge.

"You sparkle like a new wedding ring on a bride, Dante. You're supposed to be downtrodden, looking at life with a chip on your shoulder. Slump a little and wipe the grin off your face."

"I'm cocky, it's part of my character. A boxer's supposed to swagger. And stop calling me Dante," he whispered. "I'm Vittorio."

"When you're poor you don't stride around like a dancing master. Observe them, steal their gestures. Watch me, I'll show you." She took a large gulp of her bitter ale and suppressed the urge to spit it on the floor. She wiped the foam off her lips with the back of her hand, sighed as though delighted, then belched loudly.

"I don't see the woman," she whispered as her eyes raked the crowd.

"That was a disgustingly authentic display," he said, sipping his Black and Tan. "She's probably in the back."

Dante guided Cesca through the back room, where he spotted Giuseppe Colombo watching a group of men playing cards. Colombo waited until the hand was finished and the pot claimed, then, while the cards were being shuffled, he bent to talk with the winner. The man wore a mossy green cap pushed back on his head and chewed a wooden matchstick.

The man glanced up eagerly when Colombo gestured in Dante's direction, but the man's searching eyes didn't pick Dante and Francesca out of the crowd. Amid loud protests he scraped up his winnings and left the table with Colombo. In a moment the two were joined by a woman with long dark hair. At the sight of the woman Cesca's hand squeezed Dante's arm like a vise.

"That's her! That's the one Bevilacqua described. Oh, my God, do you think it's her?" Cesca felt like a ventriloquist's dummy. Her voice and gestures seemed to belong to someone else.

"Calm down. If she has the earrings, it'll be your job to determine how she got them."

"They're not going to buy your being a boxer," she whispered distractedly. "This whole idea's half-baked . . . *Vittorio!*"

"It'll work. With the purse we're offering I doubt they'd turn down a fight with you if it were suggested. Let me do all the talking. Colombo and I worked it out during your performance."

The woman cleared a table and the two men sat down. In a moment she returned with a pitcher of ale and some glasses.

"Here's Vittorio now," Colombo said expansively as Cesca and Dante walked up.

Introductions were made all around. Cesca smiled blandly at the black-haired woman and shook her hand. She caught a twinkle of stones behind a dark curtain of curls. It was just a glimpse, she couldn't be sure, but she thought she saw the earrings. Her heart beat rapidly.

The Irish brogue immediately told her the woman, Kathleen, wasn't Italian, let alone Maria Grazia. Cesca felt shattered. She'd hoped this meeting would be the end of her search, not the beginning. How had this woman gotten the Lampone heirloom earrings? She examined Kathleen closely, searching for any clue of dress or behavior that might answer her questions, while Kathleen's sharp eye examined her in return. She was grateful the lighting was dim.

Dante had roughened his aristocratic accent and bearing, but for all his fantasies about being a savage under the skin, he was still a gentleman dusted in an ash bin. The man introduced as Tonio didn't seem to put it together, but Kathleen asked pointed questions. She wasn't fooled by Dante's demeanor and was aggressively trying to uncover Vittorio's roots. So when the opportunity presented itself, Cesca tried to offset the obvious with a little subterfuge.

"Even though Vittorio's had a run of bad luck, it no mean he fight for nothing," she said using broken English. "He's champion in *Napoli* before he comes this country."

Dante and Colombo were startled by the interruption. Dante openly scowled at her.

"*Napoli?*" Tonio asked with interest, immediately reverting to his native tongue. "*Come ti chiami?*"

"The name I fought under is Vittorio Fusco," Dante replied in Italian.

"We don't want to bring the family name into this," Cesca continued, laying on a thick Neapolitan dialect. "There's no love lost between the stepfather and the son. He got rid of Vittorio by educating him out of the country. Then he stole his inheritance, leaving Vittorio with nothing. We just want a good match with a good purse for both fighters."

"I don't know what the hell yer going on about in that dago twaddle, but if ya ask me, this fellow's a dandy down on his luck," Kathleen said, looking Dante over hard. "Or perhaps the two of ya are looking for an adventure. Is that it? You're down here slumming?"

"Do you let your wife do the talking for you?" Dante asked Tonio in his nastiest slang. "Perhaps we should be dealing with her instead of you."

"This woman's not my wife. My wife knows her place."

"Tonio, speak in English, damn it!" Kathleen shouted, losing her temper.

"Shut it, Kathleen."

"We speak English or Italian," Cesca said, switching back to English for Kathleen's benefit. "Your friend she is right, Vittorio's real father was *padrone* in *Napoli*. He raise him a gentleman, but now we make our living this way."

"That's correct," Colombo added. "Besides, what difference does it make if he's a gentleman or a day laborer? The purse is the same."

"Better!" Cesca said. "We make the difference to stir up excitement. It will make a big crowd and more cash for our pockets."

"True," Kathleen said, focusing on Cesca. "Yer a clever woman. But I don't know . . . we don't want no truck with dandies looking for pleasure at the expense of working men, do we, Tonio?" Cesca felt Kathleen's eyes dig into her like a dart.

"I don't care who I fight as long as I get paid," Tonio said.

"The Polack bar wipe you fought the other night wasn't much of a challenge for you," Colombo said.

"What do ya mean bar wipe?" Kathleen snapped, shifting her focus. "He went nine rounds before Tonio was able to take him down."

"Only because Tonio wanted him to go nine rounds. A more sophisticated crowd would have seen through the performance you gave. Vittorio won't be such an easy match, but if you're afraid of a real fight, that's different," Colombo offered casually.

"I'd lay odds that Tonio can take any man currently in the game. Why, I think he's as good as a Corbett or a John L," Kathleen asserted.

"My fighter's a Neapolitan champion. It won't be a cakewalk," Colombo added dryly.

"Tonio's hungry for a good opponent. If we make the date he'll eat yer man with a spoon," Kathleen shot back.

"I see the woman has him by the balls," Colombo whispered to Dante in Italian just loud enough to be overheard. Cesca saw Tonio stiffen at the insult. "Do we deal with her or walk away?" Colombo asked.

"I'll take the fight," Tonio said, reverting to Italian. "Let's set up a time, place, and purse." To Kathleen he barked in English, "Get another round of beer and whiskey and get lost. We talk business, better I talk Italian."

"Don't be a fool," Kathleen whispered in his ear. "They're leading ya by the nose." He shoved her off roughly. She could see they'd hooked into him by the way he pushed back his shoulders. Damn him, she thought, his head's already swimming in whiskey, beer chasers, and pride. "Tonio, listen to me—"

"Kathleen, do what I say!" he shouted, banging his fist down on the table. "This business ain't for a woman."

"Who d'ya think yer bawling at, that stupid wife of yers? I set up this here meeting in the first place. Ya don't talk to me like I'm yer dog to kick around." She put her foot up and shoved back his chair, ready to strike.

"Mimi, get me something to drink," Dante said, pushing Cesca toward Kathleen. "I want to talk . . . alone."

"I can use a drink and a change of company," Cesca announced. She stepped between Kathleen and Tonio and whispered in Kathleen's ear. "Let them have a talk, we have ours. Is more important what we say. Let them flap and crow, we hens . . . we the ones that hatch the eggs."

Kathleen glared at the intruder. Who'd this bitch think she was, interfering the way she had? The woman's eyes held hers unfazed. Every fiber of the stranger's body seemed as resolved to violence as her own. She would fight, and Kathleen could see that her opponent had a very nasty temperament. Kathleen cooled down. "Yer a woman after my own heart. Smart and tough, I like that!" She slapped Cesca on the back, the stalemate over.

"And you, Mr. Tonio," she said, hitting him on the top of his head with the flat of her hand, "are a big, stupid wop!" She leaned over and put her mouth against his ear. "Ya just try and make yer own arrangements! Ya'll come begging me for my help before yer through."

He batted her away, but let her walk off without a retort. It was an obvious victory that he'd gotten her out of the negotiations and he was content with his prize. The rest would be as smooth as a virgin's thigh.

Chapter Seventeen

ESCA WAS UP TO HER CHIN in hot water, her wet red hair lathered and piled in shampoo while foam streamed down her back. She scrubbed her arms diligently.

"I thought I'd forgotten the smell of poverty, but the minute I stepped through the door, twenty years vanished like smoke."

On the floor of the mauve and black tiled room lay a trail of discarded costume pieces from the evening's "performance." She'd gone directly from the front door to the tub, peeling off layers of mock poverty.

"My throat is raw from shouting in that smoke. And that whiskey . . . like swallowing splinters. I hope it hasn't injured my voice."

She vocalized, standing Dante's hair on end in the close room; then, satisfied her vocal cords were unharmed, she asked, "How can they stand to live that way?"

"It isn't a choice, Cesca. They can't help being poor."

Dante was sitting on the opposite side of a folded floral screen removing his dark mustache and sideburns with spirit gum.

"They *can* help it," Cesca said stubbornly. "Look at that man tonight, the boxer . . . disgustingly crude, yes, but he's got ambition. He's going to use his proclivity for violence to force his way out. I admire that. He'll succeed just as I did."

"I don't agree. His love of alcohol and brutality will destroy him."

"Oh, alcohol," she sighed. "I used to drink."

"What? A little wine, some champagne?"

"Champagne? Ha! I drank cheap whiskey and rotten wine. You don't know that side of me. In the early days, I drank my dinner. I'd gobble a handful of *polenta* and spend the rest on drink. I sang in waterfront bars for a few *scudi* and slept on the docks under the stars. Usually I passed out. But like him, I chose to fight. I made choices I don't like to think about now. Choices that still make my skin hot with shame on sleepless nights. When I think back to those hungry days in Naples and the bargains I was forced to make . . ."

She shook her head, surprised at the power of her memories and the rueful thought that she'd survived. "Maria Grazia was one of those bargains. You understand? I had to be hard, emotionless, savage. I wanted to tie a stone around my ankles and dive into the bay . . . but I stayed alive . . . my ambition was a cruel goad that made me demand more. Now everyone looks at my position, my career, my wealth, and they think, A great lady . . . blessed with a gift from God. God? I trod a path with the devil and he taught me to cheat and lie. There's a way out of poverty . . . but it might cost you your soul."

"You're strong . . . still intact."

"You see my act, my facade. You don't think I still tremble inside? It was ignorant luck in the beginning that I wasn't murdered for the few coins I had in my purse. If I had known then what I know now, I would never have attempted the ascent. Become *diva assoluta?* Impossible! I made mistakes, so many . . . doing things . . . I don't know how I did them. Disgusting things . . . degrading things . . ."

"You wanted to make a place for your daughter."

"I had to prove I was good enough. I wanted to show Emilio that I was better than his coat of arms, his heritage, his estate, his money . . . and I used every crumb of chance that fell on my path."

"Are you acknowledging destiny's helping hand?"

"Which of God's hands does the helping and which throws the stones in your path? Eh?"

"You had no help? You're a goddess unto yourself?"

"What do you mean?" she asked, slipping below the surface to rinse her hair, then shooting up quickly, "Are you, like Emilio, implying that it was my destiny? I could have sat back and had it handed to me on a platter?"

"If it had not been willed by God, you wouldn't be a diva."

"You don't believe in destiny any more than I do, and if you continue in your circular argument you'll only succeed in making me furious."

"I'm simply pointing out that the initial clue came from Sister Anselm, and a hand more powerful than yours led you to the earrings. Do you deny it?"

There was truth to his argument. She'd been puzzling over the earrings for days. How strange it was that they'd been led to them so quickly; first Madame Zavoya, then the sighting in the market. All the logical methods had been tried in Italy and New York without success.

She'd tried to use her will like a machete to force a path back to her daughter, but no scrap of information had been forthcoming.

No one at the convent or in the village knew where Maria and her family had gone. Civil records were useless. Dante had found only dead ends. Then a little clue from Sister Anselm, and the trip to America. So far the records had also failed to yield a trace of Maria, and yet the earrings had appeared and had led them to the saloon. Had it been kismet, as predicted?

"I'm loath to admit it, but perhaps there is something . . ." Cesca said. "Some power greater than our own, spinning our destinies. But I don't believe in a white-bearded God who directs every move. If he existed, he would be too cruel."

Her tone had changed. Dante thought her voice sounded younger, more vulnerable, and a bit sad. "When my parents died I definitely saw His hand taking away all that I loved. I grew up in an inflexible convent orphanage, begging Him on my knees every night for help, but the places where His presence should have been most palpable were devoid of warmth and love. His voice didn't speak to me within those stony walls or from the mouths of priests. His hand didn't touch me."

"What of Sister Anselm?"

"If it hadn't been for her love and friendship I would have ended my life. I didn't want to go on, but she was an artist and believed in my gift. Her passion and instruction eventually led me to opera."

"Why did the convent eject you and force you to become a servant on Emilio's estate?"

"They didn't eject me. I'd decided to become a nun."

His laughter bounced raucously off the tiles as she stepped from the tub and wrapped a big towel around her body. "A nun? You!"

"*Cretino!* What do you know? I'd have made an excellent nun."

"You might have been all right for a year or two—you're stubborn— but you'd never have made a career of it."

"Anselm taught me to be still and find His voice in unlikely places. Music became my form of worship. And being raised in the convent, I knew little else. I believed God had planned for me to be a nun: that's obviously why my parents had died. But before I could become a postulant I was required to live in the outside world. I needed to test my vocation. When I was fifteen the nuns got me the job on the estate." She twisted the water out of her hair with her hands. "Do you see the large pitcher on the stand?" she asked.

"Yes."

"Fill it, please, and come here to rinse my hair."

He poured the water over her hair and gave her a towel to wrap it up. "So you failed your test when you got involved with Giulio."

"He was so handsome and I loved him so desperately," she said with a laugh, "yes, I quickly forgot all about God."

Scrubbed clean she didn't look like a grand diva. He envisioned her solemnly striding the halls of a convent. The towel wrapping her hair resembled a wimple; all she needed was a dark veil and habit.

"So *that's* why you lost your belief in God," Dante said.

"I believe in God, but I think it's up to us to battle the devil."

"You don't trust God to defeat him?"

"God needs us to help, and I'll fight any of the devil's agents to get my daughter back."

Dante took off his shirt. "I assume Emilio's his main henchman," he asked, amused.

"He's as irrational as the devil in his grief. He could have made peace long ago . . . we could have found her together, but no, he must have someone to blame for his own arrogance, his own failure. In his eyes Giulio never loved me. I forced a wedge between him and his son and stole the earrings. I'm the devil's henchman too."

"Eve and her apple."

"Just so!" She suddenly turned serious. "Colombo gave that woman, Kathleen, money, didn't he?"

"Yes, for the hundredth time. It was enough to show her we're serious about a match, but not enough to make her suspicious. She's supposed to use it to pay for a larger arena. We'll continue setting up the event until we get all the information we require."

He ran a bath for himself. "Tell me again *exactly* what she said about the earrings?" Dante asked.

"She got them from Tonio as a present."

"You didn't find out who *he* got them from?" Dante tiredly stripped off his shoes and socks and began unbuttoning his trousers.

"I told you, I tried. She said she didn't know. I couldn't keep pressing her without stirring up suspicion. She was already asking pretty incisive questions." Cesca's eyes were fastened on him, but her mind was far away. She was remembering the day Giulio had given her the earrings.

"Cesca, do you mind! We may pretend to be lovers, but is it necessary to see me naked?"

She came back from her memories of Naples to find Dante standing before her annoyed, waiting to take off his trousers. "Who knows, one day I might be asked a very personal question about you," she joked. "Oh, take off your pants, half-wit! I assure you, you have nothing special to hide . . . do you?" She waited expectantly with her hands on her hips while he refused to remove his pants. "You forget I'm a fallen woman of the stage. Traveling with stock companies, dressing in limited space, I've seen the long and the short of it, my dear! Oh, *Madonna!* Just to please you . . ."

She salaamed, with her right palm to her forehead, like a courtier bowing before a pasha, and slipped around the screen. She plopped down at the mirrored console to towel and comb her hair as they talked.

"So she didn't say anything of use," Dante concluded, turning off the taps.

"She knows plenty she's not telling. She doesn't realize the earrings are valuable. Thinks they're junk he picked up in the market."

"We must find out where he got them." Dante eased himself into the steaming water, which was hotter than he'd anticipated. After he sat, he washed the mock dirt and grime off his skin with a fat, slippery cake of soap that got away from him, plunking into the water.

"Colombo wanted to know everything I learned," Cesca said, "so he could report to Bevilacqua. He said they'll follow Tonio and find out who he knows, the places he frequents . . . and they'll put another man on her."

"Yes, I know. I'm on her."

"You! How can you follow her when she knows you?"

"Cesca, you're as thick as pudding," Dante said, fishing around for the dropped soap. "Didn't you see her flirting with me?"

"You think every woman's flirting with you."

"I've already arranged to see her again."

"I'm coming with you."

"Certainly, come right along. The presence of my 'girlfriend' will loosen her tongue completely," he said, depositing the soap in the wire dish. He leaned back against the porcelain and closed his eyes with a sigh. "All I need is to find out where Tonio got those earrings." It was so peaceful in the hot tub. He wished he could fall asleep and forget the case for a while.

Suddenly he was underwater, then he was yanked up by the hair. He grabbed the sides of the tub, sputtering. Through the soapsuds he saw Lucifer's paws hanging over the edge of the tub at his feet. The cat's green eyes watched him mischievously and he grumbled softly at his mistress's temper.

"Find out where those earrings came from *presto, presto!*" Cesca ordered, holding him by the hair. "I won't stand for any more of your amorous maneuverings. Service her if you must, but get the information quickly, or instead of beef steaks from Delmonico's, I'll feed *you* to Lucifer."

Chapter Eighteen

I DON'T UNDERSTAND WHAT YOU mean, signorina," Mina said as she reheated the curling iron on the dressing room stove.

"I mean, in the throes of passion we all think we're climbing the Matterhorn, but after we've reached the pinnacle we usually realize we've been stumbling up a hillock with the village idiot." She laughed merrily as Mina tested the iron; it wasn't hot enough. "Take, for example, André. I met André in Paris when I was appearing . . ."

The Signorina had been telling intimate stories, but today Mina wasn't listening. She kept drifting away. Slipping back to the encounter she'd had with the attorney earlier in the week, the one whose name the Signorina had slipped into her apron pocket.

*   *   *

T H E day after receiving the address of the lawyer, Mina found her-self passing his building on her way to work. She paused to watch his shingle, printed plainly in black, swinging in the wind. Should she go in and ask? She'd hesitated on the sidewalk, glancing up and down the street to see if anyone might recognize her. There was no one familiar on the street, so she quickly slipped inside. Her heart was pounding with trepidation as she climbed the two flights of stairs.

The lawyer was a small, nervous man with glasses who shuffled his pa-pers around without meeting her eyes. His cursory glance over her said he thought she shouldn't be bothering him. "What is it you want?" he challenged.

"I wanted to ask about a divorce," she said. "Signorina Frascatti sug-gested I talk with you."

His manner changed immediately when he heard the Signorina's name. He stopped shifting paper and became very attentive, adjusting his horn-rimmed glasses on his nose.

"Of course, of course," he said, smiling broadly. "A friend of the Signorina's is always welcome. Please sit down, won't you."

Mina sat on the edge of the chair and wondered where to begin. She glanced around his office, feeling acutely embarrassed by her problem.

"You were married in this country?" he asked.

She nodded and explained.

"I see," he said, jotting down notes as she spoke. "Sent for . . . the Church of the Transfiguration . . . yes, yes, go on."

She'd explained about the arranged marriage and braced herself for his questions, afraid of what he might ask. She kept her head down while he explained the divorce procedure. He'd told her that without Antonio's agreement, she'd have to prove either abandonment or adul-tery. Since she'd been intimate recently and thought she might have been pregnant, a divorce would rest on his affair. It saddened her to think the law didn't recognize cruelty as a valid reason for divorce. Just as Teresa had said, women were the property of their husbands, to be dealt with as the husband saw fit. Antonio's cruelty, although repugnant, was a nonissue.

"He might claim you've refused him sexually, driving him to his adulterous behavior. If that's the case," he coughed, "no divorce will be granted since you'll be at fault."

"I've never refused him," she said, her head coming up, her face flushing with embarrassment.

"Good!" he smiled, writing it down. "In that case we must prove adultery. Rumor is inadmissible. You must have strong witnesses. Perhaps the mistress herself will testify."

He looked up, arching an inquisitive eyebrow. She felt panicked. "I couldn't ask her to—"

"Surely she'd like your husband to be free," he interrupted. "Perhaps a monetary settlement of some kind for her and your husband's cooperation?"

"I don't have money for a settlement," Mina said uncertainly. "Signorina Frascatti didn't—"

"Perhaps your friend Signorina Frascatti can make you a loan. In any case, we can deal with money later."

The Signorina wouldn't loan her money for a settlement, and she couldn't go to Antonio's mistress and ask her to testify. Antonio might actually beat her to death if she tried something like that. The whole idea of getting a divorce was ridiculous.

"Bring me your papers and we can begin the process immediately," the lawyer said, poking his glasses back onto the bridge of his nose. "You can pay me a retainer at that time."

"My papers?" she asked. "You need papers?"

"Yes, of course. Your marriage and birth certificates, immigration records . . ."

"Oh, yes," Mina said. "Mmm . . . my papers. I need *all* those papers?"

"You already have your birth certificate and immigration papers, the ones you came with. They wouldn't let you into the country without them." He laughed. She kept her eyes on her hands in her lap. "Look through your records. I'm sure you have them. You'll simply need to go to the courthouse and get a copy of your marriage license if you don't already have it."

She got up abruptly. "I have to go. I'm late."

The lawyer sprang up and came around the desk. She pulled open the door and hurried into the hallway, thanked him, and left. All the way to the opera house she'd felt numb. Even if she got the money somehow to give to the lawyer, she didn't have the proper papers to begin a divorce proceeding. The papers were her real undoing, and there was nothing she could do. She'd have to stay married to Antonio.

"ISN'T that so?" the Signorina asked, breaking in on her reverie.

The curling iron sizzled. Mina swiftly uncurled a lock of the Signorina's hair before it burned. She'd been so involved in her dilemma she hadn't been paying attention.

"I'm sorry," Mina said. "What did you ask me?"

"I said, Antonio, your husband, saved you from those boys in the field and you loved him for it?"

What could she say? Had she loved Antonio? She'd thought she had. He'd been presented to her as a god, a savior. He'd been so loving and attentive the first few weeks that he'd won her easily from Mario. All the pieces had fallen into place and she'd married him. But now she wasn't sure of anything. She felt exhausted. She was tired of trying to figure it out, tired of constantly struggling to stay positive and not give in to despair. She didn't want the lies or the life she was leading to continue. This wasn't what she'd planned. Why was it so important to others where she came from or who her mother was? What did it prove? She'd wanted to escape all that when she came to America. She didn't want to be like her mother . . . or an illegitimate outcast . . . or a whore. She wasn't her past. She'd planned to start over with a clean slate, but it wasn't working.

She wanted to scream and throw the iron the way the Signorina had thrown the hairbrush on the first day she'd started work. She wanted to pull God down from his cloud and make Him explain why He was making her life a living hell. Why did others have the things that she could only dream of? Simple things, like a loving husband, a family, children, respect. She wanted to throw herself on the floor and weep, weep for all she'd hoped for, but she couldn't act like a child just because things hadn't turn out the way she'd dreamed.

Wasn't it her fault that she was so far away from her true self? She should never have agreed to the marriage in the first place, but now she was required to be content with her lot in life. The priests and her friends always told her to count her blessings and be submissive, but what did they know? They weren't being beaten. She'd asked about a divorce, but it wasn't possible.

She felt desperate, but she had to act as though she were content. It was funny, really. The Signorina acted on stage, but she acted in real life. She had to pretend to be someone she wasn't, pretend to feel something she didn't. If only she could leave the role behind. But who was she really, behind her facade?

I want to truly be myself, without anyone's sticky fingers clinging to me, she thought. Without another woman's past casting its shadow over my life. Every day she pulls me back into her life, making me do something I don't want to. If I were free . . . I'd do other things. I'd learn to read and write properly. I'd sell lace. I'd become a designer of costumes or dresses. Simonetta used to tease that one day I might take her job. I have skills to make money, Signor Dante said I could. . . .

"Well," the Signorina asked, "is that why you married Antonio? He was your hero?"

She thought about confessing to the Signorina, asking her for a loan, begging her for help. But she was afraid. The Signorina would be shocked by what she'd done. She'd never understand, and as for loaning her money, Mina was a stranger, an employee. She bit her lip. It was better to stick to the path she was on and hope to find a way out later. "The hand of fate brought us together," Mina said as cheerfully as she could manage.

"Nonsense! He saved you that day by chance. Life is a series of chance events. We make what we can of them. You choose. If you don't like your choice, make another."

It frightened her to hear the Signorina say the very thing she'd been thinking recently. She crossed herself and kissed her bunched fingers. "Oh, signorina, don't say that. *Gesù* and *Sant'Anna* wouldn't understand."

"Do *Sant'Anna* and *Gesù* tell your husband to beat you?"

Mina hurried to reheat the iron and avoid any further questioning.

"I know you think it's a secret," the Signorina continued, "but I've seen the sling, the marks on your neck, and the cut on your temple those carelessly cut bangs are supposed to hide."

"When he drinks he has a temper—"

"This has nothing to do with temper. Your husband's behaving like an animal."

"Signorina, I . . . I—"

"You must stop him, even though you feel you owe him still. He has no right to strike you."

Mina met the Signorina's eyes in the mirror. They were as piercing as nettle spines, and although the Signorina's voice was low, there was a constriction in the tone that Mina had never heard before. "You must end this *casino*," the Signorina admonished.

Mina nodded. Of course I must, she thought, but what can a woman in my situation do? The Signorina tapped her foot with impatience. "Did you go to that lawyer I gave you the name of?"

"Yes, but he said, 'You can't divorce your husband because he beats you. The law doesn't allow it.' "

"Then you must leave him."

Mina tested the iron. It wasn't hot enough. She suddenly found tears in her eyes. "I know, but I'm afraid."

"Of course you're afraid," the Signorina said, and came to stand next to her. "Leave that iron alone and come sit for a minute." She pulled Mina to the chaise longue and they sat. "You know you should have left him long ago, when he first hit you. Why did you allow it?"

Mina plucked at her skirt. "It wasn't supposed to be . . . you see it was arranged for someone else . . . but he married me."

"And marriage to you is so horrible he must beat you to be able to stand it?"

Mina twisted her wedding band and stared down at her hands. "No, you see, there was another match."

Once again she thought about blurting out the truth, but she feared the Signorina would send her away and she'd lose the extra money. How should she tell this part? She had to explain her obvious inability to see through Antonio's evil temperament and to stand up for herself. How could someone who had everything possibly understand having no options? The marriage offer had been a wonderful chance for a new life, and once she'd made the bargain she was trapped by circumstances.

"The original agreement had been to marry his best friend, Mario," she hedged. "He'd sent a letter—"

"So he too felt this hand of fate?"

"Yes," Mina said, shaking her head and slipping into her storytelling voice.

"Mario wanted to get married, and Antonio suggested that he send for . . . a bride from the old country. Antonio knew of a girl . . . from his village. You have to understand, the day I was given the letter I was so happy. I believed God was offering me a new destiny. I didn't need to pretend to be afraid of Mario like I'd planned . . . when I arrived. . . .

"Mario was a stranger, so it was believable that I would be afraid and prefer Antonio. I thought I would have to work hard to win Antonio over, but when he wanted me . . . I couldn't believe it was all working out. Antonio wanted me when he saw me—you can't know what that meant— and I thought . . . I *knew* that *destino* had arranged it all. *Destino* would see to it Antonio and I were married and that we would be happy."

Cesca saw the joy go out of Mina's eyes. Why hadn't she realized that day in the field that Antonio was a violent man capable of murder, or that it had been a blessing that his best friend had sent for her instead of him? Why had she been so desperate for love and acceptance that she'd willingly trade her life for it? "But Mina, *he* didn't send for you, his friend did."

"Can't you see? A stranger saves a young girl in a field and becomes her hero. She dreams of him her whole life only to have him reappear years later. It's out of a fairy tale! There are thousands of people in New York Mario could have chosen for a best friend, yet he chose Antonio . . . and Antonio had been sent by *Sant'Anna* to save that girl from being stoned to death. It was *destino!* Obviously he'd been given back to her . . . to marry."

Cesca closed her eyes and pursed her lips. It was ridiculous, the whole thing had nothing to do with fate, it was only a confused romantic notion, but she declined to argue the point.

"So *Sant'Anna* arranged for you to be a mail-order bride. How clever of her. But surely your family objected to this arrangement?"

"Oh, no, signorina, the family was happy."

"Happy! To have a daughter marry a stranger, never to see her again?"

"Mamma Rosa was pleased about the marriage proposal, but Papa Vito cried. He'd never cried before. The girl was sobbing so much, he had to lift her into the cart that carried her to Naples."

"You accepted a marriage proposal from a complete stranger, not knowing if you could win your savior over? And your family approved it?"

Not wishing to meet the Signorina's eyes, Mina got up to get the curling iron and started working on her hair again.

"I don't understand. Wasn't there any other man in all those years you could have loved? To take such a risk . . . and come so far . . . what would you have done if he'd refused to marry you?"

"I couldn't fail. Too many sacrifices had been made . . . too many lives lost. But you see, because of my past, in Italy I could never have a decent life. I could never have married."

As she wound a strand of hair around the iron, a strange agitation crept over her. She hated telling these stories, stirring up the departed. There was always the possibility of saying too much.

"What do you mean? Why couldn't you marry?"

"No man would have me for a wife. I wasn't suitable."

"That's absurd. You're perfectly suitable."

"You don't understand, I can't say. . . . I lit candles, made novenas to Our Lady and *Sant'Anna* to find a way. I asked for forgiveness . . . for my sins, my life . . . I . . ." She stopped. Just tell it and get it over with, she thought. Then she'll stop poking around and leave you alone. Get the past out of the way and get on with living truthfully in the present. She gave in to the urge to hide and started her story.

"Papa Vito tried other villages. I was engaged once, but gossip travels. I was almost past the age where anyone would want me."

"Past the age? A pretty young woman like you, kind, hardworking . . . Why, anyone would be lucky to marry you. What foolishness!"

"Not if you have a sinful mother. That destroys any chance for a good marriage. You don't know how people treat those who traffic in sin . . . how men treat women . . . they see only whores. That's why when the letter was given to me and the marriage suggested, I knew it was the right thing to do."

"But why did the villagers hate your mother so? Was she a murderess? A psychopath?"

"She had a terrible reputation. The whole village claimed her daughter was just like her . . . that she too had hot blood, that she too wasn't to be trusted, for she too was a thief and a whore—"

"Those are harsh words. . . . What do you remember of your mother, besides the gossip?"

"I would've been eight the last time I saw her. I don't remember everything. Some things I recall."

"Tell me about her. Tell me what you remember."

Mina looked down.

"Her hands," she said, staring for a moment at her own. Cesca heard Mina's voice take on the distant tone it always did when she talked about her past. "Her hands were small . . . soft and white. The daughter's hands were calloused from the fields . . . stained with dirt. The mother's hands were covered with rings. I can tell you a story about that last afternoon, if you like. It was a warm spring day . . . unusual for that time of year. . . ."

In a moment Cesca was whisked to the village. She felt the uneven ground under her buttocks and the rough bark between her shoulder blades. She sat, leaning against the tree, with Mina and the others. She was covered by the only shade for acres in an endless sea of curving furrows.

Chapter Nineteen

*O*N THE GROUND the women had spread their lunch of cheese, hard salami, bread, olives, and fruit. They shared what they had, told stories, and swapped advice. After they ate, they rested, dozing in the parched landscape, dreaming of weddings, christenings, lovers, and the like. These moments and the dark night were their only escape. Their lives were as hard as the stones they used to sharpen their hoes. The noonday rest was a welcome break from reality.

"Look! Can you see, on that rise? There! Someone is coming."

"Who's coming?"

"I don't know. . . . It's a woman. . . . She's carrying a parasol."

"A parasol? Carrying a parasol in the middle of the country?"

Mamma Rosa sat up, her tired bones alert. "Where?" she asked.

"There!"

The women shaded their eyes with their hands. It was true, a small figure with a swaying skirt approached. The stranger wore a large hat and carried a bag in one hand and a parasol in the other. The girl stood up abruptly, her heart quickening. "Oh, Mamma, is it her?"

"I wouldn't be surprised," Nedda giggled. "Who else would traipse around the countryside dressed as though she were the mayor's wife, carrying a parasol?"

"Hush, Nedda," Rosa said firmly. "It is hot and there is no shade on the road."

The women glanced uneasily at Rosa and the girl, then traded barbed looks. A woman with a parasol meant one thing. Why didn't the disgraceful creature leave them alone? The girl stared intently, ignorant of the women's curiosity and insinuating looks.

But Rosa was aware of their contempt. After a moment she got up.

"*Basta!* We should be getting back to the fields—they cannot prepare themselves for the wheat."

The women moved slowly, hoping to hear firsthand what would be said. Rosa's eyes were flinty. She returned the sharp looks the women gave her daughter.

"Oh, Mamma—"

"Hush! You stay here. Visit your *Mammina*. Enjoy the time you have. Come, Domenica, get up. Nedda, hand me my hoe."

The girl watched with growing excitement as *Mammina* approached. It had been almost a year since she'd seen her last.

On the crown of her big hat, one large yellow ostrich feather danced with each step. Her face was in shadows, but the girl could see her dark brown hair peeking out and her swinging gold earrings. *Mammina*'s dress was deep purple with pink flowers, trimmed with bows and puffed up with petticoats, a bit short in length.

The sun glinted off a thick gold chain hanging across her bosom, pinned to a pocket watch that dangled at her waistband. A parasol wavered overhead, like a tightrope walker's prop. She struggled to keep a red shawl, heavy with fringe, from slipping off her shoulders, and she grasped a heavy canvas bag with grim determination and a set jaw.

Mammina was a swirling mélange of colors as garish as a circus poster, but to the girl's eyes she was a great lady from Naples. As she approached on the rutted wagon path, picking her way carefully in her bright green high-topped heels, she represented all to which the girl aspired.

She ran the last few yards to meet her. "Oh, *Mammina*, you've come back!"

"*Figlia mia! Figlia mia!* My daughter!" *Mammina* dropped the canvas bag in the dust and pressed the girl to her breast. "You're getting to be a lady, let me look at you," she said, stepping back. "That dress is torn and too tight for you." *Mammina* glared toward the workers in the field. "What's the matter with these people, don't they have eyes?"

"Mamma says I'm sprouting like wheat. This old dress is only something I wear to work in the fields. I have others—"

"*Mamma* says!" She cocked an eyebrow and wrinkled her face in disgust as she removed her daughter's scarf. "And when was the last time you washed this hair?"

"Come, *Mammina,* it's hot. Come out of the sun and sit."

The girl quickly retied her scarf and hefted the canvas bag with both hands as she climbed over the wall and resettled under the tree. Words sped forward like mice before the scythe and the hours passed quickly. They shared the pastries—crumbled but delicious—*Mammina* had brought from the city, ate bruised fruit cut with a penknife, and licked their fingers clean. It wasn't long before the sun grew fat on the horizon.

"Did you bring me something special?" the girl asked hopefully.

The mother had forgotten to bring a gift. "Yes, I . . . I almost forgot. I have something for you."

"A present!"

"Yes, I got it in . . . a little shop in, ah, Capri. Yes," she said as she searched around in her bag. "I was in Capri and I saw it in the window of a shop. I thought to myself, that ring would be the perfect gift for my daughter."

She drew out a man's ring that glinted dully on her palm. "It's a little big . . . but you will grow into it."

"It's beautiful!"

"Put it on."

The girl put it on her middle finger and the heavy face slipped to her palm. It was hopelessly too large.

"See how it catches the light? I told the . . . shopkeeper, 'That's just the ring for my wonderful daughter.' I told him, 'I must have it, no matter what the cost.' So he put it in my bag and I've brought it to you. It's a little big, but later when you wear it in the city—"

"You've come to take me? We're going to Naples like you promised?" She jumped to her feet in excitement, but *Mammina* wouldn't meet her eyes.

"You ungrateful girl! You don't understand what I've had to do, to come here. In Naples I barely stay alive. In order to hire a carriage I had to—"

"But you promised. You promised to take me away. I want to go with you to the city—"

"And I'll take you, *cara,* just—"

"I don't want presents," she said, flinging the ring to the dirt. "I want you!" She threw herself into *Mammina*'s lap and wrapped her arms around her waist. The folds of her skirt smelled of flowers, sweat, and dust. She could feel *Mammina*'s soft hands stroking her hair.

"Your father and I will come for you. You must believe me."

"You've seen him?"

"He lives with me now. He's sick, but getting stronger. He wants to see you. As soon as he's well, he'll come. We'll marry, then you'll come live with us."

"He'll never come. He doesn't exist."

"He exists. Have you forgotten what I told you?" The mother lifted the girl's chin, but she refused to acknowledge the question. "You must remember who you are. You're not a peasant, like those women there."

Mammina tipped her head toward the women leaving the field. The girl saw Mamma Rosa smile uncertainly and wave. The girl loved Mamma Rosa even if she was a peasant. She sniffled, burying her face in *Mammina*'s lap.

"Be proud. You're a lady, and someday you'll have everything. It won't be much longer. Your father, how he suffers, poor man . . . he would rather forgo his future, his wealth, his family, everything . . . because of us. You must remember and be patient. If your papa and I can be patient, you must be patient too. Come, let me see your face. Let me see you."

Mammina lifted the tear-streaked face from the folds of her skirts, but the girl stubbornly kept her eyes closed. "You know I love you more than anything in this world, don't you?" *Mammina* asked.

The girl jerked her chin away and stared down at her big, heavily calloused hands, ingrained with dirt. She hated her hands. She took *Mammina*'s tapering fingers and delicate rings into her hands and rubbed the calloused fingertips where the mandolin strings had pressed. She tried to burn this moment into her memory. Their hands were so different. They were so different.

Perhaps they would never come together. She'd always trusted and hoped, but it was always next year, next month, in a while. Perhaps she was a peasant like the others and *Mammina* was ashamed of her. Overwhelmed, she hid her hands in her skirt. Oh, how she wished she could be a different person entirely. "Let us sing something together, *Mammina*."

They sang an Italian folk song the girl loved as they shook the straw from their skirts and headed toward the village, trailing behind Mamma Rosa and the workers. Their sweet soprano voices floated over the darkening countryside and cheered them.

I N the dressing room the song died on Mina's lips and she lifted her hands wide, palms up, in a gesture of embarrassed confusion.

"It was the same story she told every visit. She'd always bring some little trinket. Some useless gift. There would be a few lira, a day or two together, sometimes only a few hours snatched from an afternoon, and then she would disappear for months, years. Until finally that last time with the ring when the child . . . was about eight. She never came back."

The Signorina was sitting at the edge of her chair, clutching a bouquet of roses that had arrived during the story.

"She caught influenza when the girl . . . when I was almost fourteen," Mina said, coming back to herself and hurrying to finish. "I was told that she died. She's buried someplace in Naples."

"Ah, yes, influenza." The Signorina's voice was barely a whisper; it sounded pained to Mina's ears.

"So I was told," Mina added.

"There were so many women forced to give up their children. I'm sure there are many stories like yours. Did you love her very much?"

Mina heard fear in the question. What did she expect her to say? A mother who abandons her child and taints her with disgrace . . . it was a nasty legacy. But Mina had stories that were worse. If she'd wanted to, she could've told a story to make the Signorina wither with disgust. "I guess . . . yes," Mina said. "She . . . I must have loved her."

"It's difficult to make those trips," the Signorina said. "Few carriages are willing to go to the mountains."

"She said . . . it broke her heart to leave—"

"I know it did." The Signorina's eyes were moist; she shook her head sadly and plucked petals from the bouquet as she paced back and forth. "This woman, your *Mammina*, what did she do in Naples?"

"Supposedly she sang and played the mandolin in waterfront cafés, but I think that's only a story."

The Signorina stopped pacing. "She had a mandolin?"

"It was the only thing left from her father. He was supposed to be a mandolin maker."

"Oh, *Dio!*" The Signorina's voice was high, shrill. She seemed very upset.

"Signorina, it was a lie," Mina said with a laugh. The idea that the Signorina would believe such a lie amused her. "My grandmother knew the truth," Mina continued. "You see . . . she was really a . . . a . . ." She turned away, not liking this part of the story.

"A what?" The Signorina grabbed her shoulder and forced her to turn around. "What did they tell you about your *Mammina*?"

The fingers were like a claw, a cruel claw digging into the past. Mina was tired. She was tired of the lies, of avoiding the truth, of hiding behind stories. Her eyes overflowed with tears. "She was a whore, signorina. A prostitute and a thief, that's how she got pregnant. She lied to her daughter to get love."

"Who told you that?"

"My grandmother said she liked living in sin—" Mina caught herself and steadied her emotions. "*Mammina*'s daughter was in the way, she didn't love her enough to keep her."

"Perhaps she gave up her child to give her a better future."

Mina shook her head. "I'm a whore's daughter, not the daughter of a wealthy *padrone*. That's all a lie."

For some reason the look of shock on the Signorina's face made Mina laugh. "On a dark night even a fool can see a candle in a window," Mina said. "I know this kind of woman. I understand her ways. *You* lived in Naples, you can understand the truth. There was never any wealthy landowner. *Mammina* sold her body on the waterfront. The girl's father was a customer who paid for sex, and the rest were fantasies told to soothe an ignorant child. The ring she gave . . . the pocket watch that supposedly belonged to the father . . . stolen. When I agreed to marry Antonio, I gave the watch to Mario, as payment for the passage money he sent, without a flicker of regret for her memory."

The Signorina shook her head in disbelief. Her eyes were far away.

"I *know* about Naples, believe me," Mina continued heatedly. "Its streets, the waterfront. To survive you descend into a horror no decent woman should . . ."

The Signorina sat down slowly, her face twisted with . . . what? What was she feeling? Disgust, anger . . .

"You've lived there," Mina said. "You know about the slums. You can understand why I had to get away. Mamma Rosa hoped to shield her daughter. In a new place no one would learn the truth, but of course . . . a dog digs up his . . ."

She trailed off, aware that a strange mood had overtaken the Signorina. She looked feverish and the flowers in her hand were trembling. Stop talking like a fool, she told herself. Can't you see you're ruining everything? You've said too much. All that talk about Naples . . . she'll wonder how you know such things. Torn rose petals lay scattered across the carpet and around the Signorina's feet. The remains of the twisted bouquet lay in her lap and she had blood on her fingers from the thorns.

"Are you ill, signorina?" The Signorina seemed in a trance. "Please don't be angry with me."

Mina was frightened. Clearly she shouldn't have told the story. She hurried to explain.

"I know how the past can destroy any hope for the future. I've prayed and done penance, but you can see now why I had to get away. A mother's sins are a terrible burden to carry. I'm paying back a debt . . . a debt of sin. Satan's purse is deep and tightly tied. He watches every *scudi*. He wants payment for any pleasure. I should've known payment would be due and never made the bargain."

Mina sighed as a wave of regret washed over her. If only she could go back to the day she'd died. The day she'd accepted another woman's fate as her own.

"Sometimes, even though I know she's dead, I wish . . . I wish I could see her again. Just once—"

"If you could see her one more time, what would you say, what would you do?"

"I would give her back her destiny with both hands. It isn't right that I suffer because of her life. I have my own sins, my own destiny. It was false hope she gave me . . . this marriage gave me false hope. Because I accepted it, my life is ruined. I thought he was a good man, but I married someone who is evil. I should have known he—" She was doing it again.

Mina bit the first knuckle of her hand to stop her tongue. Everything was coming out wrong. The Signorina suspected something. She could see it in the eyes that dug into her like screws into soft pine. Does she think I'm a liar and a whore too? Have I ruined everything?

Cesca didn't see Mina standing before her, didn't feel Mina's fingers clinging to her sleeve. She was far away, climbing back over a stone wall encircling a wheat field, a carpetbag in her hand. Her eyes were focused on a young girl. It was the last time. The girl was eight, proud and able to care for herself. The girl insisted she could help in the city. . . .

"*Mammina,* can't you see I won't be in the way? I must go with you or I cannot live!" the girl had cried.

Cesca had pulled the little fingers from her dress and tried to back away. "I'll come back for you, *figlia mia!* I swear it. Do not doubt me . . . I love you!"

She could feel the desperation in the little hands that drove her rings into her flesh. Tears of anguish were steaming down her face, but it was the best thing to do. Leave her daughter in a safe place . . . with a good family . . . even though it broke her heart. . . .

In the dressing room Mina stood before her with accusing eyes.

"That . . . that woman . . . never meant to cause you pain," Cesca whispered.

"My life before the letter was hell . . . a shame no woman should suffer. I had to get away and find a new destiny. But I made a terrible mistake, and now my life has become a series of stories told to pass the time."

"Do you still have the ring?"

Mina shook her head. "The girl threw it into the wheat and never saw it or her mother again. Six years later she was handed some trinkets wrapped in paper. *Mammina* had died. It was finished forever. I tell you one thing, and I swear it on God's holy Bible, I'd never want to be blood of that blood."

Something was gravely wrong. The Signorina stood up, looking pale. The torn bouquet tumbled to the carpet and she pressed her hands to her heart.

"I have said too much and have upset you," Mina said. "Forgive me."

Mina snatched up the ravaged bouquet and busied herself collecting the torn petals from the carpet.

Inside Cesca's breast something was burning like a comet . . . in a moment it would burst from her flesh. Someone help me! I need help! Her throat felt as if it would explode with screams in a minute. Where was Dante? She needed help! Oh, God! Someone!

"I think we should have some tea," Cesca said, doing her best to sound normal. "Mina, get the tea things ready."

"Yes, signorina, tea, *subito*."

She watched Mina fussing with the teakettle and gripped the chair for support; her hand was as weak as an old woman's.

"But I don't understand. You told me you come from the mountains near Salerno. The town, you said . . . *Fitenza* . . . and your name is *Rossi* . . . and you speak of Mamma *Rosa* and Papa *Vito* who sent you. I . . . I . . ." the Signorina stuttered.

The Signorina seemed so strange. Mina wondered if she'd gotten the names mixed up again. It was so hard to remember all the details. Or did she suspect something else?

"That's where we moved . . . after she died, to start over. We even changed our names. All of them, even Mamma Rosa and Papa Vito."

"Changed names?"

"Yes. We left . . . to start over." Mina was busy in the pantry, bending down to search for the tea. Cesca moved precariously toward the chaise longue. She heard the water rattle into the teakettle. The blood pounded behind her eyes. She felt as though she were choking, as if there weren't enough air. This couldn't be happening. It was all a mistake, a misunderstanding, a joke.

"The village that you come from," Cesca asked, "originally, the one where you were born, what's it called, do you remember?"

"Rocca San Felice."

"Near the sea? Near Salerno?"

Mina was humming. Cesca realized it was the tune from that day in the wheat field. It was *"O Marenariello,"* the tune she'd hummed to Maria Grazia. Mina shook a match out of the tin, her anger and that day long ago forgotten.

"It's true there are two villages with the same name, but I'm almost certain I told you we *moved* to Fitenza near Salerno."

She used the excuse of lighting the stove to avoid the Signorina's eyes. "I was born in the mountains near Sant'Angelo di Lombardi, not far from your village of Lioni," Mina said as she settled the heavy kettle to boil. "Remember the first night, backstage, you told me we were practically neighbors, you even said we were countrywomen? Did you forget?"

She adjusted the burner, thinking she'd said it with just the right note of gaiety. Hopefully the Signorina wouldn't delve into her background anymore. She could stop telling lies. As she bent to check the flame she heard a loud thump. Turning toward the sound she glimpsed the Signorina's head hitting the edge of the piano bench and her body slumping to the floor.

Chapter Twenty

*S*IGNORINA! SIGNORINA!"

Mina dashed to pick up her hand. It was cold and limp. Oh, *Gesù*, Mina thought, looking at her lying on the floor, she's dead. She rushed into the corridor calling for help: "*Aiuto!* Someone come quickly! Something has happened to Signorina Frascatti."

Frantically she pounded on dressing room doors. A few cast members seeped into the narrow hallway to stare at her blankly. She beseeched them, but either they didn't understand her Italian or didn't know what to do. She thought of Signor Hammerstein and turned to rush up the stairs, her head down, skirts up. She ran smack into Signor Dante.

"Signor Dante," she said, falling gratefully into his arms. "Thank God you're here!"

"I'm happy to see you too, little dove, but what is it?"

"It's the Signorina. I think she may be dying!"

"What's all this racket?" Oscar Hammerstein asked, coming up behind them. "We can hear you screaming in my office."

"Something's wrong with Cesca," Dante said as he rushed down the hall.

In a moment they were at Cesca's side. "Cesca, *cara*, can you hear me?" Dante patted her cheek, but she didn't respond. He put an arm under her back and cradled her against his chest. "Get that chaise cleared off and get something to wrap her in."

Mina responded immediately. "Is she breathing?" Mina asked fearfully.

"She's breathing, but she's like ice." He put his other arm under her legs and lifted her easily, carrying her to the chaise. "Get some pillows."

"The curtain is less than an hour away," Hammerstein said, hovering. "What shall we do?"

"Cancel the performance," Dante said.

Mina arranged pillows as Dante tucked the edges of Cesca's fur coat around her body.

"Well, of course I can cancel the performance," Hammerstein replied indignantly. "But we'll have to give refunds, and she's agreed to eight performances." Oscar bent over Cesca, examining her ashen face. Fear gripped the purse strings of his heart at the thought of having to refund the money for the night's receipts.

Dante grabbed the lapels of the impresario's jacket, glaring at him. Hammerstein stood firm, puffing up like a toad, his teeth clamped on his cigar. "You mercenary bastard, I ought—"

"Signor Dante, please," Mina pleaded, putting her hand on Dante's arm. "Shouldn't we get a doctor?"

"Of course!" Hammerstein replied, remembering his humanity. "I'll go get the doctor immediately."

Perhaps there was still time to salvage the performance if the doctor came quickly. He headed for the door, the tails of his Prince Albert coat flapping, when a steely voice stopped him.

"A doctor won't be necessary, Oscar, stay where you are," Cesca ordered, sitting up.

"Thank God! Are you all right?" Oscar asked.

"I'm fine, just a dizzy spell. I didn't eat much this morning."

"Cesca, you frightened us," Dante said, chafing her hands.

"Signorina, what can I do?" Mina asked, kneeling next to the diva.

Cesca glanced away, forcing gaiety into her voice. "Dante, release me. Mina, such a fuss! I'm fine. Truly! I'm a little hungry, that's all. Not eating has made me a little weak."

"You're as strong as oak, Cesca. It isn't like you to faint. We should send for the doctor."

"Yes, a doctor, at once," Hammerstein chimed in.

"No, no doctor," Cesca said with authority. "I tell you, I need something to eat. We were rushing so, Dante, you know . . . to finish our errands this morning, and I completely forgot about lunch."

"I'll go at once," Dante said.

"No, Dante, I need you here." She clung to his hand, squeezing it in an odd series of jerks. He knew she wanted to tell him something, something she didn't want to share with the others. He signaled back his comprehension as she turned artfully to Mina and said, "Mina, perhaps you wouldn't mind getting some things for a quick supper."

"*Subito*, signorina!" she said, jumping up.

"Get some cheese, bread, fruit, you know, something like the little supper you were telling me about in your story." Mina tore off her apron and threw on her coat. "Dante, give her some money so she can get some wine from that . . . that Sicilian shop."

"It's not necessary, signorina, I have money," Mina said, heading for the door. "I'll only be a moment."

"Wait! Mina," Dante called. He took her out into the hallway. "Get some red meat and red wine," he whispered, pretending to be conspiratorial. "There's a special wine shop not far from here on Eighth Avenue: *Vendemmia*. They have a strong Sicilian wine she sometimes takes for her blood. Tell the shopkeeper it's for Signorina Frascatti. It shouldn't take you long to get there. Hurry back!" He pressed a ten-dollar bill into her hand. She flew down the corridor and up the steps, leaving the three of them staring after her.

"I really must insist, Signorina Frascatti, that the doctor be summoned," Oscar stated flatly. "We can't be too careful with our prima donna's health; after all, we have four more performances of *Tosca* and the possibility of a *Butterfly*. . . ."

Cesca hesitated. By the time the doctor was summoned, and finally arrived, she would be onstage performing. She turned to Oscar with a weak smile. "If you think it necessary, dear friend, I consent. But I assure you I'm fine."

"Very well," Oscar said, concern for his investment plain upon his face. "I'll go fetch him now."

As soon as Oscar closed the door, Cesca turned immediately to Dante. When she spoke, hysteria edged her voice. "Make sure the hall is clear. We must talk."

In a moment he returned, closing the door silently behind him.

Cesca was on her feet, bursting with emotion. "You're positive the hall is clear?" she whispered.

"Yes, what is it?" he too whispered.

"Dante, it's her! And she told me she despises me!"

Dante looked flummoxed. "Who despises you?"

"Maria Grazia . . . Kismet! How I laughed at the idea, but the Russian was right. The trail had ended and we didn't need to look. She's from Rocca San Felice. My daughter was here the whole time. In my dressing room . . . as my servant. Oh, *Gesù!* What can I do? There's hatred in her heart, and the things she said . . . she said she wished I were alive so she could give me back my destiny. She says she doesn't want to be blood of my blood." Cesca broke into sobs and collapsed onto the chaise longue.

Dante had never seen her so unnerved, not even that night outside Rome when she'd shot Emilio. He thought she must be ill, for she was talking in circles. How could Mina be Maria Grazia and be from Rocca

San Felice? He had a copy of her marriage certificate in his pocket. "Cesca, I've just come from the courthouse. She's not your daughter. Not one statistic matches," he told her.

"It's Maria! Damn you! Don't you think I know the truth? She's changed her name, she moved to another village. . . ."

She was pacing the room frantically. Dante put his arm around her and guided her back to the chaise. "Listen to me, *cara,* I think you have a fever. You're not making sense." He pressed a hand to her forehead. "The doctor will be here shortly."

She slapped his hand away and furiously pushed him back. "Stop treating me like an idiot and *listen* to me. I'm not sick! We've been stupid enough. I tell you, Mina is Maria Grazia."

Although she was frantic with joy, a terrible sadness cloaked the emotion. Dante sat down, took out a cigarette, and tapped it three times on the case. "Very well, explain to me how you know Mina is your daughter."

"She was talking . . . talking about a ring I gave her and—"

"A ring?" he interrupted, lighting his cigarette.

"I stole that stupid ring, but I forgot all about it . . . oh, Dante, I never realized I did her such harm."

"She has this ring?"

"She threw it away and —"

"Cesca, you've decided Mina is your daughter based on a ring she mentioned? It's another ring, another girl. Situations like yours are not unique. There are thousands of babies abandoned in Italy, with thousands of stories—"

"This story is specific, it has names and places and a ring I stole. Millions may have been cast aside, but none would have the details that Mina has. She's my daughter, and Dante—oh *Gesù*—she told me she despises me."

"*Cara,* she can't despise you, she doesn't know you." Dante blew a cloud of smoke at the ceiling. "Stop being dramatic for a moment," he said, "and listen to me. I've just come from the courthouse. I have startling news myself." He pulled out a folded paper and opened it. "This is her marriage certificate." He handed it to her and she looked at the certificate without comprehension. "Look at the name." He pointed. "She's married to that brute of a man we met last night."

"What? She can't be."

"She is. Her name was Filomina Rossi, but her married name is DiGianni. It wasn't important at the time you hired her who she might be married to, but there's some kind of strange connection here. Some plan we're not aware of. I feel it has Emilio's stamp all over it."

"No, Dante, she knows things, things she couldn't possibly know unless she was Maria."

"We don't know where her information came from. I hate to hurt you, Cesca, but it's possible she's another spy. He could have given her information, and she could have cleverly filled in the blanks—"

"For what purpose?"

"Who can say? He holds you responsible for Giulio's death and wishes to pay you back. What better opportunity to hurt and confuse you?"

"Dante, what are you saying? You're half in love with her. You don't believe she's a spy."

"We need to be positive."

She nodded, her face now devoid of joy.

"When there's no doubt, we'll know what to do," Dante said.

"What should we do first?"

"We must question her and uncover her true identity. If she is Maria, Emilio must not find out. If she's another spy sent to torment you, we must get rid of her. I'll cable Italy immediately. It'll take a few days, but we'll have the truth."

"I want to be alone with her. We must think of a scheme to get her out of this opera house."

"You're right, it's too public," Dante mused.

"Another errand of some kind . . . perhaps we should—"

"I'll take her uptown to prepare the house for your arrival. We can use the excuse that your help has quit. . . . No—they've run off, yes . . . they've run off and now you're ill and need her help. Let her go right after the third act costume change," Dante suggested.

"Never! She must go as soon as she returns. Go, release our servants. Make sure there's no one lurking about. Then hurry back to get her."

"I'll take her to get a few things at her apartment, then take her uptown," Dante said with enthusiasm. "I can accomplish it quickly with the Pierce-Arrow and question her on the way." Even with this fearful turn of events he was pleased to have an excuse to be truly alone with Mina.

"What about her husband?"

"We'll send a message. He's sure to be at the saloon with his mistress. He's greedy, so if you give her another generous raise to compensate him for the separation, he won't interfere. If he doesn't see it your way, I'll be happy to convince him."

Chapter Twenty-One

SEATED AT A TABLE in the Palm Court, Emilio Lampone looked benign. His fine silver hair, his subdued wool suit, and his manicured fingers gave the impression of bored gentility. He wiped the last trace of a late supper from his lips and placed the linen napkin on the table. Immediately a waiter appeared at his elbow to remove the plates and scrape the crumbs.

At least the service at the Plaza Hotel was civilized, but he preferred his own table in his villa in Naples. He ordered an espresso and accepted a light for his cigarette, wishing this whole business settled quickly. He checked his watch: nine fifteen. The man would arrive shortly.

As he waited impatiently he examined the people coming and going. He disliked this brash country and its people and had often pronounced over a stem of port that "l'America was peopled with the refuse of Europe." *Contadini* who'd scraped passage money from the dirt. Italian, Irish, or Polish—it didn't matter. They were all animals, vainly hoping to advance, but animals couldn't escape their nature. They'd always be inferiors no matter how much money they amassed.

His contemporaries agreed as they puffed cigars and sipped fine liquor. They'd all seen upstarts return to Italy with fat wallets to purchase fancy villas and fill them with expensive objects. *Contadini* with stones for pedigrees! Emilio was no different from most cultured Italians when he called them *cafoni* and refused to do business with them. So the irony of the present situation made him squirm.

A wealthy man could usually purchase what he wanted from those beneath him, but he feared that this time his money might not be enough. Last night he'd bent his knee to ask God to make the man he was to deal with base, greedy, and amoral. Make him want money more than honor, more than common decency, he'd asked, and if you must, make him truly evil so that I might buy what no man has a right to sell.

Emilio had been offering large sums of money for information about Francesca Frascatti and her entourage, and greed had quickly surpassed integrity. Several days ago one of Francesca's hired men had come forward, confirming his suspicion that Francesca was in New York searching for his granddaughter. But the informant added new information as well. Francesca had hired Giuseppe Petrosino to help her in America, and Dante Romano, the man posing as her lover, was actually an Italian detective in charge of the search. The informant promised that, for the right price, he could provide Emilio with an important clue he'd been holding back. It was a clue that had just been discovered and would lead to his granddaughter's whereabouts.

Emilio hired the informant and paid him handsomely. The informer told him, "I saw a woman wearing stolen heirloom earrings in a downtown market and secretly traced her to a Cherry Street saloon." The woman was the mistress of Antonio DiGianni, a day laborer, who was newly married to a Filomina Rossi.

Swiftly Emilio had his Pinkertons wire Italy. The records for DiGianni and Rossi had been checked. It was an incredible coincidence. He quickly discovered that his granddaughter was working in the costume shop of the very opera house in which Francesca Frascatti was performing. Thanks to his informer Francesca wasn't yet aware of her luck, but Emilio was certain that as soon as Francesca discovered the girl's true identity she'd spirit her out of the country. He feared he'd never see his granddaughter again.

Emilio's immense wealth had aquainted him with the greed of men, so he'd decided to act covertly. Once again he'd sent out his hired Pinkertons—this time, to spread a distasteful rumor. He'd cast a wide net and brought in his prey. Let the animal come, he thought impatiently, stubbing out his cigarette. I know how to deal with him. Soon Francesca Frascatti will suffer the way I've suffered, and when she does . . .

"Whaddaya mean I can't come in? I got a meeting here."

"I am sorry, sir, but a tie is required apparel—"

Across the room his informant sprang to his feet, slipped a crisp bill into the maître d's hand, and told him, "It's all right, Dennis, this gentleman is with me."

"Oh, sir, I didn't realize. I believe I may have a tie in the cloakroom. I'll go fetch it." He scurried off. The informant guided Tonio DiGianni to a table screened with palms, just behind Emilio's. Emilio would remain unseen, but hear every word. A waiter appeared.

"Would you care for something to drink?" the informant inquired in Italian.

"Yeah, swell, a whiskey. Two fingers."

The faintest suggestion of an arched eyebrow from the waiter caused the informant to add, "I'll have a neat whiskey as well."

"And don't give me watered down slop, I want Three Feathers." The waiter left and Tonio continued in Italian. "Pretty fancy joint, supposed to be a jungle, right?"

"Exactly right. Would you care for a cigarette?" He offered an open case. Tonio's eyes popped as he examined the oval rolled cigarettes. He scooped up half the case, put one in his mouth and the rest in his coat pocket. After the waiter brought their drinks, and a tie, the two settled down to business. "I understand you're an expert boxer."

"You might say that."

"I would say winning all the fights in which you've competed is pretty much the mark of a champion."

"Yeah, so? What're you greasing me about? You got somebody you want me to fight?"

"Not exactly."

Tonio looked him over—the gold ring, the fancy suit, the soft hands. *Frocio!* he thought. "I get it. You want me to rough somebody up."

"Do you do that sort of thing?"

"I might." Tonio looked around the dining room. The room was pretty much deserted. He didn't see Emilio on the other side of the thick palms. He did see a waiter clearing a table on the far side and flagged him.

"Do you need something?" the informant asked.

"Yeah, another drink. So who do you want roughed up?"

"Nobody."

"Look, mister, this cat-and-mouse might be interesting to you, but it's Saturday night. I got things to do."

"Tonio—I may call you Tonio, yes?"

"Bring the bottle, Charlie, and leave it," Tonio said to the waiter. The informant nodded his consent; the waiter left annoyed.

"I ask these questions because I've a rather delicate issue to discuss with you, and I . . . I'm a bit fearful of your reaction. You see, I've heard of your reputation—"

"You're afraid I'm going to slug you? Is that it?"

"Exactly."

"What're you going to do, insult me?"

"Maybe."

Tonio took the bottle from the table and poured two more shots. He looked the man before him over. "Shoot," he said.

"Let me start by saying I have a lot of money at my disposal—more than you can imagine—and I'm willing to pay you a handsome price."

"Money don't insult me. Keep going."

"I don't know how to put this . . . it concerns a woman you are involved with."

Tonio sat back in his seat and pushed his hand through his hair. Kathleen. The man obviously meant his mistress, Kathleen. "Oh, I get it," he said, thinking it over. This must be the man from that saloon above Fourteenth Street. The fancy place she'd had her eye on. She'd told him she'd been up to see a man several times, but he wasn't interested in selling. "Why are you offering me money? She's the one—" He stopped, confused. "You're talking about Kathleen Shaunessey, right?" The man shook his head. Tonio's confusion deepened. "I don't understand."

"I'm representing a very wealthy and powerful man. An *Italian* man," he said, tipping his head and raising his eyebrows suggestively. "My employer has fallen in love. He realizes that he's older, more than twice her age, but from the moment he first saw her he was captivated. He's been obsessed with her day and night. We've been informed, through our contacts, that you don't live with her, and I believe, from the information we've uncovered, that you don't love this woman and actually wish to be rid of her. He's willing to pay you five thousand dollars."

A surge of excitement flowed through Tonio. Five thousand dollars! It was a fortune! The amount of money fogged his mind. Why was he being offered five thousand dollars? "What's he want?"

"He wants you to divorce your wife and allow him to take her back to Italy."

"Divorce my wife? You're talking about Filomina?"

"Yes."

This wasn't at all what he'd expected. It had to be the man he saw a week ago at the opera house. That fancy man had "put horns" on him after all. The insult seared his gut like grain alcohol. "I knew it! That bitch's been lying to me." He shot to his feet, knocking the table edge into the informer's chest. "He's been screwing my wife."

"Of course not. He hasn't touched her. Believe me! Sit down, you're making a scene."

"I'll kill him if he's touched her—"

"No, I assure you. Sit down, please . . . you're attracting unwanted attention."

Tonio sat down reluctantly, his fists spasmodically clenching with rage. I might have married her on a bet, he thought, but nobody, nobody's going to call me cornuto! Not Antonio DiGianni.

"He's seen her, yes. Many times, at the opera house. He's spoken to her briefly."

"I saw them together," Tonio snapped. "A pretty boy in his late twenties."

"No, no. He's an older gentleman with silver hair."

Tonio was completely bewildered. "Silver hair . . . but she knows him, right? She knows all about him?"

"No. Look, he saw her working at the opera house and fell in love."

"She knows about this, this meeting?" he asked, fanning his hands across the cloth.

"No, she does not."

Tonio put his hands on the table and leaned toward the man belligerently. "You're saying she doesn't know about him? At all?"

"No! Don Lampone has not—" The man was momentarily flustered by his slip. On the other side of the thick palms Don Emilio cursed inwardly. The fool had given away his identity. Tonio made note of the name.

"—my boss has not . . . told her his feelings. She knows nothing and he wants to keep it that way. I know it sounds absurd, but he's hoping that if she's free . . . because she's so young . . . He can offer her everything, but being in his sixties, he hopes that she'll come to care. He's well aware that she's a respectable married woman . . . pious. . . ."

"The old lecher. My wife looks sixteen. Why—"

"He's willing to compensate you handsomely for the loss of your wife. A woman you married by mistake and would happily be rid of. You are, after all, involved with the owner of the saloon on Cherry Street, are you not?"

"You know quite a bit about my business."

"Yes, we do. And as an added incentive to agree, we add that we also know the police are in on your side business. Your illegal boxing matches in the back room. My boss's connections in the city might not look so kindly on profits being made in a back room brawl, even if your Fourth Ward police friends turn their heads. Why don't you think it over?"

Tonio nodded shrewdly. The old man would see to it that the matches stopped. Bye-bye to any championship bouts, but . . . five thousand! He'd never heft a pick again. It was a fortune!

"I'll think about it," he said, trying to hide his enthusiasm.

"This is a one-time offer, not open to negotiation. I'll come by the site again to hear your decision. Don't discuss this with anyone, your mistress included. We don't want the authorities to interfere with our agreement. My employer wishes to win the young lady over; he wants her to love him, not fear him."

Tonio looked at the man keenly. Why did the old man want Filomina? If he was so wealthy he could have anyone. Something more was going on. "Your boss is *la mano nera?*"

The man said nothing, just a flicker of eyelashes.

"You know *la mano nera,* right?" Tonio whispered, jerking his chin. "Black Hand? Mafia?"

The man got to his feet and put out his hand. Tonio took it, pulled him close. "Let me see if I have this right," he whispered in the man's ear. "Your boss is offering five thousand dollars to *buy* my wife."

"I suppose you could put it that way."

"Is he going to marry her?"

"What he does with her after the exchange is his business."

"If I agree, when do I get the money?"

"When the details are settled you'll get one thousand . . . as a token of good will. But you must convince her to divorce you and leave the country. You'll get two thousand when my employer takes possession and the other two when the divorce is final. That's a total of five thousand dollars. He's planning on leaving for Naples next Sunday."

Tonio thought it over for a moment. Something was definitely going on here. Fancy gentlemen didn't just show up to offer large sums of money for poor working girls. He wasn't going to lose the opportunity by challenging the setup, but perhaps it was some kind of trap. It was essential to find out the reason before he agreed.

"Think it over carefully. The money would set you up for life."

"Yeah, it just might," Tonio said, rubbing his stubbled chin. He snatched the liquor bottle off the table, turned on his heel, and strolled out of the Palm Court still wearing the maître d's tie.

W H E N Tonio arrived at the Cocked Hat, Mario was partnered with Biaggio for the usual Saturday evening pinochle game. Biaggio immediately gave up his spot and Tonio threw himself down to play, but he was too jittery to concentrate. He tossed in his hand, insisted Mario quit the game, then uncharacteristically suggested they go out for a walk.

Mario was curious about Tonio's strange behavior. Something important must be brewing. "The fresh air will do us both good," Mario agreed, snatching his jacket from the chair. "I think this might be the moment I've been waiting for," he whispered meaningfully to Biaggio as he passed.

"Remember, he's a wolf," Biaggio whispered back. "Watch his teeth."

Mario followed Tonio as he made his way across Cherry to a dive they both knew two blocks from the river. Tonio was uncharacteristically silent, and the tension Mario felt, waiting to discover the source of Tonio's agitation, coiled in his stomach the same way it had when his father had gone cold and brooding. As he followed behind in the dark, his mind slipped back to the terrible days of his father's last week of life.

His mother, *Madonna* grant her peace, had been forced to tie his father down. She'd bathed his forehead with cool cloths and tried to soothe him with gentle words, but the nightmares his ravaged brain invented gave him no peace. He'd lain, pulling against the restraints, cursing and begging for God's vengeance to destroy his wife and only child. Mario had been eleven when he watched from beside the bed.

For almost two years he and his mother had been bewildered and embarrassed by his father's bizarre behavior. At first his father had simply been suspicious of careless gestures and nervous laughs; then he'd been certain there were plots behind everyday conversations; and finally he'd seen devils lurking in every encounter, waiting to ensnare him. Mario tried to reason with him, but his father had turned away from his family and friends, refused to wash or eat, and sought solace in wine with invisible companions. After awhile Mario gave up trying to help him. He told himself his father was a fool. A weakling.

Mario had felt cheated. Where had his easygoing father gone? Friends had pitied Mario and his mother, then they'd deserted the family. Mario and his mother had scraped along on the little Mario had earned working at the mill. They'd kept to themselves and rarely went out, for even in church his father had raved. During the last week of life he had become lame and unable to walk. A doctor had finally been called and discovered a tumor pressing on his brain. Mario's contempt dissolved when he realized his father had only been sick, and he'd never recovered from the guilt he felt over his desertion.

After settling in and ordering a bottle of whiskey, Mario could stand the tension no longer. "Tonio, what's the matter, are you in trouble?"

"I need a favor, Mario."

"Sure, sure, if I can—"

"First, I want you to be in my corner for the big match on the barge Saturday night. I don't trust those sheeny Irish bums of Kathleen's." Mario nodded, watching Tonio's eyes. "It's going to be a tough fight. The guy has fifteen pounds on me and two inches of arm. I want to make sure nothing goes wrong. There'll be a good cut of money—"

"That's not necessary," Mario interrupted, waving away the offer.

"You're my best friend, you deserve it." Tonio paused a moment and took another drink. Mario waited anxiously. "And I need your 'old friend' to investigate a man who's offered me a lot of money to do a job. His name is Don Lampone."

Mario knew that the "old friend" Tonio was referring to was his connection to the Black Hand.

When Mario had first arrived in New York City he'd stayed with his cousin Vito. Vito paid him to write some letters: requests for money, mostly. He'd been paid well, but when he'd discovered that a secret society, *la mano nera,* was behind the requests and that the society was involved in extortion and sometimes worse, he'd quit. He'd done it diplomatically, laughingly telling Vito, "I don't think it's wise of the Black Hand to write threats down on paper that can be used later as evidence." Vito and his friends had agreed. They'd continued making threats, but used the imprint of an inky hand on paper to achieve compliance, and had allowed Mario to move on.

"Who's this man to you?"

"I'd rather not say, but he wants me to . . . ah . . . make a delivery for him. I want to know his background."

"What kind of a delivery?" Mario watched Tonio's eye twitch. The tick told him it was more than a petty crime. He wondered if he'd been asked to murder someone. With Tonio's reputation he wouldn't put it past him. Whatever it was, it was serious. Tonio wasn't easily shaken.

"Not a delivery exactly," Tonio hedged.

"Tonio, I need to know what's going on or I can't help you. You said I'm your best friend, you know you can trust me. Is it murder this man is talking about?"

"He's offering me five thousand dollars and—"

Mario whistled. "Five thousand!" he whispered. "Who does he want you to kill?"

"I'd rather not say."

Mario was shocked by the amount. It couldn't be a simple murder. Someone might pay five hundred, but thousands of dollars, never . . . unless . . . "It's political?" Mario asked.

"This man might be connected to the Mafia in Italy. Can you check his associations?"

It was possible. Mario could check his identity with the Black Hand, but first they'd want to know the reason for the interest, especially if the person was heavily connected, and they'd want money for the service. Mario could press his cousin, but he wanted the details from Tonio, for perhaps this might be the way to settle his debt with Tonio.

"Look, Tonio, we've known each other for years. I gave you my fiancée to marry. We have no secrets. If you don't trust me—" He shrugged as though he could go no further.

"No, no! I trust you. It's just that it's got to be secret. The man told me."

"I can't go to my friends and ask them to do a job with vague information. You know it doesn't work that way."

Tonio thought it over. "I've got to have your word that this stays between us and your friends."

"My word!" He pulled back, insulted by the request. "You ask me for my word after all these years?"

"When I explain you'll understand."

Tonio whispered the news. Mario averted his eyes and sank his teeth into his thumb to keep from reacting. Their relationship had finally hit bedrock. Until recently he'd always given Tonio the benefit of the doubt, but in the back of his mind there had been a shaky case against Tonio. Now it was clear his "friend" had never been swept away by Mina as he'd always hoped. Tonio finally admitted he'd betrayed their friendship by tricking him to win her, just as Biaggio and the others had claimed.

Tonio went on to tell him Mina was a *cafona,* a country boor and a religious fanatic who hated sex. He said he might have had children with her, but he would never have grown to love her. The money he'd get for selling her would set him up for life. He didn't care why his "worthless wife" was being purchased or what might happen to her, he simply hoped that Mario could get the Black Hand to uncover some useful information so he could apply leverage and get more money.

It was infamy! Mario thought of Mina's beauty, sweetness, and innocence. He remembered the scent of her perfume as he rode in the carriage with her that day from Ellis Island, the shy touch of her fingers on his palm, and the encouragement in her eyes when she'd teased him at Biaggio's sister's house, before Tonio had ruined his chances. He'd known how vulnerable and alone she'd been, but he'd trusted his friend. Now that he knew how little Tonio cared for her, it infuriated him. It's my fault, he thought, I should've seen through his lies.

Why hadn't he seen the truth? He'd seen him cheat others; what made him think he was immune to Tonio's evil? He should have been smarter; he should never have allowed her to make such a terrible mistake. He should have had a showdown with Tonio and broken the friendship. Mina should now be married to him, safe and happy, but his foolish loyalty had doomed her to unhappiness and only *Gesù* knew what else.

Tonio was planning an unthinkable depravity and his only concern was how to get the most out of the situation. Mario wanted to smash the whiskey bottle across Tonio's head and stab him through the heart with the shards. How dare Tonio confess he'd purposely cheated him of happiness, then tell him he was planning to sell the only woman Mario had ever loved for five thousand dollars?

"The man's coming back to the work site to get my answer," Tonio said. "I'm supposed to deliver her on Sunday."

Mario tasted blood on his tongue and realized he'd bitten through the flesh of his thumb trying to hold in his temper. He shoved his hand into his pocket and met Tonio's eyes with a smile. Mario was the only one standing between Filomina and Tonio's evil. The best thing to do was to keep up his charade until he found out the stranger's plot. "Okay. I'll go see Vito tonight," he promised.

"You know as well as I do that there has to be more to it than him lusting after my wife. What is she? Not even good for a fuck. If I can—"

"Don't say more," Mario said, clamping his teeth together. "I know what I have to do."

Mario left Tonio near the work site and headed across town toward Elizabeth Street with his clay pipe glowing fiercely in the dark. The Black Hand had long fingers and would get the information he needed quickly. He'd find out what this *padrone*, Don Lampone, was up to and put an end to it. Then he'd find a way to settle with Tonio. All the hurt and rage he was feeling would be revenged. Suddenly he thought of Mina's sweet face. He wondered if she would curse him or be relieved when he made her a widow.

Chapter Twenty-Two

‿☜☞~

ꞭOOK AT MY FACE, don't look down," Signor
Dante coaxed.

Mina shook her head and squeezed her eyes shut. "No, no, I can't do
it." In her tightly laced skates she felt as stiff as a new shirt collar, but allowed him to draw her onto the ice.

"Am I that bad to look at? Thank you very much. And I thought I was
rather a handsome fellow."

Hearing the disappointment in his voice, her eyes flew open to search
his face. After all the confidence he'd shown in her since they met, the
last thing she wanted to do was hurt his feelings. "No, no, it's just—"

He crossed his eyes and puffed out his cheeks, making a face that reminded her of the monkey she'd seen in the market with a tin cup and
tasseled fez. It was such a ridiculous image—handsome Signor Dante as
an organ grinder's monkey—that she laughed.

"That's better! Just let yourself go."

She took a deep breath and felt a bit of the panic leave her as he
pulled her out of the shadow of Bow Bridge into the whirling crowd. It
was a Sunday morning at the skating lake in Central Park, and every-
where she looked the rich and poor were rubbing shoulders, unified in a
childlike desire to master the ice on two shining blades of steel.

Both male and female couples held each other about the waist and
skated in unison. Single men in bowler hats darted about, their hands
clasped behind their backs, and even the old and infirm had a chance,
warmed by lap rugs and pushed in small sleighs. All were dressed in their
best and seemed to be having great fun. She was bundled against the
chill in her new dress and coat and felt part of the crowd, until she hit a
bump and flailed wildly.

"I've got you. I won't let you fall. Try not to think about your feet."

Not think about her wobbling ankles in the unfamiliar rental skates?
Impossible! The thin blades were tossing her back and forth like a shut-
tlecock. She was sure she looked like a fool, but Signor Dante smiled at
her so encouragingly she bit her lip and determined to make him proud.

Before they went on again he attempted to put his arm around her waist, but she purposely turned aside to adjust the new handbag on her wrist. After all, she was a married woman; his arm around her waist would be too intimate. They began again.

"See, you're doing wonderfully."

She scraped along for several yards, sweating and struggling. It was hard work, but she felt she was starting to get the hang of it when someone hit her from behind. Suddenly her skates flew out from under her and she dropped onto her backside, hard. Signor Dante helped her scramble to her feet.

"Maybe we better sit down," she said, embarrassed by the fall.

"Absolutely not! You're not hurt, are you?" His eyes were anxious. Nothing seemed damaged, except her pride. She hoped she hadn't ruined her new clothes. "Don't worry, it's only a little snow." He brushed off her coat. Next she tried walking on the ice, but she slipped sideways and almost fell. "It's okay! I've got you. You need to lean forward a little and push off."

Push off? What did he mean? A smartly dressed young couple waltzed in curlicues around them. She watched two boys weaving in and out of the skaters, playing tag. Antonio always said she was stupid, so maybe Signor Dante was wrong. Maybe she wasn't smart enough to skate.

"I see," he said, inclining his head toward the boys. "You think because those ragamuffins can skate, and you can't, that you won't be able to learn?"

"Perhaps I'm not smart enough to—"

"It has nothing to do with being smart or stupid. You're learning a totally new skill. It would be like me trying to work on your lace. I wouldn't know where to start. Would that make me stupid?"

"Men don't make lace."

"And women don't skate? There are lots of women here. Just look at those two over there. You can do it; you just need to learn how. I'll get behind you, it'll be easier that way."

She felt his strong hands encircle her waist and gently push her forward.

"I'll guide you around and tell you when to start moving your feet."

She gave up her pride and allowed him to maneuver her into the throng. He kept up a steady stream of encouragement and it didn't take long for her to catch on. After a while it was natural for him to switch to a side-by-side skating position. He slipped his arm securely around her waist to guide and support her while his other arm stretched out to hold her hand and give her balance. She finally felt comfortable, for she realized his intent wasn't sexual.

She hadn't been held this tenderly since she was a child. It felt so good. She stole an occasional glance at him as they glided around the lake and under the bridge. It made her blood thrill to see his shining face so close. His presence felt like the Mediterranean sun warming her soul with hope. He'd been kind and encouraging from their first meeting and he had so much faith in her abilities that he made her believe she could accomplish anything.

Why hadn't he been the one to send for her? Why hadn't fate put him in Mario's place? She would never have been able to turn him down if he'd asked to marry her. Once again she glanced at the other couples, imagining what it might be like if she were married to him. He would never beat her, never treat her like an animal or steal her pay. He'd be a true partner, someone she could rely on and trust, who would help her take her rightful place in life.

He'd encouraged her to read and write, to improve herself and find a better job. She knew he'd be a tender lover and a good father. If only they truly were a married couple. . . .

"We should stop now and warm up," he said, interrupting her thoughts and leading her to the side.

She didn't want to stop, didn't want the fairy tale to end; the time was passing too quickly. She was unfettered, like a child again. True, it still felt awkward, but she hadn't fallen since the first time and she was happier than she'd been since leaving Italy.

He clomped onto the wooden sidewalk and helped her up. Her legs trembled. "It feels funny to walk."

"Wait till tomorrow," he said, laughing. "Muscles you didn't even know existed will howl for attention." He helped her into the noisy shelter and she sat down on a bench. He knelt down in front of her and unlaced her skates.

"My feet feel prickly."

"You need to get the blood circulating," he said, putting her foot on his thigh. He rotated and rubbed her cold foot between his hands. "The laces sometimes cut off the circulation."

She felt herself blushing at the intimacy of the gesture, but enjoyed his attention. All over the shelter men were helping women take off their skates. Everyone was playful and merry. This is a normal part of skating, she thought, putting the anxiety she felt out of her mind. She purposely waited before suggesting she put on her high-topped boots.

He wasn't at all like Antonio as he guided her to the refreshment area and paid for her drink. He's a gentle, loving man, she thought, the kind of man every woman hopes for in a mate. In his presence I'm a delicate flower or a precious treasure. She sat across from him at a little round marble table.

"Thank you so much for bringing me here," she said, suddenly shy. Oh, how she wished this day would never end. She looked down at her cup of cocoa and then out the window. The lake was still crowded; there was plenty of time left for skating. This is something people do frequently, she thought, shifting her gaze to the couples enjoying hot drinks. Men treat women with care and attention, they laugh and have fun together. She felt sad. How different it was from her life downtown.

"I've never known anything like this, except perhaps a feast day."

"There're many new things to learn. Your little village had this many adventures," he said, crossing his thumbs and wiggling his fingers like wings. "New York City . . ." He spread his arms and flapped.

She laughed, savoring the moment and her cocoa. "Have you ever wished you could run away from your life?" she asked, suddenly serious.

"All the time."

It wasn't what she'd expected him to say. He sounded as though he meant it. "You've imagined what it might be like to be another person?"

"Of course! My life isn't perfect, I'd like to be smarter, stronger . . . more handsome."

"You couldn't be more handsome." When she realized what she'd said, she looked away, fiddled with her handbag, drew out the hanky the Signorina had given her, and pretended to dab at her nose. She hoped he didn't think she was flirting with him. She liked him too much to have him think she was common or forward.

"How did you come to America?" he asked.

"Excuse me?"

"Why did you leave Italy?"

"I wanted a change," she said evasively.

"Your engagement to your fiancé was broken?"

"I see you've been talking with the Signorina." She saw his face color at the reproach in her voice. She busied herself stuffing her hanky into her sleeve.

"Small villages can be unkind," he said simply, offering her a warm smile.

"People go to church on Sunday and think that makes them Christ's equal."

"Ah, the problem of the Pharisees."

She was pleased; they were on common ground for once. "Yes, you quickly become a harlot, without anyone understanding the truth."

" 'Ye shall know the truth,' " he said, jabbing his finger toward the ceiling like a parish priest, " 'and the truth shall set you free.' John, chapter eight, verse thirty-two."

From what she'd heard she'd expected him to be godless, living for the moment. Yet he could quote scripture, chapter and verse. She realized that the gossips' sordid comments were still coloring her thoughts. Ashamed, she lowered her eyes.

"So you understand how important it is to know the truth before judging someone?" he asked. She nodded. "You have to take your time and discover a person," Dante said. "Like finding a new flower in the field. You examine every petal, every leaf. People have reasons for their choices and actions that we don't understand. To understand why a person chooses as she does is to understand her heart."

She was startled to realize he was speaking her own convictions. "Yes," she said eagerly. "Others might try to guess, but only God sees into someone's soul and has the right to judge."

His eyes sparkled with delight. "I'm pleased you believe in allowing God to be the final judge," he said. "Sometimes we play a role, we pretend to be someone we're not, but we have reasons others might not understand. Often when we look closely, the person we thought we knew ends up being someone else entirely."

He took her hand from the table and her heart jumped. She tried not to let him see how frightened she suddenly felt. Was he deliberately commenting on her marriage to Antonio and the lies she'd told? She could tell he meant to say something deeper, something beyond surface conversation. He was clearly implying that someone was masquerading. Why not accuse her now of being false and get it over with? Now was as good a time as any to end the charade. "What do you mean?" she asked.

"Remember to let God be the final judge of why someone might not be who they appear to be," he said. She wrinkled her forehead in confusion. "It's only something to think about for the future." He turned her hand over and traced the lines on her palm with his index finger. It wasn't at all what she'd expected him to do, and now her heart raced with a sweeter fear.

"*Destino!*" he sighed. "Do you know they say the past and future are written on our palms? Are you happy, Signora Filomina?"

"It's been a wonderful day."

"I don't mean right now, right this minute. I mean . . . in your life . . . in your marriage."

His hands were warm. She felt lulled, safe. Once again she looked out at the twirling skaters. "Life isn't about being happy," she said. "It's about doing God's will, keeping your word."

"Do you know His will?"

"I can't seem to hear His voice anymore." She saw the scene before her darken as the sun went behind a cloud. I've made bad choices and turned Him away, she thought. You'd never understand. And even though you said we shouldn't judge, you're judging me now.

"God gave us a heart not only to pump blood, but to hear His voice," he said. "We can't listen for His voice with our ears, can we?"

She shook her head and looked at her palm resting in his hand. His soft voice, his tracing finger, sent tongues of flame shooting through her veins.

"Is it God's will when we are hurt, signora?" he asked. For some reason her eyes were stinging with tears. "God never takes pleasure in our pain," he continued. "Suffering is caused by our own choices."

She had no answer. She knew only too well that past mistakes caused present pain, but hadn't she sought His help every night through prayer? If God didn't want her to suffer, why didn't He answer her when she asked for guidance? Lately she'd been thinking He might not exist at all.

Perhaps He was only a plaster figure with gold trim, created to make people do what they were told and give false hope to those who were never going to have anything better than what they already had. She'd been thinking perhaps she'd have to give Him up, take a new path, alone. If she was brave enough to leave Him behind, she might escape and fashion her own destiny.

If only I could sprout wings and fly, she thought, like I do in my dreams. I'd fly away from so many things. She savored the thrill of Signor Dante's warm hand holding hers. Then reality intruded itself again. Her hand was so different from the hand of the beautiful Signorina he loved. He could never belong to her. She could never win him. He was only being kind, being a friend. She looked away, afraid of showing her fierce desire to stay in this moment forever, holding his hand without the interference of gloves or morals. Unexpected tears overflowed her eyes at the impossibility of everything.

"Tell me why you're crying," he said, brushing a tear from her cheek and guiding her chin back to face him.

"I've tried to listen for His voice. It isn't easy to know what He wants me to do."

"Perhaps He wants you to listen to your heart." He leaned toward her, still holding her hand, and the table between them seemed to disappear. She felt a strange impulse, an undeniable urge flooding up from her toes, like water rushing into an irrigation ditch after the board had been pulled. It was pulsing in the same way, threatening to spill over when it reached the top.

She was barely aware of her chin tilting up, her rib cage lifting. . . . A chill rippled up her spine and neck, arching her breasts toward him. She drew a long, slow breath as the current drove her forward . . . closer, closer. . . . She cocked her head to the side . . . her eyes fluttered down . . . she could hear her heart pounding. . . .

"God gave you free will," he whispered, pressing her fingers. "You decide in your heart what's right. If you listen to your heart, it'll tell you what to do."

Through a searing veil his soft lips brushed hers. A thrill of longing eddied around her. She felt naked, as though she were standing beneath a shivering tree of golden coins and the breath of God caressed her. She felt as though she were plunging into a dizzying vortex. Deeper and deeper she dove, until she felt the hard metal of her wedding band cutting into her flesh.

In an instant she snapped out of her reverie. She was shocked to discover that her body had tricked her into kissing him. True, the kiss had ended as a peck, but if she hadn't been reminded of her vow by her wedding band, she would have kissed him eagerly, wantonly . . . in public! What was wrong with her? Didn't she have control of herself anymore?

"Excuse me. I'm—I don't know what I . . ." For a moment she'd forgotten about the Signorina and the loyalty she owed. She'd forgotten about Antonio and her vows. She felt like a terrible traitor.

"Sometimes we're sent messages, even given orders," he said, shaking his head, "but we refuse to hear them."

She pulled her hand away from his and busied herself with putting on her gloves, afraid of what he might be trying to say. "Signor Dante, if I'm receiving orders, it's to go immediately and get the groceries."

"You know I care about you, Signora Filomina."

Her emotions were so confused she had to strain to hear him. "Signor Dante, you're a . . . good friend. The Signorina trusts and loves you. She and you are engaged to—"

"But you don't understand. Cesca and I . . . it's not . . . we're ."

She stood up and quickly put her gloved hand over his mouth to stop his words. "God, in His wisdom, has given us our places. My marriage may not be what I expected or make me . . . happy, but I must believe it's His will that I—"

He too stood up and gently took her hand from his lips. "Even if you're being mis—even if it's not good for you?"

"I've made a vow. I promised. I mustn't break my word in so sacred a contract. And you mustn't tempt me to think otherwise. If you do that, I can no longer be your friend."

"I wouldn't want to lose your friendship, signora."

"Nor I yours, signor."

She followed him to the automobile. Snow crunched under her boots. It was amazing how quickly things could change. Earlier she'd been so comfortable, wishing that her time with him would never end. Now she just wanted to get away, to be alone to think. The air inside the Pierce-Arrow was heavy with unspoken words. He had his driving to concentrate on while she busied herself watching the people in the street. As he headed the automobile across town to Second Avenue she thought how strange and unreal everything seemed all of a sudden.

He turned south to the Essex Street Market where she would do the week's shopping. Mina tried to make light conversation, but her feelings seemed exaggerated and her voice sounded funny to her own ears. She was all mixed up and didn't know what to say. She picked at a loose thread on her sleeve and silently brooded. What if the kiss and tension that now existed between them ruined their relationship forever?

He pulled to the curb and hopped out to open her door. He pressed a roll of cash into her hand for the groceries and mumbled an apology for his earlier breech of etiquette. Then he helped her descend and impulsively hugged her, brushing her cheek with a kiss. "I'll be back to pick you up in about three hours. Same spot."

As he drove off, she stood on the curb staring after the automobile, with her hand against her burning cheek, until he was lost from view. She should have been angry that he'd kissed her cheek, but she was happy. Thrilled. It was suddenly clear she was losing control of her feelings, and she didn't know what to do about it.

During the day, chores usually kept her mind occupied and she didn't take up fantasies of Signor Dante, but at idle times or late at night she found herself constantly thinking of him, wondering in what ways her life would be different *if only* . . . Today those fancies had almost become physical, and if she couldn't control herself, she knew she would have to leave her job and go away.

He wasn't making it easy. Like a spoon in coffee, the kiss on her cheek had stirred the sweet emotions to the surface again. She needed to put him firmly out of her mind. He belonged to the Signorina, and Mina was a married woman. She adjusted her wicker basket on her arm and started toward the market, trying to concentrate on her errands and the merchandise she needed, but her mind continued to turn over images.

The golden brown of his hair, like the rubbed leather of her wallet . . . his smoky blue-green eyes that sparkled with amber when he read poetry to her . . . the scar that crisscrossed his lip at the base of his perfect nose . . . the delicate way he held his cup in his angular hands . . . his deep laugh . . .

She remembered the feel of his lips on her knuckles when they first met. A surge of energy shot through her body at the thought of his hands on her waist at the skating pond . . . that strange rush of feeling that pushed her toward his lips in the café . . . the blind, searing heat that made her knees weak and the soft touch of his lips when—

"Signora DiGianni! Watch out!"

The shout cracked into her consciousness. A hand grabbed her arm and pulled her back. She tumbled against someone as an ice cart, hurrying from the market, passed inches from her face. She realized she'd stepped off the sidewalk without seeing the oncoming cart.

The driver pulled his horse up short. "God damn stupid woman!" he shouted, shaking his fist at her as he rushed away. "Do you want to get killed?"

Oh, *Sant'Anna,* she thought, my soul's in mortal danger. Take away these images. Let me not remember his lips or long for his touch.

"Thank you! I'm so sorry—I—" She pulled back, surprised. "Signor Catanzaro!"

Mario Catanzaro released her arm; he'd saved her from being trampled. "Are you all right?" he asked, sweeping his well-worn fedora from his head.

She was trembling but unharmed. "Yes, yes I am. Thank you, Signor Catanzaro." He smiled at her kindly.

She'd seen him many times at the work site when she brought Antonio's lunch, but she'd always rushed away before he'd had a chance to speak with her. She remembered how kind he'd been when he helped her convince Tonio to accept her promotion. She was suddenly ashamed. She'd lied about being afraid of him so she could marry Antonio; how ironic that she'd given up this gentle stranger thinking Antonio a better choice.

"You must be careful. An innocent woman is unaware of the dangers that lurk in a city like this."

"You're right, Signor Catanzaro. I wasn't paying attention."

"It was lucky I saw you. You're shopping for your new position?" he asked politely.

"Yes, I am. But how did you—"

"When the note came this morning, Tonio called me. You're advancing in your work for the opera singer Francesca Frascatti, aren't you?"

He seemed impressed with her new position. She felt pleased. "Yes. I've come to do the grocery shopping for the week."

"Do you need help? May I carry your basket?"

"Oh, no, Signor Catanzaro. You're very kind, but I can manage by myself."

He made a slight bow. His liquid brown eyes were brimming with affection and she realized he still cared for her. "It was a pleasure to see you again, Signora DiGianni."

"*Arrivederci!*" she said and crossed the street. She felt him watching her, and before she slipped into the crowded market she heard him shout her name. She turned to see him still standing on the corner, waving his hat over his head.

"*Addio!*" he called. "Go with God, Signora DiGianni! I'll be watching out for you."

Chapter Twenty-Three

$\mathcal{A}$FTER THE MATINEE PERFORMANCE, Cesca entered her empty house like a sleepwalker. She'd given a poor performance, and only her reputation as *diva assoluta* had saved her from ridicule. With only a few hours of fitful rest and a light breakfast hastily prepared by Mina, she hadn't been able to control her wildly vacillating emotions on stage. She'd soldiered on until the second act confrontation scene with Scarpia, when she was finally overwhelmed in a fervent and tearful "*Vissi d'arte*."

Even though the audience loved the novelty of a prostrate Tosca whose voice cracked with emotion, Hammerstein hadn't been fooled. It wasn't an artistic interpretation, he insisted, but a physical collapse. She'd quickly switched the blame to him, claiming her raw emotions were a direct consequence of his insistence on an imaginary illness.

As she opened the front door the dogs rushed into the foyer, yapping wildly. Their shrill voices tore at her nerves. A sedative would calm her, but she needed to stay alert. The dogs followed her up the stairs to where Lucifer waited, ever patient. He rolled over so she could scratch his stomach, then sprang to his feet and followed her into the bedroom, claws clicking softly. There he lay down again to watch her change.

Without servants bustling about, the house felt like a mausoleum. She had no lady's maid to help her change. No one must know of her daughter's presence. Dante had taken Mina out, ostensibly to shop, but mainly to get to the bottom of her story. He'd promised to question her casually and keep her safe from Emilio's machinations. They were due to return around five o'clock for supper.

She checked her watch. It was after three. Two hours to reflect on a course of action. While she was certain that Mina was her daughter, Maria Grazia, Dante wasn't convinced. He'd spent most of the night arguing that there might be other explanations. He'd asked Giuseppe Colombo to check the shipping records for the date Mina supplied and had put in a phone call to Petrosino's headquarters. He'd left a message asking Bevilacqua to contact Cesca as soon as possible.

Cesca refused to listen to Dante's arguments; she was beside herself with joy. Even though she knew her daughter would be angry with her for "dying," now that she'd been found, somehow everything would set itself right and Cesca would make up for lost time. But Dante had burst her bubble. "Time has passed," he'd said. "Lies have been told and feelings have jelled. You must move slowly. The grown woman won't be the child you left in the village so long ago."

She knew she'd need to win her daughter back. Mina wasn't just going to tumble into her arms and thank the stars and God for her *Mammina*'s return. They weren't going to take up where they had left off. Negative opinions *had* been formed that would be difficult to change. She shook her head. Somehow it had never occurred to her that her daughter would forget her and build a life of her own.

In her imagination, Maria was always waiting in Rocca San Felice, magically hovering around the age of eight. Of course, intellectually she'd realized her daughter was growing. She'd ticked off the birthdays on her engagement calendar and imagined each milestone—Holy Communion, confirmation, her teen years. Many times she'd tried to envision her face, but it either looked the same, like her own, or like Giulio's.

She'd considered herself a realist, but had to admit that in this area she'd completely deluded herself. Time had passed swiftly and Maria had grown into a woman—a woman Cesca didn't know and hadn't recognized. Maria, or Mina, as she now called herself, was a stranger.

The situation was worse than ironic. Cesca's only desire had been to ensure her daughter's happiness by providing her with a family and stability. She'd sacrificed her own happiness in deciding to remove a disgraceful mother from the equation. The adoption should have guaranteed a good marriage and bright future, but it hadn't worked out as planned.

Her heart-wrenching sacrifice had been misinterpreted, and her daughter had been shamed. Mamma Rosa had labeled Cesca a whore and a thief who cared more for carnal pleasure than her daughter's welfare. But wasn't there some truth to her daughter's beliefs? Wasn't it possible that she'd been greedy for wealth and fame . . . willing to give up everything, perhaps even her own blood, to obtain power?

Wasn't it possible that mixed in with her altruism was a large dollop of ambition for her own advancement? She couldn't paint herself in shades of the Holy Virgin. She wasn't pure. There was plenty of gray, and yes, even black in her portrait. It was true, her daughter wouldn't have been safe in Naples, but she also would have been in the way. Ambition demands its sacrifices. Perhaps her choice had been a convenient excuse for selfishness and nothing more.

She remembered the first weeks, leaving Maria at the convent with Sister Anselm and trudging on foot to find work in the surrounding villages. No one would hire her. She was suspect, at the mercy of wagging tongues. Finally, weeks later, overcome with shame, she'd run off to seek anonymity in the teeming streets of Naples.

When she'd returned, a little less than a year later, she discovered that Anselm had placed her daughter with a family named Muscillo. The woman's baby girl had been stillborn. The woman was kind. She'd offered to give Maria a family life while Cesca continued saving to bring her to the city. It had all seemed so logical. A better environment than a convent orphanage, a happier life . . . but the woman had become attached, and Cesca's plan had spun out of control. . . .

Lucifer nudged her legs and grumbled. She was pacing the floor in her chemise, gnawing her fingernails. "Yes, I know, sweet Lucifer. I'm upset, you can see." She bent to scratch him under the chin and stroke his soft coat. He rumbled his appreciation as she slipped on a house-dress. In her distraction she picked up her mandolin with the faded ribbons of former suitors trailing from its neck. Her mood immediately altered, and Lucifer plopped down on the carpet, pleased. Music would relax her, and Lucifer could stalk the swaying ribbons when he wasn't keeping time with his tail.

She took the tortoiseshell plectrum from the neck and strummed the strings, tightening a peg or two to correct the pitch. The mandolin traveled with her everywhere, for it was the last remnant of her family. The last time she'd played was aboard ship with Madame Zavoya. She strummed the opening of "*Marechiare*," an old tune with improvised lyrics she'd sung in the waterfront bars. Her fingers flew over the doubled strings, recalling the chords even as her mind traveled elsewhere.

She rested the instrument on her hip, singing the risqué chorus as she had in the old days. As she dipped in a dance movement, the light bounced off the intricate pattern of ebony and shell, and for the first time in many years she thought of her father. They'd made the mandolin together when she was only seven—about the same age Maria had been when they parted.

She struggled to remember his face, but only remembered his dark hair, rough hands, and the smell of wood chips. Resting her wrist against the varnished wood, she remembered his patience as he guided her in the trimming and sanding of the mother-of-pearl needed for the inlay pattern around the sound hole. The bittersweet memories of their time together filled her heart with longing.

Perhaps it was the same for Mina, and that was why she hadn't remembered. Mina had no photograph to remind her, just as Cesca had none of her parents. If she, who had a memory that could take her back to crawling among the wood shavings, could not recall her father's face, how could Mina remember her *Mammina* when she'd only seen her a handful of times? Cesca tried to remember what she could of her father, a master mandolin maker who had studied under Vinicacci.

She remembered the shirt she'd "stolen" and hidden. Its scent of shaving soap kept away the loneliness when he traveled. She remembered his small toothed saw, used to cut ebony, swinging from a nail on the workbench, and how she would look up at him as he stood beside her. He was tall as a tree, his face too far away. She remembered wiggling toes in an icy stream . . . they both had long second toes. Mother had said that made them stubborn. But there was only the feel of stubble on her cheek when he kissed her good night. No image was conjured.

Her father had taught her to play and read music, and her strong-willed mother had given her perfect pitch and the gift of an operatic voice. In the early mornings, when the coffee was brewing and the coats of varnish they had applied the night before were dry, father and daughter tested their creations, performing wild duets as her mother's fine soprano soared above the sound.

Those were happy times, before life fell apart and she lost everything. After her father's horse slipped and crushed him to death, everything changed. Her mother gave up every cherished item they owned, but refused to sell the last instrument for food and shelter. In the end, her mother was sacrificed too, broken like a crust of bread for the poor. The mandolin was the only concrete memento she had.

Cesca's name had been Giuseppina Checci when she'd walked the fifteen kilometers to Sant'Angelo di Lombardi. She'd been ten years old. She'd pulled the bell cord at the convent's orphanage, bitter and angry at "God's will." Five years were to pass before Cesca would return to peaceful mornings of song. It was the crotchety old nun who answered her raucous summons who would lead her to a new life.

Sister Anselm was the convent's cook, and Cesca was assigned to her care. Every day as Cesca worked in the stifling heat she learned patience and humility while scraping potatoes or pummeling dough or washing endless pots and pans or fetching water or chopping kindling. Anselm used every trick to frighten, goad, and guide her.

Anselm insisted that Cesca accept God's design, and because of Anselm's insistence, Cesca eventually came to believe that He was guiding her to a better life. As she worked, she sang, and Anselm, who had a keen ear, insisted on vocal training for her. Much later, Anselm confessed to having been "a wicked woman" who had spent most of her life onstage in France and abroad. She was a reformed *diva assoluta,* now in charge of the choir.

Cesca's naturally gifted voice was honed by Anselm to pierce the heavens and give glory to God. Without the nun's iron determination and expert coaching the gift would have been lost. Few women found training outside of the convents, and study with expert male teachers would ruin a woman's reputation for life.

But Cesca didn't want to study with an impresario. She didn't want a life upon the stage. She wanted only to serve God and use her voice to praise Him. She felt secure in the religious life and in the kitchen. Anselm was pleased when she confided she wanted to become a nun.

Cesca had finally found happiness after the loss of her parents, but powers greater than Anselm's decided that she must go back to the "impenitent world." Mother Superior ordered a "trial" and sent her to work as a servant on an estate near Naples. She was to work for a year, and if after that time she still wanted to join the sisterhood, she would be accepted as a postulate.

It might have been only a song ago, so fresh was her memory of his teasing blue eyes. A boy of seventeen . . . acres of grapes . . . yards of cloth billowing in the dry wind . . . the vineyards on the slopes of Vesuvius . . .

As she lay back on the bed, waiting for Dante and Mina to return, she stared at the blue ceiling and remembered the clear summer sky. The tune she was picking carried her back to the vineyard twenty years before.

Giulio stood before her, his bare feet in the soft earth, his eyes blindfolded with her scarf. She could hear him laughing.

"**PEPPINA,** *tesoro,* don't tease me, my treasure. I'm dying. You're killing me." He turned, trying to peer out from under the blindfold.

"Stop cheating. Don't use your eyes," she ordered, pulling the blindfold tighter, "or your hands." She slapped his hands that reached for her breasts and playfully circled him. "Find me using your senses," she purred, running her hands up his legs to her target, "and *all* your senses."

When Giulio's hands reached out for her she whirled away. They staggered around the vines like children playing blindman's buff.

"Over here, *bambino*. Yes, that's it. Smell me . . . use your nose . . . that beautiful Neapolitan nose of yours. . . . No, no, to the left . . . the left . . . use your ears, *angelo,* hear how my heart is pounding for you."

He stumbled, tangling himself in the white muslin covering the vines. To steady himself, he threw out his arms and clutched the juicy grape clusters. He fell backward pulling handfuls of them with him. She took pity on him, catching him as he tumbled to the soft earth. Once in her arms he yanked off the blindfold.

"Let me find you with my lips," he said. He kissed her breasts through the material of her bodice, starting the quivering sensation she loved. She hurriedly unfastened her top and cast it aside, then loosened the cotton blouse underneath and pulled it down. Giulio pulled off his shirt and lay on top of her, the fallen grapes were crushed between their warm flesh and he licked the juice dripping from her body.

"This is the best way to have a wine harvest," he said. "Use our bodies as the press."

They rolled in each other's arms, twisting in the muslin, smashing grapes, and laughing in the joy of their union. That was how Emilio had found them, but in a matter of minutes he'd destroyed their happiness forever. He'd thrown Cesca off the estate and she'd returned in shame to the convent in the caretaker's cart.

Hugging her body for warmth in the back of his cart, with the stars spread across the velvet sky like dice thrown from a gambler's cup, she hadn't known she was pregnant. She hadn't known that her sensual diversions with Giulio could create a child. She'd been that innocent. As the old man encouraged his donkey to climb and the wooden wheels bounced over the ruts, they ascended the steep path back to Anselm singing hymns.

She'd been overcome with shame when she'd realized how seriously she'd sinned against God, but Anselm had blamed herself. She hadn't prepared Cesca for the world. After she discovered she was pregnant, Cesca returned to look for Giulio. The servants told her he'd ridden off to Naples the same day she'd been dismissed. She found Emilio and told him about the baby, but he wouldn't believe the child was his blood.

"Get off my land, you slut!" he'd shouted over the stomping of his horse's hooves. "Only sixteen and spoiled. Like a broken melon in the dirt. Only a starving fool would take you up now."

The word *slut* had shocked her, but she'd clung to his bridle and fought for her unborn baby's future. Emilio had finally wrenched the bridle from her grip and she'd fallen in the lane. He'd galloped away, leaving her in a dusty heap.

She'd felt nothing. Above her the blue sky had remained arched and empty. When the shock had ebbed away sufficiently for emotion to return, she'd felt the sharp stones of reality cutting into her shoulder blades. Just as after the death of her mother, she was alone. She would have to make her own way in the world.

Chapter Twenty-Four

QUESTA SCATOLA ANCHE ... This box too ... to the address I gave before," Mina said, speaking Italian with the vendor.

"Signora, there are four melons here. They are imported from South America. The cost—"

"Please don't worry about cost. I'm shopping for Signorina Frascatti."

"Frascatti, the opera singer? Of course, of course, I've heard of her, she's in all the papers," he said with a grin. "I have some beautiful grapes here too." He lifted a canvas cover to show the plump fruit. "They're sweet and juicy," he continued, to tempt her. He pinched off a tiny spring of grapes, rubbed away the waxy bloom, and handed it to her. She tasted one and nodded, pleased. They would be perfect for Signor Dante. "Thank you, they're delicious. Put in several bunches. Don't forget, I want everything delivered this afternoon."

She crossed the street to the butcher's shop and passed inside. "*Buon giorno, Signor Vitelli. Come stai?*" she said to the man behind the counter.

"*Bene, signora, e lei?*" he replied, reaching across the counter to shake her hand. "*Tu stai bellize oggi.* You look beautiful today."

Signor Vitelli beamed as he looked at her, making her feel like a queen. She was proud of her new clothes and touched her new hat self-consciously. "I need to order some—"

Behind her the bell above the door tinkled loudly, the door slammed, and a woman with a plaid scarf pulled close around her face pushed up to the counter. Mina didn't understand what the woman said, but it was clear that the stranger wanted to be taken care of first.

"*Uno momento, Signora DiGianni,*" Signor Vitelli said. "*Questa donna è una disgraziata.*"

Mina turned away to examine a display of canned goods while he showed the "disgraceful woman" several cuts of meat. The woman fussed and argued until she finally picked the piece she wanted. He started to wrap it, but she stopped him. Mina could tell Signor Vitelli was disgusted with the woman's manners, but he said nothing as he expertly cut the meat. She waited patiently, checking the cases and stealing a glance or two in the woman's direction. The fringed woolen shawl hid her face.

She'd seen that same shawl several times in the market today, always a few steps behind. Was the woman following her? The woman paid, tapping her foot impatiently as he counted the change. Then she paused as though she couldn't decide if she wanted something more. She barked something at Signor Vitelli and began examining other cuts of meat in the case.

"Okay!" he sighed, as though exhausted. He turned to Mina with pleasure. "*Mi dispiace, Signora DiGianni.* What can I get for you today? We have nice pork chops."

She surprised him by ordering a large roast, plenty of cold cuts, lamb chops, five strings of sausages, several pounds of ground meat and steaks, and three chickens. The woman hovered in the background, forgotten. He was confused but pleased as he wrote down the order.

"Signora, where will you put all the meat? Are you having a party?"

"No, Signorina Frascatti's having a gathering. I'm doing the weekly shopping for her. You've always been so generous, I wanted to repay your kindness."

"Ah, Frascatti! What a goddess. I went to see her just the other night. . . ."

Suddenly the woman wearing the plaid shawl pushed past them and slammed out of the shop. The brass bell sounded wildly. Mina stared out the glass door as the woman melted into the crowd. "Who was that woman?"

"I assure you, no one you want to know, signora. She's just one nasty customer."

He focused his attention on a piece of broken twine caught in the dispenser above the counter. Mina noticed that he wouldn't meet her eyes and suspected there was something about the "nasty customer" that Signor Vitelli didn't want her to know. She finished up her business feeling a bit deflated by the sudden change in the butcher's behavior, and left the shop, heading toward a wine shop she knew on Houston Street. There was definitely something the butcher wasn't telling her, she thought. Why would he be embarrassed? Perhaps she's a prostitute . . . or a thief. Maybe he's involved with her . . . having an affair. Signor Vitelli? Never! She stopped her racing imagination right there. Other people's problems weren't her concern. She was expected to prepare a grand meal tomorrow and she had too much on her mind to worry about such nonsense. Even though the Signorina had made menu recommendations, Mina was nervous about her cooking skills.

The famous tenor Enrico Caruso was to cook pasta, and her responsibilities were the making of the linguini and the preparation of the sauce. For the second course she was to prepare a roast and some potatoes, then a little salad of mixed greens. It was all to be very informal. She took out the note the Signorina had given her for the owner of the wine shop. Barolo, Chianti, and Asti.

The carts thinned out as she approached Houston, and just before leaving the market, she came upon a cart displaying handmade baby clothes. She smiled shyly at the old woman who sat bundled up, working a crochet hook and thread. It was the first time she'd thought about clothes for a baby. She still hadn't gotten her monthly flow of blood. It had only been the trickle after her brutal encounter with Antonio. It was possible she might be pregnant after all. She decided to look, even though she knew she should wait.

Her heart swelled with joy as she looked over lace-trimmed dresses, warm crocheted blankets, stuffed toys, and silver cups and spoons. There was an elegant christening gown and cap, hand-stitched and trimmed with tiny rosettes. She picked up a pair of blue baby booties. They were so tiny. Perhaps if it was true, in six months she might have a boy.

But she put them down. She believed, like her fellow Italians, that buying baby things before a birth would tempt fate and cause a miscarriage. She started to move away, but noticed a filigreed baby spoon. It was so beautiful. She picked it up. A silver spoon didn't really count, did it? It wasn't clothing or furniture. Besides, it could be used for something else—jelly or sugar. Buying a spoon wouldn't harm her chances for having a child, she told herself.

The old woman offered to wrap it in a scrap of tissue, but she hesitated. Perhaps she shouldn't risk even a spoon.

"It's an antique," the old woman encouraged her. "This I can't make for you in six months."

Quickly, before she could change her mind, Mina made the purchase and slipped the packet into her purse. Then for a few minutes more she indulged her fantasy, discussing the items she might want reproduced when her child arrived. She was so involved fantasizing about future purchases that she took no notice of a woman standing on the opposite side of the cart, sorting impatiently through hand-knit sweaters.

The woman said something sharply and threw a sweater down on the pile. Mina wasn't sure she was being spoken to, but she smiled in the woman's direction and nodded her head politely. Then she saw the plaid shawl. It was the same shawl she'd seen at the butcher's only a few minutes earlier. The woman had obviously followed her. Perhaps she's a thief or a pickpocket, Mina thought. Perhaps she saw Signor Dante give me money and she's going to try to steal my purse. She held on to her basket and bag and moved away.

"*Grazie, signora, che vi diamo dopo sei mese. Arrivederci.*" Mina thanked the old woman, saying she'd see her in six months. As she tried to leave, the woman with the shawl blocked her way and said something in English.

"*Mi dispiace*. I sorry. I no speak English." Mina tried to get around her, but the woman countered. "No speak," Mina said, her fear rising as she pushed past.

The stranger grabbed her wrist. Mina pulled backward toward the other side of the cart, but the woman held on tightly. Perhaps, Mina thought, this woman's mentally unhinged. Maybe she wants to harm me. What did she want? Why did she grip her arm so firmly?

The old woman could see an odd glint in the stranger's eyes. *Pazza,* she thought. There were crazy people wandering the streets, many of them homeless and looking for a handout. The pregnant lady seemed frightened and obviously didn't understand a word the woman said.

"You need help, miss?" the old woman asked.

"Ya talk dago?" the *pazza* demanded, still holding the lady's arm across the cart.

"Italian, *si*. What you want?"

"Ask her name."

"Signora Antonio DiGianni," Mina replied proudly to the old woman's query.

"Ya used to live on Mulberry Street, didn't ya?"

"*Si.*"

"You work for some opera singer? Uptown?"

Perhaps this woman has something to do with the Signorina, Mina thought, but she discarded the idea quickly. The butcher had said this woman was trouble. She tried to twist free, but the woman held on like a bulldog. "What does she want?" Mina asked, her heart pounding with fear. "Why is she following me?"

The old woman translated. "She says she wants to know if you're going back to Italy," the old woman told her.

"What?" Mina stared at the old woman, trying to understand what she'd just said.

"*Si,* she says she wants to know *when* you're going back."

"I'm not going to Italy."

The strange woman insisted she was. Mina tried to get a look at her face, but the woman kept her face turned away and hidden by the shawl.

"Miss, she say no!" the old woman insisted. "She no go!"

"Ha," the *pazza* said. "She don't know yet, that's all."

"Who are you? Why you bothering her?"

The *pazza* moved swiftly to whisper in the old woman's ear. Mina watched her curiously. "Between you, me, and the lamppost here, her husband's sending her back. And being paid quite a handsome sum to boot."

Mina was astounded by the woman's statements. Who was she that she would say such horrible things about her husband? She *had* to be a crazy woman.

"Lies!" the old woman said. "She say you *pazza!*"

The crazy woman finally flung Mina's wrist aside. "Crazy, am I?" she cried, shoving her back on the old woman.

The action was unexpected. Mina instinctively grabbed the fringed ends of the shawl as she staggered back and tried not to fall. As she yanked it off the woman's head, loose black hair spilled out. Mina gasped. It was Antonio's mistress, and dangling from her ears were ornate seed pearl and ruby earrings.

"Tell the stupid bitch her husband's name is Tonio. He's a ditchdigger, twenty-three, married to her on a bet after he took her away from his best friend, Mario Catanzaro." The old woman translated as Mina, shocked by the raw hatred oozing from the woman's eyes, stood transfixed. "Tell her I know why he don't come home at night. I'm the reason why, because Tonio's in love with me. It's me Tonio loves, not her. Ask her if she thinks I'm crazy now?"

"You go from here," the old woman shouted, refusing to translate. "You *pazza!*"

The old woman used her body as a shield. If she didn't block this woman, something bad was sure to happen. There was a cruel look of triumph in the *vergogna*'s eyes. She obviously wanted to fight.

"Where did she get those earrings?" Mina demanded, struggling to reach past the old woman and get at Antonio's mistress. "What did she say about Antonio?"

"She's crazy, signora."

"Tell me!"

"Sssh!" the old woman said, stroking her arm. "*Calme ti!* Be calm. Let me find out what she's talking about."

"I feel sorry for her, that's all," the crazy woman responded indifferently. "Her husband's out-and-out selling her to a rich old wop. He's going to send her back to Italy and she don't even know it."

"She says your husband's selling you," the old woman said, too shocked by this revelation to act as censor.

Mina knew it couldn't be true. No one could sell another human being. Maybe what Antonio had said the day she'd caught him at the saloon *was* true, maybe this woman's mind was unhinged and she was trying to upset her. But what was she doing with her earrings?

"No Italian man sell his blood, his child," the old woman said.

"What child? Tonio don't have no child."

"This lady three months pregnant."

"She ain't pregnant," Kathleen shouted belligerently, putting her hands on her hips. "He don't have sex with her."

The old woman shrugged her shoulders and spread out her hands toward her cart and the baby items displayed. Kathleen realized the nature of the merchandise in the cart for the first time.

"She order today. You information no right."

Pregnant? Tonio's wife was pregnant? It couldn't be. Tonio said he hadn't touched her after their wedding night. That was almost six months ago, and she was three months pregnant? Kathleen's brain was churning. He'd lied to her! And if she was carrying his child, he'd never go through with the plan. He'd never divorce her and send her away.

"Where did you get those earrings?" Mina shouted, slipping away from the old woman and grabbing a fistful of dark hair with the earring. "They're mine."

Tonio's self-proclaimed mistress shoved her off, but Mina held on, determined not to let her get away. Her pent-up anger at the inhuman treatment she'd received for the last six months shattered her ladylike demeanor. She wanted her earrings back, and if she had to beat the mistress the way Antonio had beaten Gaetano in the field, she wanted an explanation of how she'd gotten them. She shouted questions in Italian as she pummeled the arrogant *vergogna,* demanding to know why she'd said Antonio was selling her and sending her back to Italy.

The meeting quickly turned into an old-fashioned catfight, and the crowd pulled back to give the women room and shout encouragement. No one moved to interfere as the two jerked each other around, screaming and swinging wildly. Mina was able to get in a lucky blow and knock her opponent to her knees.

"*Puttana!*" she shouted, spitting on her.

"You bitch!"

The mistress jumped to her feet, wielding her meat packet in its string sack like a mace. It hit Mina in the shoulder and pitched her backward into a cart, where she banged her head against a sharp corner. She lay on the stones under the cart stunned, trying to catch her wind. The chin ribbon on her hat was caught on something. The restraint made her feel like a goat on a tether. She slipped out of the noose and backed out from under the cart on her hands and knees.

Kathleen didn't wait for Tonio's wife to get up, but booted her in the backside and sent her flying. The old woman caught her before she fell and shouted something in Italian to the crowd that Kathleen couldn't understand, but whatever it was the bastards turned on her, booing and shaking their fists. They surrounded Tonio's wife, effectively cutting Kathleen off from further action, and jostled her ominously, forcing her back even as Tonio's little spitfire struggled to get free and fight.

"That's enough!" a man's voice said against Kathleen's ear. She felt someone pick her up and lift her out of the fray.

"Get yer filthy hands off me," she screamed. She kicked and fought to get free, unable to see whomever it was who held her from behind. "That bitch attacked me."

Abruptly she was set down on the sidewalk. Her face was pushed against the brick wall of a nearby alley and her arm was twisted into the small of her back, but she continued to struggle and sputter.

"She attacked you? I find that a bit hard to believe, Mrs. Shaunessey."

At the mention of her name Kathleen halted. The voice sounded familiar. "Let me go!"

"Not until you calm down."

"I'm calm," she barked, going limp and pliable.

"Can I trust you to stay calm?"

"I said, I'm calm!"

When her arm was released, she spun around with her fists up. It was Vittorio, the dandy boxer. He moved in quickly, pinning her to the wall with his hip, and blocked her attempts to strike him. She and Tonio were to meet him at his gym in a few hours to go over details for the upcoming match. "What the hell are ya doing here?" she demanded, relaxing enough to rub her sore wrist.

Dante saw she was breathing hard and bleeding from a torn earlobe. Her eyes were as bright as brass plates in the sun.

"Don't you remember, you mentioned meeting me here?"

"I never said any such thing."

"You told me you shopped in the Essex Street Market on Sundays."

"So what if I did?" Her chin went up defiantly as he continued to push his body against hers and smoothed the tangle of hair from her sweaty face. Caught in her dark hair was the ruby and pearl earring matching Cesca's description.

"It wasn't difficult to spot your splendid mane of hair. You're quite a contender, Mrs. Shaunessey. Perhaps I should be making a match with you instead of your mate."

The nearness of his body caused a different surge of adrenaline to shoot through her now. She'd been hoping to see him today; she'd mentioned the market on purpose. She could see that away from his girlfriend's watchful eye, he gave off a sexual energy that felt pleasant, but dangerous.

She could handle Tonio, but this man was a different story. He was smarter, more cultured, and sure of himself around women. The sexual heat radiating off him was like an overstoked furnace.

"Whaddaya mean, interfering in a personal matter the way ya just did?"

"I don't think it's a good idea to draw the police down on us now, do you? Not with the match coming up so soon. Besides, I'd hate to see your lovely face get all smashed up."

"By that cup of sour milk? Yer daft!"

His index finger traced a curve from her eyebrow to her chin. He pushed her chin up, then gently untangled the earring from her hair. She could smell bay rum and tobacco and see a dangerous light in his eyes. The nearness of his body made her knees wobble.

She snatched the earring from his hand and drew her breath in sharply. If she didn't get away from him soon, she'd let him lift her skirts and they'd do it here in the alley with the market a step away. The sudden surge of desire made her feel giddy. She hadn't thought anyone but Tonio could make her feel that rush of excitement.

"Who was that woman?" he asked, releasing her.

He took out his cigarette case and lit up as she put her clothes in order.

"It's personal and no one ya've a need to know."

"Would you like me to take you back to the Hat?"

There was something in the way he phrased the question and something in the way he held his cigarette that told her he wasn't just offering to see her to the saloon. She'd love for him to "take her back," but it wasn't the time. After the match, when she had her cut, she'd be more independent, and if she liked she could step up in class in more ways than one.

"No. I can make it on my own."

"That's a shame, Mrs. Shaunessey, but I'll look forward to a future meeting," he said, brushing close. "Anytime you have a yen, call on me . . . I'm the man for you." He touched the brim of his hat and winked.

"I'll see ya at the gym," she said. She turned to go, then stopped and turned back. "If ya've a mind to stop at the Hat . . . another time . . . come in the mornings, after ten or before seven at night. I can always spare time then." She elbowed her way through the packed crowd heading in the opposite direction from the fight, knowing her shawl was either lost or pinched.

The whole way back to the Hat she alternated steam and lust. Was it possible Tonio's wife was pregnant? If she was, it was an end to all her plans, and that lying bastard would pay. Not having sex with her indeed. Unless . . . she could turn the whole thing around. Then there was that handsome stud boxer, Vittorio. He wanted her. She knew it. She wondered what it would be like to have a go with him. Time would tell. He'd be around. Plenty of time to dance to that fiddler's tune.

DANTE had hurried back to the car, removed his mustache, and changed his jacket. He pulled his fedora down over his darkened hair to hide the color and hurried back to find Mina shivering on the old woman's chair, her face as white and stiff as a new sheet. Her thick hair had slipped its pins; one braid snaked across her bosom while the rest hung down her back. Her eyes were blazing, but as he walked up, carrying a packet of books, she didn't focus on him.

"Mina? Little dove, is that you? What's happened to you?"

"She was attacked, signore," the old woman said when Mina didn't answer. The old woman smoothed her hair into a knot and secured it with some pins. "A woman, escaped from a madhouse, attacked her. She was raving! She said you were selling her back to Italy."

"Selling her back to Italy?" Dante asked, amused.

For a moment he wondered why Kathleen would say something so ridiculous. Then it hit him. Emilio! She must know something about Emilio's plans. But what? He'd have to hurry and get Mina back to the protection of Cesca's rented brownstone.

The old woman shook her head sadly and continued, "I tried over and over to tell her it was all the fantasy of a sick mind and the black-haired woman knows nothing about you two, but your wife doesn't believe me."

Mina was sitting rigidly, her hands pressing something into her lap. He watched as she clenched and unclenched her jaw.

"She doesn't look bad, considering what's happened," the old woman said, retying Mina's hat. "Go with your husband now and forget this whole incident."

"Yes, come," Dante said, pleased by the word *husband*. "We will go back uptown." He put his hand under her elbow and urged her up, but Mina's face shrank into itself like a slip of paper set on hot coals. She remained hunched over her white-knuckled hands.

"What is it, little dove? Are you in pain?" he asked, kneeling down.

She didn't respond. The old woman shrugged and turned away. Dante put his books down on the cobbles and gently pried her hands open. Tangled in a woolen scarf, he found Cesca's other seed pearl and ruby earring.

Chapter Twenty-Five

ESCA STILL FELT THE BITE of the rocks on her back from the road she'd fallen upon so long ago. She could still smell the dust. She pushed aside her mandolin and rose from the bed, wiping the tears from the sides of her face. The room had grown dark.

She switched on a light. How different everything would have turned out if only Giulio had been strong and able to stand up to Emilio.

She wouldn't have had to leave Maria in the orphanage or wander as far as Naples to find work. She wouldn't have had to sleep in the open, beg for food, or do any of the degrading things she'd done to stay alive. Maria could have lived on the estate, or she and Giulio could have made a home. But Giulio had not been strong. She'd had to leave her daughter and try to make it alone.

She felt exhausted. When would Dante and Mina arrive? What would she say to Mina when they did? She dropped into a chair to wait and her mind returned once again to those early years.

SEVERAL months after she found work in Naples she happened upon Giulio. He was sitting at a table in front of the Porta Capuana among the vegetable carts and vendors, earning a few *scudi* reading and writing for the illiterate. She almost didn't recognize him. The falling out with his father was allowing depression to gnaw into his spirit the same way the tuberculosis was gnawing into his lungs.

She took him to live in her basement apartment near the waterfront. The damp couldn't have been good for him, but he knew he was dying and it was the only place they could afford. He was too stubborn to take the money left for him on account by his father, and he forbid her to return to the estate for help. He'd lost all interest in life, and only for the sake of his daughter did he rally bravely for a few months.

In the evenings, she wandered among the diners in the waterfront bars, singing and playing her mandolin. In the past she'd occasionally stolen from the customers to get little extras to take to the mountains, but now she stole to pay for Giulio's expensive medicines. The drugs didn't help. The doctor whispered that he needed a sanitarium. In desperation she began to use the men, who made so many indiscreet advances. She had hoped her sacrifice might save Giulio and reunite them as a family, but it wasn't to be.

At the sanitarium before he died, Giulio married her, making their union legal and giving the Lampone name to Maria Grazia. He also gave her the ruby and seed pearl heirlooms he taken the day she'd first left the estate. The necklace and earrings purchased by his great-grandfather in Sicily sealed their union. He put the precious stones around her neck with trembling fingers, but he couldn't fasten the clasp.

"The eldest son gives these to his bride. I'd hoped I would pass them on to our son one day . . . but now, that will never be. Give them to Maria from her father."

He penned a shaky letter telling his father of their marriage and their daughter's birth, insisting on Maria Grazia's right to inherit his portion of the estate. A few days after their marriage he died. She cut a lock of his hair and buried him. All she had left were his pocket watch, the letter, and the seventeenth-century wedding gifts.

Giulio's love had been her shield against shame and the reality of her life, but when he died, anger and grief fixed her eye on a different kind of man. She strummed her mandolin and became brazen, offering the illusion of love to the powerful men who sought her favors. With skillful manipulation she used them for a new goal. Instead of medicine, her body bought influence . . . connections. . . .

Within a few months of Giulio's death, Giuseppina Checci's soft heart was walled up behind a stone facade and Francesca Frascatti had taken her place. On her last trip to the mountains, she saw clearly that her scandalous life and her comings and goings were causing Maria pain. She could take her daughter away, but how could she expect to raise an innocent child in the slums of Naples? She reasoned that if she were dead, Maria would have a normal life and make a happy marriage, so she hardened herself and told the family taking care of Maria that they could adopt her. She instructed them to inform her daughter, when she was old enough, that she'd died of influenza and to give her the earrings and pocket watch. Then she forgot past sorrows and began her climb up fame's dung heap.

She became a gypsy traveling Europe to appear in music halls, on bandstands, and in other venues. Elocution and etiquette lessons followed, allowing her to lose her Neapolitan accent and manners. Her paramours encouraged her, hiring expensive coaches to improve her technique and enhance her interpretation. She was driven by her flayed pride to win a place in society and gain enough power to grind Emilio and his disdain beneath her satin heel.

One evening in a music hall she was "discovered" and taken under the wing of a wealthy impresario. "Your voice," he'd said, "is unique and your beauty too great to escape such subsidy for long. Fame will find you no matter where you hide. I have connections, so why not accept my help, my protection?"

He adored her and dedicated his life to building her career, putting other business interests aside. For two years they traveled across the continent and to South America for performances, but jealousy and a desire for iron control eventually led him to attempt suicide. It wasn't an uncommon story, but it hurt her nonetheless when she was forced to leave him.

She was already notorious, but it wasn't her scandalous reputation that propelled her to stardom—it was an unusual bit of luck. In Paris, while attending an opera she was studying, Cesca was pulled from the audience when the soprano's voice failed. Hastily pinned into the still-warm costume, Cesca was shoved onto the stage. The public loved her bravura performance and the newspapers were filled with the Cinderella triumph. Francesca Frascatti burst like a skyrocket upon the opera world.

Shortly after, she made the acquaintance of Giacomo Puccini. Always a ladies' man, the composer was taken with her spirit and beauty. It was rumored that their love affair served as inspiration for several of his operas, including *Madama Butterfly,* partly based on the story she'd told him about giving up Maria. Giacomo adored her and she him; life became easy.

In a rowboat near Torre del Lago, in late summer, it was easy to drift and forget her purpose. She was resting against silk pillows, enjoying life, the slums forgotten, while Giacomo penned her next great role. Under the shade of a cherry pink umbrella, Maria Grazia was a hazy fantasy that had never really existed. Emilio's censure was submerged beneath undulating reeds. She was *diva assoluta*.

The world lay ready for her, like a naked eager male, but after a few short years her love affair with fame and wealth went limp. One dress was very much like another; a delicious meal pleasing, but ultimately just food to be digested; a rich home and furnishings merely objects that gave shelter and comfort; a new opera role . . . a part to be played . . . for money.

Soft living made her forget vindication and pride. Without the salt of her struggle, the wound scabbed over and was forgotten. Surrounded by fawning hangers-on, she discovered she was bored and lonely. And men . . . After Cesca was forced by the horrible scandal surrounding Giacomo to break off her liaison—his wife had accused him of having an affair with his young housekeeper, the housekeeper had committed suicide and was discovered to be a virgin—after that horrible scandal, all the men in Cesca's life became interchangeable windup toys.

She was now the boots others tried to slip on to climb to opera's high C. There was no one to trust and no one to care for, no one to love— only the vague memory of a daughter she'd given up. At least, she thought, Maria Grazia has remained untainted. Her daughter had a simple but honest life in the mountains. She contented herself with the idea that her sacrifice had meaning.

But after some reflection, she thought she might have made a terrible mistake on her last visit to Rocca San Felice. She decided to sneak back, see her daughter, and make sure she was safe and happy. If she wasn't content, there still might be time to be a proper mother. Why should Maria remain poor if she wasn't happy? Cesca was powerful enough now to face Emilio and reclaim her daughter's birthright. These ideas shot new life into her veins and she acted swiftly.

First she went to visit Emilio. He was cordial at first, not realizing to whom he was speaking. She presented Giulio's letter and showed him the jewelry, but time hadn't changed him; even his son's death had not dented his arrogance. He denounced her once again. She left Giulio's letter and shook Emilio's dust from her heels. She rode on to claim her child, but in Rocca San Felice she made a startling discovery. Her daughter and every trace of the adoptive family had disappeared.

It was then that she realized—

LUCIFER jumped to his feet, his ears cocked, his eyes bright with curiosity. Below she heard voices in the entry. She shoved her mandolin behind the dresses in her closet and glanced at the clock. It was well after five.

"Francesca?" Dante called. She heard a note of alarm in his voice.

"I'm coming down."

She hurriedly descended the stairs to find a disheveled Mina sobbing on the sofa. Her new coat was soiled, and her crushed hat, with its broken feather, sat askew on her head.

"What's happened?" Cesca asked in alarm.

"She's had a little accident in the market. I'm going to call the doctor."

"A doctor? She's hurt?"

He went to the phone as Cesca snatched up a coverlet and rushed to her daughter's side.

"I'm all right, signorina. I . . ." Mina put her head down on the arm of the camelback sofa as Cesca tucked the blanket around her.

"What is it?" Cesca asked gently. "Can you tell me?"

"I don't think you should question her, Cesca. She's a little hys—Dr. DiBella?" Dante turned his back, giving his full attention to the telephone. Cesca untied the ribbon around Mina's neck and smoothed back her hair.

"My husband—Antonio—gave this to his whore," Mina said, thrusting something into Cesca's hand. "Why?"

Mina's eyes were filled with anger and troubled petition. Cesca was shocked to find Giulio's gift lying on her palm.

"Where did you get this?"

"I—I brought them with me from the ship along with the watch that—"

"—you gave to your former fiancé," Cesca finished, feeling a quiet rush of excitement.

"Thank you, doctor," Dante said, hanging up the receiver. Cesca turned to Dante, her open palm outstretched. "Yes," he said. "I've seen it. He's on his way."

"She told you *who* they belong to?"

He shook his head and gave her a look of warning as he poured a brandy. She knew he wanted her to tread carefully.

"Signora DiGianni was attacked in the market by a madwoman wearing those earrings," he said.

Mina's head came up from the sofa's arm. "She admitted she's his mistress and that he only married me on a bet."

"How terrible for you," Cesca said.

"Sip this." Dante held the pony glass to Mina's lips. She coughed as the brandy seared her throat, then pushed the glass aside, trying to shake off the covering, but Dante restrained her and pressed the glass back against her lips. "Drink some more," he urged.

"I suspected them, of course," Mina said. "I saw them together at her saloon. He said he doesn't come home because he's working two jobs, but it's because—"

"You must stay quiet until the doctor comes," Cesca urged.

"—because he loves *her* that he doesn't come home. I've got to see my husband."

"On the way here," Dante said, "she insisted I take her to the board-inghouse where her husband stays."

"You didn't go?" Cesca asked, sounding alarmed.

"She couldn't be dissuaded, but I made her stay in the Pierce. He's gone to meet with some boxer. She wanted to go looking for him, but I convinced her to come back here."

"I have to see him," Mina said, struggling to get up. "He's got to explain why that woman would say such terrible things to me."

"You've had a nasty shock," Cesca soothed. "Be still. A doctor must look at you before you can go anywhere."

"But I don't need a doctor," Mina said, turning away from Cesca. "You'll take me back to Mulberry Street, won't you, Signor Dante?"

"Yes, of course I will."

Cesca regarded Dante as though he'd lost his mind. The look in his eyes indicated she should play along.

"Of course we'll take you there," she said, "but first you must wait for the doctor. Please, do it for my sake." Mina consented and lay limply back. Urgently, Dante motioned Cesca toward the hallway. "I'll make tea," Cesca whispered to Mina. "It will help relax you. I'll be right back."

In the hallway, she regarded the earring in her palm. "This is my earring. Oh, Dante! Maria Grazia has truly been found." She collapsed against him, sobbing with joy. "Our search is over," she continued. "Isn't it wonderful?"

"Yes," he said, but he didn't sound happy. "Cesca, there's more. Kathleen told Mina her husband's selling her to a man wishing to take her back to Italy."

"Emilio!"

"That's what he meant at Delmonico's."

"Then her husband knows about us?" she asked.

"No, he would've forbidden her to work for you. Emilio must be keeping him in the dark, afraid of a tug of war. Antonio and his mistress have gone to the gym. Colombo and I are to meet them"—he paused to look at his watch—"in about fifteen minutes."

"Emilio's planning to leave for Italy on Sunday."

"You'll have to tell her everything immediately."

Cesca looked as stricken as a character from an opera. "Immediately? I can't, I'm not ready."

"She swore to me, 'If what that woman says is true, I'll leave my husband.' "

"That's exactly what we want," Cesca said.

"Yes, but if she confronts him, he'll make sure she doesn't come back to us. He wouldn't lose the opportunity to make money. Tell her the truth while I'm gone." He charged up the stairs, unbuttoning his shirt and cuffs as he went.

"I can't do it alone. Don't leave me."

He leaned over the banister. "I must find out what they're up to. I'll be back as quickly as possible. Get Bevilacqua on the phone. Explain what's happened. Get him to send someone over to guard the house."

Cesca helped Mina to her room and put her to bed. She took the tea things up and sat beside her making small talk, trying to think of a way to break the news, but before long Dr. DiBella arrived. He closed the door and examined Mina while Cesca paced in the hallway.

Later, as Mina was dressing. Dr. DiBella walked Cesca down to the entryway. "She's had a shock, but is uninjured."

"Nothing's broken?"

"No. Can you tell me how she got those fading bruises on her body?"

"Her husband."

The doctor shook his head with disapproval and took a small vial from his bag. He placed it on the table. "Mix this powder with warm milk or broth. You must keep her calm and quiet tonight. She's delicate and small-boned. Another beating like the one she suffered at her husband's hands and . . . well, it will be a difficult pregnancy for her without the shock of physical trauma."

"Pregnancy?" Cesca was dumbfounded.

"About three months, perhaps less. She's small, so it's difficult to ascertain, and she's had some bleeding—I suspect from her former injuries."

"She didn't tell us." This was a terrible complication.

"With the periodic bleeding she wasn't certain. She had been hoping, of course. With what she's told me and the physical examination, I'm almost positive. I have a sample, I will run a test, but you should know there is a risk of miscarriage in her present state. She must be kept from any physical or emotional shocks."

"But I have some very important . . . information. She must be told—"

"If it's something that may upset her, I suggest you save it for a few days. No matter how important it might be."

"Then she should be confined to her bed?"

"No, no, just for tonight. Though small, her body's sturdy; emotion plays a large part in these situations. It's just a precaution. Let her stay occupied with normal household activities. Use the sedative if she becomes overwrought." The doctor put on his coat and hat. Cesca saw him to the door.

"Thank you, Doctor."

"She wants to see her husband and tell him the news, but I've ordered her to remain in bed tonight. She doesn't need a confrontation, especially with that brute. Remember, keep the atmosphere light and unemotional. She needs reassurance and security."

Part II

NOVEMBER 15, 1908

New York City

THE PRICKING

Chapter Twenty-Six

A DRAPED PACKAGE, the size of a side chair, sat on the circular table in the foyer of Cesca's brownstone. The double doors were open and the curtains billowed in the breeze. After a moment Dante appeared in the doorway with a ten-foot Christmas tree bound with twine like a mummy. He half dragged, half threw the tree onto the marble floor and slammed the doors with his foot.

He stared down with disgust at his new pigskin driving gloves covered in dark sticky sap. Ruined. He stripped them off and childishly threw them into the umbrella stand, poking them to the bottom, in the hope of forgetting their existence and the exorbitant amount he'd spent on them at the market only the day before.

After hanging up his coat and hat, he combed his hair and straightened his tie before the hall mirror, savoring the sweet scent of baking wafting from the kitchen. The sound of Cesca singing scales floated down from the music room. He checked his pocket watch; she would be up there practicing for another hour and three-quarters. If he worked quickly he'd have time.

Nervous as a schoolboy about to read a report, he peeked under the canvas cover. He hoped Mina would be pleased with his choice. He'd been vacillating for a week, but the fiasco at the market had decided him. A perfect gift, he thought, as delicate and sweet as Mina herself. He picked up the light but bulky package and headed down the hall to the kitchen.

Mina was mincing onions at the chopping block, her hair pinned up, her dress covered by a long bib apron. Her red nose and swollen eyes showed she'd been crying a good part of the morning, and Dante knew it had nothing to do with the onions. She'd be made of wood if she didn't cry, he thought. Finding out, in the vilest manner possible, that your husband doesn't love you and is planning on selling you, who wouldn't cry?

"Good morning, little dove. I see you've gotten an early start," he said, regarding her fresh pasta hanging over broomstick handles to dry.

"There you are," Mina said, quickly turning. She wiped her eyes on her apron. "Onions always make me cry," she laughed. "The Signorina was asking for you. You left without coffee."

"I had a few errands."

"You can have a cup now," she said, forcing a smile and indicating the pot on the back burner. "I made fresh espresso for Signor Caruso."

In the morning's excitement he'd forgotten Errico was coaching Cesca for her role as Cio-Cio-San in *Madama Butterfly*. Errico had been touting his special breathing technique for years and Cesca had finally caved in and asked to learn it. Dante knew he'd have to act quickly. Jack Johnson and his wife would arrive in a few hours for lunch and *Tre Sette*.

"Coffee will be perfect, it's frigid outside."

Mina heated some milk for *caffè latte,* his favorite morning coffee. "What do you have there?" she asked, eyeing the cloth-covered mound.

"A little something for you."

"For me?"

With a flourish he removed the covering. Inside the three-tiered split bamboo cage a nervous little yellow bird flitted from perch to perch, twittering loudly.

"Oh, Dante! How wonderful!" she cried, looking into the gilded pagoda that was almost as big as she was. "She's so delicate."

For the first time she'd forgotten her formal address. It was a good omen. He so wanted to take away the pain he knew she must feel. As they watched, the bird took a turn on one of the unstable swings, then hopped from perch to perch, and finally grasped the bamboo bars of the cage. Joy and wonder replaced worry and pain on her face.

"How do you know it's a she?" he asked, amused.

"She looks like a she . . . oh, she's lovely." Her eyes were shining with delight.

"I neglected to ask the sex, but the shopkeeper assured me . . . she can sing beautifully."

"She sings?"

"Yes, and she's from the tropics, so you must keep her warm. I thought it might be nice for you to have company."

Mina slipped a fingertip through the slats to stroke the tail. The bird's reaction was swift. "Ouch!"

"Be careful. She has a sharp little beak."

"She must be hungry," she said, inspecting her undamaged finger.

"I bought some seed and a stand. They're in the Pierce. I'll fetch them later. What will you call her?" He cracked the oven to see what she was baking.

"How about Inquisitive Dante?" she asked, bumping the oven door closed with her hip. She took the hot milk from the stove and wagged her finger in his face. "That's *my* surprise!" She poured him the promised coffee.

"Ah, to be a loved pet, with an endless supply of seed and a kind mistress."

"You'd tire of a cage, even a big one like this."

"Never," he said, stirring some sugar into his cup. "If you were the keeper, a tiny cage would feel like a universe."

She watched as the canary cocked its head from side to side. "That's very poetic, but I think you don't know how it feels to be in a cage." Her voice was melancholy and her eyes glistened with tears. Here was the very emotion he'd been hoping to banish.

"Let's open the door and set her free." He playfully whisked up the cage. It was light as dry cork without its cover, but she snatched it away. The bird squawked and flapped.

"No, no . . . she'll freeze outside. She's all alone. I must take care of her. I'll make her happy, and in the summer . . . if she's still sad, I'll set her free."

"Shouldn't we set her free now?"

Mina shook her head and set the cage down. "She has nowhere to go," she said.

"You must find her a name. How about Peeper?"

"She's going to sing, not peep like a chick," she replied indignantly.

They watched as the canary puffed out her chest. With her beak she enthusiastically cleaned her feathers and stroked her wings.

"She preens just like a diva," Signor Dante said. "Diva! That's a perfect name."

Mina laughed. The bird did give as much attention to her feathers as the Signorina did to her toilet. "Prima Donna," she said, "because she'll sing as sweetly as the Signorina." Mina clicked her tongue and made kissing noises. "Sing, Prima Donna. Sing!" She waited, feeling a bit disappointed when the bird didn't respond. "Will she sing?"

"Not on cue. But I think when she's happy and adjusted she'll sing."

He took the cage. Mina scooped up the onions to add to the skillet. "Prima Donna must be hungry. You should get her food from the automobile." She was humming as she stirred the onions. Dante felt relieved—her sorrow seemed momentarily forgotten. He slipped his jacket onto the back of a chair, rolled up his sleeves, and soaped his hands in the sink.

Now the next step. He'd planned to give her the pet, cheer her up, and then broach the subject of yesterday afternoon, but now as he dried his hands he realized the hopeless inadequacy of his little present. How could he hope to offset the discovery of her husband's villainy with a canary? He stalled, pawing noisily through the pantry's bottom cabinets, feeling like a fool. "I brought an early Christmas tree for you and Cesca to decorate later," he told her.

His plan, hatched in the early morning hours, had been to suggest that Mina stay at the brownstone indefinitely. He'd bring up the subject early in the day, explaining how badly Cesca needed her help. Good, honest help was impossible to find, and Cesca had grown very fond of her.

She'd have the afternoon to mull things over, and then, in the evening after the card party, as they were decorating the tree, Dante would withdraw. Cesca would stress the importance of getting away from her violent husband for the sake of her child. Hopefully children and mothers would be discussed, breaking ground for the revelation and reunion later in the week.

"I need a saw and hammer. Where are tools kept in this house?"

Mina stepped back, avoiding the hot grease spitting from the sausages. "In the cellar."

In the dry cellar he found what he needed quickly, but resisted returning. Fear of saying the wrong thing sat heavily on his heart. He wanted so much to protect her from further harm. He had a plan of his own, but he didn't know how she'd receive it.

Last night, after several sherries, he'd gotten the courage to mention it to Cesca. Surprisingly she'd been open to his suggestion, but she'd cautioned him to wait. It had all seemed so logical and easy last night in Cesca's room.

Hammer in hand, he entered the kitchen purposefully. Talk to her immediately, he thought. Get it over with quickly. No use dillydallying. But when he saw her face he changed his mind. He set down his tools and rushed, coatless, out the back door. "I'll get the stand and seed."

He returned, but avoided her eyes as he handed her the packet of seed. He hurried out to the sitting room to set up the stand and stall a little longer.

While Mina was adding the tomatoes and finishing the sauce, she wondered what might be troubling Signor Dante. He suddenly seemed so shy and uncertain.

She took her cake from the oven, stoked the fire, and added more fuel. Then she put the tied roast in the oven and turned the sauce to simmer. She folded her apron and placed it over a chair. She only had to add the potatoes and carrots and decorate the cake. Everything was ready.

Carefully she lifted the birdcage and went to ask Signor Dante what was wrong. He'd set up the stand next to the sitting room window. From that vantage point, Prima Donna would see the trees and feel the sunshine. As Mina hung the pagoda on its hook she could hear him cursing softly as he struggled with the tree in the entry. She decided to wait until he'd finished, and instead put a handful of seed in the feeder. The bird immediately began showering the bottom of the cage with husks.

"Maybe after your stomach is full you'll sing, eh?" Mina asked her little charge.

She checked the sunny room. Every detail for the card party was in order: ashtrays for the men's cigars, several decks of gilt-edged cards, a thick pad and two silver pens for scoring, and on the side tables, dishes of candies, fruit, and nuts. Mina would bring in champagne when the guests arrived. Now she had a little time to work on her lace and try to think.

She began to twist and knot her threads, advancing the pins of the Duke's Garter swiftly. It was one of her favorite patterns, and lately, as she worked on its simple yet elegant design, she thought of Signor Dante. Hadn't the Signorina said he was a duke disowned? Normally she'd have lost herself in fantasies of him, following the tough gimp thread as it wound its way through the delicate webbing, but today her lace couldn't take away the vile images and revelations of yesterday.

She tossed bobbins and placed pins, floating straws of hope in her mind. Perhaps, she thought, the woman isn't really his mistress but insane, like the old woman said . . . or maybe he needed cash and sold the earrings—the woman purchased them and concocted a story. No, no, she thought, too far-fetched. If she continued to grasp at ridiculous self-deceptions she would drown. I must face the truth, she thought. Antonio's a cruel, callous man who never loved me.

She looped her thread under the gimp thread, gave it a twist, and set in another pin. Tomorrow morning, early, I'll find him and confront him with the earring. I'll tell him I'm pregnant . . . perhaps he'll get rid of that woman and settle down. Won't a child make him return home and become a proper husband?

With each shift of the bobbins she heard the old woman say, "She says your husband is selling you!" It was a preposterous idea. A husband couldn't do such a thing; besides, who would buy her? Slavery had been abolished. His mistress—how she hated the word—was only trying to upset her, to scare her away so she could have Antonio for herself. She would say anything to get him.

"He's selling you, selling your. . . ." He couldn't be that vile. She pulled the bobbin too hard and broke the thread. With it her denial snapped and she dropped her shoulders in defeat. She knew she was deluding herself. Her shaky fingers tied and trimmed the reef knot, the fine threads blurred out of focus as tears filled her eyes. She stabbed her scissors back into her basket, squeezed her eyes shut, and wiped them with the backs of her hands so as not to dirty the lace.

No tears, she ordered herself sternly. It doesn't help to get weepy. When she began again her eyes caught the dull gleam of her wedding band. She could still hear Signor Dante in the entry working on the tree. Prima Donna greedily cracked seeds. Her eyes shifted from her ring to the birdcage.

He's worried about me and purchased the little bird to cheer me up. Signor Dante cares for me ... cares what happens to me. ... She stopped. How could Signor Dante care about her? A duke in love with a *contadina*? How ridiculous ... another stupid delusion. She'd foolishly believed Antonio loved her, even though he'd treated her with little regard. Now her muddled brain wanted to believe an elegant gentleman loved her. Absurd!

She worked the bobbins fiercely, irritated with herself for inventing such fantasies. The flash of sunlight bouncing off her ring repeatedly caught her eye. Antonio's wife ... Antonio's wife ... it shouted as it flickered. Trapped, trapped ... as trapped as the little canary in the golden pagoda. She gazed at Prima Donna sitting on her swing. It wasn't the cage that trapped Prima Donna. No, it was that she'd been taken from her real world and had nowhere to go.

Where could she herself go? *If* what the woman said about her husband was true, it meant he was an evil man who'd deceived her. She wasn't the only one living a lie. In God's eyes they'd never been married. She wrapped her arms around her body, feeling in the pit of her heart that his mistress had spoken the truth. He was planning to get rid of her and she was in danger. She should get a divorce and take her chances. She needed to free herself. Her fingers twisted the band of gold.

But what of her pregnancy, confirmed last night? How could she make her child a bastard? Who would rent a room to a lone pregnant woman? She could claim to be a widow, but she'd have to work to survive. Who would care for the child while she worked? She'd need to find a man willing to marry her even if she carried another man's child.

She thought of Mario. He'd been gracious even after she'd rejected him. Yesterday in the market she'd seen he still cared, and he would probably marry her if she wanted. Oh, what a fool she'd been. She'd been fooled by romantic illusion and stupidly rejected an honorable man for a young girl's fancy. True love?

Reality dictated that people marry for practical reasons, to raise a family or, if they had wealth, to form an alliance. She should have known better. All over the world marriages were arranged without love, and people accepted their mates and married. That's how the bargain with Mario had been reached—love hadn't entered into it—but she hadn't wanted a loveless marriage. She still hoped, someday ...

She twisted the band off and stared at it. The Signorina came to mind. How she envied her. She had everything—a career to support herself, the love of Signor Dante. . . . She didn't have a child, but surely she could have one if she wanted. She would make a kind and generous mother. And Signor Dante? Signor Dante was a dream come true . . . he would be a perfect father. . . .

In her mind she saw his smiling eyes and they transported her back to her fantasies. Whether she was alone under the dowry sheets at her Mulberry Street apartment or asleep under the canopy of the bed on the fourth floor, she dreamed each night of being Dante's wife. It was his fiery kisses she wanted on her lips and his gentle hands she longed for on her body, even if those desires made her a brazen whore.

Chapter Twenty-Seven

*W*HETHER SHE RESISTED HIM in her dreams or boldly took charge, at some point she always melted passionately into his arms. The heat invoked by such visions caused her to kick the covers from the bed, awakening her with a chill. After retrieving the blankets, she would lie awake guiltily savoring the images until she fell back to sleep.

In the morning, shamed by her imagined transgressions, she wouldn't look at her flushed face in the mirror as she brushed her hair. For a while, loyalty to the Signorina and embarrassment at her wicked nature kept the images from her mind, but as she moved through the day the passionate images stole back into her mind.

Since coming to the house it had gotten worse. As she dusted the beautiful porcelains or drew back the lace curtains or laid logs in the marble fireplace, it was easy to think she lived in an altered universe. Her fantasies whispered that she could be Dante's wife in this house. As she made up the beds she wondered how he'd touch her if they lay beneath the sheets and made love . . . how he'd undress her, where his lips would linger, and where his fingers would trespass, would he moan in the throes of passion if—

"Signora Filomina?"

She jumped at the sound of her name. "*Sant'Anna!*" she cried as the ring slipped from her fingers. It rushed across the polished floorboards, rolling on end. "Signor Dante, you scare me. I no look for you," she murmured in English.

He quickly retrieved her ring. It surprised her that he didn't give it back. "Sorry, I didn't mean to frighten you, but I've been speaking. You didn't answer."

He seemed upset. She tried hard to remember the English words that he was teaching her. It always pleased him when she tried to speak them. "Something is wrong?"

His face softened and he smiled warmly. "Let's speak in Italian today. It'll be easier that way."

"Sure. I practice Italian too."

"I want to talk to you about what happened yesterday in the market."

The pain of the incident rushed back to fill her throat like hot bread. She turned back to her lace and fussed with the bobbins, rewinding and straightening the threads. She didn't want Signor Dante to see how helpless she felt.

"Cesca and I are hoping you'll stay here for the time being. She needs help with the house, it's difficult to get trustworthy servants, and she's so fond of you. She's a little nervous about approaching you, afraid you'll say no."

"Well, I've been thinking, Signor Dante, that I might return to my village."

"Yes, of course, but last night after . . . The doctor, ah . . . he told Cesca about the child. Well, we thought perhaps you might postpone any decision for a few weeks, until Cesca finishes her contract. If you stay, she's promised a generous bonus. It'll help with your expenses to Italy, and you'll be safe here, away from your husband and, ah . . . that woman."

She could feel a vein throbbing at the base of her throat. She put her hand against it to calm her nerves. Of course, she thought, the doctor would have discussed my condition. It embarrassed her that Signor Dante knew she was pregnant. She took up her bobbins and began to work the lace, shoving the pins into the pillow quickly, crossing and knotting, doing her best to shut out the whirling emotions his suggestions evoked. "I must talk to Antonio."

"Do you think that's wise?"

"He's my husband. No matter what I decide, I must tell him about his child. But I also want to know if what that woman said is true."

"In your heart you know the answer."

"I want to hear it from his own mouth. That he stole my earrings from my bureau and gave them to his whore. I want him to tell me to my face that he was planning to sell me to some old man."

The vehemence in her voice surprised him. "And then?"

Prima Donna chirped. Mina turned to look at the canary. It cocked its head as though waiting for her to answer. She felt a hard coldness creep over her. "I wasn't sure"—her voice was low, almost inaudible—"about the baby. He must decide if he wants to know his child." She felt Signor Dante watching her as she flipped a cloth over her lace, to keep it free of dust, and got up. "You and the Signorina have been kind to me, but this isn't my home. If he doesn't care about his own flesh and blood, I'll return to my village."

Now was his chance. He and Cesca had worked it all out. "Why not stay with us indefinitely, signora?"

"What would I do? I'm not a trained domestic servant."

"Surely you realize you're not a servant. You're a friend . . . a helper. I—Cesca loves having you here."

She shook her head uncertainly and went to the window. The sun coming through the shirred curtains cast her face in dappled shadow. She seemed very far away from him. "I've been weak and foolish, thinking I was a lily in the field, believing *Gesù* would provide, if only I were meek enough. Now I must take up a jawbone, wage a war, fight for my child. If Antonio won't take responsibility, I'll go back and make my own way."

"No one doubts your courage, but I want to suggest—"

"He wants another woman, I can live with that, but I know how it feels to be alone in a strange place . . . to be no one . . . because of your past . . . and to yearn for something . . . something you believe you can never have. I won't let my child suffer the same fate."

"I hope you'll consent to stay with us while you decide what to do. Will you?" Dante held his breath, his heart as tender as a lace maker's pillow stuck through with pins, as she considered the proposal.

"I'll stay, but only until the end of the Signorina's contract. I want to be in Italy for the birth of my child."

He sighed, relieved; he'd gotten past the first hurdle. "Thank you. You'll make Cesca very happy." He slipped the wedding band he'd been clutching into his waistcoat pocket and swallowed hard in an effort to push down the nervous lump in his throat. "Signora Filomina," he ventured, "I want to offer an alternate suggestion to your going back alone to Italy."

"Alternate?"

"What if someone wanted to take care of you?"

She turned to look at him, confusion plain upon her face. "Take care of me?"

"Yes, there are other men who are in a position to help you raise your baby."

He saw uncertainty leave her face as disdain swept over it. Her laugh sounded bitter and her eyes flashed like diamonds in the sunlight.

Mina was strangely moved by the sincerity she saw in his eyes. He means well, she thought, but his lofty ideas are borrowed from his books. He doesn't understand the real world or its sordid ways. He believes in brave heroes who fight dragons and save damsels in distress. I'm no damsel, she thought. Real men run from my kind of trouble. They want easy adventures and untouched women, not women with swollen bellies. A pregnant woman with a violent husband was at the top of the list of adventures to be avoided. She knew he wanted to ease her fears, but no one in the real world was going to step forward and rescue her. She adjusted the feeder on the cage and sighed.

"Who would want a woman pregnant with another man's child?" she asked.

"I, for one, would want to keep you safe . . . I'd want to help raise your child."

For an instant, hope cut into her heart like a cruel thread, but she knew it was pity he felt. He was trying to give her hope to go on. "You live in books, Signor Dante," she said. "People despise men who offer such kindness."

"Would you?"

Prima Donna hopped to the feeder. Mina watched the bird pick at the seed, refusing to meet his eyes. He was cultured, handsome, rich. Eager young women came backstage every night seeking the Signorina's autograph, and if he chose to be disloyal to her, he could have any one of them. Even a man like him would never dare to take on a problem like hers.

"A wise man must choose better," she murmured, "when he can have his choice."

"Men don't want paper dolls cut for today's fashion," he said.

The thread sank in a little deeper, tangling around her heart, making it beat in an odd, jerky way. Was he trying to say there were men who might want to keep her? Take care of her and her child in exchange for sexual favors? Like the men in Italy? Perhaps like the man her husband had been planning to sell her to?

"You're wrong. Men must have women who fit them like clothes cut for those dolls."

"I'm not saying I'm the one. If you were free there would be others who have the resources to care for you—"

"If I were free I'd only want you."

The words were out in an instant, blowing away her carefully clutched facade like smoke. His turbulent face and startled eyes showed how badly she'd blundered. She was a clumsy fool. He'd been saying if . . . if . . . supposing, giving her hope. She'd meant to reply in kind, but the truth had slipped out. Oh, *Sant'Anna,* she thought, I know he doesn't really want me, he only feels sorry for me, but now he'll think I've taken his ideas seriously.

"I meant I *would* want you," she said hurriedly. "Someone like you. You're trying to make me feel better, I know, because I'm with child."

She fumbled, becoming as stiff as a frozen petticoat on a clothesline. "I thank you for your kindness."

She couldn't look at him now. Not after she'd been so foolish as to reveal her heart. She put her hand out. "Please, give me back my ring. I need to go back to the kitchen and check the roast." She had to get away—get away before she said something else she'd regret.

"Signora—"

"This conversation's foolish, I—" She slipped past him and hurried toward the hall.

"Stop!" he cried. "I need you to listen to me."

The urgency in his voice made her pause, but she didn't turn around. "Signor Dante, wealthy gentlemen don't keep pregnant peasants," she said coldly. "They cast them out to fend for themselves. Ask the Signorina, she'll tell you what I say is true."

"Mina . . . I don't want to keep you. I'd never do that. I want to marry you."

The statement hit her in the stomach like a full scuttle of coal. It buckled her knees. She was sure she hadn't heard him properly. She turned and saw that he was flushed with excitement, his eyes wide with expectancy, and an uncertain smile hung on his lips.

"What—what did you say?"

"I want to marry you and take care of you and your child."

The blood seemed to rush from her toes to her head. Its force pushed every thought and sensation out. How strange, she thought. Such an extraordinary statement, and everything seems so dull and colorless.

Dante saw an odd yet blissful expression cross her face. Then her eyelids fluttered and she collapsed. He caught her before she hit the floor and berated himself as he set her down in a wing chair. Damn it! The doctor had told him not to upset her. Cesca had warned him to wait. He dampened his handkerchief in a vase on the mantle and placed it on her forehead. He thought about fetching Cesca, but in a moment she stirred.

"Are you all right?" he asked, blocking her retreat. "You fainted."

"I did?" She lifted a hand to the damp cloth, unable to remember how she'd gotten into the chair or what had just taken place. "I'm so sorry. It must be because of all the preparations. Perhaps I have a fever." She put a hand on her cheek. "I've been cooking and rushing. . . ." She laughed, remembering that they'd been talking about her duties and staying in the house. "I must be overheated."

It took another moment for her thoughts to travel to his proposal. I must have dreamed it when I fainted, she thought and laughed at such a foolish idea. "I guess I had a dream. When I fainted, I thought you . . . Well, it's witless what I thought—"

He picked up her hands and held them very tightly. He leaned toward her and she wondered what the matter was. "I know the timing's bad, I wish it could be under better circumstances, but I want to marry you."

She straightened up and the cloth fell to her lap. It hadn't been a dream. "Don't say such things. When Signorina Frascatti hears she'll—"

"About Cesca and me I . . . well, you know, there's a big difference in our ages. . . . Ah, for two years I have been covering for—. You see, there's a woman she's been searching for. . . ."

Mina's face spoke of her confusion. He stopped to think for a moment. He was rushing to get it out and upsetting her, but anything he essayed in his mind led immediately to the disclosure that Cesca was her mother and he, a detective in her employ.

He tried again with more restraint. "Everyone thinks I'm a cad and that my life with Cesca's scandalous," he said, chuckling. "All the affairs . . . it's amusing, really, because the real shock is we're not lovers. Our relationship's only for show and the newspapers. There have always been other women in my life as there have been men in hers. She pays me to—"

Mina looked thoroughly frightened by what he was saying.

"Damn it! I'm making a mess of it, but you must realize that all this . . . this relationship nonsense is a facade."

"Please," she said, trembling, "the Signorina has been so good to—"

"Cesca knows how I feel about you. She's known for some time. We discussed it last night and she agrees. She thinks we'll be happy together—"

"Approves? That you leave her? That you support me? No, no, no! I don't want your pity."

"Pity? What does pity have to do with it?"

"It's impossible! Please, I know you're trying to be kind, but this is hurting me. . . . You don't know how I—" She finally pushed his arm aside and escaped from the chair. "I'll leave today, I'll go back to Mulberry Street."

"You can't go back there, you're in danger. Your husband's planning—"

"Stop it!" Anger flashed through her. "I may be poor and ignorant, but I'm not helpless. You don't need to say things you don't mean. This kind of talk is foolish. It's for fantasies . . . operas. You don't understand what you're suggesting."

"Fantasies? Mina, from the first day—"

He put his hands on her shoulders, but she pushed him away. "No! Don't say any more! Let me go!"

"What's all this excitement about?" Cesca asked in English, striding into the room with Errico lagging behind. One look at Dante's sheepish face told Cesca he'd bungled his assignment. Mina glanced at her fearfully, looking pale and sick as she steadied herself by holding the side table. Cesca hurried forward to put an arm around her waist. "Dante! Have you forgotten DiBella's orders?"

"Who, may I ask, is this fiery beauty with the flashing eyes?" Errico asked.

"This is Signora Filomina DiGianni," Cesca said in Italian, guiding her forward. "And this is the great Enrico Caruso."

Errico bowed. "Such a lovely young lady, I hope you'll quickly become a friend of my heart."

Mina's body trembled in Cesca's arms as they exchanged pleasantries. Cesca regarded Dante sternly. He winced slightly, but his tone was defiant.

"We've had a little misunderstanding," he said. "Signora DiGianni's set on returning to her home."

Cesca couldn't believe her ears. Returning home? She'd been unwise to trust such an important discussion to lovesick Dante. What had he done? If she could get Mina alone, perhaps she could smooth things over. "You're not going this very moment? With guests coming?"

"Of course not, signorina. I can leave after lunch. If you'll excuse me I'll check on the preparations."

Like a marionette, Mina turned to Dante and held out her hand. "May I have my ring?"

Dante fished her wedding ring out of his pocket. She snatched it and hurried out.

"What were you doing with her ring? What have you done to her?"

"It looks like a lover's spat to me," Errico chuckled, helping himself to a sugared date. "Have you been playing Don Giovanni?"

Cesca gave Errico's hand a slap. He dropped the fruit back onto its platter.

"What does Mina mean, she's leaving after the card party?" she demanded.

"She'd rather return to that savage husband of hers than marry me."

"Marry you?" Errico asked, glancing back and forth between the two. "Why, my dear Cesca," he said, chuckling at her discomfort, "it seems your fiancé has defected for a housemaid. How very operatic of you, Signor Dante."

Chapter Twenty-Eight

*I*MMEDIATELY AFTER TAKING BACK her ring, Mina rushed into the kitchen with her mind churning. She fumbled around, vacillating between hope and fear as she finished the last-minute details of the meal with a thousand questions shooting through her mind. Could it be that Signor Dante really did care for her and wanted to take care of her and the baby? Or was it just his poetic nature and soft heart? She didn't have long to consider the question, for within moments the door chimes sounded and she rushed to the foyer to open the door.

She was surprised and a bit frightened to find an ebony giant with flashing gold teeth standing on the porch holding a bouquet of bright flowers. The first Negro she'd ever seen had been on the ship coming over. She'd been curious, but didn't have a chance to get up close. Later she'd seen Negroes on the fringes of the Essex Street Market displaying their wares on blankets. Once, she'd purchased a squash from a Negro woman, but while she was getting the coin out of her purse the police had appeared. The woman snatched up her blanket and ran off.

She was curious about the dark people her neighbors called *melanzani,* eggplants. The whites made nasty remarks about how they smelled and lived and told her they were stupid and lazy. Teresa had even whispered, "Stay away from the men. All they want to do is have sex with white women." She'd kept her distance and learned quickly that blacks and whites never mixed. It took her a moment to notice the elegantly dressed white woman on the Negro's arm.

He said something to Mina and winked, but she didn't understand.

While she stood gaping, Lucifer brushed past and playfully jumped up on the Negro, knocking him back. He laughed and stroked Lucifer's coat as Mina struggled to pull the cat back. Then the Signorina appeared and introductions were made: "This is Jack Johnson and his fiancée, Etta Duryea. The man I told you would come to play cards. Come in, I've been expecting you."

Mina took charge of the coats and hats. The Signorina had told her to expect company, but had said nothing of this unique pairing. Dante and Errico greeted Jack and Etta warmly and exchanged pleasantries while Mina openly stared. Cesca sent Mina to put the flowers in water and bring back the champagne as everyone, including Lucifer, made his way to the card room to play *Tre Sette*.

Mina escaped into the kitchen. She cut the stems and arranged the flowers, then set up the champagne the way the Signorina had shown her, but she dreaded having to go back to the group. Although they'd included her in the merriment, she'd felt jittery and false, like a boxed puppet on a spring. She didn't know how to behave among these exotic people, and now she felt terribly awkward around Signor Dante and the Signorina.

She swallowed hard, reminding herself that she only had to make it through lunch. She took up the ice bucket and champagne, thinking Signor Dante's proposal couldn't be more taboo than a marriage between the black giant and the fragile, aristocratic white woman. When she came into the room, clutching the flowers in one hand and the ice bucket and champagne in the other, Signor Caruso jumped to help her. He managed to make everything she did appear effortless as she opened the bottle and poured out the glasses.

She kept her eyes on Signor Caruso as they made toasts, but she couldn't help darting looks at Jack Johnson's fiancée. She seemed so happy. Was it possible to find happiness with someone so different from you? What if Signor Dante knew about the lies she'd told? Would he still smile at her, the way Jack Johnson's fiancée smiled when she looked at her unique partner? Out of the corner of her eye Mina saw Signor Dante moving in her direction. She quickly excused herself and slipped out the door.

It made her cringe to think he might find out about her past. She knew he'd run away as fast as any other man if he knew the details of her life in Italy. Then there was the Signorina. When she'd come into the room with Signor Caruso and caught them together she'd been furious. Even though Dante believed their relationship was all for show, the Signorina didn't. Mina's heart sank as she thought he might have lied to her.

She felt sure he'd only offered his help to take the sting out of her terrible discovery in the market. He'd reconsider his offer. Even an idealist like Signor Dante wouldn't be happy with a woman like her. He couldn't forgive her past and create a scandal by marrying her. It was a preposterous idea.

She fretted in the kitchen until Signor Caruso came in rubbing his hands together briskly, a wicked grin upon his face. She'd just taken the roast out of the oven and was putting it on the sideboard to rest.

"Etta and I trounced Cesca again. She plays *Tre Sette* like she sings *Tosca:* all fire, no finesse."

The Signorina crowded into the kitchen after him. "Look who's talking about finesse! Your Pagliacci's nothing but melodramatic ham. You haven't a subtle bone in your entire body."

"Ah!" he cried, dropping to one knee on the tiles. He grabbed Cesca's skirt to dry his eyes and put his other hand over his heart. "Your critique has sliced me to the hock!"

"*Buffone!* Get up! Next week you'll weep in earnest, when I offer you a generous helping of crow."

Mina laughed at his melodrama. Signor Caruso was such a nice man;

she knew he was trying to lighten her mood. He groaned as the Signorina pulled him to his feet.

"Now, Mina," he said, turning to her eagerly, "let's get the pasta pot boiling. I'm starving!" He pushed the Signorina toward the door. "Go! We great cooks have great secrets. Don't come back till you're called!"

It wasn't long before the water was rumbling in the pot and Mina was heaping linguine noodles into the salted water. Signor Caruso had tied one of her aprons loosely around his middle and was twirling a slotted spoon, chatting about his love of fine food and his abilities in the kitchen.

"Never add oil to the water to keep the pasta from sticking, like the Americans do," he said. "It coats the pasta and the sauce slips right off to lie miserably in the bottom of the dish."

"Signor Enrico, may I ask you a question?"

"Please, please! Mina, my dear, no Signor and call me *Err*-ico. The way my friends do."

She went to get more noodles. "Very well, *Err*-ico, have you known Signorina Frascatti a long time?"

"A very long time. We met years ago at the Café dei Mannesi in Naples when we were both struggling singers working for a few lira."

"Was she always—?"

"Hard-headed? Yes!" he said, waving his wooden spoon. "She only gets worse with each success. I told her then that she was gulping air, she—"

"No, no. I mean free with her lovers . . . with men?"

Her fingers were trembling when she dropped the last of the noodles into the pot. Errico interpreted her blushing face and downcast eyes. He'd been thoughtless. She obviously feared Cesca's hold over Dante. "Oh, you're referring to her arrangement with Dante."

There it was, he'd said "arrangement." So he was aware of the situation.

"That's just for the newspapers and prying eyes."

"Oh!" Mina cried. "That's exactly what Signor Dante told me."

"You thought him a liar?"

She shook her head and weakly sat down, pressing her apron to her face to hide her shame. "I mean I didn't, but I thought perhaps I'd misunderstood. I can't believe that she . . . that he could be . . . that he wouldn't be interested in—"

"Cesca?"

"Yes . . . but . . . do you know he asked me—?"

"You mustn't worry. She's not his type at all. She's too bossy! With her temperament he's had a tough time these last two years, I'll tell you that. But frankly he knows how much she needs him, so he's patient with her. He's not really an artist, even though he paints, so her artistic temperament is unsettling. He's more a philosopher. Loves hunting, boxing, mucking around in the dirt like a farmer. . . . He absolutely hates opera. Imagine how that makes her feel?"

"He's never been, ah, involved with her?"

"No, no."

Mina didn't believe him. How could Signor Dante not be involved with the Signorina?

"Then why does he travel with her and live in her house?"

"Oh, she pays him very well," he said.

"Is . . . is there something wrong with him?"

"Wrong with Dante?" he laughed. "In the two years I've known him he's had his fill of petticoats . . . I mean, until now."

Her face had turned the color of a scalded shrimp. He handed her a strand of linguini to test, then crouched, in his patent leathers, to look into her eyes. He rested a hand on her knee, to keep his balance.

"But I thought you said she and Signor Dante had an arrangement?"

"He's a detective. Didn't you know?" She looked very surprised and shook her head. He got up quickly, realizing his mistake. "Well, perhaps I shouldn't have told you," he said, stirring the pot. "You'll keep that between us, won't you? I hate to deal with Cesca in a temper."

"Signor Dante's a detective?"

"Yes. But you didn't hear that from me."

She put the strainer in the sink, wondering what the Signorina was doing with a detective. Errico was humming as he lifted the heavy pot off the stove. Now all the funny little awkward scenes she'd witnessed between them began to make sense. So he was a detective . . . of course that would put them in close proximity. But did it mean they weren't involved? Perhaps he did care for her after all. Why did the Signorina need a detective? She tried to think of a way to ask Errico what Dante was detecting while she cut cheese into manageable pieces for grating.

"I want to say one thing," Errico said, resting the pot on the edge of the sink. "And I hope you'll forgive my butting in, but . . . Dante is in love with you. If you haven't succumbed to his charms already, you should. I encourage you to accept his proposal immediately."

"Signor Caruso! I'm a married woman."

"So? My Ada's married. Italian law may have stopped me from making her my legal wife, but it can't stop me from loving her."

She came forward with the pasta dish and cocked an eye at him. He was confessing that he was in love with a married woman and thought it was suitable? As she warmed the dish with ladles of hot water from the pot she thought her whole world was turning upside down. If she agreed with him, what would happen to morals and rules?

"Has Dante done something terrible by loving you?"

"No, but it's an indecent suggestion, to live with a man without being married."

"But this is America," Errico said as he started to dump the contents. "What if you married him?"

"Without an annulment, God says it's a sin."

He rested the heavy pot back on the edge of the sink. "Ah, ah, ah! Be careful what 'God says.' Sin has little to do with God and a great deal to do with sanctimonious idiots and politics. Why should people who are miserable together be forced to stay married? Should the Holy Church force us into a lifetime of mental and physical sin? God surely didn't intend for His creatures to live in pain, sneaking around to satisfy the natural urges He invented for them."

"That particular urge was meant to be controlled," Mina asserted.

He cleared his throat, taken aback by her tone, and dumped the linguini.

"Of course it is, but I'm talking about man's desire for joy, communion, mutual respect, and friendship . . . his desire for peace and serenity."

The steam swirled around them and evaporated. Hope struggled with the doubt in her breast as she ladled sauce onto the pasta. Would God condemn her to hell for loving Signor Dante?

"Love is capricious," Errico said. "We don't choose who we're going to fall in love with."

He was right; she hadn't chosen to love Signor Dante.

"I tell you this because I suspect you feel the same way about him. It *would* be a sin to discard a man so worthy, because of antiquated beliefs. You know, sometimes we're supplied with a solution we never anticipated."

He left to call the party to the table, and within a few moments the tensions and worries she'd been feeling over the past few hours began to dissolve. At the Signorina's insistence she was seated as a guest next to Signor Dante, and one by one they passed their plates to the head of the table where Errico dramatically lifted strands of sauced linguini into minihaystacks.

Signor Dante played waiter with a towel over his arm and grated cheese for each person as the Signorina poured the rich Barolo Mina had purchased at the market the day before. The first course was devoured with gusto and a smattering of chatter, but gaiety broke out in earnest when she brought out the succulent roast served with golden oven roasted potatoes.

"This is delightful!" the Signorina cried. "I'm so pleased my cook ran off. I'm having more fun than I've had in years."

"Your cook ran off?" Etta asked.

"Yes, it seems she and Dante's valet were stuffing *calzoni* in the kitchen," Errico joked as he tore off a hunk of bread and handed the remainder to Mina.

She broke off a piece and turned to pass it to Signor Dante.

"Signora Filomina has kindly consented to . . . to help us," Dante said, "ah, in the meantime."

Mina put her hand on Dante's arm to get his attention and passed him the flat loaf of bread. When his eyes met hers, she held his gaze and smiled, shaking her head slightly and fluttering her lashes boldly. She hoped he could see she wasn't angry anymore. The boldness of her actions sent a current of excitement through her veins.

"Mina has a firm, even hand with the rolling pin," Errico said, tucking his napkin in his collar. "And knows how to cook pasta *al dente!*"

"And this meat's as tender as newly churned butter," Jack said. "Don't you let her get away, Cesca."

Mina was filled with pride. She'd succeeded in preparing a perfect meal and was embraced as part of the company. They stuffed themselves and drained four bottles of wine. After several glasses of wine her confidence grew and she joined in the banter, forgetting her troubles and her clash with Signor Dante.

The red wine warmed her blood and several times she found her hand on Signor Dante's arm when she leaned over to make a small comment or joke. Touching him didn't seem strange or abnormal. Everyone seemed to be encouraging them to respond and answer as a couple. Signor Dante seemed especially pleased that she'd relaxed and was taking part in the festivities. She added this day to her handful of happy days spent in America.

After lunch, over her protests, everyone helped clear the table. Signor Dante was up to his elbows in soap, washing dishes, and Errico and the Signorina led the merriment, taunting each other unmercifully as they had in their youth. They tossed dishes back and forth, sang snatches of operas, and told tales of past mishaps, both onstage and off.

Mina's former reserve was discarded with the scraps. She silently blessed Errico for his tact as she bustled about the kitchen and put away pots and pans. After a terrible day of confusion, she unclenched her stomach and laughingly announced she'd prepare *pollo cacciatore* for the next card party.

Chapter Twenty-Nine

OW, IN HONOR OF that wonderful meal, I'm going to sketch you like I promised," Errico said. Jack Johnson's fiancée watched as Errico arranged Mina. "Just relax and let me pose you."

"Yes, do let him," Etta said, lighting a cigarette. "He's very good. I've seen some of his caricatures."

Mina didn't have to try to let her body be pliable. After the wine and the aperitif she felt like overcooked pasta. Errico seated her in profile, with her arms resting across the back of a Victorian sweetheart chair, next to the fire. He adjusted her skirts and tilted her head.

"Do you mind if I watch?" Etta asked.

"Not at all," Errico said. Etta took a seat on the sofa as Errico began to work. "Don't move a muscle. Sit perfectly still," he coached Mina.

The others had gone into the sitting room for fruit and coffee. Mina could hear them talking while Errico sketched. In between bits of conversation she could hear Signor Dante snapping walnuts. There hadn't been a chance for her to speak with him alone. She was anxious to have the card party over.

"I don't believe a word of it!" she heard Signor Dante exclaim in Italian to the Signorina. Then the Signorina laughed gaily.

"When do you sail?" Signor Dante asked.

"From California in two weeks," Signor Johnson replied. "It's going to be—"

Mina heard no more when the door between the two rooms closed.

In the sitting room Dante took another walnut from the dish and waited for Cesca to gather her nerve. She was leaning against the closed oak door, staring at the back of Johnson's head. Something about the intensity in the room made Johnson swivel to face her.

"Jack, is it possible to kill a man in the ring?" she demanded, her tone changing as she switched to English.

"Of course! Several men have been killed, a few died after . . . from complications. The human brain wasn't meant—"

"Those were accidents," she said.

Dante saw Johnson examine her keenly. "Nobody purposely kills an opponent, no matter what's said beforehand."

"What if you wanted to?" Dante asked soberly.

Johnson's eyes moved questioningly from Cesca, who stood challenging him with her hands on her hips, back to Dante, who pretended nonchalance, lounging in his chair. Lucifer lay snoozing at Johnson's feet.

"Is it possible to kill, for sure . . . dead, no question?" Cesca asked.

Johnson looked troubled in the half-light coming through the shirred curtains. "If you want someone dead . . . for sure . . . in the ring . . ."

"Yes?" she led, cautiously.

"No. It can't be guaranteed with fists."

"Damn it!" she exclaimed. She turned away to pour herself a sherry.

Lucifer's head came up. He watched Cesca's movements through sleep-glazed eyes.

"Why are you asking?"

"We've had a little bet going. Cesca thought, perhaps, if a skillful boxer were matched against a weak opponent . . ." Dante cast around for a moment while picking the meat from the walnut shell. "You see, we've been—"

"Don't bother, Dante. I recognize rage when I see it simmering just below the surface of my friend's lovely face." Johnson's gold teeth glittered. He leaned back, crossing his long legs, and delicately raised his demitasse cup. "Who do you want dead?"

"A dangerous . . . evil . . . bully," she said.

"*Cara*, I don't think—"

"Just between the three of us, Dante, I have a very bad memory. Getting knocked in the head'll make you forget your own name." He laughed and sipped his espresso.

"No one knocks you. You're too fast for that," she said, taking a jab at an imaginary opponent. Then she turned serious. "He's a backroom brawler, making an illegitimate income in saloons."

"Well, they've made boxing illegal again, except, of course, in clubs," Johnson said.

"Cesca's arranged a barge fight on the state line in the middle of the Hudson River for next Saturday night."

Johnson seemed cautiously amused. "That skirts the law comfortably. You're promoting a boxing match to kill this here fellow?"

Dante could hear the disbelief in Johnson's voice. Cesca might be the boldest and most determined of women, but obviously Johnson didn't believe that her confidence extended to arranging murder in the ring.

"You could say that," Dante said. "I might have to compete in a fifteen rounder. If our current plans don't work out."

"You? I didn't know you boxed."

"Growing up I had a temper. Later in France, at school, I polished my style."

Dante remembered "polishing his style." He'd taken quite a few beatings at the hands of the older boys because of gossip about his mother's new husband. Once he'd learned to use his fists he'd silenced the bullies, but he'd never forgotten the taunts and had preferred, thereafter, to keep to himself.

"I was wondering if you might be able to give Dante some pointers."

"Pointers?" Johnson asked. "On how to kill a man in the ring?"

"He's a worthless bastard," Cesca said, fuming. "A wife beater. He's going to sell her out of the country."

Johnson looked astounded. The smile left his face. "Sell! Come now, slavery was abolished in 1865."

"Nonetheless, he plans to sell her," Dante said, "and if he finds out she's the granddaughter of the wealthy man who's offering to buy her, he'll never give her up."

"She's pregnant, and the law won't protect her from his brutality."

Johnson shook his head as he set his cup and saucer on the end table. He uncrossed his legs and rested his forearms on his knees. "I forget," he said softly, "this is a free country." He was silent for a moment as he watched Cesca pace the carpet. "Stop dancing like a cat in heat," Johnson ordered. "Cesca, come sit down. Let's chew a little fat."

She sat like a schoolgirl on the edge of a tufted armchair with her drink. The room resonated with her tense anticipation as though a pebble had been tossed into a well to measure its depth.

"Plain to see you love this woman very much."

"She's my daughter, Jack. And it's a bad match. A doctor has already been called once. Her husband and his associates are violent and greedy. He'll sell her to her grandfather and I'll never see her again. Or if, God forbid, her husband finds out about the familial connection, he'll never let her go. His brutality will eventually kill her or the child. Of that, there's no doubt. Something must be done."

"The police?"

She snorted. "The law says she's his property," she said. "She'll be reprimanded for upsetting him and told to go home and behave."

"And if she should take his life," Dante added, "even in self-defense, she'll most likely hang."

Johnson smiled sadly. "Women are, after all, the final slaves, aren't they?" he asked himself more than them. "How about throwing a scare into him? Roughing him up?"

"He doesn't scare easily," she said.

Dante mentally reviewed the information he'd recently collected about Mina's husband. "He's a tough bastard, a ditch-digging, drunken bully who's hoping to make a fortune and a name for himself in the ring," Dante said. "Now that he's met the grandfather, Don Emilio Lampone—"

"Oh, yes, it's coming back to me . . . Rome, wasn't it?"

Cesca nodded grimly.

"Rumor has it that Emilio will pay him off and take her to Italy on Sunday," Dante said. "If that happens she'll be out of our reach. Emilio has high officials in his pocket there."

"In Italy," Cesca said, "even my political friends couldn't fight Don Emilio Lampone. The only answer is to kill her husband. His threat forever nullified."

"Well, you can't kill him in the ring—"

"I wish I could shoot him!" she cried, jumping up to stamp her feet. Lucifer growled and snuffled.

"As you know," Dante said dryly, "Cesca wants to shoot everyone!" They laughed, cracking the tension.

"Cesca, you'd only wind up in jail," Johnson said, leaning forward. "Too bad you can't feed him to Lucifer." He stroked the cat's fur and watched the muscular animal arch and stretch in appreciation. "If this man's as violent as you say . . . use his own kind to subdue him. A barroom brawl would be best. A knife in the ribs during a dispute. No one would see it . . . no one would be sure. A knife's a sure thing. A fist is not."

"A barroom brawl . . ." she mused.

"A violent man has many enemies. Perhaps—" Johnson started.

There was a rap on the door. Lucifer jumped up.

"Jack? Are you ready? You still have to finish packing."

"Yes, sugar!" he called. "A very organized woman, my future wife. I still have another two days."

Cesca opened the door to admit Etta.

"Have you reduced the world to a thimble?" Etta asked.

"We have," Cesca said.

"That's what I love about Jack, he cuts right through the bull." She slipped her arm around Jack's waist as they moved into the hallway.

"Australia's a beautiful country," Cesca said. "Do you realize the next time I see you, you'll be Heavyweight Champion of the World?"

"That he will!" Etta said proudly, her eyes shining.

"You promised me a boomerang," Dante reminded.

"Will do, but I want to see you Wednesday at Owney Geagham's. You know where that is?" Dante nodded. "Let's say around ten. No point in getting your head taken off. We'll spar a little and I'll show you some combinations."

"That'd be great. Thanks, Jack."

Johnson led Cesca ahead of the others to the foyer. "Be careful, Cesca," he whispered. "This is a dangerous business. Get your daughter away if you can. Forget revenge and taking the law into your own hands."

Errico and Mina entered the foyer to say *bon voyage*. " 'Lil' Artha,' " Errico said, clasping Johnson's hand and using his nickname. "I'll be wagering on you against Tommy Burns."

"Make it Texas-sized," Etta said, embracing Errico. "Jack won't let you down. We're looking forward to seeing you two in an opera soon." Dante helped her into her fur coat.

"I'm afraid *La Grande* Frascatti will have to come to the Met for that," Errico said.

"Imagine hotheaded Cesca working under her temperamental friend Toscanini again," Dante mocked as they all laughed.

Mina moved shyly forward to say good-bye.

"It was a real pleasure to meet you, Miss Mina," Johnson said, taking her hand. "You're a beautiful young lady, blessed with grace and charm. Only surround yourself with people who cherish you."

"Good-bye and good luck," she said carefully, shaking the boxer's hand.

"Ah, you do speak English!" Everyone laughed. Mina blushed. "And," Jack whispered as he hugged Cesca good-bye, "she's as beautiful as her mother." Cesca looked startled. "The way you look at her, any fool can see she means the world to you."

"*Andiamo!*" Dante said. "Jack, wait until you see my new Pierce."

"A Pierce-Arrow! That's the car for me. Have you had it up to speed? I hear it'll do sixty!" They started out the door.

"Do you mind dropping me at the Knickerbocker?" Errico shouted over his shoulder as he rushed into the sitting room to retrieve his portfolio.

The two women huddled together waving good-bye from the stoop as the Pierce-Arrow screeched away, a merry Jack Johnson with his golden smile at the wheel.

Chapter Thirty

*S*IGNOR DANTE LIKED TO RELAX by doing botanical studies in the early morning hours before the Signorina arose: flowers, bulbs, fruit, and seeds. He'd told Mina he used the time to dream and plan: "A watercolorist needs to discipline himself to paint every day. If he neglects his paints, they will dry up and what little talent he possesses will blow away." It wasn't yet eight, but the sun felt strong, the light would be good for painting. Mina knew he'd enjoy his meditation today.

She watched unnoticed from the doorway as he took a few sheets of smooth, fine paper from his folder and tacked one into place on the easel. On a stand next to the window he placed a scrap of turquoise cloth and one of the plants he'd taken from the opera house. He turned the rustic wicker basket, which held three white orchids with purple-spotted throats spiraling above thick moss, until he found an interesting angle. Then he removed his jacket and tie, rolled back his sleeves, and sat down to study the flowers.

Dante's breathing slowed as he compared the colors and contrasts in the sunlight. He arranged the small white saucers for mixing, water jars for rinsing, rags, pencils, rubbers, and the abundance of paintbrushes on his desk. He folded out the white glass palette of solid colors inside its sparse wooden case, and immediately a sense of peace settled over him. The paints were still moist from Saturday, still waiting for him patiently.

He picked a paintbrush, dipped it into the jar of water, shook it slightly, and applied it to the color. After mixing the right hue on the saucer and touching it to his rag a few times to blot up the excess liquid, he applied the brush to the paper and in one smooth calligraphic stroke delineated the spiral of the orchid's stalk.

He had a sharp eye, a steady hand, and a rapidity of execution that came from many years of practice. And with just a few strokes, he slipped into a state where Dante Romano vanished from the process and only the orchid, backlit by the sun, existed.

Mina stood in the doorway, rolling and unrolling a ribbon from the bodice of her dress around her index finger. She wanted desperately to believe the things Errico had told her about Signor Dante. She needed to talk to him, but had no idea how to approach him or what to say. Was it possible Signor Dante loved her and that she returned those feelings? Could it be true?

He sat in front of the window, his sandy brown hair shimmering in the morning light. The white cotton of his shirt was open against his naked tanned throat and was dazzlingly bright. The short hairs on his thick muscled arms glimmered as he moved gracefully back and forth from the palette to the water jars. A soft sheen of sweat appeared on his forehead from the intensity of his focus. She'd never seen him so vital and yet so filled with peace.

She came softly into the room, her small heels clicking on the hardwood until she reached the carpet and stood behind him, wishing to join the holy space his creativity created. She knew he was far away, lost in concentration, and didn't sense her looking over his shoulder. She dared not break into the beauty of the moment with a word.

Mina watched in fascination as the orchids in the basket came to life on the chalk-white paper. There was a tender current of emotion running through him that showed in his delicate treatment of the flower petals and leaves. While he worked, his mood seemed to darken as he contrasted the elegant blossoms with the rough wicker basket and springy moss. She was surprised that Signor Dante, who seemed so untamed, could show such a depth of understanding and restraint.

It felt like only minutes, but the clock on the mantle indicated that almost an hour had passed when he added a few quick, dry strokes of bright turquoise to represent the table scarf. He put down his brush.

"It's so beautiful!" she whispered. "It sits on the paper just right. Like a little piece of creation."

Startled, Dante turned to find Mina standing before him with the ribbon of her dress twisted around her finger, her eyes moist.

"Ah, signora, what a nice surprise."

"How do you do it?"

"I've practiced for a long time."

"No," she said, sounding wounded. "How do you feel their beauty? The men I've known would pass them by unseen."

"Those men don't have time for flowers, signora. Flowers don't buy bread."

She released the ribbon from her fingers and pressed her palms against her skirt. "I came to apologize for my behavior yesterday."

"It was my mistake," Dante said gently. "I'm sorry I confused you."

"No, no. It's not your fault. I know I'm a coward, running from the truth."

"You, signora? I don't believe it."

"I always thought I was behaving nobly, enduring the pain of my destiny. I used to believe that it was God's will, but now I think it may be a coward's way."

"Won't you sit down?"

Mina sat. "I prayed for so long," she said, nervously plucking at the ribbon again. "I asked Him for help, but I decided He couldn't hear me or didn't want to. I was wasting my time."

"Prayer can help clarify desires," he said, resting against the desk's edge. "It's never wasted."

"Do you pray, Signor Dante?"

"For me, painting is prayer."

She turned to look at his watercolor of the orchids. It does look like a prayer, she thought, so beautiful. She sighed.

"Until I got the letter," she said, "I was sure He hated me for my sins."

"Who hated you? Your husband?"

"No. God. Until then He never answered me."

"Perhaps you were asking for the wrong things," Dante said.

He turned and picked a clean brush. She watched him curiously as he dipped it in the water and blotted it on a rag. "Perhaps," she said.

"Why don't you try my way of praying?"

He held out the damp paintbrush. Mina smiled slowly, a little wrinkle on her forehead.

"It looks difficult. I'm not an artist."

"Watercolors, making a roast, sweeping a floor . . . they can all be prayer. Anything you do completely with your whole heart and soul is prayer. They say there are people whose entire life is one long conversation with God."

Mina laughed. "I don't have that much to say."

"Oh, you'd find things. With watercolors, once the brush touches the paper you can't take back a stroke, you must move forward, think ahead, not back. You make your strokes the right choice by your next action. It's an excellent exercise in self-determination."

"Self-deter—"

"Choosing your own destiny."

"I'd like that."

"Here, take this brush. Let me show you what I mean."

She did as he suggested. "I made a mistake about before—" Mina started to say.

"And forget about 'before.' Let's enjoy the present."

"But I insulted you by implying—"

"That moment's past, we're in a new one. I don't need an apology for this moment. Dip the brush in the water and pick a color that you like."

"I'm so ashamed of myself. It's the second time I've misunderstood you."

"Hold the brush a little more loosely, like a pencil when you write."

Mina tried to copy his grip, but she was too nervous. "You see, when you said you wanted to marry me, I thought, how could a man like you care about a woman like me? If you only knew who I really am . . . you and the Signorina . . . No one knows what I've done, where I come from. I'm an orphan . . . nobody special. Destiny gave me a chance to become someone else, to marry. I wouldn't have had that opportunity if it wasn't for—"

He put a finger to her lips and took the brush out of her hand, setting it across the saucer.

"But I want to tell you the truth, about my past," she insisted.

"You're too tense. Stop trying to explain and let everything be loose. Your arm, your hand, your fingers . . . your mind. Loosen your mind and let go. Let go of the past."

She examined the cleft in his chin. His eyes twinkled mischievously. He took her hands, extended her arms, and flapped them around. She laughed nervously.

"Close your eyes."

She did as he asked, anxiously thinking he might kiss her again. A strange hope was stealing over her as she listened to his resonant voice. Perhaps Errico was right.

"Breathe slowly. Long, steady inhalations and exhalations. That's it." He stepped slightly behind her, taking her right hand in his. "Keep them closed, I want to show you something."

Her hand trembled as he folded her fingers back, leaving her index finger free. He reached forward and pressed her finger into something soft and wet.

"You say you're not special, but you're wrong. You're unique, Signora Filomina. There's only one of you. Just as there's only one of me."

Leaning against her, he gently rolled her finger upon the paper, leaving a smudge of color behind. "Open your eyes. Do you see this blot? It's the signature of your identity. No one else in the whole world has it, only you. Look at it closely. It's dactyloscopy, fingerprinting. I'm studying this wonderful new science because it clearly illustrates that we're all different. Special."

He handed her his magnifying glass. She looked at the smudge through the glass, feeling confused. It was nothing but a mass of lines running around an oval in the middle. Nothing so special at all.

"Do you realize that even identical twins don't have the same imprint?"

He put his own finger in the paint and rolled it on the paper next to her impression. She examined the new blot under the glass. His print didn't have the oval; instead there was a pattern that looked like several hills tucked inside each other.

"If I looked the whole world over, I'd never find another woman like you."

His soft lips brushed her ear and the touch of his breath on her skin made her tremble. Through the cloth of her dress she felt his heart beating against her back.

"I'm no one, Signor Dante. I don't have my own identity—"

"Your print tells me differently."

"If you knew, if you understood about my past . . . I've been living a lie . . . a mistake. . . . I'm only an ignorant girl from the mountains. I can barely read, I can't—"

"You're everything to me. Your heart is filled with beauty and it contains all I've ever wanted."

She turned toward him, her eyes filling with tears. "I'd never be your equal. My past would shame—"

He swiftly pressed his fingers to her lips. "You'd never shame me."

Tears leaked from the corners of her eyes and ran down her cheeks. She pulled back from him, shaking her head in negation. "But I—my child would—"

"Be ours. Yours and mine."

She looked at his earnest face. She wanted him so. Did he know how she felt inside? As if she would wither and die if his light were taken from her. "I don't want to go back to Mulberry Street," she confessed.

"Then you won't."

"He—he doesn't want me."

"But I do, Mina. I want you. All of you: the good, the bad . . . the tearful." He touched the tears on her cheek. "I want to share your laughter, I want to be with you as we are now, when you feel sad or lost. I want to spend my days building a life with you and our children. I want to marry you. You. The special, unique woman I see before me, not any other. I want to spend the rest of my life with you."

"But—"

"There are no buts," he said, putting his index finger against her lips again. "The past, the future—they're illusions. There is only this moment. This reality."

He took her forearms in his hands the way he had that first time in the dressing room when he'd saved her from the flames. She searched his face frantically. Was it true? Was love going to be hers the way she'd hoped? Part of her was terrified of what would happen next.

"No. Please let me go. I—" she said, pressing her palms against his chest.

He pulled her to him, putting one hand on her back to press her against his chest while his other hand grasped the back of her neck and drew her face against his shoulder. "Don't be afraid," he murmured against her hair.

Dante stroked her back. He knew she was frightened. It crossed his mind that she'd probably never had a man touch her with love. He brushed his lips across the top of her forehead and kissed her hair, holding her gently in his arms. The thrill of finally holding her almost overwhelmed him. He desperately wanted to kiss and touch her, but he moved cautiously.

For her it was like her dreams. The touch of his hands on her body, his lips against her hot skin.

"*Cara,*" she heard him whisper urgently, "hold me. I need you so."

His lips brushed against her throat, sending a cascade of chills over her body. In an instant, her head tilted reflexively into the press of his lips and her eyelids lowered, shutting out everything but his touch and the feelings it created. Without being aware of it, her feet pushed her up onto her toes and pressed her body against his hips. She felt that odd twisting that his nearness always started returning even more strongly.

His chest muscles were firm under the palms of her hands. Her fingers slid up tentatively across the cotton of his shirt and the warmth of his skin streaked through her body like honey drizzled into a cup of hot tea. By the time her fingers reached the base of his neck she was clinging to him, rhythmically stroking his hair while he pressed fiery kisses against her throat. Her heart was beating like a length of cloth flapping in a storm and she heard a soft moaning that could only be coming from her own throat.

Inside her fevered skin she was climbing, climbing a ladder, moving in the dark toward a shuttered window. She didn't know what lay on the other side, but she was going up, up. Above, through the cracks of a window's sash, came a golden light, soft and pure. She couldn't resist each rung that brought her closer to the top. She wanted to see, to see what she would find up there at the top.

She mounted the last rung, released the latch, and pushed the shutter open. As she leaned over the sill to get a glimpse of the other side, abruptly, the ladder and the window disappeared. She tumbled forward into a blinding sweet tangle that touched every secret recess of her body and soul. She turned toward his questing lips, and when his mouth touched hers, she plunged into a deep pool of emotions.

She returned his first kisses timidly, but never having been kissed with such a mixture of tenderness and need, she responded with growing boldness. Unlike Antonio, his hands were gentle and his body trembled slightly as he caressed her. Perhaps he too was afraid of this moment; perhaps he too had fallen into a blinding liquid light. His restraint made her feel brazenly secure, removed from harm.

She opened her mouth under his, shamelessly exploring new sensations and delving deeply into each new thrill. She found they were speaking silently with their lips and tongues, communicating in a language she hadn't known existed. It was a strange and magnificent language he was speaking and she was surprised to find that she understood and spoke it fluently. Her blood was searing as it coursed through her veins, nicking against them like sharp knives. To draw a breath was painful, but somehow delicious.

She'd never felt such a rush of joy and wonder. She was a beggar starved for food, and the stranger who stood beneath her closed eyes took nourishment from the lips and hands of this man in her embrace. She couldn't get enough of him. She felt she was being drawn . . . drawn like a thread from a bobbin. Destiny held the gimp thread and its hand was stronger than her own.

It was the Master's hand working the lace, shifting the bobbins. She and Dante were being knotted together in a web of love that could never be untangled, and the world beyond the loops and whorls was blocked from her senses as the Master placed the pins.

"Tell me you love me."

"I—I—"

His lips moved over her eyes, her cheeks, her neck, but came back again and again to dwell on her lips, pulling her into the swirling threads of desire, this way and that, until she was lost.

"I love you," she said. She was surprised by the naturalness of the words; there was no artifice, no sense of duty, and no fragment of doubt in her mind.

"Say my name."

"Dante," she said softly, opening her eyes to look at him for the first time since they had touched.

"Ah, Mina my love, finally the Signor is gone."

She looked quickly down, embarrassed by the intensity of his gaze and the uncertainty of the situation, but he lifted her chin up and kissed her reassuringly. As the passion once again flowed through her, Prima Donna warbled her first notes, and their immaculate beauty knocked aside the fleeting doubts hidden in the shadows of her heart.

Chapter Thirty-One

"SILENZIO!" THE OLD DOORMAN hissed as he guided Mario to a seat at the back of the inky opera house. Mario gripped the envelope he'd used to gain admission to the opera house. "A message for Francesca Frascatti from Don Emilio Lampone that needs to be delivered in person," he'd told the old doorman. It had been cold in the alley and the *paisano* had taken pity on him.

"They'll take a break. Deliver your message then," the old doorman whispered as Mario sat down.

Onstage, in bright light, several men and two women stood around a grand piano. One woman was a short, thickset brunette, the other a flaming redhead he recognized from the Pierce-Arrow that had dropped her at the stage door.

The redheaded woman was singing softly, stopping occasionally to demand clarification in the music or argue imperiously over a notation. The pianist was deferential, giving her the respect her position demanded. She must be Francesca Frascatti, he thought, a strong, beautiful woman. She'd make a formidable enemy.

Suddenly, in full voice, she began an aria whose music seemed familiar, but he'd never noticed the words before. "*Un bel dì, vedremo le varsi un fil di fumo* . . ." Her rich voice hit him like a tidal wave of honey, crashing against him and vibrating his bones like the elevated train he'd ridden uptown. The Italian was precise and unblemished, the voice full of longing that tugged on his heart.

She sang of a beautiful day when all would be perfect. On that day a thread of smoke would float on the horizon. Attached to the thread a ship would appear carrying a lover across a wide sea and on that day the lovers would unite in bliss. He understood the woman's longing; he too had felt it. For he too had waited and held hope in his breast. He too had dreamed of being united on a beautiful day.

The moment was magical. It transported him back to the weeks before Filomina's arrival, to the days when he'd been conjuring her from the darkness of his solitude, dreaming of a time of bliss. He felt tears slipping down his cheeks. How beautiful the music was, how—Then, on a high note, her voice broke harshly. She put a hand on her throat, clutching the sheet music to her breast. The pianist whispered something.

"No, no." She shook her head sadly. "I can't. Oscar, it's hopeless."

In the front row, a fat man wearing a top hat shot to his feet and bounded up the steps. "Ladies! Gentlemen! Let's take an early lunch. After that, perhaps Signorina Frascatti will—"

"*Testo di cazzo!*" she hissed, glaring at him. "*Tu non capisi nente!*"

She snatched a leather case from the piano, barely missing the fat man's head with it as she stalked away into the wings. Hat in hand, the man hurried after her. Mario followed the argument through the backstage maze and down the stairs. In the lower hall he moved into a little alcove to listen.

"But I have a signed contract, Cesca. You signed it Friday."

"On Friday, Signor Hammerstein, I didn't know I was headed for nervous collapse."

"Perhaps a second opinion—"

"I went to a specialist! Errico's doctor insists I need peace and quiet. The cold and damp aren't helping my condition. A hot, dry climate for three to four months. I must leave for Sicily immediately or risk damaging my voice *permanently*."

"Signorina . . . Cesca, please, the—"

"No, no, Lucifer, get down. Down I tell you!"

"But—"

"Against my doctor's orders I'll fulfill my contract tomorrow evening for *Tosca*, but that's the extent of my obligation. Today I tried for friendship's sake. I cannot go further, contract or no, impossible!"

"I'll come back later when you—"

"Get out! Get out or I'll release Lucifer's leash." Mario heard something smash against the slamming door before the man hurried away grumbling. Mario stepped forward and rapped cautiously. "I told you, go away!" He knocked again.

The door jerked open and a small leopard sprang forward. "*Dio!*" Mario shouted, jumping back in alarm.

The cat pawed the air and snarled a few inches from his face. Francesca Frascatti jerked the leash, reined the cat in, and wrapped the slack around her hand.

"Lucifer, down!"

The leopard dropped to the floor, snuffling softly. He watched Mario with cautious eyes.

"Signora Frascatti?"

Cesca recognized the man at the door and her heart skipped a beat. She couldn't remember his name, but it was Antonio's second from the Cocked Hat. What was he doing here?

"I am Signo*rina* Frascatti. Yes?"

"I have a message from Don Emilio Lampone."

She watched him pull a crumpled envelope from his pocket. Don Lampone? She stared at the envelope in his hand. Since taking Mina into her brownstone she'd been waiting for Emilio's move. Obviously the moment had come, but what did Antonio's second have to do with it? She pulled Lucifer back inside and gestured for the man to enter. "Fine. Come in."

Trembling inside, she secured Lucifer's leash around the leg of the piano and picked up her portfolio. She knew she mustn't show fear, so with an attitude of impatience and boredom she sat on the piano bench and took out her music. "So give me the message." She put out her hand, but he folded the envelope and shoved it back into his coat pocket.

"In a manner of speaking, ah, I'm carrying a message to you." He eyed the cat at her feet while his hands made a circuit around the brim of his hat.

"Ha! I see! He doesn't dare to write it down. Very well then, out with his threat. What does the bastard demand?"

"So you two *are* enemies." He took a step forward, obviously surprised, but pleased.

She swiveled on the bench, her elbow striking the keys discordantly. Her portfolio fell to the floor, scattering its contents. "What do you mean?"

He stooped to collect the papers. "First I have some questions," the man said.

"Questions! How dare you! If you have a message, deliver it. Otherwise get out."

"Pardon me, signorina . . . I'm not your enemy. I've come to safeguard Filomina Rossi."

His particular choice of words stopped her. "What do you mean 'safeguard'?"

"Do you know why a wealthy patrician wine maker would purposely have false rumors spread that make him out to be a 'perverted abuser of young women'?"

Like a tambourine in a tarantella, her heart began to bang against her ribs. So that's Emilio's cover for "buying" Mina, she thought, he's making himself out to be a lecher. This man's question clearly showed he knew Emilio was no pervert. Then, she mused, he must know Emilio is Mina's grandfather and he understands the real reason why the money is being offered. That's why Antonio has sent him: to taunt me. Obviously, Antonio has figured out that Mina is my daughter.

She met the man's eyes levelly. "There's no message from Emilio, is there?"

The man boldly stared back. "No, there isn't."

She quickly decided there was only one reason for the sudden visit. Money. Now that everything is in the open, she thought, Antonio will squeeze me first, then Emilio. Back and forth. He'll play his little game until the highest bid is reached. "All right, whatever Emilio's offering, I'll double it. Let's make it easy on everyone."

"He's offered five thousand, but—"

"Ten thousand," she countered coolly.

"Signorina, this is not lira, but doll—"

"Yes, ten thousand American. I'll do whatever's necessary to keep my daughter away from that bastard."

"Daughter!" The man looked shocked, then pleased. "Is Signora DiGianni truly your daughter?"

His astonishment seemed genuine. She was confused for a moment, then it hit her; My God, he didn't know. I've given this man the leverage Antonio needs to take Mina from me. My plans for a simple divorce or an offer of money to outbid Emilio are finished. When she stood up her legs wobbled. "You bastard! You tricked me!"

Lucifer jumped forward, snarling. She felt his leash taut against her leg.

"Signorina Frascatti, please!" The man dropped to his knees, making the sign of the cross and throwing his arms wide in a gesture of supplication while still clutching the papers from her portfolio. "I haven't come to harm you or your daughter. I swear by the *Madonna*. I come only to help."

His face was earnest. She hesitated; the leash against her leg went slack.

"Who are you? Why are you here?"

"My name's Mario Catanzaro. Filomina DiGianni was my fiancée. Antonio DiGianni stole her from me. I pledge my life to protect her."

So this was the bridegroom that Mina had rejected in favor of Antonio. "Does your friend Antonio know you're here?"

"That animal is not my friend," Mario corrected her. Lucifer grumbled at the loathing thick in Mario's voice. "He's a cheat and a liar who pretended to be a brother. He betrayed my friendship and dishonored me for money. Now he wants to sell the woman I love. I hate him for his evil and would gladly see him dead."

"*Vendetta?*" Cesca asked.

"*Sì. Vendetta.*"

She turned the idea over in her mind. Mina had already told her about Mario's sincerity and kindness. And she knew it was a sacred obligation to seek vengeance when a man's honor had been defiled. If no court of law would help, it was incumbent upon Mario to restore his honor. Antonio's betrayal would make Mario a strong ally; he'd fight to repay the treachery. As if to further her trust, Lucifer plopped over onto his side and lazily began licking his coat. She sat down again and gestured for Mario to do the same. She would listen to what he had to say, then she'd decide if she should trust him. "All right, Mario. Perhaps together we can find a way to defeat those who wish us ill. Tell me what you know."

Mario explained that late Sunday afternoon Kathleen had arrived at the Cocked Hat wild-eyed and disheveled. She claimed to have seen Tonio's wife at the market with a gigolo from the opera house: "I saw her leaning against his Pierce-Arrow, fancy as ya please, the two of them groping and tonguing each other in front of the whole bloody market."

Mario knew she was lying because he'd been close enough to see the innocent exchange between the two. He'd said nothing, purposely letting Kathleen go on spinning a web of lies aimed at firing Tonio up against his wife. "I followed yer wife in the market, to see what else she might be up to, but she accused me of being yer mistress and attacked." She'd shown Tonio scratches and a torn, bloody earlobe. Tonio hadn't believed her until she'd pulled an antique earring from her pocket.

"Yer wife claims this belongs to her. Now why would the darlin' girl say something like that? Where'd ya get the little present ya gave to me, Tonio?"

The two had gone on arguing, but Mario couldn't take his eyes off the red stone earring in Kathleen's hand.

Only the night before, his cousin Vito, a member of the Black Hand, had sent for him. Vito had told Mario there might be a connection between the stolen earrings belonging to Francesca Frascatti and Don Emilio Lampone. "Frascatti's ruby earrings are heirlooms, reputed to be worth a fortune, and she's so desperate to get them back she's followed the thief to America and hired detectives to search, but I don't believe it," Vito had said. "I've recently gotten information that suggests Frascatti and Lampone are connected. Something's going on with this woman he's offering to buy and the earrings."

Mario wondered if Mina was somehow involved with the theft of the earrings. After the quarrel had ended he'd taken Tonio aside. He didn't tell Tonio what he'd learned from Vito, but instead suggested that Antonio allow him to go uptown to the opera.

"I'll get to the bottom of her story about the gigolo without jeopardizing your wife's sale," Mario had promised. Tonio trusted his "best friend," so he'd sent Mario to "dig up the truth."

"I want to protect Signorina DiGianni, so I came and hid in the alley to wait for you," Mario told Cesca. "I was going to use the earrings as an excuse, pretend to be looking for a reward, but when the driver got out of the Pierce-Arrow and came to help you inside, I recognized the man from the market. You see, there was something else I'd neglected to tell Tonio. I followed Kathleen in the market and saw everything. I saw the man she was with strip his disguise and change into the gigolo. He's the same man who's been passing himself off as a boxer. Isn't he?"

Francesca Frascatti smiled. "I should have known a clever *cavallo di razza* like you would recognize him," she said, putting on her Neapolitan accent and using the expression for *stud* that she'd used at the Cocked Hat.

He looked at her uncomprehendingly for a moment, suspicion mixing with fear, until she let loose with a raucous laugh like the one she'd used at the Cocked Hat.

"I knew I was right!" he shouted, slapping his thigh. "You—you're Mimi, the boxer Vittorio's girlfriend."

"*Eccola!* I am she."

"But why did you disguise yourselves?"

Francesca explained that Dante was a detective in her employ and that they'd traced her earrings to the Cocked Hat.

"So the earrings were never stolen?" Mario asked.

"The earrings are from her father's estate. I gave them to her as a child, before she was adopted."

Mario thought he understood. "Don Lampone's the father? That's why he wants to 'buy' her for five thousand dollars?"

"No, Emilio's her grandfather. Mina was born illegitimately. She's Emilio's only heir. He blames me for his son's death, so he wants to punish me by taking her away so that I'll never see her again." She filled him in on the details of all that had happened since they had come to New York to search for Maria Grazia.

Mario was troubled. He began to pace. "Is Don Lampone as rich as my cousin claims?"

"He's as rich as Croesus."

"Tonio'll never give her up if he finds out the truth. He'll stay married to her and bleed the old man for money and power."

"That's what I'm afraid of. I have a lawyer working on a divorce. Mina thinks we're going to Italy, but I've purchased tickets for South America. We'll be safe there."

Mario stopped pacing. "Don Lampone can tell him the truth and use him. If he does, Tonio'll never agree to a divorce. He'll never let her escape with all that money."

"You must speak to Dante, the man you know as Vittorio. He'll know what to do with your information and your offer to help us."

"I must get back. Tonio will be suspicious," he said, checking his watch.

For an instant she worried that she had said too much. Then a sudden calmness touched her heart. The watch that had been Giulio's was resting in Mario's palm. This is a sign, she thought, that I have placed my trust wisely. Mario will help me defeat Emilio.

She put her hand on his arm. "Please, Mario, Dante's training for the boxing match on the Lower East Side. Meet him for a moment. We'll take a cab downtown, it'll be faster than the train."

On the way to the gym they completed their pact for revenge. When the cab reached the Bowery she pulled back against the upholstery and put down the oilcloth flap, hiding her face from view. "Go. Ask for Vittorio Fusco. He's sparring with our friend Jack Johnson. Use Vittorio's real name, Dante Romano. Tell him you know everything and that Cesca sent you. Hurry, I'll wait here."

Mario went up the steps to Owney Geagham's Boxing Club. At the top of the stairs a man leaned back in a chair, his foot upon the doorframe, blocking the entrance. He was studying a racing form. Mario scanned the room. A few feet away, a snowy-haired trainer held a patched heavy bag for a busted-up pug. Nearby a stocky Irishman worked a thudding speed bag, and in the middle of the room an Italian kid, all arms and legs, determinedly skipped rope. In the far corner, two men were sparring in a raised roped ring.

"Yeah?" the man growled without looking up.

"I'm looking for a boxer named Vittorio Fusco?"

"Over there, dancin' with the jig."

Mario crossed the uneven boards and leaned against the wall to watch the two men spar. They were sweated up and working hard, throwing jabs and practicing combinations. Johnson was teaching Dante his trick for slipping punches. Mario had never seen a finer athlete, so natural, so powerful. He wished with all his heart that the black man were fighting Tonio on Saturday.

"Boxing's not about taking a punch," Johnson said. "That's bull. Boxing's about avoiding the shots, having guts, and being smart. It's about confidence and relaxation. A small move, a fraction of an inch, that's all it takes. The glove skims past, meets air. You need to slip, then get in and under."

"Like this?" Dante shifted to the left, missing the punch just as Johnson suggested.

"Terrific! That's it! Again!" he shouted. "Again! Good, good. Now the right. Excellent!"

"Such a small thing."

"Yeah, but it takes confidence and courage. You trust me. What'll happen when fear grabs you by the balls? The other guy's shorter than you, right?"

"He's small, but wiry and fast."

"Unless he's a gorilla, you'll have a couple inches of arm on him. You can pepper him and he can't hit you back." Johnson corrected Dante's footwork. "Don't cross your feet. You'll knock yourself down without him laying a glove on you."

Dante learned fast. He didn't look bad, but he didn't have the fire in his belly. He was a gentleman boxer, and Mario knew that Tonio was going to eat him up.

"You've got a solid punch, but you need more force. Put your hip into it every time. A natural lefty like you has got to watch his opponent's right. See, it's fairly easy for me to come in under your punches. Either pull back or block."

Dante blocked the next right punch, but then Jack jabbed him on the chin with a left.

"That's better," Johnson said, "but I can still get to you with my left. Block your head, not your stomach. Let him punish the body if you have to, but watch out for haymakers."

"Haymakers?" Dante asked.

"Wild swings. He's going to be tough. If you hurt him he'll turn vicious. One ferocious haymaker will take your head off."

They stopped. Johnson removed his leather helmet.

"You're better than I thought, but you've got to use your anger. Practice putting rage in your fists. Show him no mercy. Remember, you've only got to go fifteen three-minute rounds. Pace yourself. Try not to be afraid. Fear'll defeat you before he lays a glove on you."

Dante spit the wet strip of cotton that protected his teeth onto his glove. "I'm not afraid of the bastard."

"Good! Fear'll sap you. If you're afraid, you won't breathe, your muscles'll feel like lead, you'll tire out fast, and he'll destroy you. If you get into trouble, lie down. You're not a professional, there's no shame in saving your brain or your life."

"Right."

"The best thing's not to fight him at all," Johnson laughed.

"I've no plans to fight him, but we need to keep up the charade to keep our information coming in. Chances of my actually having to throw a punch are slim."

Dante removed his protective headgear and shook the sweat from his head. Johnson nodded toward a man leaning against the wall. "Who's that?" he asked.

"Jesus Christ! It's the bastard's best friend. What's he doing here?" Dante pulled off his gloves and slipped between the ropes to the floor. He grabbed Mario by the lapels and slammed him into the ring support. Johnson was beside him in an instant.

"Easy!" Johnson cautioned.

Mario put his hands up over his head in a show of surrender.

"It's okay, Signor *Romano*. I know everything," he whispered. "I come as a friend to Filomina Rossi, the Signorina's daughter. *Cesca* said to tell you you can trust me. She's waiting for you and Signor Johnson downstairs in a cab."

Chapter Thirty-Two

AT FOUR O'CLOCK on Friday afternoon, shadows filled the trees and lay long on the snow-covered lawns of the uptown brownstones. Dante was in the garage behind the house, working on his temperamental Pierce-Arrow, and the Signorina was in the music room running scales. Mina was busy tidying the Signorina's room, dusting and ordering everything before the trip.

She'd sent her pay envelope to Antonio by messenger, having been convinced by Dante and the Signorina to wait before meeting with him and telling him about their child. The following days had been spent discussing her options. The Signorina offered her a generous bonus to become her assistant and accompany her back to Italy, all expenses paid. Once she reached Naples, if she chose she could continue working until her baby's birth or go back to the mountains. It was a chance to become independent of a man's protection and still give her baby a future.

What kind of future would her baby have with Antonio? The only legacy he had to offer was drunkenness and cruelty. Now she realized that what the Signorina had said was true. The boy in the field wasn't a god sent to save the girl, but a devil. She'd decided a divorce would be the right choice, not only for the baby's sake, but her own. With the bonus she'd been offered she could begin the divorce process. She had two concerns, the main one being her papers. She would need to speak with the lawyer again. Perhaps he could find a way around her problem.

In Italy, if God willed, she might be able to get an annulment and start over. Her other worry was Antonio. How would he react? Would he fight the divorce? Could he stop her from leaving on Monday? The lawyer would know. She was going to see him tomorrow with Dante and the Signorina on her way to the Mulberry Street apartment. She was going with them to retrieve her few belongings and tell Antonio about her decision to leave.

Dante's proposal of marriage hadn't been discussed further, but her love and respect for him grew deeper every day. She was going to have to tell him her secret if their relationship was going to develop any further. She wondered how he would react to the news. He said he loved her heart and all it contained, he wasn't in love with any of her outward trappings, but did he really mean that?

She picked up the Signorina's wrapper and nightgown, which had been left lying on the chair, and took them to the closet. She was beginning to feel hopeful. A new life was beginning. Not just in her belly, but in her head. Because of the choices she was starting to make, her duplicitous life might almost be over. She shoved the tightly packed dresses aside to hang up the peignoir set, and as she did, something dark tumbled out. It flashed in the light and made a small thunk, vibrating like a wild thing. She jumped back in fright.

It took a moment to realize it wasn't anything alive and wouldn't attack her. She bent down to investigate. She could see it was a musical instrument of some kind. She tried to pull it from behind one of the long skirts brushing the carpet, but it was stuck on something. One of its pegs was caught in some lace edging and she disentangled it.

This must belong to the Signorina, she thought, backing out of the closet. Why does she store it behind her dresses and not on the shelf? She took it into the light. It was a beautiful mandolin! Its body was made of subtle alternating light and dark ribs of wood curved into a pear-shaped body. The front had a sound hole rimmed with mother-of-pearl and ebony. She strummed the strings. Oh, how she wished she knew how to play.

The only time she'd seen a mandolin up close was on the docks in Naples. She began to dip and sway the way she remembered the man had when he'd played, and she hummed "*O Marenariello.*" Maybe the Signorina will teach me to play, she thought, smoothing the faded ribbons that Lucifer stalked as she paced about the room discordantly strumming.

Mammina had played a mandolin in the cafés of *Napoli*. She remembered the story she'd been told about how the mandolin had been passed down. It was the only instrument left from *Mammina's* father, who'd been a master mandolin maker. It was the one his daughter had helped design and make. *Mammina* had carefully scratched her lover's name onto the ivory bridge so that whenever she played, her lover would speak to her through the strings.

Without thinking, Mina turned the mandolin onto its side to examine the creamy bridge that held the strings up from the face and away from the sound hole. In the afternoon sun she thought she saw something carefully carved into the ivory. She wasn't sure she actually saw writing. It was probably a design, flowers or fruit. Perhaps her mind was playing tricks. She took the mandolin to the window to look more closely.

Yes, under the strings she could see that someone had carved a name into the bridge. G-I-U-L-I-O. Her heart began to pound. It couldn't be. This couldn't be the same mandolin. There were hundreds of mandolins in the world . . . thousands perhaps. She wasn't so good with letters. She looked again. G-I-U-L-I-O. *Sant'Anna!* That's his name . . . that's the name of *Mammina's* lover, the one—

She jumped when the door chime sounded, suddenly afraid of being caught with the secret she'd discovered. Lucifer forgot the ribbons and padded toward the hallway. She pulled the dresses aside and thrust the mandolin behind them next to the wall, arranging the skirts hastily.

She pushed a growling Lucifer back into the bedroom and closed the door on him, then hurried to the foyer, thinking Dante had probably locked himself outside again. Peeking though the curtained windows, she was shocked to see her husband standing on the porch.

Antonio looked as respectable as the day he'd walked to the Church of the Transfiguration to get married. He'd bathed and given his clothing a thorough brushing and now stood bareheaded, clutching his cap to his chest. With the setting sun casting a crimson glow around his head and shoulders, she remembered the story she'd told the Signorina: Antonio at seventeen, balancing the bundle of wheat on his head, after saving the girl from dishonor in the field.

"Mina? Who's at the door?" the Signorina called from upstairs.

"No one, signorina, I'm—I'm cleaning the chimes, sorry."

The last thing she wanted was a scene. If she said Antonio was at the door, there was sure to be an afternoon of drama. Besides, this would be a perfect opportunity to settle things. In this neutral setting, supported by her friends, she'd offer him the last chance her conscience insisted he deserved. If he remained unbending, as she believed he would, everything would be over and settled. She would have a clear conscience.

Impatiently, he reached for the bell, and on impulse she opened the door. "Excuse me, miss, I look for—" He stopped, a look of surprise on his face. "Filomina, I almost no recognize you."

The words tumbled out in English, shock overtaking his natural inclination to speak Italian in such foreign circumstances. His wife stood before him dressed in a lovely purple dress with silk flowers tucked into the pleats of her blouse and across the skirt. Her hair was sleeked back artfully, shiny curls adorning her temples, and she wore intricately worked gold earrings. If he'd passed her on the street he wouldn't have recognized her.

"Antonio, what are you doing here?"

"What's the matter, I can't come to see my wife?" He slipped back into Italian, taking the simple question as a challenge, but he sweetened the ending, remembering Kathleen's harping: "Be nice, charm her, get her to come back of her own free will."

"Of course you can."

"It's cold out here, can I come inside?"

She hesitated, but she was far from the tenements. Here she was in control. She widened the door to let him in, but before he stepped fully inside he stopped to peek between the brick wall and the large planters flanking the door at the top of the porch.

She followed his gaze to a gentleman leisurely walking his dog. The man's back was turned to them as he stood under a horse chestnut tree. His dog sniffed around the trunk, then lifted a leg. Antonio quickly slipped past her into the foyer.

He looked around and whistled under his breath. "Nice place!"

Several porcelain pieces captured his eye and he snatched one up eagerly to examine it. Carelessly he turned it over to find the mark, a blue fleur-de-lys. "Capo-di-Monte! This stuff costs a fortune."

"Yes, the Signorina has many beautiful things." She took the piece out of his hand and put it back before he could drop it. "Come into the kitchen where we can talk," she said.

Antonio walked carefully across the parquet floor, feeling like a clod of dirt on a silver platter. The whole setting, with crystal chandeliers, marble floors, and carved wood, was too elegant for his comfort. He was relieved when he entered the familiar surroundings of a kitchen. He closed the door firmly.

"Why did you come here?"

"I miss you. I wanted to be sure you're all right. That you're happy."

She hadn't heard this kind of talk from Antonio since her first week in the country when she was still engaged to Mario. The sudden switch made her stomach sick, especially coming so rapidly after her admission of love for Dante and her decision to get a divorce. *Gesù* was staging a bad joke. "You miss me? You haven't been home two days in a row in over six months. You only come to see me on payday."

"Don't be that way, Filomina," he said, trying to put his arms around her. "You know I work hard. Do you think I want to stay away? I want you to come back home. We're man and wife. It's not good that you stay up here and I stay downtown."

She shook him off and moved to the other side of the kitchen. "Are you in trouble with gambling again? Do you need money?"

He rubbed his hands together, hating the part he was playing. He was used to taking what he wanted, no questions asked, but he remembered the five thousand dollars and sweetened his voice. "That's just it. I—"

The tight knot in her stomach relaxed a little. He wanted money; the rest was just a trick to get it. The sickness that had been rising in her throat started to ebb away and a sudden sadness overcame her. After all her efforts to be a good wife to him, to make up for the lies she'd been forced to tell, he didn't want her.

"—I've come into a good amount of money," he said. "I don't want you to work anymore. You work too hard. I want you to give up this job and come home where you belong."

She was astounded. He'd come into money? He wanted her to quit and come home? After he beat and rejected her? He expected her to drop everything and go back to hell?

"I have a good position here. I don't want to give it up."

"I'm your husband, I decide." His voice took on a nasty edge, his veneer of sweetness slipping. She saw him shove his hands into his pockets. He's trying to hold in his temper, she thought. Good, now I have the upper hand.

"Does your visit have anything to do with the woman in the market on Sunday?"

He prowled around the kitchen, refusing to meet her eyes. "You got something to eat? I came from work." He uncovered the remains of a pie, but pushed it away and opened some cupboards. "I need meat. I didn't have lunch, Filomina," he said, giving her a hangdog look, "you don't bring my lunch anymore."

It was a poor attempt to make her feel guilty, but she no longer wanted responsibility for him or his stomach. "There's meat in the pantry."

"I'm starving. Get me some, please."

Please? He'd never said please. What was going on? Perhaps he'd sensed her decision to divorce him. She decided to fix him a sandwich and tell him everything. He peered out the curtained window as she went to fetch the meat, but when she returned he was leaning against the sink smoking a cigarette. She set the platter down and sliced off a few pieces of roast. Uncovering a loaf of bread, she held the heel against her breast and deftly cut two thick slabs. "I want to know if you're here because of that woman in the market."

"I don't know who you're talking about."

"The dark curly-haired woman who said she was your mistress. She told me all about you and swore you were selling me and sending me back to Italy."

He jerked away from the sink, his eyes blazing. "That stupid cunt! I knew she was lying to me."

"It's true!" Shocked, she set the loaf of bread on the table. She'd believed they were lovers, but selling her, sending her back to Italy, never.

"You attacked her in the market," he shouted, doing his best to put her on the defensive. "She wanted to call the police."

"I attacked?" She gestured with the bread knife, her anger finally rising after all the inhuman treatment she'd suffered. "And you believe her?"

Antonio shrugged. He tapped his ashes indifferently onto the tiles. "Why should she touch you? Who are you? Nobody."

"I'm your wife!" She wasn't afraid of Antonio now, not here in this house where she was safe. "You accept that disgraceful woman's word over mine?"

Tonio was shocked to see his wife lean across the table and wave the knife under his nose. Her eyes were as hot as rivets. She'd never fought back, not after the first beating he gave her. Obviously, he'd lost control just as Kathleen had predicted he would. "These people have been putting ideas into your head. I don't have anything to do with her. She's a friend of Mario's."

"Like I was a friend of Mario's?"

This wasn't going the way he'd planned. She wasn't as trusting as she used to be. "No," he said. "She's a whore, Mario's whore."

"That isn't what she told me. She said she's your whore. She said you never loved me, that you only married me to win a bet, and she said that you're selling me to an old man who—"

"Lies! She's always wanted me, and when I married you, her mind snapped. She's a slut who sleeps with every man who comes to the saloon. I wouldn't have anything to do with her, so she's angry."

"You're telling me you were never with her?"

"Never," he said, thrusting out his chin defiantly.

"You're saying she came after me in the market because she wanted you and was jealous because you married me?"

"Exactly, yes. She runs the saloon downstairs from the boardinghouse where Mario has a room. We drink there and play cards. You know I stay with Mario when I don't come home."

"So you say."

"She knows me from there . . . you saw her that day hanging all over me. Ask Mario if you don't believe me. He'll tell you she's a slut, a liar, crazy."

"And the earrings?" she asked softly, the sadness and anger caused by his lies clawing at her throat. "How did she get the earrings, Antonio?"

"What earrings?"

"The earrings I told you had belonged to my mother!"

He shifted his weight. He'd forgotten the earrings. He could never explain them. Then in a flash of anger he thought, Why should I have to? His wife and all her property belonged to him, to do with as he saw fit. She'd no right to accuse him—he was the master and she must obey. How dare she reproach him?

"I have the one I took back, upstairs," she said. "Shall I get it? How did she get them if you didn't give them to her?"

He could see that she was going to be difficult, just as Kathleen had predicted. "How do I know?" he said, stalling. "Maybe she stole them."

"Stole them! No. You took them from my bureau and gave them to her. How could you? Have you so little respect for me?"

He was tired of wasting time arguing over nonsense and trying to be nice. "Those earrings are junk. I'll get you better ones. Stop breaking my balls with bullshit." He was shouting.

It was clear he wasn't sorry; his only concern was for himself. The story about selling her had to be true. Righteous anger streamed through her, filling her with strength. She was justified in divorcing him. God could damn her to hell, but she wasn't going back to him.

"I have a child in me, Antonio."

Antonio gasped involuntarily; his face went purple.

It was Kathleen's second prediction: "She'll try to tell ya she's pregnant so ya won't sell her, but if she is, it'll be that gigolo's kid." Antonio had only had sex with her a handful of times, and Kathleen's words hammered in his skull.

"You've been fucking that Casanova!"

"God forgive you," she said, making the sign of the cross.

"You expect me to believe they gave you a job, clothes, money because you can sew and keep house? Something's going on with you and that man."

Mina's underarms itched with nervous tension and she felt nauseous. She'd kissed Dante and declared her love for him. She couldn't deny it. She looked down in a panic, unable to disguise the rush of guilt that covered her face. "I have not . . . done what you accuse me of. The child I'm carrying is yours."

He didn't miss her averted eyes or the subtle spots of color on her neck. "You did something, I see it."

He viciously flicked his lit cigarette into her face. It stung her cheek but didn't burn and bounced clear. After all his mistreatment, her temper finally fired. Dante and the Signorina were right, Antonio would never change and her baby would be in danger. She felt a strange sense of elation as she stepped from behind the kitchen table still holding the knife.

"I was coming to see you tomorrow. I thought you should know about your child and have a choice in its future. I'd hoped for a real marriage, but I see your child means nothing to you. You deny your responsibilities as you always have. I know you don't love or want me. So I've made other plans."

"Other plans! You! A woman no man would marry, who had to come to this country because she was a whore in her own."

"I've tried to be a good wife to you, but our marriage was cursed from the start. Someone else wants me, and I want a divorce from you."

"Listen to me, you little bitch, you're my wife. You'll do what I say, when I say it."

"No!" she cried. "I won't!" She held the knife out with both hands. "I'm not afraid of you," she said evenly. "I don't have to do what you say. I can make other choices now."

"You're coming back with me." He tried to grab her, but she instinctively circled away behind the table, remembering the girl in the field. Mina could be strong like her; she could defeat him.

"Put that knife down," he said.

"You get out of here!" She jabbed the knife at him menacingly. He drew back, surprised by her intent. She'd stab him; maybe even kill him if she could. His reaction was swift. He shoved the table over violently. Then he grabbed her wrist, broke her grip, and twisted her arm behind her back. The knife clattered to the floor.

"A divorce, eh? Who's been filling your head with shit? That gigolo?" He gave her a stinging slap in the head as he forced her clenched fist between her shoulder blades.

"Antonio! Stop!" She thought her bone would pop from the shoulder socket. She screamed, but he covered her mouth and yanked her toward the pantry. He pulled a knife with a mother-of-pearl handle from the drawer and held it against her throat.

Mina heard the Signorina's shoes clatter in the upstairs hall.

"You scream again," he hissed, "and I'll cut your cheating throat. Are you going to be quiet? Are you?" He shook her savagely until she nodded.

Outside an automobile engine raced noisily, sputtering and backfiring. The racket was coming from the garage where Dante was working on the Pierce-Arrow. "Let me pack some things," she whispered, trying to stall for time as he edged her toward the door. "The Signorina and Dante will wonder what happened if I leave without my things. They might—"

"Dante, is it?" His laugh was nasty. "Nice try. The other whore who lives here and your boyfriend can't help you where you're going. I've watched and waited. I made my own plans." He checked the curtained window, then dragged her out the back door and down the icy steps to the hedge.

It was cold, and the streetlights oozed a feeble yellow light. He crouched low and shoved the branches of the hedge apart. Through the tight maze she glimpsed the dog walker at the far end of the block conversing with a couple near their stoop. Antonio eyed the threesome closely.

She heard the door of the Pierce-Arrow slam above the rumble of its engine. Help was at the back of the house, blocked from view, or just up the street. She could scream, but no one would hear her over the noise, and the point of the knife was sharp against her collarbone. Her heart felt as though it had pushed into her throat. This couldn't be happening to her. Someone was sure to see.

"Stay down and do as I say."

Antonio's eyes flickered between the garage and the stoop up the street. His hand tightened on her wrist painfully. When the man bent to stroke his dog, he rushed her along the hedge toward the cobbled street.

Chapter Thirty-Three

*L*ADIES! GENTLEMEN, PLEASE!" Dante shouted. "Quiet, please!" He stood in front of an improvised blackboard in the parlor of the brownstone. "I need to give you information as a group so that we can act in concert. Then you'll spread out across the city to search for Signorina Frascatti's housekeeper."

The milling agents quieted immediately upon hearing Cesca's name and darted glances in her direction. So this was the "secret client with bottomless pockets" searching the city for a woman with antique earrings: Francesca Frascatti.

She's handling herself fairly well, Dante thought, considering the circumstances. Cesca was leaning against the back wall of the parlor for support, blotting her red-rimmed eyes with a twisted handkerchief, her face as white as the chalk dust on his fingers.

"As you know, for two weeks we've been searching this vicinity," Dante said, circling an area on the board, "for Signorina Frascatti's stolen earrings. The earrings have recently been traced to the Cocked Hat, a saloon below the market on Cherry Street." He marked a spot bordering the East River on the map he'd drawn. "The person seen wearing them is the saloon's owner, Kathleen Shaunessey."

There was a murmur of confusion as everyone stole another look at Cesca. The group that had been searching the city for the earrings concluded that the case was now closed, while the other faction, which had been searching the records, wondered what had happened to Maria Grazia Muscillo or Checci.

"Silence! Listen to Signor Romano," Bevilacqua said, stepping forward. "Time is short."

Dante nodded his thanks to Bevilacqua and continued hurriedly. "Kathleen Shaunessey is the mistress of Antonio DiGianni, a ditchdigger and a backroom brawler involved in this case. He is married to Signorina Frascatti's dresser and housekeeper, Filomina DiGianni."

More murmuring. Dante made connections on the blackboard to clarify relationships.

"Filomina DiGianni was taken from this house by force," he said, raising his voice with emotion, "exactly"—he checked his watch—"eighty-six minutes ago."

The detectives glanced at one another and buzzed with disbelief. Bevilacqua covered his mouth and cleared his throat to hide an amused grin. How could Dante claim such accuracy? Colombo, the detective who'd acted as Dante's fight trainer and the one who'd been guarding the house with the schnauzer, stepped forward and gave a sharp whistle. The room quieted.

"A *hand-rolled* cigarette was found smoldering on the kitchen tiles," Colombo said. "The back door had been left open to the elements. As you know, hand-rolled cigarettes extinguish almost immediately if left unattended. Eighty-six minutes is feasible."

The group regarded Colombo quizzically, then glanced at Bevilacqua. Who was this upstart? Bevilacqua gave Colombo a look indicating that

Colombo should keep his mouth shut and leave such clarifications to the detective in charge.

"That's right," Bevilacqua said, taking back control. "Signor Romano is grounded in scientific fact. Eighty-six minutes is an accurate reckoning. Let's hear the rest of his briefing."

The amusement ceased and solemn attention turned again to Dante.

"We've uncovered a plot to kidnap and spirit Signora DiGianni from the country on Sunday," Dante said. "Don Emilio Lampone of Naples is paying Antonio DiGianni a substantial amount of money to turn his wife over against her will. As you know, many of Don Lampone's hired Pinkertons have been interfering with our search and are now facilitating this abduction. It is our job to uncover her hiding place and foil their plan to take her back to Italy."

"Perhaps she's still secreted in the house," an operative offered eagerly.

"The house has been thoroughly searched," Dante said.

"The Plaza Hotel?"

"Our agents still on duty there have informed us that neither Signora DiGianni nor her husband has been seen entering the Plaza. Don Lampone is currently dining at Sherry's and has been unapproached all day."

"If Don Lampone *is* contacted, our agents will immediately inform me by telephone," Bevilacqua said. "The Plaza's too risky a hiding place, too public."

Dante nodded his agreement. "The Lower East Side or a building adjacent to the docks is more likely," Dante said. "We must move quickly. Inspector Bevilacqua will give you new postings. These next few hours will be critical. You gentlemen and ladies know the lower part of Manhattan intimately. Don't hesitate to come forward with ideas."

Dante handed his chalk to Bevilacqua and went to join Cesca. Then as an afterthought he added, "Signorina Frascatti and I thank you for your prompt response." He wiped the dust from his fingers and tucked his handkerchief back into his pocket. The chattering group surged toward Bevilacqua for clarification and new assignments.

"Colombo, come with me," Dante said, cutting him off from the group. "I wish to speak with you."

"Yes, sir." Colombo quickly followed Dante to the sitting room.

As he attempted to close the door, Cesca pushed in. "Tell me everything you know," she demanded. She shoved Colombo into the middle of the room and slammed the door with her foot.

"I told Signor Dante everything, signorina. I was walking the dog and watching the house. I saw no one enter or leave."

"Don't lie to me! Only three people knew about the earrings: you, Bevilacqua, and that Vincenzo person. You're the one who's been helping Emilio. She didn't fly away!"

She surged toward Colombo looking as though she might box his ears; Dante stepped between them. "Cesca, melodrama must be kept out of the equation. Be logical. Shouting accusations won't help." Dante felt overwhelmed. He couldn't deal with her dramatics and search for Mina at the same time, but his attempt to pacify the situation backfired.

"You were in the garage and saw nothing?" Cesca demanded, turning on him. "I can't believe your incompetence! You're supposed to be the best Italy can offer! Did your mother buy your reputation?"

Dante was stung by her rebuke, but he held his tongue and swallowed her insult. It was more important for him to find Mina than protect his ego.

"Don't you see?" she continued heatedly. "This is the informant who let Kathleen slip away in the market."

Colombo was startled by her insinuation. "No, no, signorina. There was an accident . . . a horse broke his leg."

"So you say, but your 'accident' cost us a week. We know that someone is giving Emilio information."

"Someone may be giving information, but I swear it isn't me." Colombo appealed to Dante, his palms up and open. "How could I?" he asked. "That day I knew only that a woman might be found in the market wearing stolen earrings. You were working the market with me, Signor Dante. You saw the horse."

"It's true," Dante said. "I was with him when the horse stumbled. Colombo stayed with me until almost midnight."

Colombo seemed sincere, but Dante knew Mario's information was correct. There was an informant in the group. If it wasn't Colombo, who was it?

"How do you explain her disappearance?" Cesca asked.

"I cannot, signorina. I was watching the house the whole time."

"Impossible! You're telling me she disappeared into thin air?"

They'd reached an impasse. Colombo's defense was implausible, but Dante believed him. If Colombo were lying, he'd have made up a more credible story. Dante pulled Cesca to the side and explained his reasoning. He watched Colombo surreptitiously as he spoke. Colombo turned self-consciously aside. Nothing in the man's manner spoke of guilt. He looked self-assured, but dumbfounded. Finally Cesca reluctantly agreed that Colombo didn't appear to be the informant.

"Very well, Colombo, I'll continue to place my trust in you," she said. "Now let's go outside and retrace every step of your watch."

Colombo showed Dante the positions he'd occupied, while Cesca fetched lanterns from the cellar. Dante studied the house from different vantage points. In the growing darkness two peculiarities jumped out.

From under the chestnut tree tall amphora planters flanking the front door blocked the light that should have spilled from the entrance windows. And when they looked back at the house, from the stoop where Colombo had conversed with the neighbors, a dark line of bushes cut across the white of the snow-covered lawn and hid the drive.

"You stood here," Dante asked, "and talked with the occupants?"

"Yes, but as I told you I kept my eyes on the house at all times."

Dante felt a flicker of excitement as he scrutinized the sight line of the hedges. "At any time did you notice a carriage or automobile parked in the street?"

"No, sir."

At that moment Cesca exited from the kitchen door carrying two bright lanterns. When she passed into the drive, the snowy hedge suddenly hid the lanterns' light. It was clear from the stoop's angle that the hedge acted as a low screen from the side door to the middle of the street.

"You're sure there was no carriage in the street?" Dante asked excitedly.

"Until you called me to the house, no one entered the drive or parked nearby."

Dante and Colombo rushed back to join Cesca and searched the driveway and the hedge. The driveway had been shoveled that morning, so there were no footprints, but near the sidewalk on the wrong side of the snow-packed barrier Dante noticed a slender curved shadow at the base of the hedge. When he brought the lantern close he saw that something had cut into and sunk beneath the crust of ice. He plunged his hand in and pulled out a crude iron tool.

"What is that?" Cesca asked fearfully.

"It's used to lift manhole covers," Colombo said.

Dante rushed into the street with Cesca and Colombo following. "That's how he did it," Dante said, indicating the loosened iron disk. "Antonio took her through the sewer."

"Of course," Colombo said. "He's a ditchdigger, a sewer man, he knows the systems well. If there's a connection to the new subway system he'd know it. He could take her anywhere."

"The Plaza Hotel!" Cesca said. "My God, he could take her to Emilio and our agents wouldn't see him. Dante, call the hotel."

"Immediately," he said, moving toward the house.

Colombo grabbed Dante's arm. "Your first instinct is the right one. If he hides her in the tenements or somewhere in the sewers we won't find her."

"Why not take her directly to Emilio?" Cesca insisted with irritation. She still hadn't given up the idea that Colombo was the informant. "The sewers run all over the city."

"They do, but Colombo's right, the Plaza's too public," Dante said.

"We should go downtown," Colombo offered, "to the saloon and question the mistress, Kathleen."

"Yes," Dante said. "Antonio's behavior, if he's there, may tell me a good deal about where he might be hiding Mina."

"I'm coming with you," Cesca said.

"No," Dante said. "As Vittorio I'll work more effectively without you. You must go to the Plaza. Insist on seeing Emilio, use any pretext. Keep your eyes open for any clue, any scrap of information. There's an off chance you may be right, but it's the last place they would take her."

"Shall I go with you, Signor Dante?"

"No. I'll operate better alone. Go inside, follow Inspector Bevilacqua's orders, but say nothing of our discovery or my planned investigation. Nothing! You'll suffer his wrath, but from now on you'll report only to me. This is a chance to uncover the informant and for you to redeem

yourself. Show me my faith in you is not misplaced." He patted Colombo on the back reassuringly as he and Cesca hurried into the brightly
lit house.

HALFWAY across the city, several feet below ground, Mina
shuddered, hurrying along behind Antonio in the dark, claustrophobic
passageway. She'd pulled up her skirts and held them against her nose,
but it didn't stop the fetid odor. It seemed like an eternity ago that they
had entered this reeking hell.

She was totally lost, but Antonio unhesitatingly dodged subway cars
and navigated a maze of stifling passageways, squeezing through open-
ings, some of which were little more than shored-up excavation tunnels.
Now with a lantern held before him, he raced along within inches of a
dark, glinting channel she knew was choked with excrement. Their steps
resounded against the bricks, alerting rats the size of bread loaves, which
waddled before them in panic. She could hear them plunging into the
stream and occasionally she glimpsed one as it swam gracefully away.

Antonio stopped. In the flickering light she saw that they were about
to enter a large, arched corridor. She straightened up, easing her
cramped back.

"You see that opening over there?" he said, pointing. "That's where
we're going. Jump the channel after me." He made the crossing easily and
waited for her. "Come on, come on," he gestured impatiently. "Be careful, the bricks are slippery, and you're no good to me with a broken neck."

She glanced around. What could she do? Run back down the passageways? She had no idea where she was. In this hell, there was no one
to save her. She'd have to help herself, but escape down here was hopeless; she'd have to wait. It crossed her mind that he intended to kill her,
but she reminded herself that he was selling her, sending her back to
Italy. She took slim comfort in his love of money and his statement
"you're no good to me with a broken neck."

"Hurry it up! It's not wide."

When she jumped, her foot caught the edge of the channel and she
lurched backward. He grabbed her sleeve, pulling her roughly against
him. She'd only been apart from the filth of the tenements a week, but

it surprised her how strongly he smelled of stale sweat and liquor. His touch was disgusting.

"Can't we go up, please?" she implored softly. "Why are we down here?"

"I had to lose that private dick with the schnauzer watching the house. We're almost there."

Once again he shoved her behind and began moving. Obviously he wasn't worried about her following. Where could she go? Finally he came to a shaft leading up, and set the lantern down. "This is it. You try to run and I'll leave you in the shit with the rats for a while. Then I'll come get you and fix you good." He climbed up.

She clutched the ladder, alternately watching him and searching the gloom. She was afraid he might change his mind and leave her down below. She listened intently. Silence. Then she heard him grunt with effort as he slid the iron manhole cover onto the cobbles. Once again there was silence.

"Leave the lantern. Climb up!"

At the top she poked her head up fearfully. He yanked her out and shoved the cover back. She knew they were near the East River, for she could feel the damp and smell the water. In the distance she saw the lights of the Brooklyn Bridge. It was growing increasingly dark as he pulled her along the waterfront. Her eyes swept the streets; she hoped to find someone who might help her, but there were only deserted warehouses and decaying, boarded-up buildings.

"Antonio, where are we?"

"Keep yer mouth shut. I'll do the talking."

His grip was crushing her wrist bones, and her lungs were burning with the effort necessary to keep pace with him as they sped forward. She felt dizzy and disoriented, but she knew he was guiding her steadily downtown toward the bridge. What was he planning? She suddenly heard the clatter of a passing hack. Antonio whistled sharply. The carriage halted and he shoved her inside. She strained to hear what he was saying to the driver, but she couldn't make it out. She felt as though she were in some horrible nightmare. If only she'd wake up. When Antonio climbed into the coach she had only to look at his hard, set face to know the situation was all too real.

"Antonio, I've saved some money. It's under the floorboards on Mulberry Street. You can have it all. Just let me go."

"Shut up or I'll fix it so you don't talk again." He raised his hand threateningly.

She pulled back into the corner of the cab and remained silent. After an eternity of silent dread the cab stopped. Antonio guided her through a dark alley littered with garbage and shoved her up some rickety steps. He pressed her tightly against the barred door as he worked the lock and when he released the latch she half-stepped, half-lunged into a deserted kitchen. He caught the back of her skirt as she fell forward and yanked her toward a swinging door. He held her and stuck his head out to shout something, then he shoved her back against a cluttered sink and paced the room impatiently. After a minute he went to the door and called again.

When the door swung open, the first thing Mina saw was his mistress's shocked face. The dirty glasses she'd been carrying crashed to the floor. Here's the cause of all my trouble, Mina thought. His vile mistress ruined my marriage, disgraced me in the market, and now he brings me to face her. Mina's fury at Antonio and his mistress coalesced into a white-hot goad for vengeance. Here's my chance to repay her *mal'occhio*, Mina thought as she lunged forward. "*Carogna!*" she shouted, her hands extended like talons.

Kathleen screamed in answer, hefting an iron skillet from the stove to protect herself. Antonio pulled Mina up short by her hair. "*Stai zitto!*" he shouted, yanking her back.

Mina struggled to free herself, biting, punching, and squirming until Antonio savagely hit her in the side. The blow knocked her wind out and doubled her over. As she gasped for breath, she quickly rethought her strategy. She wasn't going to get out of this predicament by fighting. If she kept resisting he'd beat her into submission. She might be able to get in some good blows, but he'd win, and might harm her child. She'd have to outwit him.

"*Fermati!*" he cried, holding Kathleen back. "Stop it! I'm no have a catfight. Put down that pan. You hear me? Put it down."

"She called me a bitch!"

"Good," he said, wrenching the skillet from her hand. "You finally learn some Italian." As he threw the pan down, Mina tried to jerk away. "Get me some rope, something to tie her up."

"Ya stupid guinea," Kathleen yelled, grabbing a soiled bar towel. "What the hell do ya think yer doing bringing her here?"

Mina didn't understand their words, but their manner told her everything she needed to know. For the first time she was truly frightened, for if he really was selling her back to Italy it meant she'd end up a prostitute or an indentured servant and God only knew what would happen to her child. She thought of the Signorina's offer of money, her desire to help with the divorce.

"Please, Antonio," she begged. "I can get you all the money you want. Signorina Frascatti will pay you. Let me go and I'll give you a divorce. You can marry this woman."

His mistress gnawed the edge of a rag, then ripped the cloth in half. "What's she going on about?" Kathleen demanded.

"Nothing. It ain't important."

"You can be happy together," Mina urged. "Don't sell your child into slavery."

Kathleen looked at Mina distrustfully. "Whatever she's saying, don't ya believe her, Tonio," she warned. "She'll say anything to save her hide."

Antonio held Mina by her forearms while his mistress wrapped the strips around her wrists and tied the knots. "It's not my child," Antonio said in Italian, "even if you *are* pregnant."

"How can you say such a thing?" she asked, but she knew he'd been listening to his mistress's lies and didn't want to know the truth. He was totally corrupt. She swung her tied fists at Antonio, cracking him across the jaw. He lurched sideways as she charged toward the swinging door and what she assumed was the barroom.

"*Aiuto!*" she screamed. "*Aiuto!*" Antonio sprinted after her, covered her mouth to muffle her shouts, and dragged her back.

Kathleen took grim satisfaction in forcing a filthy bar towel into his wife's mouth. As she watched her gag on the cloth, Kathleen felt little pity. "Yer going home, ya dago bitch," she said. "Just like I said ya would. Back to the old country, where ya belong." His wife jerked her head away and kicked her in the shins. Kathleen grunted in pain and pulled back her fist to strike. "Why, you little bitch, I oughta—"

Tonio grabbed her arm. "Don't mark her. He ain't gonna want her bruised up."

"Get her legs, ya fool!" Kathleen ordered.

While Tonio held his wife, Kathleen ripped up another bar towel and tied her ankles together. When Kathleen finished she stared at Tonio's wife, annoyed. "Yer crazy, kidnapping her. Ya'll have them uptown cops down on us. I told ya, *charm her.*"

"She's my wife," he said stubbornly. "I can no kidnap a wife."

Kathleen smiled and bobbed her head pensively. "There's a point. Well, just the same, they'll be looking for her, and we ain't supposed to deliver her to the old man until early Sunday morning."

His wife leaned against the sink, bound like a sack of potatoes, with her eyes darting around the room like a trapped animal's. I'll bet she's petrified, Kathleen thought, but the twinge of pity she felt quickly faded. Well, who gives a bloody fuck? I didn't tell her to come to this country, she told herself, and I sure as hell didn't tell her to marry Tonio. Everything would've turned out different if she hadn't come over to marry Mario, but then Tonio made that stupid bet and ruined everything. Well, his wife's going to pay for it, and Tonio was—

"I waited until nobody was watching, then I took her," Tonio said, cutting into her thoughts. "You was right all along. She says she's pregnant and that it's my kid, but she's getting a divorce to marry that gigolo."

Kathleen rubbed her thumb against her lower lip. "They'll come looking for her. We got to hide her."

"I got her, you hide her."

"Me? What the bloody Christ am I supposed to do with her?"

"You said, 'Go get her.' You said, 'Tie her up.' Okay, she's tied up." He started toward the bar.

"Ya can't leave her here, ya idiot. Help me carry her down to the beer cellar. It's got a lock."

They hauled his wife down into the cellar where they retied her hands behind her back and set her on a beer cask. Tonio turned to head back up the stairs, but Kathleen grabbed him. She kissed him and ran her hands intimately over his body, watching his wife's response in her peripheral vision. It gave her a thrill that shot to her toes when she saw his wife's dark eyes go cold and hateful. You might have married him, she thought, but I'm his woman. You can't lord it over me, wife or no wife.

After a bit of lustful groping, Tonio pushed her away. "Later. I need a drink."

Without a backward glance Kathleen followed him up the steps and padlocked the door. She'd deal with the baggage after she had a drink. She tucked the keys between her breasts and went into the bar with Tonio.

Chapter Thirty-Four

MINA AWOKE GROGGY, with a piercing headache. She felt bruised all over, but the pain was strongest in her shoulders. When she tried raising a hand to her head she realized her wrists were lashed together behind her back. Her feet were numb and bound to spindles on either side of a straight-backed chair. A gag had made her mouth dry and sore, but she wasn't blindfolded.

In a rush, the panic she'd felt during the kidnapping returned. Her eyes frantically searched the shadows, sure that Antonio and his mistress were just out of sight. Perhaps they'd already sold her to the old man and this was a room in his house. She listened intently for a moment, certain she would hear conversation—Antonio's voice arguing, the mistress laughing—but she heard nothing, not even the sound of mice.

When her heart stopped racing and her mind focused she saw that her chair had been placed at one end of a long, narrow room. Dim light from a street lamp seeped in the floor-to-ceiling window at the other end of the room and silhouetted a mountain of tables and chairs. The room reminded her of the pantry at Signorina Frascatti's house, only bigger. Its counters were also covered with hammered tin and there were open cupboards above and below, but interrupting the long counters were two doors directly across from each other. The right counter was jammed with dusty glasses, mugs, and plates, and near the left door were rows of shakers for salt and pepper. She assumed she must be in the pantry of a bar or restaurant.

Her stomach rumbled in the silence. How long had it been since she'd eaten? In the rank cellar Antonio's mistress had offered her greasy stew, but she'd refused. She'd gratefully gulped the water offered, attributing its bitter taste to the metal cup, but now she realized the water must have been drugged. How long had she been unconscious? Was she in America or Italy? Was she Antonio's prisoner or the old man's?

It had been late afternoon before the kidnapping; now it was dark. Dante would have finished working on the automobile and come into the kitchen to wash up. The Signorina would have come down to see what was for supper—Mina had heard the clatter of her heels in the hall above before Antonio had taken her from the house. Surely she would have been missed by now.

Perhaps they didn't realize Antonio had taken her . . . but Signor Caruso had said Dante was a detective and Dante had said she was in danger. They would see the mess in the kitchen—the overturned table, the half-made sandwich—and realize she'd been kidnapped.

She wiggled her wrists, but they were bound too tightly to work the knots. How ironic it was! She was a lace maker and could work knots blindfolded, but the ligature was so tight it was impossible to reach them. Next she tried bouncing, but her efforts didn't move the chair much and the action sent shooting pains through her shoulders. By experimenting she found that if she pulled forward sharply, then quickly slammed her upper body backward, she could inch forward slightly.

Sant'Anna, give me strength, she prayed, to get out of this room and find help. She jerked toward the door on the right, wood on wood screaming with each tortured attempt. The noise frightened her: what if they heard? She stopped to listen, but no one came to answer the chair's complaint, so she continued on, grunting with each effort. After what seemed like hours she was drenched and every muscle in her body felt raw. The sweat ran down her face, burning her eyes and tickling her neck before it soaked into her collar.

She'd moved the chair only a few inches and was feeling overwhelmed. It's impossible! You can't do it! her mind nattered wildly when she stopped to catch her breath. You don't have enough strength; you're only a woman. Give up, where will you go tied up like a pig? Can't you see Antonio's won? She rested, trying to still the negative voices and gain enough courage to continue.

In the stillness she heard Signor Dante's voice say, "If you listen to your heart, it will tell you what to do." She remembered the talk in the café and the walk they'd taken in the park before he'd suggested skating.

It had been so cold that day; the snow squeaked under her boots. She'd been chatting nervously about her new duties at the elegant brownstone, trying to put up a brave front but feeling incapable, when they'd suddenly come upon a beautiful double fountain topped by an angel with outstretched wings. She'd been breathless with wonder.

"It's so beautiful!"

"A woman named Emma Stebbins sculpted it," Dante said.

"A woman hammered and chiseled such a wonder from stone?"

"Yes, a woman," Dante said. "Don't you think women are capable of great deeds, just as men are? All that's needed for success is a plan and determination."

She hadn't quite believed him and teased him about being a suffragette, but he'd refused to hear any argument about men being superior.

"Do you really think women are the equals of men or are you saying it to be fashionable, Signor Dante?"

"I think women are better than men, signora," he'd said. "They bear the children and shape their progress day after day. That takes incredible patience and bravery. I could never be so brave."

"Oh, having babies," she'd said, embarrassed by what she considered a little deed.

"It takes a great deal of strength to bear and raise a child. Don't let men fool you. We minimize women's accomplishments and strut like peacocks over the slightest feat of physical strength, but we could never accomplish such daunting tasks. If women can survive child rearing and the arrogance of men, they can accomplish any goal they set their minds to."

She'd been thinking about his little speech for a week and had decided he was right. She wasn't weak and worthless, as Antonio insisted. She was strong. Dante's words had resparked a fire Antonio had banked down in her soul. His faith in her ability had given her courage to fan that spark into a flame, and when Antonio had brutally tried to stamp it out she'd blazed into action. Only Antonio's physical strength had defeated her.

She realized she hadn't really given up on herself, she'd only gotten sidetracked. After the loss of her mother and the change in fortune caused by her death, Mina might have doubted her ability to care for herself, but she wasn't about to give up the fight. Not now, not since she'd rediscovered her strength and found love. Hadn't she survived in spite of all her losses—her father, her mother, her grandmother? Hadn't she risked her life and everything she knew to leave Naples with a few pennies in her pocket?

On that last day in Naples she'd stood on the pier watching the half-naked children dive for tourists' coins in the garbage-choked harbor and realized that she too had been a beggar, grateful for the scant coins life offered. She'd known her spirit was dying in this city of despair and she had to get away.

Her first tentative step toward self-reliance had been to sell her dead grandmother's cache of antique lace. She'd taken what money she could get and had entered uncharted terrain. Forcing her legs up the gangplank, she'd left the familiar streets, the smoking charcoal braziers, the women plying their trade under the arches, and finally sought love with a stranger. She'd gone on to survive Antonio's brutality.

As Dante said, she'd found a way to thrive even though she'd been foolish enough to believe that past sin would doom her to suffering. On the streets of Naples she'd prayed that God would make a miracle and save her, but her marriage to Antonio was a test that taught her she'd have to rely on her own wits. She'd been desperate to take her life back, but she'd thought she was unable, a coward.

In the stillness of the cold room she marshaled her strength. This moment would be her greatest challenge. Not the past, not the future, but this instant. This reality. She was strong enough to fight for her baby and her real love, Dante. She began again.

NOT far from the pantry where Mina was being held, Emilio was battling with the throng in front of Sherry's for a cab. He and Solange had just finished a leisurely supper and were heading back to the Plaza. He slipped the doorman a five-dollar gold piece and, over the protests of the crowd, climbed into the next carriage. Within a few minutes he was standing at the front desk of the Plaza, checking his messages. The clerk handed him an envelope. He tore it open eagerly. His informant was brazenly waiting for him in the Palm Court.

Solange went up to the suite while he made his way to the lounge. He found his man finishing dessert. "You have news for me?" he asked as he settled.

"I do." The informant sat smirking before him.

"It was foolish for you to come here."

"I'm beyond reproach; after this evening they depend on me more than ever. Besides, tonight my post is the Plaza. I'm keeping an eye on you." The informant laughed and sat back to enjoy his cigarette. Emilio waved the waiter away. "What's your news?"

"Your granddaughter has been taken from under their noses."

"*Grazie Dio!*" Emilio cried. "Where is she?"

"Her husband is hiding her downtown."

"He's signed the papers allowing her to leave the country? Everything's set for tomorrow?"

"Yes. I went down to meet with him before coming to you. But there's a small change in plans. He wants to meet you tonight. He and his mistress have instructions for your ears only."

Emilio was suspicious at once. "At this hour? What kind of instructions?"

"They refuse to say. Perhaps the final details for the switch on Sunday." The informant took a card from his jacket pocket and leaned forward. "Go to this address," he said. His ring twinkled in the subdued light as he slipped the card across the table. "Be there at eleven thirty. Do you have the money ready?"

"It's in the hotel safe," Emilio said.

"Get it," he ordered. "I'll arrange for a cab. It's to be a short meeting. They insist on seeing the cash."

"Is it wise to take the money?"

"They don't trust that you actually have it. You must remember, all this is very strange to them. Rumors are circulating that you buy women for your pleasure . . . you're 'a perverted abuser.' "

Emilio gripped the card, his heart racing with excitement. Soon he'd be reunited with his only remaining blood. "That lunatic husband of hers will not harm her?"

The informant laughed and crushed his cigarette in the ashtray. "He's a madman, it's true, but his mistress understands your granddaughter's value. Don't worry, everything'll go smoothly. Just call on me if you need me to help with the transfer."

After the informant went to hire a cab, Emilio retrieved the money from the hotel safe and took it up to his suite. He took the case with the money into the bedroom and instructed Solange not to bother him.

Solange knew that Emilio was agitated by something important the moment she saw him, but she remained in the sitting room doing her needlework. Whatever it was, he would handle it the way he always did—his way. After a moment she was startled by a knock on the door. "Yes?" she inquired softly, not wishing to disturb Emilio.

"Emilio Lampone?" The familiar voice of Francesca Frascatti inquired. "Open the door, please, I must see him."

Solange checked the clock on the mantle; it was after ten thirty, a little late for a social call. She put her needlepoint down and went to the bedroom door to get him, but changed her mind. She'd wait to see what Francesca wanted. "Signorina Frascatti, please come in," she said, opening the door.

Francesca's dress rustled stiffly as she brushed past. Her eyes flickered over the fine furnishings and the fire burning in the grate, then darted between the two doors leading out of the room. "Where is she?" Francesca demanded.

Her manner was highly agitated. Solange thought her close to hysteria. "Emilio's changing," Solange said. "If you wait just a moment I'll get him for you."

Solange followed Francesca's gaze around the room, seeing it from her point of view. Several new steamer trunks and cases stood open, bulging with expensive dresses, skirts, and waists. Piles of hatboxes and shoe boxes were grouped together and tied for transport. Over one of the chairs a complete cream and sage outfit was set out, with underclothing and outerwear arranged. On another chair a similar assortment lay ready in shades of rose. Jewelry, gloves, and handbags sat on a side table. It was obvious that a decision about Mina's traveling costume was in progress.

"I'm afraid I've been very naughty," Solange said with a forced laugh. "I've been shopping incessantly and simply can't decide what to wear tomorrow. Please excuse the clutter." She hastily closed several of the cases on her way across the room.

"Where's he hiding her?" Francesca demanded. "Is she in there?" Francesca darted toward Emilio's room.

"Signorina Frascatti! Stop!" Solange cried, blocking her path. "I don't know what's troubling you, but just a moment, I'll get Don Emilio." Solange tapped on Emilio's door, then disappeared inside. Francesca was examining a glove she'd picked up when Solange returned. "He'll be right out," she said crisply. "Won't you sit down?"

Francesca plucked the pearl buttons on the glove distractedly and remained standing. Solange sat down and bent her head to her needlework. Her fingers were trembling from Emilio's hasty confession. He'd told her his granddaughter had been kidnapped from Francesca's home. Even though Solange was being paid handsomely to help take the girl back to a life of luxury in Italy, it didn't remove the guilt she felt for her role in his twisted plot. She pitied Francesca, for she knew that Emilio's vast fortune and unbending temperament would cheat her of a relationship with her daughter.

When Emilio had told her the story in Paris and hired her to accompany his granddaughter back to Italy, he'd cast himself as the victim and the diva as the villainess, but Solange eventually read between the lines of his self-pity. It was his arrogance and pride that had caged him in loneliness and fear. For all his money and power, she thought him a rather sad, pathetic man. He longed for communion with others, but the death of his son had destroyed his slender connection to the world. Anger over his loss had snuffed out any compassion for the suffering of others. Only his plan for revenge kept him alive. Perhaps, Solange thought, I shouldn't go along with his plans, even though he's getting me a solo role in the next ballet.

"The weather has changed again," Solange said, hoping to still her guilty thoughts. "Just yesterday it was snowing and tonight it's as balmy as a June evening. They say tomorrow's to be the same. New York is so unpre—"

"Please, mademoiselle, it isn't necessary to discuss the weather," Francesca said as she threw the glove back onto the table.

Solange was about to apologize for her part in this calamity when the door to Emilio's room opened.

"What a surprise!" Emilio said, advancing. "Good evening, Signorina Frascatti. To what do we owe this pleasure?"

"What have you done with her?"

"Done with whom?"

"You know very well what I mean," Francesca cried, pushing past him.

"No, signorina, I'm afraid I don't."

"Then you won't mind if I search your rooms?"

He gestured that she was free to look if she chose. Francesca threw open the two doors and searched, but the bedrooms were unoccupied. She came back to find Emilio sipping a glass of brandy.

"You gave Maria Grazia's husband five thousand dollars to kidnap her from my home."

He threw up his hand and turned to Solange in mock surprise. "I? Pay a husband to kidnap his wife?" Solange heard the satisfaction in his voice. "Have you ever heard of such a thing, Solange?" he asked. "Surely she's thinking of one of her opera librettos, *n'est-ce pas?*"

Solange pulled the floss through the webbing with annoyance and held her tongue.

"Emilio, I beg you," Francesca said, "give up this *vendetta*. You don't realize how dangerous and depraved he is. I've seen the bruises, as you have not. He treats her worse than a stubborn horse, savagely beating her for minor indiscretions. If she should refuse to obey him now . . ."

Emilio sat down and crossed his legs casually. He rested the hand holding the brandy snifter upon his knee. "Your years as a diva have destroyed your sense of reality. Surely you don't believe this person you're—"

"Think, Emilio. If you're posing as 'a perverted abuser of women' and he's willing to sell—"

"I, an abuser of women! Solange, do you hear? The plot gets thicker with each—"

"Stop it!" Francesca cried, slamming her hands down on the side table. "She's pregnant with his child!"

The snifter wobbled and slipped from his fingers. The liquor soaked his pants as her words reverberated in his mind. "Pregnant?" he whispered. His sardonic demeanor crumbled. He stood up and took a faltering step toward the door. Solange, still clutching her work, sprang up to support him.

"Yes. And a doctor has warned she may miscarry. Where are you hiding her? Is she in a decent place? She must be terrified. Please, Emilio, have pity!"

Francesca's tears spilled down her cheeks. Fear was plain upon her face, but he refused to believe she was in earnest. After all, wasn't she an actress, able to cry on cue? Wasn't this melodrama her stock and trade? "I'm not holding her," Emilio said stubbornly. "I resent these accusations. You'd better go."

Francesca's tears vaporized to fury. "*Bastardo!* You still haven't found a heart. You think you can buy her, the way you tried to buy Giulio?"

"Don't speak to me of my son."

"I'll speak of my husband if I please."

"Husband?" Solange turned to Emilio.

"You're surprised?" Francesca asked. "Emilio still won't acknowledge our marriage or his son's happiness in my arms. He offered Giulio only money and fear. That's why Giulio left. Not because of lies, but because of love."

"My son was naive. You used your body and tricked him with lies."

"It was your inability to see past your selfish desires that lost you Giulio. You wanted to control him and refused to compromise. You didn't know how to love, so you used manipulation and guilt to bind Giulio to you, and when that didn't work you tried to buy him outright. Yes, you tried to buy Giulio, just like you're now trying to buy Maria. If you filled these trunks with gold ingots you couldn't buy her love, though you may be able to buy her body from this madman who married her."

She snatched up the rose dress. The carefully arranged pieces of the costume scattered across the carpet. "This is not affection." She shook it in his face, then cast it aside to snatch up other items. "Nor this nor this! Is your heart so shriveled you cannot feel her pain, her fear? She's been kidnapped, locked up, *Gesù* knows where, and she is trembling in terror waiting to be delivered to you like a parcel. She has feelings, Emilio, fears. If you love her you'll give her your protection and not cause her more pain."

For a moment Emilio wavered. He was touched by pity, but then he remembered the day Giulio ran off. How dare she lecture him? This vixen was just as haughty as the day he'd denounced her in the stable yard. "Leave before I summon hotel security."

"Emilio, listen to her," Solange pleaded, but he shook her off and went to the telephone.

"What if I tell her husband, Antonio, about your little charade?" Francesca asked.

His hand was poised to lift the receiver, but her tone of voice stopped him. "What would be the benefit?" he countered.

"He might make a deal with me."

"You know you haven't enough money to outbid me."

"What if I told him that Mina's your granddaughter? That he'd have legal rights, not only to her, but to her child," Francesca said.

"You'd never do that. You'd chain her to him and his malice."

"Yes, but I'd watch him bleed you of what you truly love. You wouldn't control her or her child, and every precious penny piled up over the years would go to him. Then he would take your name and your land—"

"I cannot be bled, and he can be dealt with," Emilio replied ominously. Her suppositions weren't anything he hadn't already turned over on a sleepless night. There were risks attached to his plan, it was true, but in Italy a mad dog could be disposed of, no questions asked. If Antonio were to discover his ploy and follow him, well . . . Don Emilio Lampone was no fool.

"I warn you, Emilio, if he adds one bruise to her body, I'll kill you. I wounded you once, I'll finish you this time."

Emilio picked up the phone and requested hotel security. Francesca swept out of the room and slammed the door.

"I'm going downtown," he announced to Solange, grabbing his case and topcoat. "Finish the packing and go to bed. We leave tomorrow night. It'll be a difficult day."

"Emilio," Solange called, catching him at the door, "she's right. Your money won't buy Maria's love."

"Then I'll settle for her freedom."

Chapter Thirty-Five

*S*EVERAL HOURS AFTER THE KID-
napping, Dante, disguised as Vittorio Fusco, swaggered through the front
door of the Cocked Hat. He knew his best chance for getting information
about Mina's whereabouts was to try to finesse it from Antonio or Kathleen.
Their presence at the Hat, or lack of it, would give him an indication of
Mina's whereabouts. Jimmy, Kathleen's barman, was behind the bar.

Dante checked the back room. Kathleen wasn't there, but as planned,
Mario had arrived ahead of him and was seated at a corner table with
Antonio and his raucous cronies playing pinochle. Antonio was swilling
whiskey and ferociously arguing with Biaggio over the last trick. There
appeared to be a fair amount of money in the pot, and wherever his wife
was hidden, Antonio didn't seem concerned about her welfare.

Dante tamped down the visceral rage he felt at Antonio's nonchalance. He wished he could throttle Antonio now, in front of everyone,
but he needed information, so he'd have to tread carefully. Dante put on
a cocky smile and moved into the action. Slapping backs, shaking hands,
and sitting down to join the game, he soon had a brandy and beer chaser
in front of him. He lit a cigarette and sat back to watch the card play,
waiting impatiently for the conversation to turn.

He knew Kathleen and Antonio weren't foolish enough to harm
Mina, but he was worried nonetheless. As far as he knew, Mina hadn't
told Antonio she was pregnant and Kathleen wouldn't be choosy about
her hiding place. Mina would be terrified and the strain might cause her
to miscarry. If that were to happen, she would be in grave danger, locked
away without help.

After a few minutes Antonio suggested a change in partners so that
only Biaggio, Mario, and Dante would remain at the table with him.
"The rest of you, scram," Antonio said. "Okay," he continued, slugging
down a shot of whiskey after the men moved away. "Let's lay out the action for tomorrow night's match. We got to give the crowd a good show.
We'll be stuck on that barge in the middle of nowhere and if we don't
make it look good, we'll have to swim back to Manhattan."

They went over the plan set at the gym and argued over fine points as they played. Dante's eyes kept sweeping the room looking for Kathleen, but she was nowhere in sight. He assumed she must be with Mina. Was Mina all right? He exchanged meaningful looks with Mario, but Mario's eyes bespoke his puzzlement as he filled Antonio's shot glass again and again.

Dante purposely underplayed his hands. He could easily have taken tricks, but he couldn't show his skill and feed Antonio's ego at the same time. Antonio was as giddy as a schoolboy raking in each pot. He was having a great time, but Dante's partner, Biaggio, was growing frustrated with Dante's "mistakes."

After several losing hands, Biaggio suggested a change of partner. "You watch awhile," Biaggio offered. "Take a break. This is a different kind of game. Not so formal, like in *Italia*." He elbowed Dante aside and motioned for one of the other men to come join him. Biaggio had lost enough pay to Tonio for one night, and now that the plans for the match were finished he was desperate to win some money back. Dante graciously moved to the side to watch, but he couldn't relax. Where was Kathleen?

After a few minutes Kathleen finally hustled in through the ladies' entrance. Dante's stomach unclenched when he saw her, but Antonio didn't look up from his hand. Her cheeks were flushed with color and she was wearing an overcoat, gloves, and a woolen scarf, so he knew she had come a distance in the cold.

Now that Biaggio had a new partner, the game had become a little more challenging for Antonio and he was thoroughly involved. Dante nudged Mario under the table and kept his eyes on Kathleen as she hurried into the front room without a backward glance. Dante "carelessly" set his glass down on the edge of the table and purposely toppled his beer. The liquid cascaded across the table, the cards, and the money in the pot.

"*Gesù Cristo!*" Antonio exclaimed, swiftly pulling the money toward his chest.

Dante jumped up and made a show of mopping the spill.

"Hey, *padrone*, what's the matter?" Antonio joked, "Can't hold yer liquor?" Then he laughed and motioned for another deck of cards as Dante excused himself to clear his head and take a leak.

Dante hurried to the front room, where he spotted Kathleen behind the bar. He slipped behind a patron to shield himself and watch her. Carefully she took something from her apron pocket and put it behind the end bottles, next to the wall. Whatever it was, it was small and remained secreted in her hand. She wiped her hands on her apron, wadded it up, and shoved it under the counter. When she swung around to survey the smoky room her face was set, her eyes glittering.

Dante knew he'd need to be his most seductive tonight, to save Mina. He stepped out into the open and rapped his knuckles against the bar to signal Jimmy for a drink. Immediately Kathleen picked him out of the crowd. When she made eye contact he winked at her insinuatingly and raised his glass. A sly smile stole across her face as she self-consciously lifted her hand to her throat.

She glanced back over her shoulder to check the back room and Antonio's whereabouts. Dante saw her smile confidently and toss her head to flip back her long hair. He smiled at her as she sauntered down the length of the bar, smoothing her corset and adjusting her skirts. He just might have a chance to get the information he needed.

"So ya ain't resting up before the big match tomorrow night?" she asked.

"I thought I'd come see what the competition's up to. Might as well go over plans tonight as tomorrow."

"His lordship's in there," she said, jerking her head. "Ya can go and join him if ya like."

"I've seen him. Besides, I'm not interested in cards." He let his eyes caress her figure, then gave her a carnal stare.

"No?" She laughed. "Where's yer girlfriend tonight? I'm surprised she's not keeping an eye on her man."

"Is that what you're doing?" Dante asked.

"I go my own way." She pushed a patron aside with her hip and sidled in next to him.

"That's what I like to hear," he said.

Kathleen nodded and smiled, taking note of his insinuating tone. "She wouldn't take kindly to hearing ya say that."

"I can't help what she'd like to hear."

"I see," she murmured as she ran the side of her foot up under his trouser leg and stroked his calf with her instep. She pounded on the bar and held up her thumb and index finger. After a moment Jimmy delivered a pint of ale and a shot of whiskey. She led Dante to the far corner, against the wall, where they were shielded from view. He leaned against her and she laughed huskily.

"You're looking lovely tonight, Mrs. Shaunessey."

"Thank ya kindly, sir, but I'm not any man's property. Call me Kathleen."

"All right, Kathleen, you look positively provocative tonight."

She grinned and lifted her shot. "To provocation and the fruits thereof."

He clinked his glass against hers and watched her toss back the whiskey. She was already tipsy, her passions smoldering.

"I'd have thought ya'd be down my way before now," she said.

"I've been in training. It took me some time to lose my excess weight," he said meaningfully.

She sized him up under half-closed lids, her chin up, her lips parted, and her hand slowly rubbing her collarbone with the empty shot glass. "Ah," she muttered, "I see. The little bundle's no longer with ya? Is that it?"

"Yes, you're right," he said, smiling. "I've sent the baggage packing."

She enjoyed the joke and ran her eyes over Vittorio. He was taller and leaner than Tonio, his hair and skin lighter, and his alley-cat eyes had a dangerous glint that made him irresistible. She watched him reach into his pocket and draw out a handkerchief. He moistened the tip in his ale, shifted her chin, and rubbed her cheek slowly with the cloth.

"You look like an angel stroked by Satan's sooty finger." He showed her the spot on the fabric.

"That's a little baggage of my own that needed taking care of." She chuckled wickedly.

He tilted his head toward the back room and covered her hand resting on the bar with his. "Are you saying you've finished with Tonio?"

"Finished with his property, yeah. Where it goes from here, who cares? I got bigger plans." She caught Jimmy's eye and held up her thumb. He brought her another whiskey.

"Dare I hope your plans might include me?" he asked, kissing her hand. He noticed an odd smell mixed with the perfume clinging to her clothing. Pressing her palm against his lips, he tried to place the odor. "You smell of the sea."

"I've been down to the docks to arrange for the match." She chuck-led. "I needed to pick up some provisions."

"Provisions?" Dante asked.

"Let's just say that however this plan pours out it's going to be a vin-tage year." She convulsed in laughter and slapped her thigh. He looked at her inquisitively. "Ya don't get it!" she crowed, tossing back the new shot, "but I'm hysterically funny."

"I wish I could laugh with you," he said, drawing back and pretend-ing disgruntlement.

"Now don't be temperamental. Yer not like them others," she said, walking her fingers up his chest. "Yer a smart man. Ya know I got my business to look out for. I'll let ya in on my plan after the fight."

"I'd rather you let me in now," he insinuated. He slipped his fingers into the bodice of her dress and pulled her close, pressing his other hand against her lower belly. Her eyes closed briefly and her neck arched back. When she opened her eyes, he saw they were glazed with lust.

Kathleen gave the room the once-over. No one noticed them; only Jimmy caught her eye. Being solidly on her payroll, he was no worry. If trouble was to come brewing, he'd give a shout. She turned her atten-tion back to Vittorio. His hand on her belly made her blood sizzle. Because of the day's activities she felt reckless and the whiskey only in-tensified her audacity. She had only one desire, to get her hands down his pants and possess him.

Dante recognized her need. "Don't you have a place around here that has a lock and no prying eyes?" he whispered, slipping his hand lower into the folds of her dress.

"Not here, ya crazy fool." She moaned, gripping his hand and pulling it aside.

Giving Jimmy the nod, she led Vittorio from the room. She could see that Tonio was still engrossed in his high-stakes pinochle game. Mario sat across from him playing cards, and several men stood watching the game. As she passed, Mario's eyes flickered over her. He got the drift, but seemed indifferent to her adventure. Mario would act as a buffer, if need be. She guessed she'd be safe for at least twenty minutes.

Inside the kitchen, Dante gave her a savage kiss and used the moment to look around the room. There were two other doors, one with a barred window that led to the back alley, the other a squat door under an overhang of stairs he knew led to the boardinghouse. The small door was hung with a padlock. Most likely it led to a cellar. That was all he had a chance to see before she shoved him inside the pantry and slipped the hook.

"Nice setup you got here. You got rooms upstairs?"

"Yeah, it's a boardinghouse," she said, slipping his jacket off. "If I let rooms, I can be open on Sundays. Legally a hotel." She peeled off his jacket, her passion and the liquor muddling any sense of caution.

"So how do I fit into your plan?" he whispered against her ear.

"Tomorrow night. I told ya." She started unbuttoning his pants, but he grabbed her wrists.

"You don't trust me? That kind of thing can undermine a man's confidence," he said with a chuckle.

Sure enough the back of her hands pressed against limp flesh. Damn men, they're so touchy. Things had been steaming ahead and now he was going to go soft on her because she wouldn't share her plans with him. Well, she thought, I'll hint a little, that won't hurt nothing. She hooked her leg around both his and drew him close.

"Yer a nosy one, ain't ya? Gets ya all hot to talk and tease, does it? Well, ya see, Tonio has a wife—well, he had a wife—" She snickered and rubbed the backs of her hands against him. He gripped her wrists with impatience, trying not to sound too eager when he prompted.

"Tonio had a wife. What would I care about her?"

"If ya knew he was trading her for more than her weight in gold ya'd care."

He released her. "Trading her?" he asked as though astonished. "No woman's worth her weight in gold."

"She is. She's worth ten thousand dollars."

"Ten thousand!"

She thought his voice sounded shaky. Was it choked with lust or greed? Whatever it was it was working to her advantage. "There are countries that aren't worth that," he whispered passionately against her ear.

"Yeah, like the one she's going to," she moaned as his lips brushed her skin.

Her breasts heaved, straining the fabric of her bodice. He noticed that she had a dirty velvet ribbon tucked into the cleft. He stooped to kiss the tops of her breasts and slipped his fingers down to wriggle a knot of keys loose.

"Where is it she's going?" he asked, discovering a new brass key among the tangle.

"Back to the old country. But I got her hid."

"Hid? Here? Locked up with your mess of keys?" he teased.

She laughed and tossed the keys out of reach over her shoulder. "Never ya mind. Time's short. No more talk." She trailed kisses down his chest, then dropped to the floor. He felt her fingers frantically working the buttons on his trousers.

"Are you cutting Tonio out? Ten thousand's a fortune. I could help with the trade." He lifted her hair up and brushed it back from her face, twisting his fingers into it, feigning excitement. "It's a dangerous business for a woman alone. What do you say? We'd be partners."

When her lips touched his skin Mina's faced leaped into his consciousness. She was standing at the pantry door, her hand upon the jamb, her eyes seeped in disbelief. How would Mina judge his current predicament? He was seconds away from a sexual encounter with the woman who was holding Mina prisoner, and try as he might, he couldn't stop his body from reacting. Kathleen was moaning softly as she pressed her lips against him and pulled the fabric down from his hips.

Dante tried to stall her as best he could. "You're a beautiful . . . crafty . . . woman. Where did you hide this treasure? Tell me where she's hidden and I can help—"

"Did ya hear that?" Kathleen stopped, suddenly alert. She jumped to her feet.

"What?" He listened. "It's nothing," he said, pulling her against him. "Tell me more abo—"

"Sssh!" she hissed, putting her hand over his mouth. There was a scuffle outside, then a fist hammered against the bucking wooden door.

"Take it easy, Tonio!" Mario's voice insisted.

"Jesus, Mary, and Joseph!" Kathleen whispered. "Get yer pants up. Hurry!"

Dante quickly buttoned his pants and threw on his jacket as Kathleen tucked her breasts in. Dante saw a curved knife blade he knew belonged to Mario slip between the door and the frame. In an instant the hook was lifted.

"What the hell's going on here?" Mario shouted, holding his knife in one hand and Antonio back with the other.

"Nothing's going on," Kathleen snarled. "We was discussing tomorrow night's match. We wanted some privacy."

"Privacy! You cheating whore!" Antonio thundered, lunging forward.

Dante put his fists up—he was aching to beat Antonio to a pulp—but Kathleen stepped in front of him and Mario grabbed Antonio's collar, pulling him up short. Over Antonio's shoulder Mario gave Dante a warning look. Oblivious to their exchange, Kathleen slammed her hands against Antonio's chest and knocked him free of Mario's grip. Antonio lunged into the middle of the room.

"Who ya calling a whore, ya stupid wop!" she screamed. "Like you ain't done yer share of screwing around."

Antonio tried to push past Kathleen to vent his rage on Dante, but she butted up against him and held him off. Mario gave Dante a meaningful look just before he grabbed Dante by the hair and spun him around. Dante doubled over and played along as Mario pressed his grape knife against Dante's throat. "What do you want me to do with him, Tonio?" Mario demanded.

"Are ya both daft?!" Kathleen shouted. "There's a fight tomorrow night in case ya forgot. We was planning strategy!"

"Strategy my ass! You was about to suck his dick," Antonio snapped.

The kitchen door opened and Jimmy stuck his head in. "Mrs. Shaunessey, I've got a little problem out here. Police officers from the Sixteenth Precinct. They say they're going to make a search of the premises."

"*Madonna puttana!*" Antonio swore. His eyes darted to the beer cellar door.

"Whadaya want me to do?" Jimmy asked.

She thought it over for an instant. "Tell them we ain't got nothing to hide. Let them search."

"You crazy!" Antonio shouted, indicating the cellar with a tip of his head.

"Here, Jimmy, give them my keys. Tell them to kill themselves." Jimmy caught the keys and disappeared back into the bar.

Antonio yanked Kathleen into the pantry, whispering furiously. Mario relaxed his grip on Dante and they waited in position, listening as Kathleen's voice rose in fury. "—so get yer ass back in the bar and play some cards. Act like nothing's happened. Go on. Let me handle this."

"What about——"

"Ya gotta trust me," Kathleen insisted, pushing him toward the bar.

At the door Antonio suddenly shook Kathleen off and strode back to Dante and Mario. "Smart boy, eh?" Antonio asked, shooting a fist into Dante's stomach.

Dante's gasp was genuine as he dropped to his knees. Mario did his best to pull the grape knife back quickly, but drops of blood plunked onto Mario's shoe.

"Now's not the time!" Kathleen insisted, pulling on Antonio's jacket. "Listen to me, ya stupid spaghetti bender," she said pulling at his back. "There's coppers out there."

"I fix you good tomorrow night," Antonio said. He spat on the floor, then stalked out.

Mario watched the blood trickle down Dante's neck. It was a superficial wound, but Mario was annoyed that he hadn't reacted fast enough to avoid the nick. Kathleen pulled on his arm.

"Leave him be, Mario," she ordered, putting her hand over his on the knife's handle. "He ain't done nothing."

"Tonio said——" Mario started to say, feigning wrath.

"I said leave him be!" she snapped. Mario gave Dante a shove and Dante fell forward into Kathleen's arms, where he remained on his knees, moaning in pain. Mario couldn't tell if he was acting or truly hurt.

"Sorry, love," Kathleen said, wiping the blood from his neck with her skirt. "Ya can get even tomorrow night."

She got to her feet. "Get him out of here, Mario," she ordered, suddenly all business, "and see that he gets that wound cleaned." She strode out to deal with the police.

Dante straightened up and checked his neck in a stew pot cover. It was a shallow cut, nothing to worry about, but his stomach muscles were a bit sore. "Damn it, what took you so long? She was about to—Jesus, I almost had to—I gave you the signal, didn't you see?"

"Sure. I saw you when you passed, but I figured you needed a little time. Did she tell you anything?" Dante was working the padlock on the door under the stairs with a small tool he'd taken from his pocket. "What are you doing? That's the beer cellar. Kathleen wouldn't be stupid enough to hide her down there."

"Keep an eye on the bar. Antonio was terrified when Jimmy said the police wanted to search, and he looked directly at this door."

Mario peered through a broken slat in the door leading to the bar, his anxious attention passing to the bar and back to Dante. In a moment Mario heard the lock snap open.

"I'm going down," Dante whispered, grabbing a box of matches from the stove.

He went down the stairs. Above his head, he heard the police he'd called in from the Sixteenth Precinct clomping up the boardinghouse stairs. He lit several matches and searched the earthen cellar. It smelled of stale ale, wine, and decay. Nothing but barrels, piled one atop the other, some rusted tools, smashed wooden crates, broken bottles, and rat droppings. He bent to inspect a damp spot near the storm doors. Greenish-gray wax had coagulated on the damp soil.

He heard a rustling and glimpsed a large rat slipping between the slats of a rotten barrel. There was a small incline and a storm door leading to the street. It wouldn't have been difficult to take Mina unseen from the cellar. When he reclimbed the stairs, Mario was nervously watching the barroom.

"Kathleen must have moved her," Dante said. "There's nothing down there but barrels and rats."

"You're sure? Tonio keeps looking this way, like she's hidden there."

Dante reattached the padlock. "She probably moved her while he was busy playing cards. That's why he thinks she's still in the cellar. We'd better get out of here," Dante said.

They went out the back and moved down the alleyway, turning the corner. "Kathleen was bundled up and must have come a distance. Do you have any idea where she might have taken her?"

Mario shrugged. "She could have taken her anywhere. She's got friends."

"There was a new brass key on the bunch she carries around her neck."

"A new key?" Mario's eyes lit up. "Her dream place, above Fourteenth Street. She's been talking about buying it for months."

"You know where it is?" Dante asked.

"No, but I can find out."

"Go back inside and see what you can uncover." Mario nodded and turned to go back down the alley. "Wait," Dante whispered. "Kathleen slipped something behind the bottles, in that alcove by the cash, when she first came in. Whatever it was would fit in the palm of your hand."

"I'll get it," Mario said. "Don't worry, leave everything to me. You better get out of here now. I'll meet you back at the brownstone."

Dante caught Mario's arm. "Mario, don't get caught," he urged. "I need you. Mina's alone and in danger. You have to help me save her."

Mario saw the fear and doubt in Dante's eyes. Even with all the betrayals he had suffered Mario's heart hadn't hardened. "I know you love her, Signor Dante," he said softly, "but I love her too. No one knows the danger she's in more than I. I swear to you, even if I must give my life, I will save her."

Chapter Thirty-Six

WHEN THE CARRIAGE STOPPED, Emilio was confronted with a shuttered, fashionable restaurant and saloon. Leaving the cab in the lane, he went to pound on the door.

"Yeah, yeah! I'm coming. What do ya want? Can't ya see we're closed?" a woman's voice shouted warily through the closed door.

"I need to see Signor Antonio DiGianni."

"Are ya the man looking for the package . . . from the Plaza Hotel?"

"I am."

The bolt jerked back. The face of a tough young woman with dark curly hair appeared in the chink behind a taut chain. She looked him over, then slipped the lock. He stepped inside. Across the cavernous room the halo of a single candle illuminated the scene. He could dimly perceive tables and chairs stacked in the shadowy corners. The parquet floor was littered with trash, and crouching in the gloom was a long, grandly carved wooden bar with a dusty gilded mirror running behind. The mirror rippled with dim reflections. The place had obviously been closed up for some time.

"Ya brought the cash?" Her eyes swept over him like a pickpocket's sizing up a mark. They settled on his leather case.

"I'll need to meet with Antonio before I proceed further."

"I'm his partner. There ain't nothing to worry about."

The bully had picked a likely wench. The mistress of his granddaughter's husband was slim and attractive in a cheap, obvious way, and reeked of alcohol. "Where's the young woman?"

She laughed and shook her head. "I hope ya know what yer in for. She's as hardheaded as Tonio. I left her tied to a chair in the pantry, safe and sound, and she finds a way to fall down the back kitchen steps."

"She's injured?"

"Naw. There was only three wee steps, thank the good Lord, or she'd be cold as a mackerel right this minute."

Her harsh manner spurred him to action. "I need to see her now."

"Not so fast. I got to see the cash first." As she edged forward he pulled back, trying to see beyond her into the gloom. "Don't worry yerself. Nobody knows we're here. I put up my deed to buy this place and just got the key this morning." She backed off and went to the table. "Put it down right here," she ordered, moving the taper aside.

Kathleen looked the old man over as he came forward. Fragile as a dry leaf, he was, leaning on a cane, but coiled like a snake. I bet he's a handful in bed, she thought with disgust, a real slimy stick. She'd have to watch him: he was ancient, but not beyond jamming her up if the occasion arose. He put the leather case flat on the table next to his cane. Her hands were sweating as she unfastened the straps of the case. She'd been trying to imagine just how five thousand dollars would stack up.

"Take me to the girl," the old man coaxed, his voice like syrup. "I need . . . I need to settle our business."

"Yer hot for the little bundle, ain't ya?"

"I want to make sure she's the same woman I asked for. And then, if you're reassured about payment, we can make the exchange right now."

She threw back the top. She'd never seen so many new bills, so tightly stacked, in such a small space before. "They're yellow!" she cried in dismay.

"Yes, 1907 issue," he said reassuringly. "Redeemable in gold, just like you asked."

Suspiciously, she took one and examined it. On the back, surrounded by rays of gold, an eagle soared. She held her breath, gazing in delight at the crisp, buttery ten-dollar gold certificates.

"They've never been touched," she said with awe.

"Fresh from the bank. There's five hundred of them, and they're yours, when you deliver the girl."

She saw a new sun rising on her own horizon as she pressed the bills to her nose. "They even smell good," she said, laughing.

"Is the girl here? I'd like to see her."

"Tonio!" she shouted, unable to take her eyes from the money. "Bring yer wife. He's got the cash."

In the pantry Mina tried to resist, but Antonio forced her out the door, holding the same knife he'd used to kidnap her against her back. It pricked her skin, urging her on. The door creaked open, revealing only a dark room with a candle in the distance. She saw two figures in the shadows. A moan of fear slipped from her throat.

"Scream and I'll put the gag back," he whispered. "You can't get away. The little stunt you pulled earlier proved that. Try and you'll end up dead."

"Please, take me home," Mina pleaded frantically. "I promise I'll do anything you say."

"Yer right about that. Come on, I've got a little surprise for you."

He moved her forward and the wizened face of a man with silver hair appeared as she entered the fringe of light. His pale eyes swept over her body greedily, his hands trembled with excitement. For an instant his pleasure-creased face flickered with hostility as his gaze moved to Antonio, but she saw him snuff out his distaste. Her legs were trembling so hard she was barely able to stand. It was dark, but something about the old man seemed familiar. She thought she might have seen him somewhere before.

"Is this the woman you wanted?" Antonio asked in Italian. He took the knife from her back and slipped it into his jacket pocket.

"She is," the old man answered.

One of Antonio's hands dug into her shoulder while the other held her arm. He pressed his lips to her ear. "Say hello to the gentleman."

Mina focused on the old man's thin, smiling lips. Yes, she'd seen that smile before. Where had she seen it? Her throat felt as though she'd swallowed a chunk of dry beef. She couldn't speak. Her mind flitted in panic as she tried to place him. Had she seen him on Mulberry Street . . . or in the market? Perhaps at the opera house?

"Please excuse me," the old man said softly in Italian. "We haven't been properly introduced. I'm Don Emilio Lampone, a friend of your husband's from Naples."

Yes, that was it! It was at the opera house, in the Signorina's dressing room. He had been there with the young blond woman. He was an enemy of the Signorina, but what was he doing here? Before she had time to piece it together the old man reached out to touch her. His long, thin hand was all bone, covered with a network of bulging blue veins and a veil of milky skin. On the table she caught sight of a case filled with money; she pulled back against Antonio. Surely this was a nightmare from which she would soon awake.

"Take me away from here!" she begged Antonio. This was the man Antonio's mistress had told her about in the market. He had obviously tracked her after seeing her at the opera house. Why was he trying to buy her? Did it have something to do with the Signorina and his desire for revenge? Her fevered mind raced, inventing all sorts of horrors. Slavery, prostitution, rape, infanticide . . . She tried to twist away from Antonio, but his grip was like iron.

"Don't be afraid, my dear, I would never hurt you," the old man said. When his cold hand touched her cheek, a scream finally broke from her throat: "No, no! Help me! Somebody help me!" She continued screaming until Antonio slapped her twice.

"Shut up!" Antonio shouted. "You scream again and I'll beat you within an inch of your life."

The old man caught Antonio's arm and stopped him from striking again, but Mina dropped to the floor and cowered against her husband's legs. This evil she understood. What the old man had in mind she didn't know.

"For God's sake!" Emilio cried. "Don't strike her! There's no need to be violent." Emilio was shaken by Antonio's brutality; he'd thought Francesca overly dramatic, but she'd been telling the truth. This man was dangerous.

"She's gotten out of hand this last month, but you won't have any trouble getting her back in line if you give her a cuff or two," Antonio snarled.

Emilio's granddaughter moaned softly. Her dark eyes, so like Giulio's, were terrified, but she didn't cry out again. Antonio pried her hands from his legs and shoved her into a chair. "Sit there! Don't make a peep or I'll knock you into next week." He ordered Kathleen to guard her and turned back to Emilio.

Inside, Emilio was sick with impotent rage, but his business negotiations had taught him to keep his true emotions cloaked. His confidence in his ability to manipulate circumstances to his benefit was shaken. He was beginning to regret the depraved character he'd fashioned for himself, but he was trapped by his role. He drew Antonio aside to discuss things in Italian. "This is not what I had in mind, Signore," he said, sotto voce. "You have not explained."

"What's to explain?" Tonio asked without lowering his voice. "Did you expect me to tell her, 'Some old pervert wants to fuck you and is paying me a fortune to hand you over?' Do you think she'd have come willingly if I told her that?"

"You could have said I was a friend. That she was to work for me. The cover story about the job of companion, the one my man suggested. You could have thought of something."

"That's not my business. You want to buy her, okay, she's yours tomorrow to do with what you want, but she's going to cost you ten thousand dollars."

"Ten thousand! I don't have ten—"

"You can get it," he urged forcefully.

Antonio was sweating in spite of his bluster, and Emilio saw through his desperate gambit. Antonio would be more than satisfied with the five thousand, but he'd try to haggle for more. Emilio could easily turn down the upped ante, but it would take days of bargaining and he needed to get his granddaughter out of this hell tonight. Perhaps, he thought, if I pretend the deal has gone sour and I don't want her anymore, Antonio will panic and turn her over to me for what I've brought in the case.

"You've ruined everything," Emilio said. "She detests me. She isn't worth ten thousand dollars frightened out of her mind. I don't want her like this."

"What's going on over there?" Kathleen demanded.

"He says she's scared. He no want her scared."

Kathleen forgot her prisoner and advanced belligerently. "The deal's off? Just because she's a little upset?"

Left unattended, Mina's body tensed for flight, but before she could flee Antonio dashed across the room and pulled her from the chair. He wrapped one arm across her throat and shoved her forward. "Look at her!" he cried in English, gesturing wildly with his free arm. "Cleaned up she's even more beautiful than when ya first saw her."

Emilio's gamble appeared to be working: Antonio seemed panicked. In a moment, Emilio thought, Antonio will agree to the five thousand dollars I've brought and I'll reluctantly take her despite my doubts. Then I'll get her out of here and ensure that Antonio never has access to her again.

"She's young, just the way ya like them," Antonio said, indicating her body with his free hand. Emilio tried to keep the repugnance he felt from showing on his face. "I got her from old country, untouched—"

"Ripe and wet—" Kathleen added.

Emilio's loathing rushed out before he could catch it. "Don't be disgusting!" he cried.

Antonio laughed harshly. "You're the pervert," he said. "How old are you anyway, seventy?"

"Just get the rest of the money, old man," Kathleen said, stroking his arm lasciviously, "and tomorrow night ya can have her, any way ya been dreaming."

The woman was vile. Emilio pulled back from her touch and watched the two exchange nervous glances. This man was a greedy, loathsome animal, and his granddaughter was in grave danger. He should never have concocted this revolting ruse. He hesitated. What should he say to convince them he wouldn't bargain, or should he simply agree and try to get the money quickly?

His eyes shifted to the money and back to his granddaughter. He had to take her now—Francesca was right; her fear might cause her to lose the baby. What should he do? He decided it didn't matter, he would promise the ten thousand, then create some diversion to—

Before he could act, he heard the sound of fabric ripping and in a blur saw his granddaughter collapse onto her knees. Her husband's hand was twisted into her hair as he held her arched against his leg. The top of her dress had been torn open, exposing her to the waist.

"Here, get a good look at what yer buying," Antonio cried like a snake oil salesman. "She's got hard tits, a tight cunt, and that angelic mouth of hers ain't tasted cock but once. She don't like sex, but she ain't broken in. Ya can have yer fun teaching her what ya like. Ya want to sample the goods? Go ahead, take her in the back, for ten thousand ya got the right."

Antonio shoved her forward with his leg and she collapsed onto the floor at Emilio's feet, whimpering. Emilio exploded with fury.

"How dare you!" he shouted in Italian. "I would never harm this child! She is my blood and I, her grandfather!" He stepped over her body to block her from Antonio and reached inside his jacket. She drew the tatters of her dress together.

"Grandfather!" Antonio exclaimed in Italian. "What kind of scam are you trying to pull?"

"What did he say?" Kathleen demanded. Her eyes flickered suspiciously between Emilio and Antonio.

"I am Don Emilio Lampone of Naples and this is my granddaughter, Maria Grazia. She's the treasure of my life. I thought I'd lost her, but my prayers have been answered. Loathsome creature, you'll never lay a hand on her again." Emilio drew the pistol from his waistband and aimed it. He saw the brute's eyes light up with wrath. The mistress backed away toward the money.

"I don't give a fuck if you're King Emanuel the Second," Antonio shouted. "If you want her, you're going to give me ten thousand or you'll never see her again."

"Tonio, what's he saying?" Kathleen demanded.

Antonio advanced threateningly; Emilio thought he might have to put a bullet in him. "Maria Grazia! Come here, come to me," Emilio urged. He held out his hand, but her eyes were glazed in shock.

She'd heard what the old man had said, but his words didn't penetrate or make any sense. She shook her head and crawled toward the wall, refusing this stranger's protection. Emilio backed toward her unsteadily, pointing the gun at Antonio's chest.

"Be reasonable, old man," Antonio said. "Or I'll be forced to break your neck."

"Don't threaten me. I am not a woman you can bully."

"Give me the gun," Antonio coaxed, "and I'll forget the insult."

"Stay where you are. I'm taking her with me," Emilio ordered. In his peripheral vision Emilio glimpsed a flash of gold.

"Look out!" his granddaughter shouted, her hands flying out as if to shield him.

Emilio caught a glimpse of his lion-headed cane arcing through the darkness. He felt something violently strike his head and heard the report of his pistol shaking the room. Antonio staggered back. Then everything went black.

Chapter Thirty-Seven

ONIO SQUINTED THROUGH THE smoke-stained glass of the ladies' entrance at the Cocked Hat. The sun was up. The light made it difficult for him to see Kathleen snoring on the tabletop, her head resting on her biceps, her hand outstretched toward a half-empty bottle of whiskey and a tumbled shot glass. Her knotted hair was spread like a tossed mop, her mouth, slack and sloppy. Her other arm encircled two piles of bills like a fortress. The greedy bitch had already divvied the money while he'd gone uptown with Don Lampone.

She'd obviously passed out counting and recounting the contents of the purloined satchel. The quiet of the room was punctuated periodically by her drunken snorts and the barely perceptible sound of coal slipping through the grate as it was consumed to white ash. He hammered his fist on the door.

"Who is it? Who's there?" she called, rising up like a tigress protecting a cub.

"Fucking open the door, Kathleen."

She let him in. "Did you drop him at the hotel?" she demanded, scanning the alley to be sure no one had followed him back. "It took ya a while. Everything went okay?"

"Fine, yeah."

She rebolted the door and turned to embrace him, but he slipped away from her and went to the table. "I was just dreaming of haystacks of money," she sighed. "And you and me plunk in the middle having ourselves a sporting good time!"

Money and sex, sex and money, they were all that started her motor. "Where is she?" he asked, taking a swig of whiskey from the bottle on the table.

"Yer wife?"

"No, the Queen of Sheba. Where'd you hide her this time?"

"Someplace safe," she said. "Someplace nobody'd think of looking. Least of all you!" She slapped her thigh in amusement and dropped onto the chair next to him, laughing. He wanted to yank her hair and smack the location out of her, but he didn't dare. She wasn't meek like his wife; he'd have to use craftier means.

Kathleen was scrutinizing him carefully in the dim light. She could always tell when he was lying to her. He pulled his cap lower to hide his eyes and wiped the sweat off his forehead with the back of his sleeve. He'd need to play it close to the vest. If he wasn't careful she'd smell a cheat and bolt with his wife. "What's wrong? Did ya run into trouble?"

"A gun in the ribs?" he joked, making a gun with his fingers and acting it out. "Whaddaya think?"

She laughed and toyed with the cash while he took off his jacket. "How'd ya like that guy thinking he could take us?" she asked.

"Good thing you slugged him," Tonio said. He put a finger through the hole in his jacket's shoulder. "He could've killed me."

"Jesus! I didn't realize he'd nicked ya. Ya ain't bleeding?" He shook his head. She examined the hole in his jacket in awe. "Tell me again what he was yelling about before I hit him."

Tonio turned away from her. "Let's take this upstairs," he said, scraping half the bills into the case, "throw it on the bed, and have a good fuck on top like you say." He tried to scoop up the other stack of bills, but she grabbed it away.

"I ain't never seen yer eyes so big, I'll tell ya that!" she said, waving the bundle back and forth just under his nose. "Whatever he said put the fear of God into ya."

He pressed her toward the stairs. If he wanted to get the Don's cash back and find out where his wife was hidden he was going to have to screw it out of her. "Come on."

"Tell me what the old man said," she insisted.

"I told you. He said he was going to take her *and* the money."

"He talked all that dago just to say that?" She dug in her heels, refusing to budge. There was something strange about the way Tonio was acting.

Tonio ran his free hand over her body sensuously. Her passion surged when he squeezed her breast and bit the back of her neck. She was momentarily distracted and reached back to rub her hand against his crotch. "Oh, yeah," she finally moaned, "let's go up." She broke from him and rushed back to swipe the whiskey bottle from the table; then, clutching her pile of bills in one hand and the bottle in the other, she staggered up the steps.

Tonio shoved her up, doing his best to inflame her lust by groping under her skirts. If he got her fired up it would dampen her suspicions. Near the top of the flight, her foot slipped and she fell backward on top of him, laughing hysterically, dead weight. He struggled to keep from falling and shoved her forward into the hallway, where she collapsed like a hyena. "Come on! Get up!" he snapped, impatiently hauling her to her feet.

Drunk as she was, the conniving bitch slapped his hands away when he tried to help her with the keys to the door. Rushing into the bedroom, she fanned herself with her stack of money and sniffed the air. "Sweeter than the breath of angels!" she cried. Then, like rose petals, she scattered the packet of cash across the rumpled covers and tumbled down on top. Holding her arms up to him solicitously, she crooned, "Shower me with gold, darlin', let it piss sawbucks!"

Tonio scattered the bills as she playfully moaned and groaned in excitement. "Oh, moolah, moolah . . . give me more moolah!"

After a moment he threw the satchel on the floor and grabbed her by the ankles. She eagerly scooted to the edge of the bed. "We're fucking rich, ya know," she said, running her hands over his chest. "And after the fight, we won't ever lift a finger again."

"After I deliver my wife, ya mean."

"That's the easy part, darlin'." She tried to wrap her legs around him and pull him on top of her, but he flipped her over and shoved her forward onto the mattress. It was better if she didn't see his face while he questioned her about his wife's whereabouts. She was moaning and pushing back against him like a cat in heat as he pulled her drawers down.

"Ohhh, yeah, that's good," she cried as she grabbed two fists of cash and the sheet for support. He entered her knowing she was swimming in the delightful sensations of a hot fuck on a bed of money.

Once he got her primed he got down to business. "Where'd you put my wife?"

"Ummm . . . yeah, good . . ." She pounded back against him, groaning with pleasure.

"Where is she?" he wheedled. "In the new saloon?"

She just grunted, too deep in her pleasure to respond. He rested against her, knowing how to get her attention. "Don't stop!" she shouted.

"Did ya tie her up safe?"

She slammed her fists on the mattress in frustration. "Come on, Tonio! What're ya doing leaving me stranded?" He didn't move. "Yeah! Yeah!" she shouted. "She's safe." Even in the throes of passion Kathleen sensed something amiss. She didn't trust his shifty, insistent questioning and decided not to give up the new location. "I hid her good."

"Where?" he demanded.

"In the basement of the new saloon," she lied. "Let's go!"

The knowledge of his wife's location ignited him; Tonio began thrusting in earnest, enjoying himself. His new future appeared before him, flickering like the pictures he'd seen at the nickelodeon: a villa in the country, family crest, servants, fine clothes, a stable of spirited horses . . . all the privileges of wealth. His brain was thoroughly intoxicated with images of becoming one of the richest men in Italy.

He'd apologized profusely for his brutish behavior when he'd taken Don Emilio back to the Plaza. He'd blamed it on drink and Kathleen's greed and had begged forgiveness, pledging to return four thousand dollars of the tainted money. He sheepishly admitted he needed to keep one thousand dollars to "pay off a debt of honor." The Don understood that the money was meant to satisfy Kathleen, and Tonio found the Don agreeable to his plan.

Tonio figured that by returning the money he'd show the Don respect and win his favor. Besides, he thought, why should I keep a few paltry dollars when I have the wealth of a king waiting for me in Italy? He promised to take care of loose ends and return to the Plaza with Don Emilio's granddaughter in time for lunch. Then the three of them would leave for Italy late Sunday evening.

He came back from his bright future to the rumpled bedroom reluctantly. While he screwed Kathleen one last time he retrieved the bills she wasn't holding and coolly counted and ordered the loose cash. Then he folded it and put it into his pants pocket. He watched with amusement as she pressed a wad of bills she was clutching to her lips, biting and sucking it as she climaxed. She'd always loved cold cash better than hot cock.

She was still squirming in the afterglow when he rolled her over and grabbed the bills that had been hidden under her body. "I ain't fighting tomorrow night," he announced.

"Whaddaya mean? You, Mario, and Vittorio planned everything out before we went to meet the old man. It's a couple thousand profit, by the looks of it. No sense throwing money away."

She circled her arm around him, pressing kisses to his neck, but he pulled the damp wad of bills out of her fist and flung her arm from his neck. "What're ya doing?" she asked, pushing her hair out of her eyes.

"Settling up," he said, counting.

"Settling up?" she asked with a tipsy grin. "Are ya going someplace?"

"*Italia.*" He threw back the covers overhanging the mattress and searched under the bed for his duffel bag.

"Italy? When pigs fly!"

"I go tomorrow night." He spotted the dark fabric of the duffel behind some dusty boxes and tugged on it. "I'll get the biggest villa in *Italia.*"

"With yer piddling bit of cash? Two thousand five ain't enough for a villa. Stop teasing." While he was still crouching she threw her legs over his back and wrapped her thighs around his neck, squeezing him. "Let's do it again," she hooted, digging her fingers into his hair. "I just got a little taste."

He'd had enough of her lusty demands. He shot to his feet, flipping her back onto the bed. "Come on, stop pawing me."

She rolled over to watch him as he rifled through the dresser and stuffed the duffel bag. He *was* acting strange. "What lies did that old man tell ya?" she demanded. "He's got ya all worked up over something."

"Her grandfather say—" He jammed his fist into his mouth and bit his knuckle. How could he let that slip?

"Grandfather!" Kathleen stood up on the bed abruptly, trying to marshal her wits. Her interest in sex was gone. "Whaddaya mean, grandfather?" she demanded as she wobbled on the covered springs.

Tonio's eyes had taken on a gleam. "The Black Hand told Mario he's the richest man in Naples."

He was worked up like a racehorse coming down the home stretch, but in her drunken state she couldn't connect his duffel bag with "the richest man in Naples."

"Yeah, so he'll give ya the ten grand easy," she said. "It's perfect!"

"I don't need that money. *Sono famiglia.*"

"Famil—what are ya saying? Yer family?" The idea of Tonio being family to that upper-crust snob whacked her funny bone. She suddenly plopped down on the springs, howling with laughter. She kicked up her heels and pounded the mattress while Tonio glared at her as if she'd gone mad. "Ya think he's going to accept ya, ya stupid wop? Ya've been drinking some of that camphorized ale! Oh, that's rich!" she screamed. "Tonio DiGianni, a gentleman!"

Tonio stuck out his chin belligerently. "Maybe he don't want me, but he wants his blood. If he don't take me I don't let Filomina see him. His blood's finished."

This new bit of strategy made her pause. She stopped laughing and wiped a tear of mirth from her eye. "So that's the plan?" she asked with interest. She nervously rubbed her thumb against her lower lip. "Blackmail? Yer a smart man, that's one thing I'll say for ya. Yer shrewd. So we threaten him and don't give her up until we get more?"

"She's my wife. I take everything."

"Everything? Yer loony! Ya can't push that old man too far."

"I'll get it, you'll see. Money, villa, respect . . ."

She didn't like the way his mind was working. Drunk as she was, she could see he'd been planning to cut her out. Coming back to the Hat to take the money and pack a bag . . . he was running out on her. It was a damn lucky thing she'd held back the location of his wife. "Naw, ya better take the money he's offered," she suggested. "If he finds out that gigolo's knocked her up, where will ya be? He ain't giving no money to an outsider, married or no."

"I plant that seed . . . that's my blood. My wife's a decent, respectable woman."

"Decent and respectable, is it? The woman ya refer to as 'the mail-order whore'?"

"You hate her, so I say bad things. I was not good husband. I hit her, I stayed away. But because of our child she'll forgive me. I'll be better husband in *Italia*."

Kathleen glared at him. The bastard was going to ruin all her plans. She jumped off the bed, her fists doubled. "Don't be a fool. It's that gigolo's kid. Ya told me yerself ya couldn't trust a whore of a whore."

"You're jealous," he said coolly. "You don't want to see me rich."

"She's been fucking around behind yer back. All the men know, she's made a fool of ya."

"Nobody makes a fool of Antonio DiGianni," he snapped, grabbing her.

"That's what ya think! Ya've been cuckolded. She put the horns on ya." She laughed scornfully. His eyes went dark as he forcefully pinned her arms to her sides and shoved her against the wall.

"You think I don't know you?" he asked with soft hatred. "You think I've believed all your lies? I seen the way you eye all the men. You're so hot for a dick you lift your skirt for everyone, like a dog in the street. Didn't I catch you in the pantry with Vittorio? You think I'm stupid?"

"I told ya we was planning strategy for tomorrow night's fight. There was nothing going on."

He laughed. "You'd suck him dry in a minute for two bits like the lowest streetwalker. Whore? Whores sell themselves for money; you're the only *real* whore I know."

His body gave off heat like pitch bubbling in August and his words stuck in her heart like a broken knife blade. She'd thought she'd been sly and conned him all these years, but his cold eyes told her he'd known all along about her manipulations and dalliances.

"So ya never cared?" she asked, watching him from the corners of her eyes. "Ya never loved me?"

"Loved you?" He laughed and stepped back. "Now who's acting loony? How could you think I'd ever love a potato-digging sheeny pig like you?"

"It's a lie!" she cried.

"I used you. You spread your legs, I stuck it in. That ain't no lie."

Her body surged with rage and injured pride when she saw clearly that he meant what he said. It flashed through her mind that she'd like to kill him, but she didn't have the means. She took a deep, slow breath and made sure her tone came out even and unshaken.

"So yer tossing me aside?" she asked. "All our plans for the fight and sale finished because yer wife's got a rich grandfather? What about my saloon? Ya promised."

"There's a thousand bucks," he said, pointing to the cash lying on the exposed ticking. "I squared it with the Don. Never say Tonio DiGianni don't square his debts." He shoved her aside and shouldered his duffel.

"It ain't near enough," she howled, giving into her fury. "I gave my deed yesterday for the new saloon. Ya gotta fight tomorrow."

"I got money now, I no fight. You want a saloon, *you* earn it. Use that hungry cunt of yours to get it."

She swiped at him, aiming for his eyes. He dodged her, swearing with genuine anger when her nails dug into his neck. He swung his duffel bag and hit her, catching her off balance and propelling her into the carved bedstead. She hit sideways, slamming her head into the post. Her knees buckled and she grabbed it for support.

"Give me the key to the new joint," he ordered.

She was blinded for a moment by the strength of the impact. Her nose felt like it might be broken and when she put her hand up it came away bloody. Her mind flashed back to the beating he'd given her five years before and she was suddenly afraid. He was sober now and she didn't have a table leg handy. His eyes had the glint of a lunatic. She'd be the one to end up in the hospital this time.

"Sure, Tonio, here . . ." she said, fishing for the keys hidden in her bosom. While she stalled, he backed off just enough to allow her to squeak out the door. She gripped the knot of keys at her breast and made for the stairs. "Ya ain't getting them or her," she hollered.

She pulled her skirts up and pounded down the steps, but Tonio caught her halfway. As he jerked the ribbon around her throat she lost her footing. For a moment she desperately clutched at him, choking. Then she fell backward, pulling him down the remaining stairs, and they both landed in a tangle on the bar floor. Tonio rolled off her unharmed and sprang up. As she lay gasping for breath, he broke the ribbon and took her new brass key.

"I gave a thousand dollars," he said, pulling his cap on. "It's good, fair, and finished." The remaining keys jangled to the floor where he threw them as he banged out the back door.

She lay stiffly with her fists balled up and tears of rage puddling her eyes. She'd thought she would never care what any man said, but his words tore at her gut and made her want to retch. Lying there on the floor of her crumbling bar, she began to sob for the first time since she'd left Ireland. He'd said he'd never loved her. Said she was a sheeny whore good only for a fuck. He'd insulted her before, but not like this.

This wasn't like the last time, after he married his wife and disappeared for two weeks. No, this time was different. This time, even if he came crawling back, she knew he'd never loved her. That he'd used her. "You spread your legs, I stuck it in." The bastard had known all along she'd been cuckolding him, but he hadn't cared because he didn't love her. She hated him for that.

He'd destroyed the little comfort she'd clung to in spite of poverty and hard times: the belief that she was loved. And to top it all off he was stealing her dream. There'd be no more fights in her back room, no grand payday from the barge, no ten thousand dollars to pay off the note she'd signed the day before. He was going to take his wife, and them fancy uptown bastards holding her lease were going to take the Cocked Hat. She'd be worse off than when Jack died. He was stealing everything from her and handing it to his bitch bride. How she hated him!

It was all that guinea cocksucker Tonio's fault. She sobbed and curled her body into a tight ball. But with a start she realized how crafty she'd been—she hadn't given Tonio the real location of his wife. He'd go uptown and find an empty saloon. Tonio couldn't go back to the Don without his wife. No, he'd have to come back and make a deal with her. Kathleen began laughing as she wiped the tears from her cheeks.

"I'll fix ya, ya guinea bastard," she hollered, rising from the floor. "Ya ain't beat me, not by a long shot. This sheeny whore'll see ya get fixed good."

Chapter Thirty-Eight

CESCA HEARD THE VAGUE SCRATCH-ing of Lucifer's claws on the bedroom door and ambiguous raised voices below. When she awoke Lucifer was snuffling softly, pressing against her leg, and she discovered she was fully dressed and wrapped in a blanket on her bedroom chair. She must have dozed off while waiting for word of Mina. It was light outside the lace curtains. She sprang up and hurried down to the foyer where she found Dante, still disguised as Vittorio, in the middle of a heated exchange with Mario and Colombo.

"—work out perfectly. Now, Mario, if you stay—"

"What's happened?" she asked, cutting Dante off in midsentence. "Where is she?"

"Dante's called off the search," Colombo said.

"Don't be ridiculous! Emilio's planning to leave within hours. You can't give up," Cesca said.

"We've already searched a new saloon above Fourteenth Street that Kathleen put money on," Dante said, doing his best to steady Cesca. "Unfortunately, we've currently exhausted all possibilities."

"What new saloon? What are you talking about?"

Mario, Dante, and Colombo explained the evening's activities.

"As they played cards they planned the whole match round by round," Colombo said. "And Dante took Kathleen into the pantry to try to uncover Mina's hiding place."

"Antonio nearly caught me with my pants down. Thank God Mario came into the back before anything serious happened." He shook his head ruefully and flushed.

"I had to draw my knife to separate them," Mario said, indicating the cut on Dante's throat.

Dante looked sheepish. "I searched the beer cellar and the police searched the boardinghouse, but nothing was found," he said gruffly. "Mario also found a vial of amyl nitrate. She could be hidden in plain sight and we wouldn't know it. She's being drugged and is most likely unconscious."

"Drugged?" Cesca was appalled by this new turn of events. She knew Dante loved Mina and was doing his best, but she was too angry with him to feel sorry for his suffering.

"So, 'Vittorio,' " she said with vexation, ripping Dante's gummed mustache off, "you haven't the power over women you thought you had. Why didn't you do something sooner to stop Antonio and his crazy mistress? What the hell have I been paying you for?"

She rolled the sticky strip of crepe hair and gum into a ball and paced the carpet. Dante rubbed his smarting upper lip.

"I'm sorry, Cesca," Dante said gravely. "I know the situation sounds hopeless, but there is some good news. Emilio's offered to take Antonio back to Italy with Mina."

This latest piece of information took the starch out of Cesca's spine. She collapsed on the sofa with a thud and started to weep. Colombo and Mario glanced at each other helplessly.

"It's okay, signorina," Colombo said, stepping forward to calm her.

"Kathleen's hiding Signora Mina and forcing Tonio to go through with the barge fight tomorrow and—"

Cesca looked at him with disgust. "Who cares about the fight?" she wailed. "Don't you see? I've lost my daughter."

Dante sat down and put an arm around her. "Listen to him, *cara!*" he said, shaking her gently. "Colombo's trying to tell you good news."

"Mario went back to the Cocked Hat early this morning and discovered that Kathleen's concocted a plot to double-cross Antonio," Colombo said.

"Tonio was dumping Kathleen to go back to Italy with Mina," Mario said, hurrying the story along. "Kathleen was so mad she's devised a plot for revenge. She's going to have him arrested and sell Mina herself."

"She's hidden Mina in an unknown location and made her own deal with Emilio," Dante finished.

Cesca stared at him and then at the others. Why were they all smiling and nodding at her like clowns? What difference did it make if Antonio sold Mina or Kathleen did? Emilio was still taking her daughter away.

"Dante's agreed to fight Antonio to further Kathleen's plans," Colombo said. "But the exchange will never happen. During the fight our detectives will find Mina and take her back."

Cesca stopped crying, panic replacing her fear. "During the fight you'll find her?" she asked. "On a loaded barge? In a fight crowd? We'll never find her in all those people."

Mario stepped forward. "Dante, Colombo, and I have made our own plans," he said encouragingly. "I've been waiting a long time to get even."

Cesca looked at Mario, then Dante without comprehension. "What do you mean?" she asked Mario.

"When I got to the Hat Kathleen was jittery and tense. She had a loaded gun in her apron pocket and was trying to watch her back," Mario said. "She knows Tonio is furious, even though Don Emilio helped her get Tonio to agree to go through with the barge fight. Well, like everyone else, she thinks I can't hold my liquor because I don't drink in public. So I had a few drinks with her and pretended to get drunk. I 'confessed' I hated Tonio and played it up, cursing his good luck. I cried and said, 'Not only is he stealing my bride, but he's stealing the fortune that should be mine.' That part got her angry and she confided that Tonio was trying to do the same thing to her, but she was going to fix him. After a few more drinks I offered to help her."

"I don't understand," Cesca said, staring at Mario. "You're going to help Kathleen?"

"Mario's going to be our inside man," Colombo said, trying to dispel her confusion. "Mario'll be in Tonio's corner for the fight. Tonio already trusts him, so he'll tell him about any change in plans. Hopefully Kathleen will do the same. Mario will be able to keep an eye on both of them and tell us what they're planning. We already know that after the eleventh round Kathleen will try to transfer Mina from the barge to a boat hired by Don Emilio."

"If you know he's hired a boat," Cesca inquired, "why can't you stop him before he gets to the barge?"

"We don't know who he's hired. Besides, Kathleen can't make a transfer in the middle of the river without someone seeing her," Dante said.

"It'll probably happen immediately after the knockdown while the crowd is in a turmoil," Mario said. "She hinted as much to me."

Cesca looked mournfully unconvinced.

"Don't you see? It's good news! The *only* way for Emilio to take Mina is by boat," Dante said reassuringly. "We'll array all our detectives on the barge—"

"They'll mingle in the crowd, undercover," Colombo continued. "Our detectives have a detailed description of Don Emilio and Solange. No one can leave the barge without being seen."

"I'll stick to Tonio and never let him out of my sight," Mario said.

"Just in case something goes wrong," Dante said, "Bevilacqua has a separate group watching the ocean liner at the pier."

A spark of hope returned to Cesca's heart. "But you can't go eleven rounds with that animal," she said, silently appealing to the others for help.

"Tonio, Dante, and I worked it all out last night at the Hat," Mario reassured her.

"It has to be staged," Colombo added, "to make sure the match looks good for the fight fans."

"Antonio and Dante will pull their punches. If one of them were knocked out in the early rounds, the crowd would start a riot and demand their money back," Colombo said.

Cesca couldn't believe what she was hearing. "After all we've gone through with that animal you're not going to hurt him, Dante?" she asked, the disappointment plain in her voice. "You'll both be acting?"

"Don't worry," Dante said with relish, "in the eleventh round I'll give him the beating he deserves."

Uncertainly she looked at their smiling faces. Men were men. In spite of the gravity of the circumstances they were obviously enjoying the excitement of planning an illegal boxing match. But she wasn't feeling so enthusiastic. Could Dante stand up to a vicious backroom brawler like Antonio without serious injury? "I'll—I'll show you how to fall so you'll look convincing, Dante," she said, a quiver in her voice. "I had to learn myself so that my death scenes on stage would appear realistic. Just in case Antonio should—"

Dante gave her a bear hug, obviously relieved to have her in control again, and set about planning the rest of Mina's rescue.

IT was approaching midnight. Cesca stood grasping a restraining rope at the edge of a double-wide flat-bottom barge loaded with boisterous fight fans. As the tugboat muscled the barge away from the Battery pier and pressed toward Jersey to pick up more fans, she watched the lights of Manhattan disappear behind a haze of coal smoke pouring from the tug's stack. She trembled in the damp air, allowing the icy mist kicked up by the black waves to float over her. Perhaps the chill would clear her head. Where, she wondered, in all this rabid gaiety has Kathleen hidden my daughter?

The thrum of the tug's engine pulsated with the same intensity as the questions that flogged her exhausted brain. Was Mina trapped in a room beneath the wheelhouse? Was she tied up on the Jersey side in Weehawken? Was she sick or possibly dying? The threads of destiny were knotting together: would Maria be delivered to her arms or lost to her forever? Cesca gnawed her tongue furiously, trying to find some answers as she stood on tiptoe, struggling to see over the heads of the intervening crowd. Across the way Kathleen was setting up a makeshift bar.

"Cesca, what are you chewing?" Errico asked, presenting her with wine. "You look like a cow."

She squeezed his hand and gave him a faint smile. What a good friend he was to rush from the warm applause of the Metropolitan to the reeking docks of the Battery to lend support. "*Stai zitto*, Errico! I'm frightened to death."

"Everything's going to be all right. I told you Petrosino personally caught the rogues that tried to extort money from me."

She ducked her head and adjusted her body so she could keep Kathleen in view as they spoke. "Yes, yes, so you say. But I've never seen Petrosino, only his agents."

"I assure you his finger is on the pulse of this operation. He's most likely here in disguise."

In disguise? She quickly scanned the men in the crowd. That fat man gulping a beer; was he wearing a beard? Was that dark, unkempt hair under the cap a wig? Could Errico be right? Was Petrosino here among them? Her doubt and fear made her mouth as dry as talc.

"I have a terrible feeling," she said, sipping the red wine that suddenly reminded her of blood, "something dreadful's about to happen."

"Nothing dreadful's going to happen," he soothed. "Well, perhaps 'Vittorio' will get his mustache punched off!"

He chuckled at his joke, then added, "Seriously, *cara,* you must trust *destino*. Didn't that gypsy woman tell you?"

"But Dante said Mina's being drugged. She'll lose the baby."

"Forget these horrors you keep inventing," Errico said, putting his arm around her shoulder. "You're going to get her back."

How could a mother forget her imperiled child, even for a moment? Errico's eyes met hers evenly, sending her confidence. Then a devilish grin creased his face. "I know what'll cheer you up. Let's go wish our boy luck."

"You go. I'm going to keep my eyes on that *strega*," she said, tipping her head toward Kathleen.

"The witch can't do a thing without being seen," Errico said. "Petrosino's detectives are posted on every side."

"They've watched before and failed," she said with disgust. "I don't trust them."

"Look at her. She's as busy as a pollinating bee, and Emilio's nowhere in sight."

Cesca glanced around. Errico was right. There was no way off the barge except by boat, and Mario had confirmed that the exchange would happen after the eleventh round.

"Don't you want to see Dante smash Antonio to paste? I do. *Vendetta, cara!* The kiss of Tosca! It's not much compensation, but it's something. When it's closer to the eleventh round, I promise we'll find her again."

Cesca reluctantly allowed Errico to pull her into the crowd, but she stubbornly kept watch over her shoulder as they progressed.

Across the barge Kathleen was as gleeful as a numbers winner cashing in a chit. Everything was working out just the way she'd hoped. As she hammered the taps into beer and liquor kegs she went over her triumphs. Early this morning she'd made a new deal with Don Lampone for the ten grand. After she laid out her plan he'd agreed to help her dupe Tonio into going through with the match. She'd lined up her friends at the Fourth Ward to help her out, and to skim the cream, she'd made some hefty side bets on the winner. She was a genius! No doubt about it! Soon she'd have her revenge on that stinking guinea bastard Tonio.

Last night after Tonio left her lying on the floor of the Hat, she'd hired a hack and raced to the docks to check on Tonio's wife. She was still where Kathleen had hidden her, safe and silent. With the help of a few drops of amyl nitrate Kathleen had been able to hide the "ten-thousand-dollar package" in plain sight. Tonio'd never find her. Then she'd gone to the Plaza Hotel to make her own deal with the old man before Tonio could arrive and cut her loaf short.

"I loathe that animal," Don Lampone had said. "If you can deliver my granddaughter unharmed and keep Antonio from following us back to Italy, I'll give you the ten thousand dollars you want."

With that statement in mind she told him the scheme she'd concocted. She would have her Fourth Ward friends arrest Tonio.

"Patty Sullivan's a sergeant on the force. He's a friend of my dead husband, Jack. He'll see to it Tonio's arrested for fighting illegally. I'll make sure he holds him until ya leave the country."

"But he can follow," Don Lampone had said uncertainly.

"I'll make sure he don't leave. The Irish politicians are in my pocket and I've got my own ways of keeping him here. He won't follow ya back. Count on it."

Once the Don had been reassured, he'd accompanied her back to the Hat. She kept the old man's pistol in her pocket. She knew Tonio'd come looking, and they'd waited for him together.

Ha! Tonio! She stewed as she hammered. It hadn't taken him long to arrive in a murderous rage, but when he'd seen Don Lampone sitting in the front room having a drink he'd stopped shaking his fist and turned bootlicker fast enough. She had to hand it to the Don. The old man was a master manipulator. He'd been able to smooth Tonio's feathers and set him up perfectly for tonight's cockfight.

"I'm sorry to have come down here, but it appears my 'pervert story' has leaked out," Don Lampone had said. "The police have detectives watching me. The fools think I'm actually trying to buy my granddaughter from you. I've been warned that if I try to take her out of the country openly they'll arrest me for trafficking in prostitution."

Kathleen watched with satisfaction as Tonio's face blanched. "What do you want me to do, Don Emilio?" Tonio had asked in a humble tone.

"My granddaughter must stay hidden if we want to depart as planned, but we'll need some sort of distraction."

"I told him about the barge fight," Kathleen said. "But I know ya don't want to go through with it."

"Excuse me, Antonio," Don Lampone said, "but I was thinking that if you go through with the fight as your friend here suggests, it might be the perfect cover. In that kind of crowd no one will notice us leaving. I've already purchased tickets in both your names. Once you're aboard and leaving together, the authorities will be reassured. Everything will be legal. They can't stop us."

Thank the good Lord Tonio wasn't the sharpest knife in the drawer. He'd quickly agreed with Don Lampone and actually tried to give back the four thousand dollars.

"Keep the money," Don Lampone said. "It's all in the family. My granddaughter's husband must have some money in his pockets. Use it for traveling expenses."

The obvious show of wealth stupefied Tonio and fogged his brain.

Once Tonio realized he'd be reunited with his wife in a first class stateroom, with four thousand dollars in his pocket, it didn't matter who had her or where she'd been stashed. He hadn't even asked if she was safe and sound, but immediately made plans to go through with the fight as a cover.

The whole time, Tonio had just stood there nodding and scraping while Don Lampone thanked him and patted his "new grandson" on the back. Tonio's head had been swimming in conceit all day as he purchased traveling gear, flashed his money, and bragged to his cronies.

Kathleen wasn't sure Don Lampone had been telling the truth about the detectives watching him, but she'd decided to play it safe. She'd sent a package to Don Lampone by messenger. Then she'd phoned him and added his little blond tart to her schemes, explaining in detail how Solange could help them throw off any spies who might be lurking about. It was a tangled bit of drama, but if the actors in her little scenario played their parts well, it would make the transfer a snap. The cards, it seemed, were all falling her way, for even Mario was in on the plot.

After Tonio had left to see Don Lampone back to the Plaza, Mario had turned up. She'd suspected from the start that Mario hated Tonio for taking his fiancée, but Mario hadn't turned a hair about his bride's defection. Only an occasional glint of ice in Mario's eye when Tonio wasn't watching had fueled Kathleen's suspicion that he'd wanted revenge.

Mario looked terrible. He seemed depressed and furious by turns. Kathleen knew he didn't drink much and pressed a few drinks on him, trying to get to the bottom of his mood. She told him Tonio was leaving with his wife after the fight and poured a few more shots. Mario's tongue was finally loosened and he expressed his rage at Tonio for stealing his bride. She'd been right all along. The kidnapping and sale only added to Mario's fury and desire for a chance to pay back the insult to his honor. It didn't take too much convincing on her part to get him to help with the plan.

Oh, that Mario! What a sly dog he was! All afternoon he'd helped puff Tonio's pride to popping by telling him how eagerly the men were betting on his victory. "A knockout," Mario had said, "will be a majestic farewell and win you Don Lampone's respect." Tonio had been totally bowled over, and any doubts he might have had flew when he thought of himself leaving a champion. He told his friends he "couldn't bear to leave Kathleen on the street after five years" and had decided to go through with the fight for her sake, but everyone knew he didn't give a tinker's damn about her.

All day at the Hat the men had given her the eye while she'd been burning inside, but she hadn't shown it. She'd been all smiles and free rounds for the men, letting Tonio think she was giving him the big send-off for agreeing to her plans. But tonight she was going to see him finish with a bang.

She put the last spigot into its bunghole and hammered it with real satisfaction. Yeah! It was a done . . . deal! Mr. Tonio was going to be one . . . sorry . . . wop!

After she'd driven the last tap, her barman, Jimmy, gave her a hand up. Jimmy and a few toughs from the neighborhood dives were doling out the libations and the cash was already flooding in. It was an easy bar, only beer and whiskey, but at the last minute she'd decided to add three barrels of wine for the gentry mixing with the blue collars.

"Easy does it," she said, indicating the pour Jimmy should use with her fingers. "Don't give them too much. We're the only game on board."

"It's a great idea you had, Mrs. Shaunessey. You'll clear a pretty penny on the bar tonight."

"Yeah," Kathleen grunted with pride, "and that ain't the half of it. Between the gate and the side bets, we'll clean up nicely. We're due for some extra kegs in an hour or so. Raise prices, like I told ya, after the sixth round. By the by, this here barrel's sour. We'll exchange it when the replacements come."

"Yer the boss!" he said, hefting a whiskey keg and setting it atop the barrel.

Her eyes probed the crowd. When she spotted Vittorio her heart gave a kick. What a handsome, virile devil he was. He'd come by the saloon last night to make plans for tonight. Said he was "scouting the territory, checking out the competition," but she knew it was because he'd dumped his girlfriend and was hoping to take her on.

He insisted she go in the back and they'd gone a little one-on-one in the pantry. She rubbed the back of her neck and shivered, remembering his hot kisses on her throat. She'd had to cut him short when Tonio'd broken in on them, but after the fight tonight . . . well . . . she'd be through with Tonio for good, and Vittorio'd be a horse of a different color. After tonight why not have some fun and make money off a new stud?

She glanced over the crowd, feeling a stir of fear in her guts as she wiped a trickle of sweat from her temple. Her future would be hanging on tenterhooks for the next few hours. Everything had to go smoothly. One last time she tested the ropes holding the barrels. Everything was secure. Reassured, she stepped behind the bar. "What'll it be, gents?" she shouted, icing her grand plans until the eleventh round.

C E S C A was worried. After the Jersey stop the barge had become dangerously overloaded. As it turned downstream she nervously searched the additions. "He didn't get on in Weehawken," she said.

"Emilio's planning to take her by private boat," Errico said. "You know that."

"I don't trust Emilio. He's a slippery liar."

Errico edged her toward the circle of men watching Vittorio and his trainer prepare. Colombo was smearing the grease Jack Johnson had recommended on Dante's face and chest. The grease would make Antonio's punches slip without tearing flesh and keep Dante's sweat from revealing the true color of his boot-blacked hair.

"Vittorio!" Cesca cried. "I've made a colossal wager! Don't let me down." She pushed forward to feel his biceps brazenly. "I hope you gentlemen have made substantial wagers," she said. "I've seen this man box in Naples. He's ferocious!"

The men surrounding him backed up, regarding her suspiciously.

"Cesca, calm down," Errico whispered, pulling her aside. "You sound hysterical."

"Nonsense, I'm just playing my part." But when she paused to sip her wine she found her hands shaking. She gravitated to Bevilacqua, who was casually smoking a cigarette at the fringe of the group. "Everything's going according to plan?" she asked, sotto voce.

Bevilacqua nodded, glancing around to be certain they weren't overheard. "We've put on extra men to watch the boats that come and go."

"Who's coming and going besides Emilio?" Cesca demanded.

"Fans who missed the departure."

She scanned the sides of the barge; the dark water was sprinkled with bobbing boats and lanterns. "*Gesù Cristo!* You can't watch them all."

"Don't worry," Bevilacqua said. "I have my own special cutter standing by if we need to pursue them."

"I want him stopped here!" she ordered.

At that instant a bell clanged urgently and Kathleen's harsh voice called for attention above the hubbub. Bevilacqua's ring flashed in the torchlight as he flicked his cigarette aside. "Count on me, Signorina Frascatti," he said. The crowd surged forward, pushing them apart.

"Here we go," Errico said, rejoining Cesca.

Cesca's eyes met Dante's urgently before the crowd swept him away. "Remember Jack's advice!" she called.

"Give him the beating he deserves," Errico added.

It was time. Kathleen hoisted her skirts and climbed into the ring.

"Okay, ladies and gents," she shouted. "Clear the way! Let the lads through!"

The men followed her up a low ladder and slipped nimbly under the ropes into the canvas arena. She placed two fingers in her mouth and gave a sharp whistle. The crowd quieted. They eyed Tonio and Vittorio, who wore snug boxing trunks and were bare-chested in the brisk November air.

When she introduced Tonio DiGianni he danced forward, smacking his leather gloves together. The crowd roared and he looked fierce, raising a gloved fist in salute. The workingmen had their paychecks on him and it took her several minutes to quiet them enough to introduce the challenger.

Vittorio Fusco was taller and stockier. The women hooted and whistled their approval. When the crowd heard he was a champion in Naples the Neapolitans cheered to give him courage, but it was an anemic effort. Vittorio was the underdog and the swells had bet on him five to one.

Finally, amid a smattering of boos, she introduced the referee, Jimmy Mahar, her barman from the Cocked Hat. Jimmy inspected the tightly laced gloves, feeling for brass knuckles or tampering. He shouted a few orders about low blows, rabbit punches, butting, and the like, then they were ready.

"All right, folks, here's the way of it," she shouted. "The bout's fifteen rounds. Each round's three minutes and there's going to be a one-minute rest period allowed between." More boos. "These are the Marquess of Queensberry's rules—if ya've a mind to know—not my own. Should it be necessary, a decision'll be made on the winner by Mick Donovan here, Frank Portella over there, and Tommy O'Rourke . . . Tommy? Where the hell is Tommy?" she shouted, searching the crowd.

"I'm here!" Tommy called, shoving his way through the press, still buttoning his trousers from taking a leak over the side.

"Stop swilling the ale," she mocked. "We need ya ringside, not polluting the Hudson!" His face reddened as the crowd enjoyed the joke. "One last thing: if a man falls from the ring, keep yer mitts out of the match. These boys don't need yer help. Am I clear? All right then, let's enjoy the fight!"

The bell jangled and the men squared off warily. Each followed the other's moves and shifts of weight, looking for an opening.

Kathleen climbed down and elbowed her way steadily through the crowd, eagerly greeting friends and acknowledging enemies, a slap on the back here, a nod or handshake there. When she reached Tonio's corner she found Mario standing on a stool, shouting encouragement from the edge of the canvas. She reached between the planks surrounding the base of the ring and pulled out a tapped bottle of water she'd hidden earlier. Placing it deep in the folds of her skirt, she pulled on Mario's pant leg to get his attention.

"I want ya to give him a taste of this," she said, giving Mario a peek at the bottle, "in the *tenth round*. We need a little insurance."

"What's in it?" Mario asked.

"Amyl. Not enough to kill him, but it'll take the iron out of him right enough." She slipped the bottle into Mario's training bag.

"Don't you think Vittorio can take him?"

"Maybe he can and maybe he can't. I don't truck with maybes. I want him knocked cold. I want him ruined. I've got bets out."

It would shatter Tonio to be knocked cold in front of this crowd. His pride would never recover. She watched Tonio bob and weave. What a crafty bastard he was, crouching low, throwing out snappy punches as much to feel Vittorio out as to show off his skill. She noticed that Vittorio stayed out of his range, sliding back and forth like a puppet on a string.

"He ain't bad," she said to Mario, a little surprised by Vittorio's skill. "Maybe he can do it without the help, but don't take any chances."

"Take his head off, Tonio!" she shouted, hamming it up for him and his cronies before she moved away.

Cesca and Errico followed in Kathleen's wake to keep her in view. "Vittorio will be sorely disappointed to learn his new girlfriend's encouraging the enemy," Errico shouted into Cesca's ear. "She's a tough woman!"

"And a dangerous one," Cesca rejoined. "I'm going to stick to her like a tight pair of knickers."

"If Antonio connects with one of those punches," Errico whispered, "*bomba!* Our boy's finished. Come on, Vittorio!"

"Sssh!" Cesca hissed, pushing Errico off. "Don't give us away!"

Cesca watched the opening action tensely, fearing betrayal, but just as Colombo had explained, Antonio allowed Dante to land body punches while Dante threw his own light blows. After three minutes of dancing around, the bell rang and they took a break. She relaxed a little as time went on and it seemed to go well for the first five rounds of cagey, uneventful behavior, but in the sixth round the crowd began to boo and curse. There wasn't enough action and the crowd was shifting ominously. They began to throw objects into the ring. She had to admit it was turning into a bad show.

Up in the ring Tonio was feeling confident until Vittorio suddenly lashed out. Tonio's head jerked back from the impact of the punch and he felt a searing pain explode in his skull. Blood poured from his nose. Was it a lucky punch? He was sure Vittorio was smirking. He shook his head, spattering blood across his chest, and lunged back into the fray, lobbing punches like a catapult flinging boulders. It wasn't the pain that infuriated him, but the crowd cheering the mutt on.

He attacked in a fury. Vittorio backed away, lamely attempting to return fire, but Tonio countered easily, driving him onto the ropes. When Vittorio lifted his arms to protect his head, Tonio drubbed his chest. He'd fix the sonofabitch! One well-placed punch would stop his heart and knock the ox cold.

"Hold yer temper! Hold yer temper!" Through his rage Tonio heard a woman shouting, but the words blended with the howls of the crowd. "Tonio! Tonio! This ain't the time to let him get the better of ya!" He shifted his focus and saw Kathleen pounding the canvas with her fist.

Then he remembered the deal he'd made with Don Lampone and the reason for the match. Quickly Tonio pulled his punch, allowing Vittorio to break from the ropes and pass, but as the bastard slipped away he slammed Tonio on the chin.

Caught off balance, Tonio jerked back, tangled up his feet, and fell to the canvas in a slap-stick flop. The crowd burst into hoots and catcalls. Tonio sprang up, his pride smarting from the blow, and charged Vittorio, but the bell cut him off. As he stalked to his corner he was thinking that if he could get his hands around Kathleen's neck he'd snap it like a rotten branch.

"No more patty-cake!" he shouted to Mario over the roar of the crowd.

Mario reminded him of the plan.

"Yeah, yeah, but he keeps sneaking in shots," Tonio griped.

"He needed to mix it up," Mario said. "The crowd's bored. Besides, you stepped into that last one."

"The hell I did!"

"Make it look good, but wait until the eleventh round to get even."

Mario sponged him off and offered him a drink. He sloshed the water around in his mouth while Mario held out the bucket. "Spit!" Mario ordered. "Don't swallow."

Tonio ignored the bucket. "Don't tell me what to do! Give it to me!"

Mario watched Tonio suck down half the bottle. Tonio could never stand to be told what to do and would go against anything Mario might recommend. He smiled, thinking of Kathleen's bottle waiting in his training bag: first she'll get even, then it'll be my turn.

"Go ahead!" he shouted. "Kill yourself!"

When Tonio returned to the corner for the tenth round, his nose was still trickling blood, but it was the only indication of weakness. "I want to kill that bastard!" Tonio shouted as he sat down.

Mario watched anxiously as Colombo fanned Dante with a towel. Mario was waiting for a prearranged signal to show that Dante was all right, but as Colombo worked feverishly over Dante, he appeared completely spent. Mario knew how desperately Dante wanted to punish Tonio and avenge Mina, but as a precaution he took the water bottle Kathleen had given him from his trainer's bag.

"Here, rinse your mouth. Take him at the *end* of the next round like we planned. *Don't* drink." Mario kept his eyes on the opposite corner as Tonio gulped. Suddenly Colombo looked up and caught Mario's eye. He hit his chest three times with his fist, then gestured as though he was brushing something aside. To the crowd it looked as though the trainer was giving Vittorio instruction, but Mario knew it was the signal they'd agreed upon in Cesca's parlor. Dante was all right and ready to give Tonio the beating he deserved.

Immediately, Mario let Kathleen's bottle slip from his fingers and tumble into the crowd. "You're a mule," he shouted, gripping Tonio's shoulders. He examined Tonio's eyes to see if the amyl was having any effect. "Wait till the end of the round," he urged, "or you're going to lose everything."

"I ain't waiting till the end of the round," Tonio said, shaking his head.

The bell rang and Tonio shoved Mario away. He charged across the ring and threw a vicious roundhouse to Dante's head as though he was swinging a two by four. Mario froze. His leg was halfway over the rope; he hadn't even had a chance to climb down. He watched in dismay as Dante slammed to the canvas. He appeared to be out cold.

Tonio threw up his gloves and danced for joy.

Chapter Thirty-Nine

HOW LONG BEFORE WE COME alongside?"

"We'll see the torches any minute now," the man at the wheel replied.

The launch carrying Emilio was skimming invisibly over the water, headed in the direction of the faint lights of Weehawken. A glow appeared on the water in the distance and the boat slowed abruptly. Emilio glanced over his shoulder, barely making out a smaller craft following. He waved his handkerchief and Solange waved back, acknowledging that everything on board her boat was set. The actors he'd hired to help with Kathleen's scheme were dressed and in place beside Solange, their parts well rehearsed, but Emilio was apprehensive, for he'd made a solemn pledge to Giulio and he prayed that God would allow him to keep it.

Shortly after Antonio had left him at the Plaza and the hotel's doctor had dressed Emilio's head wound, Antonio's mistress had arrived. She'd sworn to Emilio that she'd taken his granddaughter to safety, away from "Tonio's lunacy," and that she'd hidden her in a place Tonio would never dream of looking. She'd promised to safely deliver his granddaughter in exchange for the ten thousand dollars. All Emilio had to do was help her get Antonio to go through with the boxing match.

Emilio hated the idea of dealing with such a treacherous creature, but this new arrangement offered him a modicum of peace. For Kathleen, his granddaughter was strictly a business deal. She wouldn't follow him back to Italy the way Antonio would, and she'd promised to keep his granddaughter safe from Antonio's brutality by having him arrested. Once the exchange was made her devilment would be over and Antonio neutralized. Emilio had agreed to give her the money and went to her seedy bar near the river to convince Tonio to go along.

Emilio had refused the sedative Solange pressed upon him when he returned to the Plaza, insisting he needed to stay alert to handle any exigency that might arise, but throughout the day he couldn't drive the image of his granddaughter's frightened eyes from his mind.

Her eyes had reminded him of Giulio's. As he paced his room with his head throbbing unmercifully, rehearsing the actors who had been added for distraction and handling the details of the transfer, he began to doubt his resolve for revenge. He spent the intervening hours before the transfer praying and reflecting, but snippets of Francesca's dressing-down returned to haunt him.

How much responsibility *did* he hold for the rift with his son? It was true, he'd been disapproving of the wine assays and the new grafting techniques Giulio had tried. He'd disregarded his son's hopes and plans. Emilio remembered the glow of excitement that had enveloped Giulio the day he'd dragged Emilio to the dank family wine cellar to taste his latest "experiment."

"For generations we've made our fortune selling the harvest to wholesalers," Emilio said, sipping the wine offered. "Let the other vineyards take the risks involved in producing wine."

"We can do it better. I can—"

"No, Giulio." Emilio shook his head. "No."

"But you just said, 'It's perfect! The best I've ever tasted.' "

"To make a few bottles for our own consumption, yes. But to—"

"My experiments with the new grafting techniques are producing grapes that are more robust, more flavorful. With a small investment we can buy the vats and equipment. I've found a winery that's gone bankrupt, we could get everything for a song. Father, if you let me—"

"Bankrupt! Don't you hear yourself?" Emilio asked, shaking his head. "No, my boy, you're a dilettante. Like the rest of your generation. You don't appreciate the reality of the hard day-to-day work it takes to manage this estate. Do you think I dream the lira into your pockets?"

"I don't want you to put lira into my pockets. I want to earn them myself."

"Do you lack anything? Do I keep you in tatters? Why can't you be satisfied to help me run the estate as I see fit?"

"I want to contribute. I only wish to—"

"You can contribute by obeying me," Emilio said, turning cold. "You'll inherit my fortune soon enough. Can't you wait until after I'm dead to try your little experiments?"

Emilio cringed as he remembered his harsh words. That day, the sparkle had gone out of Giulio's eyes. Giulio had been patient and pliable for a time, but Emilio could see his son slipping away, and when he later ordered Giulio to break off the dalliance he was having with a servant girl, the rift between them had deepened into a glacial crevasse.

"Don't be a fool, Giulio, she's a peasant. How many other men have plowed that field?"

"I love her. You won't succeed in taking her from me. She's from an impoverished family, it's true, but her father was a skilled craftsman—a famous mandolin maker. She grew up in a convent, and—"

"Mandolin maker! Convent! You come from the finest bloodline in Europe."

"I'm going to marry her," Giulio said stubbornly.

"I forbid it."

"You cannot control me any longer."

"Think, Giulio, think! You're heir to one of the largest fortunes in Italy. Everything will be yours when I die. Will you give it all up for a lusty tumble in a vineyard?"

"You've never wanted me to have this estate. You want it in perpetuity for yourself and your own stupid sense of grandeur. Well, keep it! I don't want your twisted heritage. She loves me. Me—Giulio Lampone—the weakling, the dilettante son. I've found someone who loves *me*, not my promised fortune, and you cannot tempt me away from happiness."

"Fine! Marry her, but you'll not get a *scudi;* I promise I'll disinherit you. And the money your mother left you, kiss it good-bye."

Within hours of Emilio's dismissing the servant girl, his son had run off to Naples. Emilio had stubbornly insisted on cutting Giulio off and blamed the crafty servant girl for his son's betrayal. She'd set him up against his father, lured him away with her body. But after a time, Emilio's anger against his son had abated. He yearned to see him again. He decided to implement Giulio's suggestions in the hope of drawing him back to the vineyard. He had associates carry word to Naples that he'd hired a retired winemaker and bought equipment, but even though he'd begun to turn the vineyard into a winery, Giulio had refused to return. Every lure Emilio had offered was spurned. The large bank account in Giulio's name had remained untouched.

The smell of coal oil was thick on the damp night air. It brought Emilio back to the present and he shook his head remembering his brusque treatment of his son. He hated to admit it, but Francesca was right, he *had* been proud and selfish. He'd driven his son away and tried to buy him back.

Looking back Emilio realized that he'd tried to force his own will on his son. He'd refused Giulio a chance to make mistakes and had denied him any support. Instead he'd used the only things he was familiar with to keep Giulio close: manipulation, guilt, and money. Time had softened Emilio and taught him new values. Now he wouldn't need to break his son and command him. Now he only wanted to love. But Giulio had been dead for many years.

"I promise you, Giulio, I will change," Emilio whispered into the dark night. "When I get your daughter away from this madman, I promise I will share her with her mother and beg forgiveness. I will protect and love her. Not with money or pride, but with compassion. Help me to open Francesca's heart, Giulio, help me to make peace. I swear! I will change."

After a few moments, the double barge loomed, its torches flaming. Emilio hurried toward the cabin at the stern, absorbing the rolling motion of the waves with his knees. He held on to the brim of his hat to keep it from blowing off in the stiff wind. He could hear the voices of the crowd and feel their excitement. Someone was taking a beating.

"Come on, Tonio!"

"Vittorio! Vittorio! Vittorio!"

He saw the edge of Solange's craft disappear around the far side of the barge as he ducked inside the rickety cabin with the doctor. He heard the boat's engine cut, felt it glide into position to be tied up. He checked his watch. They must be nearing the tenth round. He peeked carefully through the dirty curtains stretching across the portal and impatiently watched as barrels of whiskey and beer were unloaded and hoisted aboard. A roar went up from the crowd. It must be the knockout Kathleen had talked about. He hoped with all his heart that Antonio was lying smashed and bloody on the canvas.

On board the barge Cesca saw Dante jerk back and dramatically crash to the canvas. He'd purposely slipped Antonio's punch and fallen onto his hip, slamming his arm down hard the way she'd coached him.

He quickly rolled onto his back and lay as though unconscious until the count of five, then came around. He struggled up onto one knee on the count of six, on seven he attempted to get up but acted as though his legs wouldn't hold him. He played out the extra three seconds and rose with a second to spare. It was all brilliantly acted and she was as thrilled as the crowd with his performance.

He appeared alert, so Jimmy was forced to allow him to continue. Once again Antonio advanced like Zeus throwing thunderbolts, but this time Dante easily avoided the blows.

Now, Cesca prayed, deal him the hurt he's lavished on my daughter. Crush him, powder his bones, cast him to the wind! Let him bleed and suffer the way he has made my daughter bleed and suffer. With each punch that Dante slammed into Antonio's body and face she exalted.

"Yes!" she screamed. "Hit him! Give it to him, Vittorio! Yes, yes!" She'd lived in the cruel streets of Naples too long to feel any squeamishness at the sight of gore. She wanted vengeance exacted on this beast.

Jab, jab, hard and fast, Dante's fists flew out as though holding steel bars. A cut opened over Antonio's left eye and blood rushed over his face to his chest. Antonio raised a glove, trying to brush the veil aside, but it didn't help. The injury forced him to turn to the left as he tried to see his enemy with his right eye. The new position threw off his stance.

Cesca watched as Dante tempted Antonio inside by holding his fists wide. "Here it comes!" she shouted, grabbing Errico's arm with glee.

Desperately Antonio lumbered in, telegraphing a right hook. Dante bobbed below the haymaker and landed two fast, mean uppercuts to Antonio's chin and finished with a left cross to his stunned face that sent a shower of sweat and blood over the crowd.

Antonio's body lurched back. He staggered and went stiff, then his knees buckled and he hit the mat, as heavy as a block of pig iron. This knockdown was no act.

"He's out! He's out!" Errico shouted.

Gesù, what a punch! Cesca thought. Dante had given him a beating with time to spare.

Jimmy rushed in for a long count as Mario hovered anxiously and Dante leaned over, resting his gloved hands on his knees, panting hard the way they'd rehearsed. The crowd booed, hissed, and shouted insults.

"Get up, ya bum."

"You wop bastard, get off that mat or I'll kick your ass!"

"Oh, he can't do this to me! He can't! I bet me whole dowry on him!"

"Tonio! Tonio, get up!"

But it was clear Tonio wouldn't be getting up anytime soon. Jimmy reluctantly counted him out and put up Dante's arm. "The winner!"

Cesca screamed. She jumped up and down, dancing in a circle with Errico as the crowd around her seethed with fury.

Kathleen was thrilled. It was grand the way Tonio had crumpled like a sheet of paper, but she couldn't celebrate her triumph yet. She still had a lot of work to do. The crowd shifted. It was just the way she and Sullivan had figured it. The majority had bet on Tonio and lost; now they wanted revenge. In seconds fights broke out, punches were thrown, and the angry crowd began to invade the ring.

A flare streaked skyward, then a loud boom rocked the barge. Every face on board turned toward the explosion and was blushed by the glow.

"This is the police!" came a megaphoned cry from several boats on the river.

Right on time, she thought. God bless Patty Sullivan and the Fourth Ward. Sullivan was as good as his word.

The signal hung red and fuzzy, dropping slowly to the river. The fans rushed back and forth wildly as Sullivan and his crew boarded. Patty Sullivan was an old Fourth Ward friend of Jack's whom she'd been paying off for years. He was the ringleader of the cops who swarmed aboard, and he'd helped her plan tonight's charade. They'd arrest a few men, including Tonio, for taking part in an illegal fistfight and throw them all in jail. Don Lampone would get out of the country with his granddaughter and Tonio would be in the clink.

Sullivan fired off his pistol to startle the crowd, and many a man jumped overboard fearing arrest. Kathleen ignored the uproar. She jammed herself against the edge of the ring and pounded violently on the canvas, waving for Jimmy's attention.

"Jimmy!" she shouted. "Jimmy, over here! Give me a hand here!" Jimmy yanked her up and she went to crouch over Tonio, jerking a thumb at him. "He's all right?" she asked Mario.

"Yeah," Mario said. He slapped Tonio's face and applied smelling salts. "Just a little groggy."

"What happened?" Tonio asked, shaking his head.

"He knocked ya cold," Kathleen said.

"I was winning," he mumbled, trying to get up.

"Did you see those flares?" she demanded as Mario pulled him up. Tonio looked around in confusion. His legs were like rubber, and she hoped Mario hadn't given him too much amyl. "Tonio, listen to me," Kathleen shouted, playing her next gambit. "The coppers are here and they ain't my guys." He wasn't half home. "They'll arrest ya if they see ya," she said, pretending worry. "Ya gotta go meet Don Lampone. Do ya hear me? I want ya to go with Mario. Mario'll take ya off the barge before the coppers get to ya. Hurry now and go on board the tug so ya'll be safe. The cops won't find ya on the tug. Can ya make it?"

He gave her a muddled nod. "I make it." Mario helped him under the ropes as she strode across the ring to Vittorio's corner where his trainer was rubbing him down with a towel.

"Ya did it!" she cried, coming up to them. "Ya fixed him pretty, thank the good Lord, but there's going to be trouble, no way about it." She glanced back at Tonio. Mario was helping Tonio down, but as muddled as the bastard was, he was watching her like a hawk. She pointed to the tug at the head of the barge, holding it steady in the current.

"Whatever ya do, Vittorio, stay away from that tug. Once it gets to the other end of the barge it'll be crawling with coppers." She didn't want Vittorio snooping around the tug. Besides, if Tonio got pinched and Vittorio didn't, Tonio'd know she'd double-crossed him and he'd try to gum up her plans.

"Get yer duds on and melt into the crowd," Kathleen said. "I told the cops not to touch ya." She dropped over the side of the ring and headed for the bar.

Before Dante pulled his sweater over his head he saw Cesca's ruby dress weaving through the crowd as she trailed after Kathleen. Cesca was a little bulldog. He wished he had a hundred detectives like her on his team. He shook the sweat from his head and rubbed his face with a towel, then hopped down behind Colombo, and they began cutting a path toward the bar.

This next part was going to be difficult. They had to hurry and catch Kathleen before the exchange was made, but Colombo was making slow progress through the crowd. He kept stopping to glance to the left, and every time he stopped a fan would grab Dante's hand or slap him on the back. A few of the men who had lost money shook their fists in Dante's face or cursed him, but no one had the fortitude to challenge him outright. It seemed to be taking them forever to go a few feet.

"Hurry up, Colombo," Dante said. "Don't stop if you can help it."

Colombo nodded, but it was slow going until Bevilacqua joined them.

"We better split up," Bevilacqua said. "We can't get through this way. Dante, why don't you and I—"

"Inspector," Colombo interjected, "I saw a veiled woman on the left side of the barge. She may be the blond you described to us."

Dante craned his neck to see, but Bevilacqua was annoyed to have his power usurped again. "You've bungled things before with your half-baked observations, Colombo. I'm in charge of this investigation, not you. Dante and I will go straight ahead and cut behind the bar where there's less of a crowd. You go to the right and follow Signorina Frascatti. Keep her in view at all times, and help her if need be."

Colombo hesitated, waiting for Dante's order.

"Did you hear what I said, Colombo? How dare—?"

"It's okay, Bevilacqua," Dante interrupted. "Colombo, go help Cesca. We'll join you in a moment. I'll attract less attention without my trainer."

"Yes, sir." Colombo forced his way into the crowd, but didn't hurry.

Dante thought Colombo was purposely lagging behind. Suddenly the barge gave a jerk. The tug must be nudging into place at the opposite end of the barge for the push back, Dante thought. The next step was for the tug to tie up near the bar, then Kathleen's police friends would board the tug to arrest Antonio. At that point Mina would most likely be exchanged.

"Hurry, Bevilacqua," Dante urged. "We haven't much time."

As they fought their way through the crowd, it suddenly seemed strange to Dante that Colombo was proceeding so slowly. "Bevilacqua," Dante shouted, "Colombo thought he might have seen something suspicious to the left. What do you make of it?"

"He's not one of our sharpest agents, but there is a ladder over there," Bevilacqua said thoughtfully. "It's a logical place to come aboard. Perhaps Colombo knows something we don't."

"Perhaps," Dante said, put off slightly by Bevilacqua's tone. There seemed to be more to the situation than met the eye. First Colombo had started acting strangely and now Bevilacqua was—but before Dante could reflect further he heard a guttural scream stab into the crowd. *"Aiuto! Aiuto!"*

There was a sudden hush, then another scream and a commotion to the left. Those in the vicinity of the altercation drew back, exposing a man and a veiled woman struggling with a cloaked figure.

"Dante, look!" Bevilacqua said, pointing to the area Colombo had suggested. "It's Solange and Don Emilio! They've got Mina."

As Dante strained to see through the crowd, he caught a glimpse of silver hair under a top hat, and Mina's dress with purple iris trim peeping from under the dark cloak.

"They've got her! They're trying to put her over the side!" Bevilacqua shouted, rushing forward.

Was it the same veiled woman Colombo said he saw? The woman was waiting at the ladder while a man lifted the cloaked figure overboard. The woman turned toward Dante and deliberately lifted her veil to show her face. She made eye contact. It *was* Solange! Colombo had been right. Solange turned back and tried to pull the cloak together to hide Mina's dress but only succeeded in exposing it further.

"Bevilacqua," Dante shouted, trying to get through the people in his way, "that's Mina's dress. Get the cutter." Bevilacqua darted back and forth on the edge of the barge waving his arms.

"Cast off!" Solange cried. "Hurry!"

Dante tried to keep the man from releasing the ropes, but someone grabbed him from behind.

"*Aiuto!*" Dante heard the cloaked woman in the launch cry. He struggled against his captor vainly. "Don't be a fool!" Colombo shouted as he held Dante in a bear hug. The two men struggled.

A few feet away Cesca heard the woman's initial scream and turned. She'd headed back toward the sounds of the struggle, certain it had to be Mina and Emilio. When she reached the left side of the barge she saw Colombo trying to restrain Dante.

"Don Emilio's taken Mina!" Bevilacqua shouted as soon as he saw Cesca rushing toward them. "Colombo's trying to stop Dante and me from following him."

"*Traditore!*" Cesca cried.

Without a moment's hesitation she hurled herself forward and pounced on Colombo's back. She clung to his neck and struck him on the head with her fist until he lost his balance and the three of them tumbled. Dante managed to break free as Cesca rolled across the deck, gripping Colombo like a tigress clawing a water buffalo.

Dante scrambled up and grabbed the last restraining rope as it slithered past him. He heaved it around a metal bollard, but the bitt was too smooth and the engine of the launch too strong. He saw the launch holding Solange, Emilio, and Mina pull away as the rope tore through his hands, bloodied his fingers, and whipped after the foam spewing behind.

Finally, Bevilacqua's special cutter manned by another of Dante's detectives pulled alongside and Bevilacqua plunged down the rope ladder.

"Come on, Dante," he shouted, holding out his hand. His ring flashed in the torch light. "Jump! Don't let Emilio take Mina and her child."

Dante turned to Cesca uncertainly.

"Go!" she shouted. "I've got him." She clung to Colombo's jacket as he jerked to his feet. She tried to dig her heels in, but Colombo turned in a circle and pulled his arms free of the sleeves. Cesca flew backward, still clutching the empty jacket, and crashed to the deck. She watched helplessly as Colombo charged forward, hitting Dante low in the legs. The impact catapulted the two of them over the edge of the barge and slammed them into the bottom of the cutter. Cesca scrambled to the edge of the barge and saw them thrashing below.

"Listen to me, Dante," Colombo shouted, "it's a trick. *Bevilacqua*'s the informant."

Bevilacqua tottered forward with a raised oar, looking for an opening. He took a swing at Colombo's head, but the cutter jerked forward and threw him down.

"I swear to you," Colombo shouted, "Mina's not onboard that launch!"

"Don't listen to him," Cesca pleaded, as the cutter sped away, "Bevilacqua! You idiot, get up! Hit him, do something!"

Chapter Forty

MARIO STOOD AT THE HEAD of the tugboat, resting against the windows of the wheelhouse, scanning the barge crowd. From this vantage point he could easily search for the old man with silver hair Dante had described or the young blond woman, but there was no sign of them and no sign of Mina. He wondered if Emilio had succeeded in spiriting Mina away in plain sight.

"I'm sick, Mario," Tonio moaned. "I've never felt like this after a match." He slumped on the deck of the tug beside Mario, smoking a cigarette with a trembling hand.

"I told you not to drink the water." The hatred he felt for Tonio overwhelmed Mario suddenly. He moved to the railing, afraid he might do something to jeopardize Mina's rescue. Mario wished with all his heart that he could join Dante and the others, but his job was to keep an eye on Tonio and keep him away from Mina. To distract himself he peered down to watch the activity between the tug and the barge.

He was surprised to discover a small workboat loaded with kegs bobbing like a cork on the churning foam of the tug's propeller. Over the noise of the engine he caught snatches of Kathleen's voice grating orders, then saw her dark hair flying in the wind. She stood at the edge of the barge directing an exchange of beer and wine barrels. "Hurry it up there! I ain't paying that crook Bonafaccio for sour wine." Jimmy started bungling a wine barrel down to the workboat with a rope. "Watch it, boys!" she hollered. "Here it comes."

"What's she doing?" Tonio asked, coming to stand behind Mario at the railing.

"She's getting rid of the empties," he said, switching his attention between the workboat and the barge.

Tonio laughed at the inept maneuverings and poked Mario in the ribs. "Micks! Can you believe it, they can't do nothing right," he said.

There was a screeching protest when Jimmy's hastily tied knot gave way. The barrel shot down, scraped against the metal barge, and hit the edge of the waiting workboat. It flipped over and plunged into the river, kicking up spray.

"Jesus Christ!" Kathleen screamed. "Grab that barrel! Don't let it get away."

Mario saw the barrel jerk to the surface a few feet from the workboat. The men pawed at it with poles and drew it back, but it kept slipping, driven away by the potent flow of water. "I got it! I got it!" Jimmy shouted, using a gaffing hook. The men tried to pull it aboard, but it was too heavy. "Lash it to the side," one of the men offered.

"Ya sons of bitches!" Kathleen hollered. "Get that barrel aboard, now! It'll fill with water and sink, ya fools."

Mario glanced back at the workboat and saw two men in greatcoats step from the shelter of its cabin. At that moment a gust of wind took the hat off one of the men. He had silver hair.

"What the hell's she so hysterical about?" Tonio asked, still muddled and hanging over the side. "You'd think the damn barrel was filled with gold instead of sour wine."

In that instant everything fell together for Mario. He ripped off his jacket and boots, pulled his knife from its scabbard, stuck it between his teeth, and plunged overboard like a Barbary pirate.

"*Che cazzo fa?*" Tonio shouted as Mario dove.

Inside the barrel, Mina was semiconscious and trussed up like a roast. Her body shifted as the barrel dropped, and when it hit, she was tossed facefirst against the rough wood. She rested on her shoulder, at an awkward angle, with the weight of her body holding her upside down. Icy water saturated her petticoats and shocked her out of her drug-induced stupor.

The smell of sour wine brought back the memory of Kathleen ordering her to strip off her dress and climb into a large barrel. She remembered little else. The rocking told her the barrel must be on the water. She tried to turn her head, but couldn't. Like a wick the gag in her mouth drew in a steady stream. She coughed, trying to clear water from the back of her throat, but she was forced to swallow. After a few moments she heard rapping and shouts outside the barrel that jarred her more fully awake.

"Mina? Mina? It's Mario, are you in there?" Behind her gag, she screamed, but the sound was muffled. "Yes! Yes! I hear you! Stay calm," he shouted. "Don't move!"

There was a rough jerk, then another. Water flooded her nose as she flipped right side up, and she exhaled sharply, coughing on the water caught in her throat. As a child she'd often played with a cup in a bucket. She knew that once the barrel filled with enough water it would burp out a bubble and plummet to the bottom. The icy water was already creeping toward her waist.

This time her hands had been tied in front. With her teeth she immediately began tearing at the rope binding her wrists, but the gag intervened. She swiftly rotated the gag in her mouth to get at the knot and worked it with her fingers.

"Pull your head down. I've got to cut you out."

Mina took a breath and put her head underwater. She was able to get the gag off, and she used her teeth to loosen the simple knots holding her wrists while Mario hacked desperately at the staves.

Sant'Anna, help me, she prayed. Help my baby. If *Gesù* wills it, let me be spared; if not, ask him to forgive my sins. Hail Mary, full of grace . . .

As she teased the knots apart, many memories mundane and quirky came to mind. The baby's spoon she'd bought at the market . . . the taste of fresh figs warm from the sun . . . the creak of bedsprings . . . the stab of joy she'd felt when Dante kissed her . . . G-I-U-L-I-O, the name on the mandolin in the closet . . . *Mammina*'s mandolin . . . What did it mean that she'd found *Mammina*'s mandolin in the Signorina's closet?

She remembered the slats of the bunk above her on the ship coming to America, the hushed voice telling a tale . . . she saw the fuchsia flowers with yellow centers splashed across the mother's skirts . . . a girl and her mother . . . a hand clinging, longing to stay . . . we'll be joined, united . . . forever by *destino* . . .

She felt the sea. It was strong. The waves tossed and covered everything. A hand dangled a pocket watch with a box chain . . . the watch burned her palm like a searing coal . . . Sad brown eyes running with tears . . . a voice crying, "Don't leave me . . . stay!" Then "Maria Grazia . . . stay. . . ."

Mina had finally worked the knots apart. She pushed on the barrel-head, but it didn't budge. In a panic now, as she felt the barrel sinking, she rammed her hands and feet against the staves, twisting and turning. She shoved her back and shoulders up, battering her fists against the wood. She had to get out, she had to save her child. "Women are stronger than men!" she heard Dante whisper. "I need you so. Don't give up."

Her lungs were bursting. She wanted to breathe, but there was no air, only water. Oh, Dante, she thought, I've made so many foolish mistakes. I love you. I would have shared my life with you if I could have, but my child and I are dying because of another woman's destiny, a destiny I should never have accepted. Forgive me. Forgive me, my love. . . .

The current had taken Mario and the barrel out into midriver, leaving the men and the workboat far behind. In the dark, he felt the thick seal of wax Kathleen had poured over the bent nails and around the barrel's head. Frantically he pried the nails back with his knife and attacked the joint between the head and the staves, gouging and splintering the wood to force an opening.

He shoved his knife in up to the hilt, praying for God to help him. If it broke now, they'd be helpless. He levered it against the chime hoop and pushed down. The head gave way slowly, allowing water to pour in through the gap. The barrel began to plummet.

"Take a deep breath, we're going down," he shouted.

He forced his fingers through the narrow opening and braced his feet against the rim. He strained against the barrelhead, willing it to give way. At last, it pulled free, but he recoiled into the darkness. The barrel sped away from him, plunging to the bottom. He lunged forward, desperately diving down, searching for Mina. God was with him and he found her again. He pulled her from the barrel and pressed her against his chest, feeling immense gratitude for being allowed to save her, but she was limp and unreceptive.

He clawed the water and whipped his legs. Her head and torso arched away from him, pulling her back and down. He struggled to hold her up, but she was too heavy. He scrambled over her, searching for the source of the drag, and found that her hair had caught and twisted in the staves of the barrel like a web.

Chapter Forty-One

*C*ESCA! CESCA! OVER HERE!" Errico called frantically. "Officer," he said, thumping a policeman on the back, "my name is Enrico Caruso and I need your help."

After Errico explained, and impatiently sang part of an aria from *Le Nozze di Figaro* to prove his identity, the officer issued several blasts on his whistle and cleared a path through the throng. They dragged Cesca to the edge of the barge, where Errico pointed to a figure stretched upon the deck of the tugboat. "My God!" Cesca cried. "It's Maria!" She attempted to climb overboard, but Errico and the officer pulled her back. "Let me go to her!"

"Hold on just a minute, ma'am! They're trying to get her breathing."

Mina lay on her back, clothed only in a sodden corset and petticoats. Her face and limbs were gray; two men worked on her feverishly. One man kneled at her head. Gripping her wrists, he brought them straight back over her shoulders while the other man knecling by her side pressed his hands upward against her abdomen. Then they crossed her arms over her breasts and one pushed while the other pulled her into a sitting position. They let her down, repeating this pattern rhythmically. It took several cycles before Cesca realized that Emilio was one of the rescuers.

After several tense minutes, Mina coughed, took a ragged breath, and began vomiting most of the water she'd swallowed.

"Let me go!" Cesca cried.

She shook Errico and the officer off and scrambled over the hawser cables, rushing to gather Mina in her arms. Tears splashed down her cheeks to mix with the river water as she sat and rocked her daughter. She brushed back Mina's chopped hair and kissed her face, murmuring over and over, "*Grazie Dio! Figlia mia!*"

The doctor looked at Emilio, befuddled. "Who is this?" he asked.

"It's all right," Emilio said. "This is her mother."

"Excellent! We need a woman to get her out of those wet clothes immediately and raise her core temperature."

Although Emilio was willing to grant Francesca the title of mother, he was not yet willing to give up first claim on his granddaughter's life. "Can't we take her to a hosp—" Emilio started to say.

"She's hypothermic, she needs immediate care," the doctor said. "Come along, madam, I need your help." The men carried Mina out of the chill into the protection of the wheelhouse with Cesca following behind.

Kathleen had seen all her dreams plunge beneath the black water with the barrel when the knot had slipped. She'd been terrified they wouldn't be able to get her prize package breathing again, but now that Tonio's wife was tucked in the wheelhouse out of sight, she unwound a bit. She gave a sigh of relief and boarded the tug. Her package was shaken up, but deliverable. Kathleen turned her attention to Tonio, who was in the stern, surrounded by blue tunics.

"Mario, he no come up!" Tonio was shouting. "You got to find him. He save my wife—"

"Just a minute now—" Sullivan urged to quiet him.

"Let me go look for him. Please! You no understand!" he said, trying to climb over the side to a rowboat. Sullivan held Tonio's collar, but Tonio threw him off and rushed frantically from one side of the tug to the other, scanning the water. "Mario! Mario!" Sullivan's men rushed to seize him.

Kathleen looked at the dark water, then back to Tonio as he struggled with three cops. Well, there it was, Tonio was finally shaken. He'd learned the value of a friend, but too late. That poor bastard Mario, she thought. Lost his life saving a woman he wasn't destined to have, for a man who never loved anyone but himself.

Once again Sullivan collared Tonio. "Never you mind about Mario, he's probably been fished out already," Sullivan said, impatiently catching Kathleen's eye. He nodded his head and winked at her to acknowledge his role in tonight's drama, then he cleared his throat loudly and used his most official tone of voice. "Now then, ah, sir, did you take part in a—?" he started to ask.

Tonio switched his attention to the glassed-in cabin. "My wife," he cried, rushing to press his face and hands against the window, "she almost died . . . she's pregnant. I got to stay with her." Sullivan was jerked forward unceremoniously and almost lost his balance. He drew his billy club. Kathleen knew his patience was being severely tested. "How'd she get tossed in? Huh? This gentleman here says you know something about her going in the drink." Sullivan poked Tonio in the ribs and turned to Don Lampone, who stood guarding the wheelhouse door.

"I don't know nothing," Tonio said, glancing at Don Lampone. "Ask her, she knows!" Tonio pointed at Kathleen. "She knows how my wife got in the water. She set the whole thing up." Tonio glared at her, but didn't say more.

In the light, Sullivan made a show of examining the cut above Tonio's eye and his bruised knuckles. He pushed Tonio's jacket back with his nightstick, exposing a bloody chest.

"Don't ya know boxing's illegal in New York state? We got the Lewis Law, and this ain't no gentlemen's club. Yer one of the contestants all right, and yer going to jail."

"But my wife—tonight we go back to Italy—let me go," he shouted, putting up a real battle.

"Listen to me, ya mug," Sullivan said, trying to calm him. "Yer wife ain't going nowhere but to a hospital."

Kathleen hurried forward to help Sullivan. "Keep yer mouth shut," she hissed, brushing past Tonio. "I'll come bail ya out." Tonio shot her a worried look.

"What's the problem here, officer?" Kathleen demanded as Sullivan dragged Tonio toward a waiting police boat. "I know this man and he—" She followed after Sullivan to give Tonio a good show.

Emilio stood stroking his earlobe, watching disgustedly as Antonio argued on one side of the officer and Kathleen on the other. Kathleen was playing her part admirably, and if Emilio hadn't known the whole arrangement was a setup he would have assumed she was doing her best to wheedle the officer out of his arrest. The officer pretended confusion and scratched his head. Her voice floated back to Emilio. "I told ya, I'm only in charge of the liquor. I own the Cocked Hat on Cherry Street, maybe ya heard of it. . . . No, no, I don't know who set up the match—"

The officer shook his head and scribbled something on his pad, then tore the paper off and handed it to her. "Ya can tell it to the judge," the officer announced loudly, pulling Antonio away.

"Ah, Jesus bloody Christ!" she cried, throwing up her hands in exasperation as she stalked away.

Emilio was impressed. It was just as she'd assured him; she'd been issued a summons and let go.

"Good evening, sir," she said, strolling up to him. Chuckling, she tucked the summons in her pocket and jerked her head toward the glass door behind him. "I see ya got yer delivery."

"You cretin!" Emilio said. "You almost killed my granddaughter."

"She's a little wet, but no worse for wear and tear. It ain't my fault the rope slipped. I kept my end of the bargain, where's yours?"

"The arrangement's canceled."

"Canceled?"

"You're insane if you think I'm going to pay you for this farce."

"Insane, am I?" Kathleen snarled. "Ya ain't seen insane if ya don't cough up the dough." Several officers including Sullivan glanced over. She lowered her voice, but menace colored her tone. "I'll see to it that yer precious granddaughter don't ever leave the country. I know the law. She's still married to Tonio, and if he finds out yer trying to take her without him, he won't let her go. Come on, old man, a little dip didn't kill her."

He watched as her man made a show of cuffing Antonio and putting him over the side. "Kathleen!" Antonio shouted, struggling. "Wait a minute! Kathleen!"

"Hold on there, lads!" she called. She turned back to Emilio, fanning out her arms and turning her palms up. "What's it going to be? I'll get him released right now," she threatened.

Emilio was trapped. He hated giving in to this cutthroat, but Antonio's freedom would complicate his plans to take his granddaughter away safely and make peace with Francesca. "I'll give you the money," he agreed reluctantly, "but I want to be sure he's going to jail."

"Oh, he's going, but I gotta make it look good." She grinned and went into action. "Officer Sullivan," she shouted, pretending concern, "I've just been talking to this gentleman and he's pointed out that Vittorio Fusco made the knockout. He's the one ya want, and if—"

"It don't matter who knocked out who," Sullivan shouted her down, playing his part. "This man participated in an illegal contest. He's committed a crime and he's going to jail."

Emilio watched her dog the officer, putting up a vehement protest while Antonio was loaded onto a police boat. Behind Emilio the wheelhouse door opened. He stepped aside to assist his granddaughter as she stumbled forward, supported by Enrico Caruso on one side and Francesca Frascatti on the other. The doctor led them to a private cutter. Emilio followed.

Kathleen watched the patrolmen scramble to load Tonio's wife onto the waiting cutter as tenderly as they would their own mother. Sullivan had whispered that the half-naked broad clinging to Tonio's wife like a spider was the opera diva Francesca Frascatti. It was damn queer, a high-tone diva caring enough to strip down to skivvies and use her body heat to warm up an employee. Maybe what Kathleen had been hinting to Tonio about his wife and the gigolo wasn't so far from the truth. They were degenerates and maybe all three of them were humping each other.

That must be the gigolo, she thought, watching the man who was helping the diva. She'd caught a glimpse of him at the market when he was saying good-bye to Tonio's wife. Up close he looked a bit heavier than the day she'd spotted him, but he'd been a ways off, with a hat and his back turned. Her attention was captured by the cops, who were handing down steaming bottles wrapped in rags. The diva tucked them inside the officer's blue coat that Tonio's wife wore. Then they piled on a mountain of tattered, soiled blankets to cover them both. Ha! Kathleen thought, they wouldn't be so attentive if I'd gone into the drink.

"We must get her to a hospital immediately," the doctor said to the cop at the tiller. "Emilio, come. Hurry!"

Don Lampone rushed forward, carrying his case. It rubbed her heels down that he was avoiding her and making no attempt to give her the money she'd earned. As he passed by, she grabbed his sleeve and put her hand on the money case.

"Just a minute, why don't ya give me—" she started, but Don Lampone jerked the case away.

"We'll conclude the deal later," he said, getting into the cutter. "There are too many witnesses here. You know where to find me."

"Remember what I told you, old man."

She gave him a hard eye and tilted her head toward Tonio, who sat close by in a police boat. Don Lampone nodded in acknowledgment of her threat. "I've given my word," he said.

She gave over the case and let him go, but as the cutter shot away, fear washed back into her stomach. Now that he had his prize, what was to keep him from reneging? Her police friends? Naw, he was stinking rich. Only his fear of Tonio and Tonio's control over his granddaughter would keep Don Lampone in line. As the cutter faded to a speck she brushed her thumbnail back and forth against her lip thoughtfully. Something was up with the old man, she'd seen it in his eyes. She'd witnessed too many card games in her saloon to miss a bluff.

She scrambled over the tug to the barge and slipped behind the bar.

Jimmy showed her where he'd put the stuffed cash box under the raised bar boards. He'd already replaced the first one with an empty. She hauled the box out. With the gate and bar business she hoped it held close to three thousand dollars. She grabbed an empty amber bottle some swell had brought aboard, filled it with whiskey from the keg, and took a slug. A drink would settle her nerves after the tension of the last few hours.

She scanned the barge. The action was still going great guns and wouldn't end until they dropped off all the fans. She knew Jimmy would skim a little, he was a thief like all the rest, but he wouldn't skin her, maybe there'd be a few hundred more by the time they got back to the city. She trusted Jimmy to handle the men and the second box.

She made her way back to the tug, brooding. Something had gone on in the wheelhouse with Frascatti and the granddaughter, she could feel it. Don Lampone had begun kowtowing the minute the diva arrived. She'd seen it clear when the cutter shot away. She moved to the edge of the barge and caught Sullivan's eye. He was guarding the boat with Tonio and moved to intercept her.

"Hold that boat. I'm going to talk to the pilot in the wheelhouse. I might want to go back with ya." She slipped quickly inside the wheelhouse to quiz the pilot.

Moments later she emerged, hooting with glee. Don Lampone was the grandfather all right, but Francesca Frascatti was the bitch's mother.

The wheelman had told her Frascatti was hotter than a live coal and had been cursing Don Lampone the whole time she was inside the wheelhouse. Frascatti had sworn he was never going to see his granddaughter again. Kathleen thought it over. The two of them were brimming with dough and were staunch enemies. The only thing Kathleen had to do was work one against the other and up the ante. She could keep Tonio for a trump card. She couldn't wait to get back to Manhattan and tell the diva she knew the whole story. Kathleen was going to collect the pot of gold at the end of the rainbow!

Sullivan gave the order to keep searching for Mario as he swung Kathleen aboard the police boat. She jerked away from him roughly, to fool Tonio, but Tonio wasn't interested in her bit of drama. "Head directly for Catherine's Slip like we planned," she whispered. "But I don't want Tonio arrested after all."

Sullivan nodded and ducked into the engine house. The coppers had picked up a few other men to make the arrest look good. She brushed past them heading toward Tonio, who was hunched over his seat in the back of the boat looking sick and nervous. His misery tickled her pink. She shoved the metal cash box under the bench next to him and sat down, swigging from her bottle of whiskey.

"Let me see yer eye," she said, taking his chin in her hand and moving his face toward her. "It's a nasty cut ya got there." His eye was puffed shut and crusted over with blood.

"Take your hands off me!" he snarled, banging her backward with his cuffed hands. "You almost killed my wife."

The laugher from the engine house stopped. Sullivan poked his head out. "You there! Keep yer hands to yerself."

Kathleen studied Tonio. If she wanted his help, she'd have to cool him off. "Well, she ain't dead, is she?" She offered him a drink from the bottle, but he shook his head no.

"You're lucky. Or I'd kill you." He glared at her as the dark water flew by.

"Don't worry, I've fixed it so when we get back ya can go to her."

He sat sullenly for a while watching the lights of the Brooklyn Bridge draw near. Then curiosity got the better of him and he asked, "You got the money from Don Lampone?"

"Naw. The bastard ain't coming through with the dough. Where'd ya think these coppers came from, Don Lampone sicced them on us."

"*Minca!*" he swore, shocked.

She nodded her head conspiratorially and continued, "We're lucky Sullivan was in the crew. He was tight with Jack for years and promised me for a few hundred bucks he'll get us outta this mess. Give me some of yer dough. I'll pay ya back at the Hat. I ain't got the key." She nudged the locked box under her seat for emphasis.

"I ain't got money," Tonio said.

"What are ya talking?" she said, roughly digging into his pockets. "Don't be a tightwad. Ya was carrying the four thousand since yesterday."

"I gave it to Mario to hold while I was in the ring. He had the money when he jumped."

She rocketed to her feet. "Mario! Sweet mother of mercy!"

She was seized with a wild desire to grab the tiller and head back, but the money was either at the bottom of the river or in the pockets of the coppers who would fish him out. So that's why Tonio had been demanding they search for Mario.

"It don't matter now," Tonio said, turning thoughtful. "That was bad money. Cursed for trying to sell my child."

"Jesus Christ! Yer an idiot! How could ya give Mario the money to hold? What are ya, stupid or something?"

"I don't have no pockets in this getup! You got the take from the fight, what're you beefing about?"

"That money goes to pay off the coppers, the tug, the barge, and them other bums involved in this muckup. I need that money."

"You think I know Mario is going to drown?"

"Well, I hope yer satisfied, ya lost us an easy fortune."

She threw herself back down next to him and took another swig from her bottle. She didn't know who to be angry at, Tonio for giving the money to Mario or Mario for drowning with it.

Tonio watched her stew. He was full to the teeth with her bitching. He wanted to throw her overboard, but he needed her to fix things. After the coppers let him go, he'd go back to the Hat to wash and change into his new clothes and get his traveling things, then he'd never see her again. He wished he could go straight to Don Lampone, but he couldn't show up at the Plaza a bloody, ragged mess. He'd be dishonored. After all, he wasn't a *contadino* anymore. Gentlemen needed to dress accordingly.

Finally, the boat slowed, pulling up to the pier at Catherine's Slip. While they tied up Kathleen remained silent, gnawing her thumb and swilling whiskey. It didn't take Sullivan and his men long to unload the other prisoners and put them into the waiting paddy wagon. Then Sullivan came back and helped Tonio onto the wooden pier. As he unlocked Tonio's handcuffs Kathleen said, "Meet me at the Hat for yer money after ya drop yer load. I ain't got the key on me." Sullivan nodded, acknowledging the locked box in her hands.

Tonio didn't like the feeling he got between them. He watched Sullivan thoughtfully as the cop headed down the pier and clambered into the front seat of the paddy wagon. As the paddy wagon pulled away, Tonio brushed his hand against his scabbed eye. "I oughta get stitches for this," he said anxiously.

Kathleen glared at him. "Ya selfish pig, ya haven't heard a word I've been saying," she hissed, sounding like she was going to bust her pipe. "I gotta have seven thousand dollars by day after tomorrow or I'll lose the new saloon. They'll take the Hat!"

"Yeah, yeah. You got steak at the Hat for my eye? I don't want to go meet Don Lampone like this."

"Are ya being thick on purpose or are ya trying to drive me to the far side of the moon? Don't ya understand Don Lampone double-crossed ya? He had them coppers arrest ya, to throw ya in jail. He was going to take yer wife and leave for Italy without ya. Mario told me that if ya went back to Italy tonight with Don Lampone, he was going to have ya killed."

He didn't believe a word of it. She was still trying to find a way to get her hooks into Don Lampone's money and use him to do it. "Everything with you is always money, ain't it?" he snarled. "I don't think Don Lampone double-crossed me. I think you did."

She squirmed under his hot eyes, but held her ground. "I didn't have nothing to do with it. Didn't I get ya set free?"

"I no want to sell my wife, but you figure you make a deal with Don Lampone and cut me out. You have me pinched."

He shoved her back and she lost her temper. She swiped at him with the whiskey bottle, but he darted aside and the bottom of the bottle smashed against a piling.

"You promised me that money!" she cried, waving the jagged remains of the bottle at him and clutching the cash box under her other arm. "I need it and I'm going to get it one way or the other. I ain't losing my dream because of your bitch bride. Yer going to do what I say."

"You think so?" Tonio laughed at her rage. "I know how to fix you!"

In one motion he snatched the cash box from her fingers and flung it high and wide out over the dark water reflecting the lights of the Brooklyn Bridge. "You want money so bad, go swim for it."

Chapter Forty-Two

*G*ET OUT OF THE CUTTER," Colombo
ordered, holding the pistol on Bevilacqua and the other detective
who'd been at the tiller.

Dante stood in the cutter, his hands raised. The engine was idling and
they were drifting back toward the barge. He watched as Bevilacqua and
the other detective climbed over the edge with life preservers.

"You're a traitor, Colombo," Bevilacqua said as he kicked his legs and
gripped the float. "Petrosino will get you for this."

"I'll be sure to tell Petrosino for you," Colombo said with a laugh.

"Don't leave!" the other detective cried. "We'll freeze in this water."

"Head for the barge, the current's with you. You won't freeze if you
keep moving. Sit down, Dante, take the tiller. Let's go!"

Dante looked at the gun trained on him and did as instructed. He left
the two men treading water and headed into the river. "Where are we
going?" Dante asked.

"When you get back to the barge, loop behind and hug its right side
as you ease the cutter forward."

"Whatever Emilio's paying you, I'll pay more. I've got to get to that
ship before it leaves for Italy."

Colombo chuckled, amused and clearly uninterested in any offer of
money. As soon as the men floating in the river were out of sight,
Colombo lowered the gun and seemed to relax.

"Are you going to let someone know about those men?" Dante asked
anxiously.

"Don't worry, they'll be fine. Now when we come up alongside, cut
the engine midway and coast up to the end of the barge."

The cutter glided silently, hanging in the shadow of the barge. Ahead
the police were handing down two figures draped in blankets to a waiting boat.

"Good!" Colombo said. "My guess was correct." He tucked the gun
back inside his boot.

"Why, that's Cesca and . . . Mina," Dante said, startled. "There's Emilio! But the silver-haired man in the launch? I was certain he was—"

"Bevilacqua threw you off."

The engine of the cutter holding Mina and Cesca roared as it headed away from the barge toward Manhattan. Colombo had averted a wild-goose chase. But if he'd known Bevilacqua was a traitor, why had he kept it to himself? "How did you know it wasn't Mina being lowered over the side? I saw her dress. Solange lifted her veil and looked at me," Dante continued, embarrassed. "I assumed—"

"It happens to all of us," Colombo said, nodding sympathetically. "That's why surgeons don't operate on family members. When you're personally involved, emotion distorts everything."

"How did you figure it out?"

"After making our plans this morning I secretly went to the Plaza to check on Emilio. I arrived just as Bevilacqua was receiving a package. Although I wasn't able to see what he did with it, I was able to question a boy named Sean who brought it from the Cocked Hat. Being a curious rascal, he'd peeked inside. For a dollar he gave me a detailed description of the contents."

"The dress Mina was wearing when she was abducted?" Dante guessed. Colombo nodded. "You suspected it would be used as a diversion?" Dante asked.

"Yes. Emilio simply had an actress friend of Solange's put on the dress, and paid another to wear a silver wig. In your agitated state you couldn't see clearly and Bevilacqua did his best to rattle you. As he urged you aboard this cutter he shouted, 'Don't let Emilio take Mina *and her child*.' A highly emotional appeal, but Bevilacqua had no way of knowing Signora DiGianni was pregnant."

Dante thought it over. "You're absolutely right, I didn't release that information. But why didn't you tell me about the dress?"

"I've known for months the Black Hand's planning to have me assassinated and that they'd infiltrated and bribed someone in my undercover operations. But I needed the informant to stick his neck out. Bevilacqua's actions at the Plaza and his behavior tonight prove he's the traitor. I'm sorry I had to use you, Dante, but it was necessary. There are many who wish to see me dead."

It took a moment for Dante to see beneath the obvious. "You're Petrosino!"

The short fat man bowed. "At your service."

So here was the master of illusion who had spawned so many tales. "I should have known," Dante said, examining him closely. "They say you're always in disguise."

"It's necessary for my safety. What you see before you is illusion. Hair, eyebrows, sideburns, even my swarthy complexion, but unfortunately this belly of mine is real."

"A subtle disguise," Dante said, eagerly moving forward to shake Petrosino's hand and slap him on the back, laughing ruefully at his own folly.

"No one must suspect that I'm personally involved in this operation," Petrosino cautioned.

"As you wish," Dante said, rubbing his chin sheepishly. "You're shorter than I thought you'd be."

"An imposing man is always noticed. This composition works to my advantage, eh? Who would suspect a short, fat man?"

"Obviously, not I," Dante said.

Petrosino's eyes crinkled with delight. He took the tiller and eased out into the main channel. It was a while before Petrosino spoke again; when he did his voice was heavy and serious.

"I have news, Dante. I've received information from Vincenzo Manzaro."

"The man going over the immigration records?"

Petrosino nodded, looking uncomfortable with what he was about to say. He slowed the cutter, and the engine's roar subsided momentarily.

"Yes. It seems he's found an irregularity. While checking the immigration records for the ship Signora DiGianni told us she came over on, we discovered there was a serious illness during the trip, a Filomina Rossi—"

A low shout interrupted Petrosino.

"Did you hear that?" Dante asked. Petrosino strained to hear above the engine's idle. Once again a man's low shout carried across the river. "Cut the engine!" Dante cried.

Petrosino turned the engine off. The cutter bobbed, the only sound the lapping of the waves. Dante's eye snagged on something flickering on the inky water. "What's that?" Dante asked, pointing a few yards off to the left at something that glinted in the moonlight.

"Help! Over here! Help!"

"It must be one of the men who fell overboard during the confusion with the police," Dante said. The voice sounded familiar, but it couldn't be who Dante thought it was. A white face bobbed into view as the man paddled slowly toward him. "Mario?" Dante called. "Mario, is that you?"

Mario let go of the planking he'd been clinging to and treaded water. He waved the hand gripping his grape knife. In a moment Dante and Petrosino pulled him aboard.

"What happened?" Dante asked. "What are you doing floating in the river with your knife?"

"That bitch Kathleen! She almost killed Mina and nearly drowned me."

Dante and Petrosino listened in appalled silence as Mario pulled off his wet clothing and described what had happened after the end of the barge fight. He explained how he'd realized Mina was hidden in the barrel and what he'd done to free her.

"When I finally got to her she was unconscious. Her hair was entangled in the staves of the barrel and it would have dragged us both to the bottom, but I used my knife to cut her free. After I shoved her up, the current sucked me downstream. When I finally got to the surface I saw the men on the workboat pulling her body from the water. I tried to flag them, but I was too far away. Luckily I grabbed onto some debris and stayed afloat. It's a good thing you spotted me, I'd never have made it back to land against the current."

Dante was filled with gratitude. He embraced Mario and pounded him on the back.

"You're sure she's alive?" Mario asked.

"Yes," Dante said, his voice choked with emotion. "She's on her way back to the city with Cesca and Emilio right now."

Mario's eyes glistened with grateful tears.

"Thank God we found you," Petrosino said. "We wouldn't have come this way if I hadn't been heading back to Petrosino's offices on Mulberry Street. I need to find him and regroup with the others." Petrosino gave Dante a meaningful look. "By the way," Petrosino added, "Dante's discovered that Bevilacqua's the informant who's been feeding information to Emilio."

"*Cazzo!*" Mario said.

Dante was forced to take credit for Petrosino's work in order to keep the detective's identity secret, but he felt like a fool. Despite the reassurance that the person closest to the victim is the least able to help, he knew he'd been completely ineffective. Nothing he'd done had kept Mina safe from Kathleen's despicable schemes or Antonio's brutality, and if it hadn't been for Mario's bravery tonight, Mina would most likely have drowned. He took off his sweater and offered it to Mario.

"Bevilacqua used Mina's dress to distract me after the boxing match," Dante said, smiling thinly.

"Emilio hired actors," Petrosino informed Mario. "He tricked us into thinking he and Solange were taking Mina from the opposite side of the boat."

"To keep you away from the barrel exchange?" Mario asked.

Dante nodded as Petrosino tried to start the engine. It coughed and spit, but refused to start.

"What's the matter?" Dante asked.

"I don't know," Petrosino replied. "I think we may have lost pressure."

They checked the gauge. Petrosino was right: the pressure in the engine had dropped.

"I'll stoke the engine," Dante said and headed into the engine house. "We'll have to wait while it builds up again." They drifted downstream rapidly in the strong current. Dante anxiously fed the engine, but the pressure built slowly as they quickly lost ground.

"Do you think Bevilacqua and Kathleen are working together?" Mario asked.

"I doubt it. Emilio would have wanted to keep them separate. Bevilacqua could have given Kathleen information about Mina's true identity," Dante called through the open door.

Mario huddled on the bench, shivering in Dante's sweater. "Such evil, for money," Mario said sadly.

"It's a good thing Kathleen never discovered Mina is Cesca's daughter," Dante said.

"That's exactly what I want to talk to you about, Dante," Petrosino said. "Manzaro believes we have a complication with the immigration records."

"When we get this thing started can you head for Catherine's Slip?"

Mario asked through chattering teeth. "The pier's only two blocks from the saloon and my room at the boardinghouse. I need some dry clothes."

Petrosino nodded and checked the pressure gauge. It still didn't register. Well over an hour had passed as they drifted into the harbor. Mario and Petrosino lit lanterns and hung them at the bow and stern. A mist lay over the water and their position was becoming perilous. If a large vessel were to steam past they might not be seen. The silhouette of the Statue of Liberty loomed large in the gathering fog.

"Try the engine again," Dante urged. "I added more water to the boiler."

This time it sputtered, caught, and puttered tiredly. Still the cutter made little progress against the current.

"Sorry," Dante said, "there wasn't enough water in the boiler and it hadn't been sealed properly, but the pressure's building now."

"We'll take it slow until it's well up to steam," Petrosino called to Dante. "Keep feeding the engine."

The cutter limped back toward Lower Manhattan as the eastern sky lightened. The engine was still struggling as the cutter passed under the Brooklyn Bridge, but as it drew alongside the rotting piers where large pipes dumped raw sewage into the river, Petrosino was glad they'd been going slowly. The waters around Manhattan were an open cesspool, thick with discarded garbage. The stink was overpowering. Dante pulled out his handkerchief and pressed it to his nose as Petrosino inched the cutter forward.

"Take an oar," Petrosino said. "I don't want to foul the propeller. You and Mario clear a path."

Dante and Mario grabbed oars and scanned the water carefully, pushing any floating debris out of the propeller's path.

"Reminds me of Venice," Dante joked as Mario sang "*O sole mio*" and pretended to pole the boat through the water.

Progress was slow, but the cutter finally pulled up next to the pilings. Dante jumped the gap to tie up, and Mario threw him a line, but Dante couldn't pull the cutter in. Something appeared to be wedged between the piling and the pier. Dante forced his oar in and levered his weight against the object. It gave a jerk and shifted, but didn't free the space. Mario bounced on his oar while Petrosino reversed the engine and Dante pushed. The object dislodged and flipped over in the churning water. Dante bent down curiously to see what was bobbing. He poked it gingerly with his oar.

"Jesus Christ!" he exclaimed as he pulled back sharply. "Mario! It's a body."

BENEATH the canopied bed on the fourth floor of Cesca's brownstone, Mina tossed in fevered delusions. Her face was framed by sweaty tendrils of unevenly shorn hair. Emilio and his doctor had wanted to take her to Bellevue Hospital, but Cesca had insisted she be brought home to be cared for by Dr. DiBella.

When DiBella arrived, Emilio's doctor was forced to withdraw. "Mina's condition isn't grave enough to risk the diseases associated with public facilities," DiBella insisted. Emilio's doctor agreed and informed Emilio, "No one, even the police, can overrule a guardian's wishes."

Even though Emilio had begged forgiveness on the cutter, Cesca was still furious with him and ordered him from the house: "Get out! Never attempt to see Maria again."

"Please, Francesca, listen to me. I swear on Giulio's life I never intended for this to happen. I agreed to the transfer only to protect her. I was going to bring her to you. I want peace," he pleaded as Petrosino's men escorted him down the front steps of the brownstone. "I promised Giulio!"

Once the door closed, Cesca dismissed Emilio from her mind. She had her daughter to think of and she was going to make sure she recovered and stayed safe. She went up to sit beside the bed and hold Mina's hand.

"Her hands . . . yes," Mina moaned. "There's a scar . . . a moon . . . so hot. *Mammina*'s dead. She's in the ground—"

"I'm not dead, I'm here. Maria? *Mammina*'s here."

Cesca put a hand on Mina's forehead. She was burning up. "No, no, Antonio! Don't touch me!" Mina cried, throwing off Cesca's hand. "Women are brave . . . braver than men. I want to go—" Mina tried to sit up. Her eyelashes fluttered.

"Sssh, Mina, you're sick. Let me help you."

"She's in shock," Doctor DiBella said. "This will calm her." He gave her an injection and she settled back against the pillows.

Cesca tucked the blankets under Mina's shoulders and did her best to hold back tears. Time passed slowly, and occasionally throughout the early morning Mina gripped Cesca's hand so tightly she thought the bones might snap. The vigil by her daughter's bedside seemed the beginning of her penance for the years of neglect. Worry and reflection began to open a channel in Cesca's soul through which a deeper feeling crept, the wonderful feeling of being needed.

To sacrifice for something beyond selfish desire, to strive to become better, to drop your hard-won defenses and make yourself vulnerable to another human being's needs, these are transforming actions, she thought. What is there that's transforming in money or fame? They're feeble cloaks thrown over withered spirits. How sad it is to have no one to love, no one to trouble over. I can finally understand man's need for God and his hope of destiny if man is so alone locked within the hard shell of his heart.

As the ripening dawn washed away the harsh shadows on Mina's face, Cesca recalled what she'd said to Emilio at the hotel. She'd spoken the truth, just as all the great philosophers claimed. The most important element for a happy life is not money or fame, but love. Love shared, no matter what the relationship, is the catalyst that transforms a barren existence and fills an empty heart.

She watched Mina moan and shift, thinking of the horror of the kidnapping and near drowning. Poor child, how frightened she must have been. It was my pride and my battle with Emilio that created all the problems, she thought. If I hadn't needed to prove I was Emilio's better, I would never have left her and she would never have needed to look elsewhere for love. She'd never have married Antonio.

Would Mina be able to forgive and accept a mother who had abandoned her so cruelly? And what would she think of Emilio, the grandfather she'd never known she had? Cesca wouldn't be able to keep Emilio away forever. It was going to be a terribly long battle to put everything right, but a battle she must wage and win, for without her daughter to love, what was left to live for?

Help her, God, Cesca repeated over and over in silent prayer as the day wore on. Let her know how much I have come to love her. Take away her anger and rejection. She hasn't known me long, but let her give me a chance to pour out what is in my heart. I need her so much. Ease her pain and let her come to know joy in this life . . . even if . . . even if she chooses not to accept me. I'll do anything, promise you anything, so that she might know love and happiness. Cesca's desperate pleas rose to heaven even as tears slipped steadily down her cheeks. She leaned forward to stroke her daughter's cheek. At least, she thought, she's beyond the troubles of the moment.

But Mina was aware of what was happening around her, though it was tumbled and entwined with the past. Her mind recognized the creak of floorboards under Errico's weight and knew that the Signorina held her hand, but the diva's arias were entwined in the threads of her lace and ran through the bark of the olive trees on the hills.

Everything flowed in and out of the knots. Maria as a child and *Mammina* with her umbrella floated before her eyes . . . The streets of Naples resounded with footsteps and she felt the swaying of the ship that brought her to a new destiny. The hands of the past worked the bobbins and fed her crushed sweets . . . *Mammina* and Maria blew on the spoon to cool the soup . . . a silver spoon for a baby . . . that someone took from a carpetbag spewing yellow and pink snapdragons. . . .

Everything was coming together, forming an ornate pricking she'd never seen before. Her hand reached to uncover the secret pattern, but she didn't know how to find the edge of the lace. She heard voices, but they sounded like the sea, and the hand on her cheek was as hot as a crescent moon.

"Beloved, can you hear me?" It was Prima Donna's voice she heard and her wing brushed Mina's cheek. "It's *Mammina,* I'm here with you."

The image of the spiral pink conch shell covered by intricate carvings floated before Mina's eyes. It had been a gift from her grandmother. Her grandmother had died and left her the lace . . . a chance for a new beginning. The stories . . . *Mammina* and Maria . . . a gift from the sea . . .

Mina laughed out loud. "Yes," she said to no one in particular, "she gave me a gift from the sea!"

Her grandmother's hand was pressing the shell against her cheek and she heard the sound of the blue sea of Naples . . . and then . . . the gray sea of the Atlantic lapping . . . lapping like women keening. The women aboard the ship were keening, but it was the voice of the shell . . . she remembered its odd ebb and flow . . . it stirred stories of Naples, her dead mother and the sea. Maria was swallowed up and covered while Mina was deep inside the shell's smooth spiral, lost.

She slid her hands along the translucent walls of the shell, joining the dancing figures etched on its sides, twisting in the intricate tale, marveling at the steps. . . . The song of the dancers whorled in the conch's throat, the tambourines buffeted, a blast of the hurricane. She clutched the gimp thread running through the Duke's Garter and would have blown away, except for love . . . Maria's love . . . Dante's love. . . .

She tried to open her eyes, but they felt like hot seeds, baking under a summer sun in moist earth . . . the earth of a vineyard . . . the grandfather on his horse . . . her eyes were sprouting . . . opening. She could see . . . see herself rising above the shell . . . rising above the curving grape fields of Vesuvius. She was clinging to the gimp thread, heels over head, seeing things never before seen. She saw the curving letters of a name carved on a piece of ivory—G-I-U-L-I-O—and a woman who played the mandolin stood on the crest of a far-off hill. A familiar woman . . . with a crescent scar . . . who stood holding a colorful parasol, singing like an angel . . .

Everything made sense for the first time. The old man with the silver hair was the grandfather, and the Signorina was *Mammina*.

Mina's eyes snapped opened. Cesca released her hand, got up, and went to the door.

"Doctor DiBella," she called. "She's awake!"

The doctor hurried upstairs.

Mina stared at him fearfully as he came across the carpet and picked up her hand. The man smelled of peppermint, and when he pressed his fingers into her wrist her flesh felt like freshly made *torrone*.

She felt her pulse racing. Her eyes darted to the Signorina. The Signorina is *Mammina,* her clouded mind murmured. Was it true?

"How are you feeling?" the man asked.

She cocked her head on the pillow and stared at his whiskered lips. She felt like Prima Donna on her perch. The door to the golden cage was open, but she was afraid to fly out.

"Answer, my darling," the Signorina urged as she settled on the bed and stroked her hair over and over.

The truth shall set you free, she heard Dante say. Cut the gimp thread, her mind commanded, and fly away. She moved her lips, but no sound came out.

"She's still in the arms of the drug," the peppermint man said.

Mina stared at the Signorina. She felt as if she were spinning in a wild tarantella; what she was thinking was impossible. It couldn't be. Sounds banged, images blurred, thoughts were as confused as the ribbons on the shaking tambourines. She lifted a trembling hand and took the fingers from her hair. She turned the hand over and looked at the palm. *That* was where the proof would be. The Signorina is *Mammina,* a soft voice urged.

Threads were coming together. Mina could almost identify the puzzling pattern. It brought to mind a yellowed piece of lace her grandmother had shown her years before her mother had died. The lace was rich and intricate . . . too difficult for her to attempt. But now if she could only lift the bobbins she might figure out its pattern and understand. Under the ring finger on the Signorina's hand she found a scar, a crescent moon.

"*Mammina?*" she mumbled, putting her finger on the scar.

"What are you saying, *cara*?" the Signorina asked tenderly.

Mina touched the scar with her fingertip. "*Mammina?*"

"Yes, my darling. It's me; it's your *Mammina*. I've come to get you."

Mina dropped her hand and jerked against the headboard. "No, no!" she cried, pulling the covers aside and trying to escape. "You don't understand. You're not my mother! And *Mammina*'s dead."

"I am. I'm your mother, truly. Maria—"

Mina leaped out of bed and stumbled toward the door. *Mammina* had come back, but how could it be? She was dead . . . *Mammina* was dead. And the sea had swallowed the rest. This was a ghost sent to punish her.

"No, no!" she cried. "Go away. Go away!" She slapped the ghostly hands away and turned back toward the door. "I'm sorry," she babbled. "I didn't mean it . . . please." She yanked on the door frantically, but it wouldn't open. "I didn't steal," she continued. "She gave them to me . . . the earrings . . . she gave them to me before she died. I was supposed to make her happy . . . I didn't want to hurt anyone!"

Mina felt a prick on her arm. Once again the wind whipped like a sirocco. She tumbled back and fell down. Around and around she went. Down and down. Deep within the heart of the shell a voice was calling, whispering behind the gale. "Give me your soul!" it coaxed sweetly. She turned to see Satan riding the gray waves of the Atlantic, but he had Antonio's face. "Give me your soul as you promised long ago and I'll give you a new destiny . . . a destiny all your own."

"No, no! *Sant'Anna* save me!" she pleaded, pushing aside the hands that reached to take her away. "Help me, Maria . . . Maria, help me . . . take it back. Take your destiny back. I did my best. I kept my word. Don't let Antonio take my soul!"

Chapter Forty-Three

*T*HE BRASS-BUTTONED OFFICERS spilled into Cesca's foyer like hot oil from a tumbled skillet. While Petrosino's men stalled and demanded identification, Errico summoned Cesca from Mina's bedside. She came down the stairs defiantly to meet the intruders.

The lead officer came forward with a tight jaw. "Are you Francesca Frascatti?"

"I am."

"I'm Sergeant Patrick Sullivan of the New York City Police Department, investigating a crime," he said.

"A crime?" she mocked, holding Errico's arm.

Francesca recognized the thickset policeman with muttonchops who introduced himself as Sullivan. He was the police officer who had helped with Mina at the barge. He scribbled in a narrow book like a harried accountant while the three policemen accompanying him regarded her with hard weasels' eyes. "A man's been pulled from the river," Sullivan continued. "He's dead, and—"

Her hand flew to her mouth. Mario, they must have found Mario.

"Is yer daughter, Filomina DiGianni, recovering from an accident here in yer home?" he asked. She nodded, searching his face for a clue to the question's meaning. "I've got to ask ya some questions. Do ya have a private room we can use?"

Errico stepped forward, blocking her. "I must protest, Sergeant. Signorina Frascatti's suffered a shock; her daughter was almost drowned last night. She's in no—"

"This is a murder investigation."

"Murder!" she gasped. "Mario!"

"Is it Mario Catanzaro you've come about?" Errico asked.

Sullivan shook his head. Cesca clutched Errico's arm for support. She'd last seen Dante struggling with Bevilacqua and Colombo as the cutter sped away. Please, Lord, she prayed, don't let it be Dante.

"Come into the parlor," she said. Her legs melted beneath her as Errico led her forward. "We'll talk there."

Sullivan and one of his men moved into the parlor with her while the others stayed in the foyer with Petrosino's men. She closed the door and asked, "Who is it you've found?"

"Antonio DiGianni."

The shock set her down abruptly on a chair next to the fire. Her first thoughts, filled with surprise and relief, were Thank God! Mina's free! She felt wildly elated, but was overtaken immediately by guilt. Antonio might have behaved like a cold-blooded animal, but he was still a human being. She shouldn't be happy about his death.

Before she had a chance to process her feelings further, Sullivan announced harshly, "We've reason to believe the victim was wounded by yer hand."

"My hand?" she asked, stunned.

"That's absurd!" Errico replied.

"We found him floating down by Catherine's Slip. He'd been stabbed. We've information ya knew he'd been beating yer daughter and ya blamed him for her near drowning this past evening. He told witnesses he was on his way here to confront ya."

"Confront me? Why would he confront me?"

"He wanted his wife back," Sullivan said with a shrug. "A witness claims ya refused to turn his wife over and threatened to kill him."

"What witness?' Cesca demanded.

"He never came here, Sergeant," Errico said belligerently. "I'll testify to that."

Sullivan looked Errico over suspiciously. "Well, nobody said he came here, but somebody did go to a lot of trouble to make his death look like a robbery," Sullivan said. "They stripped him and emptied his pockets."

"Now you're saying I robbed him?"

"All right. Let's cut out the funny business. You or Dante Romano killed Antonio DiGianni. What happened? Did ya stab him in a rage because of him beating yer daughter and then yer boyfriend covered for ya?" Sullivan demanded sharply.

"I haven't seen Signor Romano since the boxing match earlier this evening," Cesca replied. "In case you've forgotten, that's where I first encountered you, Sergeant Sullivan. You helped me and my daughter aboard the cutter. I have my own witness who will tell you I came directly here."

He gave her a hard look. It was clear he didn't like her tone. "That may be true, but it don't prove ya didn't kill him. We know Dante Romano hated Ton— ah, Mr. DiGianni and wanted him to divorce yer daughter."

Cesca gave a chortle of disbelief. Now he's going to try to pin the murder on Dante, her mind gibed. What a farce! He knows I have witnesses who saw me leave the scene. It wasn't possible for me to murder him, and Dante—Dante had been in the cutter with Colombo and Bevilacqua when . . . She froze and glanced at Errico, suddenly afraid. Dante! What had Dante done after the cutter streaked away from the barge with Colombo and Bevilacqua?

Errico reacted to her fear instantly. "I'll put a call in to Inspector Petrosino," Errico said to Sullivan as he stepped to the phone. "He's been helping us on this case."

Sullivan smirked. "Oh, yeah," he said with distaste, "the famous detective, Giuseppe Petrosino. Naw, I don't need his help. Unless I want to dress up and play wop!"

He laughed at his own joke. Errico put the phone down and turned toward Sullivan, irritation plain upon his face. Cesca put a restraining hand on his arm. Sullivan saw the gesture and cleared his throat, pushing down his amusement.

"Officer Doyle," he said, tipping his head toward the officer with him, "see this gentleman out and bring in the witness."

Officer Doyle tried to strong-arm Errico, but he quickly backed off. There was fire in Errico's eye and steel coiled in his arm, which lay ready to strike. Whoever tried to manhandle him was headed for a thrashing. Errico exited under his own power, followed by Doyle.

"I got someone I want ya to meet," Sullivan said when they were alone. "After ya talk I should have all the information I need."

Cesca waited for her accuser while Sullivan continued scribbling in his notebook. A moment later Kathleen strutted through the door.

Cesca wasn't surprised. "That woman helped kidnap my daughter and almost killed her," she said in a fury. "Is she here under arrest?"

Sullivan ignored Cesca's question while Kathleen circled her as though she were examining a twenty-dollar gold piece. "Yeah, she's the one," Kathleen said disdainfully. "She was fancied up, but I'd recognize that hair color anywhere. Plenty of people saw her on the barge and heard her screaming for Tonio's blood." Pleased, Sullivan nodded and noted her comment.

"Sergeant, would you kindly explain why you've brought this criminal to my home?" Cesca demanded.

"She claims ya murdered Antonio DiGianni," he said.

Cesca turned on Kathleen, annoyed but amused. What made this woman think she could accuse her of murder? It wasn't as though Cesca were without connections in the city. "Are you drunk or mad?" she demanded.

Kathleen leaned back and crossed her arms upon her chest smugly. She smiled, her eyes twinkling with malice. "Tonio was going to go back to Italy with yer daughter right after the match. He'd found out she was pregnant and that her grandfather was Don Lampone, a rich eye-talyan. Ya hate Lampone, so ya secretly offered Tonio a five-thousand-dollar bribe, hoping to beat out the old man's offer. Tonio took yer money and was considering—"

"I offered? It was Emilio who offered ten thousand dollars—"

Sullivan's jaw dropped at the amount. He turned to Kathleen. It was written plainly on his face, she hadn't told him that part before.

"Yeah," she grudgingly admitted, turning to Sullivan, "Lampone's brimming." She turned back to Cesca in a temper. "Now shut yer lies! I'm talking."

Cesca watched as Kathleen strolled around the room and casually examined her belongings while she laid out her accusation. "Tonio gave yer bribe to Mario to hold while he fought; it's in his pockets this very minute. Ya see," she said to Sullivan, "like I told ya, Tonio was considering her offer because he never loved his wife . . . but when he found out she was pregnant he decided to start over. The kid was his blood, after all."

Kathleen paused to pluck a piece of candy from a dish on a side table. She popped it in her mouth and chewed thoroughly as she continued exploring the room. "That's when the rich grandfather, Lampone, offered to set him up in Naples. Tonio decided to go back to Italy with his wife and kid. The ship was leaving Sunday morning—well, this morning, right after the bout. But they was cutting Miss Fancy Britches here out and she couldn't abide that. So she tried to snatch her daughter away on the barge, but there was an accident. Her daughter fell overboard. Tonio was furious when he found she'd kidnapped his poor wife. He told me he was coming up here to get her back. So when he came for her"— Kathleen turned sharply toward Cesca—"ya killed him and dumped his body downtown at the pier."

"What nonsense!" Cesca cried. "I know why you're so interested in what happened between Antonio and his wife. You're Antonio's mistress and responsible for his murder or you wouldn't have gone to such trouble to concoct such lies about me."

"Lies? Ya hated him for beating yer daughter and ya swore she'd never go back to Italy to live with Tonio and her grandfather. Ya killed him and I'll see ya arrested and thrown in jail."

Cesca laughed, unable to take her threat seriously. "This is unbelievable, Sergeant," Cesca said turning to Sullivan. "She almost drowned my daughter last night in her scheme to get money from Emil—Signor Lampone. I'd like to make a statement about her activities thus far and protest these accusations. It's patently evident she's trying to bamboozle you."

Sullivan shook his head. "We've got a signed statement from the grandfather," he said, patting his pocket. "A Don Emilio Lampone staying at the Plaza Hotel. He's backed up her account. He says yer daughter's going overboard was a complete accident and that ya've been trying to keep him and her husband, Tonio, from taking her back to Italy."

Cesca was shocked that Emilio had signed a statement, especially after his apparent capitulation. He'd begged forgiveness, sworn he'd promised Giulio to make peace. She'd believed his surrender and had been considering a truce.

"I don't believe it. Emilio—Emilio was as outraged as I am by this hooligan's behavior." She paced the carpet for a moment. "Sergeant, it's clear this woman's responsible for Antonio's death. She's admitted he broke off their affair. Obviously she couldn't stand the idea of losing him—or more likely Emilio refused to give her the money she demanded. She killed him and is blackmailing Emilio w—"

There was a crash. Shards of a Capo-di-Monte figurine flew across the carpet and hit Cesca's skirt.

"Bollocks!" Kathleen shouted. "Better than half this house is packed up. Look around for yerself. She's done something. She's running away. Ya can see it for yerself, Pat—Sergeant Sullivan."

"Yer leaving?" Sullivan asked, glancing around the room.

"Yes, South America. I have—I may have an opera engagement there."

He took note of the packing crates filled with Dante's books.

"I told ya!" Kathleen said. "Tonio didn't have a defensive wound on him. Do ya think a tough boxer like him would go without putting up a mitt?" Sullivan nodded vigorously. Cesca watched helplessly while he wrote the coincidental information in his book. "Ya did it," Kathleen said, pointing her finger dramatically. "Or maybe ya had yer lover kill him and ya think because yer rich and famous ya can cover it up."

"You're delusional! I can prove I've been here at home. If he was murdered at the pier I couldn't have killed him."

"Not quite," Sullivan said. "Ya might have killed him elsewhere and staged the robbery to cover his murder. A coroner has the body at the morgue now. He'll get to the bottom of it."

"But how would I—why would we—Sergeant, it doesn't make sense."

"This was found in his hand," Sullivan said, unfolding a handkerchief from his pocket. "Do you recognize it?" Cesca's ruby and seed pearl earring dangled from his fingers.

"It's yer daughter's, ain't it?" Kathleen demanded, leaning eagerly over the camelbacked sofa. "Don't lie. The cops can search this house for the mate."

Cesca's mouth went dry. She took the earring from Sullivan's hand, knowing the other was resting upstairs on Mina's dresser. The blood rushed to her head so fast she thought she might faint. Kathleen had obviously planted the earring in Antonio's hand.

"It's my daughter's, but they were stolen from her—"

Sullivan had already closed his book and was putting it in his pocket "There's an old woman at the Essex Street Market," Kathleen said, "who saw yer daughter with them earrings. She'd be glad to give her word." Kathleen turned to Sullivan suddenly, as if she had a new idea. "Maybe," Kathleen said slyly, putting her hands on her hips, "Miss Fancy Britches is right. Maybe she ain't the one that stabbed Tonio. Maybe ya should go up and talk to her daughter."

"You bitch!" Cesca snapped, losing her temper. "You planned all this."

Kathleen's smile was nasty and she passed a smug look to Sullivan. Cesca felt like a fool. She suddenly realized this officer wasn't an innocent dupe—he was her partner. That's why he'd been aboard the barge last night; he'd been helping Kathleen and protecting her interests. It occurred to her that perhaps Emilio hadn't had an epiphany and realized he was wrong. He might have been planning with Kathleen from the beginning to accuse her and Dante of murder. If they were arrested, Emilio would be free to take Mina.

True, only the earring connected Cesca and Mina to the crime, but with sworn statements from others it would be enough to have them detained. Oh, how could Emilio be so low? And Kathleen was smart enough to know that because of her veiled threat to have Mina arrested if Cesca didn't cooperate, Cesca would keep quiet.

"Sergeant," Cesca said, turning away from Kathleen with disgust, "all this can be easily explained if you'd contact Inspector Bevilacqua. He and Dante Romano have been searching these past few weeks for my stolen earrings and my daughter—"

A sharp knock interrupted her. Sullivan cracked the door, murmured with someone outside, then stepped aside. "Speak of the devil!" Sullivan said. "Here's Bevilacqua now. Come in."

Errico and the men in the hallway crowded into the parlor behind Bevilacqua. Everyone watched as the two men shook hands. A cold shawl of dread settled on Cesca's shoulders. Bevilacqua's demeanor had changed abruptly.

"Bevilacqua, thank God you're here," she cried. "I was just telling Sergeant—"

She stopped. In the shadows Bevilacqua passed something to Sullivan. She glanced at Errico, feeling frightened as the two men conferred in whispers. When Sullivan came into the light he was holding her kid purse. "Is this yer handbag?" Sullivan asked.

"How dare you touch my personal property!"

Sullivan turned the edges of the purse back, revealing a bloody pearl-handled knife wrapped in a handkerchief. "Can ya explain why there's a knife in yer purse, caked with blood?"

She looked at the fancy lace handkerchief in shock. The double Fs embroidered in the corner attested to the owner's identity. Mina had kept that handkerchief in the sleeve of her dresses since the day Cesca had given it to her in the dressing room. The knife would match the set in her kitchen.

"Bevilacqua, where did you—?" she began.

"I'm sorry, Signorina Frascatti," Bevilacqua said, "but no amount of money can keep me from doing my duty."

A cruel fist seized Cesca's heart and stopped its beating. She thought about the barge, the struggle for Mina, the cutter streaking away. . . . The informant wasn't the sympathetic animal lover who'd tried to restrain Dante at the barge, but the leader of their team. "You traitor!" she cried, backing away. "You're the informant." Sullivan tried to catch her, but she slipped behind the sofa. "What have you done with Dante Romano and Giuseppe Colombo?" she demanded, her voice quavering.

"Dante Romano was arrested down at Catherine's Slip," Bevilacqua announced to the group. "He was caught wading in the river at the crime scene with the body of Antonio DiGianni. He tried to claim he was investigating the murder, but he was stripped to the waist and caught with sticky fingers. His two accomplices got away, but we're searching for them. They'll soon be in custody." Sullivan passed the handbag back to Bevilacqua and pulled out his handcuffs.

"All right, Frascatti," Sullivan said. "Let's go." He moved forward to take her, but she snatched the wrought iron shovel from the fire set and swung it wildly at his head. Sullivan ducked as she back toward the door.

"Listen to me, all of you," she pleaded, turning to Petrosino's men. "Please! Bevilacqua's a traitor. He's Don Emilio Lampone's informant and in league with this woman. These police officers are on her payroll. Stop them!" Petrosino's men looked uncertainly at her, then at Bevilacqua. "I'm paying your salary!" Cesca shouted. "They're staging this farce so Emilio can take my daughter. I order you to stop him."

One of Petrosino's men reached for his pistol, but Bevilacqua quickly countered.

"Even though we work for Signorina Frascatti, you must allow me to take her to the station house," Bevilacqua ordered the agent. "She's under suspicion of murder and will be duly questioned. If she's truly innocent she'll be promptly released." Petrosino's man nodded and relaxed slightly, but he kept his hand on his pistol. "Phone the station house if you're in doubt," Bevilacqua said. "They'll brief you on her involvement in this investigation."

The uncertain agent lowered his hand. It was plain to Cesca that the agents were all loyal men who had worked under Bevilacqua's orders too long to disobey. She'd get no help from them. Sullivan moved forward to take her, but she jabbed at him with the shovel. "You're not going to get away with this," she cried. "Errico! Errico! Someone help me!" Cesca headed for the foyer, swinging the shovel in wide arcs.

"Grab her, Patty!" Kathleen shouted.

"Get that shovel, Bevilacqua," Sullivan ordered. "Don't let her get out the door." She slipped away from Bevilacqua, but Doyle seized her as she rushed into the foyer. "Draw your weapons, men," Sullivan ordered. "Stay back!" In the melee that followed, Errico easily held off Bevilacqua while Cesca got in a few whacks, but Doyle was able to wrestle Cesca to the floor. As they handcuffed her, Kathleen sidled up to Bevilacqua.

"Just a bloody minute," Kathleen said, under her breath. "Whaddaya mean Dante Romano was arrested at the slip? Ain't that him there?"

Kathleen jerked her thumb at the man she'd thought was the gigolo from the barge.

"No," Bevilacqua said, clearly annoyed. "That's the famous opera tenor Enrico Caruso."

"He ain't!" she insisted, braying loudly. "I saw him on the barge. He's her gigolo."

Bevilacqua squeezed her biceps impatiently. He was sick of this job. It had started out as a little piece of informing for a big piece of money; now his whole position was in jeopardy because of Kathleen Shaunessey's stupid schemes. He was going to have to leave New York City for good once this fiasco blew over. He yanked her away from the others. "Listen to me, you fool. Dante Romano's at the Fifth Precinct in jail. He's been disguising himself as the boxer Vittorio Fusco," he whispered.

Kathleen was astounded by the news. "He couldn't of disguised himself," she said bewildered. "I'd of known."

"He's handy with crepe hair and spirit gum," Bevilacqua said. "Go to the jail and see for yourself if you don't believe me."

Kathleen shook her head skeptically. She was remembering the tickle of Vittorio's mustache against her neck and the stroke of his fine hands kindling a fire in her loins. "Why, the bloody mug," she cried, dismayed.

Bevilacqua's grip was like a vise. "Don Lampone wants you to take care of the rest of this nonsense quickly," he ordered her, sotto voce. "Get the charges dropped immediately!" Then he let her go and gave a nod to Sullivan.

"Francesca Frascatti, you're under arrest," Sullivan began in his official voice, "for the murder of Antonio DiGianni. Officer Doyle, help the prisoner to the Black Maria waiting outside."

"You'll never convict her," Errico said following behind. "I'll testify that Antonio DiGianni was alive when Cesca left the barge and that she was by her daughter's side until your arrival."

"They don't need to convict me," Cesca said. "They just need to detain Dante and me until Emilio gets away with Mina. Isn't that right, Bevilacqua?" Bevilacqua lowered his eyes, refusing to acknowledge her question, and hurried out the door.

"I know you're partners with Emilio," Cesca said to Kathleen as they led her forward, "but beware! He's double-crossed many men in his life. A woman, even a shrewd one like you, will prove no exception."

Errico hurriedly draped his jacket over Cesca's shoulders. "I alerted my attorney while you were being questioned," he said, squeezing her shoulder. "He'll meet you at the station house."

"Guard Mina! Keep her safe," Cesca said, clinging to the doorframe of the Black Maria. "Emilio will try to come for her."

Sullivan struggled to pry Cesca's fingers free as Kathleen hurried forward to grab his elbow.

"What about him?" she demanded, pointing back to the man Sullivan had identified as Enrico Caruso. "Can't ya arrest him too?"

"Naw," Sullivan spat out, finally shoving Cesca inside and fixing the padlock. "He's a big-shot opera guinea and friend of Commissioner Bingham's. Can't touch the bastard."

Chapter Forty-Four

*E*XTRA! EXTRA! READ ALL ABOUT IT! Diabolical diva, in love triangle with daughter, murders middleweight!"

Disgusted, Emilio passed the boy hawking papers and rushed up the steps of the Plaza Hotel's Fifty-ninth Street entrance. At the door he changed his mind, returned to flip the lad a nickel, and took a paper. In the lobby he sat on a tufted, circular divan topped with ferns. On the front page there was a splashy publicity photograph of Francesca holding Tosca's knife and on page two a lurid account of the "murder plot."

Francesca Frascatti, the Manhattan Opera House's *diva assoluta,* was being held at the Fifth Precinct on suspicion of murder along with her lover and supposed accomplice, Dante Romano. The paper revealed that her lover was eight years her junior and supposedly involved in an adulterous affair with her illegitimate daughter, Filomina DiGianni, age nineteen.

The story alluded to a sinful living arrangement between the three, amid the glittering demimonde of opera and the privileged world of Manhattan's "four hundred." It implied that Dante and Francesca had planned the murder of Antonio DiGianni, a ditchdigger and amateur boxer, at an illegal barge fight on the Hudson River, at the urging of his beautiful wife, Filomina, and had sought to cover it up with their influential connections.

The purported motive for the murder was murky. The writer suggested that Antonio had become suspicious of an affair between Dante and his pregnant wife. When the husband had demanded that his wife return to her Lower East Side home, he'd been murdered. A purported robbery was staged and his body dumped in the river.

The lover had been discovered trying to dispose of the body of the victim at Catherine's Slip. A costly antique earring belonging to the diva had been found in the victim's hand. And uptown, in the diva's handbag, the police had discovered a personalized handkerchief wrapped around a blood-caked knife matching a set in her kitchen. Armed with this indisputable proof, the police had arrested the diva at her home. She and her lover were currently in jail awaiting arraignment while the daughter remained free but under suspicion.

Emilio crushed the newsprint savagely between his fists. This was what had come from making a bargain with the devil. Kathleen had promised she would have Francesca and Dante set free immediately after their arrest, but she'd lied. And now every dirty rag in New York City implied that Filomina was pregnant with Dante's child and that she was a scheming gold digger who'd coldheartedly helped plan her "poor immigrant husband's murder." Emilio was outraged by the liberties the newspapers were taking.

"Emilio," a man's voice whispered, "don't turn around, you're being watched." Out of the corner of his eye Emilio saw someone behind him on the divan holding a newspaper shield. "It's me, Mario Catanzaro."

"Mario!" Emilio gasped, raising his own paper. "The papers say you drowned."

"Many things the papers say are false," Mario said.

"What are you doing here?"

"Petrosino sent me to get you."

"Mario, listen, I'm not involved with this. These hideous stories aren't true. I—that woman Kathleen has lied to the police. She's blackmailing me and threatening to have my granddaughter involv—"

"You gave false information, and unfortunately the police are being paid to go along with her lies."

"I retracted my statement. Are the authorities blind?"

"You of all people should know that when greed holds the keys, the gates to justice are easily locked. She's got Tammany Hall, corruption, and your money on her key ring," Mario said. His voice was filled with disgust. "Don't you see? She's Irish, the police are Irish, the politicians are Irish, and . . . she's being very generous with your money."

"But I've tried to apply my own influence. No one's willing to listen."

"We're Italians. The latest immigrant scum to wash ashore. Mina, Tonio, Signorina Frascatti, Inspector Petrosino—yes, even you. We're all under suspicion."

"Suspicion of what?" Emilio asked indignantly.

"The Black Hand . . . Mafia . . . we're all lowlife criminals just waiting for an opportunity. Petrosino's bravely making headway against discrimination, but all Italians are being crushed in the same press."

An immense wave of guilt washed over Emilio. Hadn't he felt the same way about his fellow countrymen until recently?

"Mario, immediately after Francesca's arrest I went to the brownstone to explain to my granddaughter what had happened. I offered Filomina my help and told her I was working to clear Francesca and Dante, but she sent me away. I went to the jail where they're holding them, but the police refuse to believe anything I say. This whole imbroglio is my fault and I can't seem to do anything to halt it. I never intended anyone to be seriously harmed. Antonio and Kathleen—"

"Sssh! None of that's important now. Go outside to the waiting line of cabs. Take the third one from the front. See that no one follows you."

"Where shall I go?"

"Just get in," Mario ordered. "Everything's taken care of."

A few minutes later, Emilio slipped out to the waiting line of coaches at the entrance and darted inside the third cab from the front. He was startled to see a dapper gentleman sitting on the velvet seat. The stout man was dressed in a dove-gray suit, sported a monocle and goatee, and rested his hands upon a lacquered cane.

"I—I beg your pardon," Emilio said, backing out the door. "I didn't realize this cab was taken. I must have made—"

"Sit down," the man ordered, flashing a gold tooth. "Hurry up! Don't create a disturbance."

Emilio did as he was told. "Who are you?"

The man banged the ceiling with his cane and the coach lurched away. "Giuseppe Petrosino, or someone very like him."

Emilio examined him closely. Here was the mysterious detective Emilio had heard so much about and tried so unsuccessfully to hire. "Petrosino! *Grazie Dio!* My prayers have been answered. Perhaps you can—"

"You and your partner are trying to set Francesca Frascatti and Dante Romano up for murder," Petrosino said, cutting him off.

"No, no, she's not my partner. You see," Emilio started, "I did not agree to murder. That woman Kathleen is blackmailing me. She's the one who—"

"So you still deny culpability?" Once again Petrosino struck the ceiling. The coach jolted to a stop. He put his hand on the door latch to climb out. "I've no time for nonsense," he snapped.

"No, no," Emilio said, grabbing his sleeve, "I admit it. I was involved. Please sit down. Please! I beg you."

Petrosino settled back against the seat. "Very well," Petrosino said. "Tell me what you have to do with these false accusations."

As the coach moved on Emilio hurried to explain.

"After my granddaughter was rescued," Emilio said, "Kathleen threatened to unleash Antonio and have him 'demand his wife back.' You see, the law stipulates a wife is 'chattel'—property. As long as she's unable to act or speak for herself her husband controls her. My granddaughter was obviously semiconscious, in a dangerous state of health. Antonio could easily go uptown with Kathleen's crooked police friends and demand her back. I'd resolved to end my difficulties with Francesca, but Francesca and I could do nothing to circumvent the law. If he wanted her back, he could take her. We would need Kathleen's help to protect my granddaughter from that animal. It was a terrible dilemma. I wanted to take my granddaughter away and dismiss that madwoman."

"But you didn't," Petrosino said, regarding Emilio with suspicion. "You insist you knew nothing about a murder plot?"

"At that point nothing," Emilio said, raising his hand as though swearing in court.

"Go on," Petrosino said.

"I wanted to be sure Antonio was locked up, so I told Kathleen to meet me at the Plaza for the money exchange. I returned to Manhattan with Francesca and my granddaughter. Francesca was furious with me for the accident. I tried to explain how much I regretted my actions. I told her I would do everything in my power to protect and share my granddaughter with her, but she wasn't convinced. She had me barred from her home. I returned to the Plaza and summoned my agent Bevilacqua. I thought perhaps he could do something to help me. While we were talking, Kathleen arrived at my suite highly distraught. She said her part of the bargain was concluded and I could go to Francesca's brownstone and collect my granddaughter without interference because Antonio had been found at the docks, robbed and murdered. Murdered! I was astounded."

"You never thought Kathleen might be capable of murder?"

"Please, Inspector," Emilio said, putting a hand over his heart. "I realized she was coarse and greedy, but I never realized she'd go so far for money." Emilio looked genuinely shaken. Petrosino motioned for him to continue. "I assumed Kathleen had come to collect the additional five thousand dollars she'd been promised and I gave it to her, but she wanted more. She said she knew Francesca was my granddaughter's mother and my sworn enemy. She'd been told that Francesca had been purposely keeping my granddaughter from me and that's why I had created the story to 'buy her.' She demanded an additional five thousand dollars to make sure Francesca and Dante were detained for an investigation. With them in jail I could still take my granddaughter away without interference."

"So you agreed."

"I refused! I told Kathleen I was making peace with Francesca. I wanted no more to do with her and her schemes. I said I'd go to the authorities if she persisted in her demand for money. That's when she turned poisonous. She told me Antonio had lost the five thousand dollars I'd given him and she wanted a full ten thousand for herself. She threatened to implicate my granddaughter instead of Francesca and Dante. She described an earring to me that had been found in Antonio's hand at the pier, an earring I knew to belong to my family and that had been passed on to my granddaughter. And she showed me Francesca's handkerchief and a bloody knife she said had come from Francesca's kitchen. My granddaughter had worked in Francesca's kitchen and I knew those objects would be traced quickly. I'd seen Kathleen's police connections in action at the barge. I was in turmoil. I finally realized what she was capable of and I feared for my granddaughter's life. An arrest in her delicate condition would be disastrous."

"And your informant, Bevilacqua?"

"I ordered him to help Kathleen. He went to the brownstone with her and 'presented the evidence.' "

Petrosino was perplexed. "But you just said you didn't want to continue with her schemes."

Emilio hurried to explain. "I told you I wasn't thinking clearly. She promised that Francesca and Dante would only be detained on suspicion and then released. I was certain that once legitimate witnesses like Enrico Caruso came forward they would be released. Perhaps a few hours in jail at the most in exchange for the safety of my granddaughter. I was terrified for her health, so I foolishly gave Kathleen a statement."

"You're saying the whole plot was Kathleen's idea?" Petrosino asked.

"I swear it," Emilio said. "I never expected it to go this far or the newspapers to become involved."

Petrosino nodded solemnly. He could see the abject devastation in Emilio's teary eyes. "Your *vendetta*'s fulfilled," Petrosino said. "Francesca and Dante are in jail and your granddaughter's free. What's to stop you from taking her and leaving? Certainly not regret."

Emilio was overcome with emotion. "I deserve your rebuke. I'm disgusted by my own conduct, but you must believe me, I never thought anyone would be killed. Yes, I sought to punish Francesca and I blamed her for my son's death, but I swear on my granddaughter's life, and I cherish her blood more than my own, that I never plotted with these vile people to kill anyone. I promised Giulio and God that I would keep his daughter safe . . . that I would change, that I would make up with Francesca and share his child, and now this has happened."

Petrosino cleared his throat uncomfortably, moved by the once proud aristocrat. Emilio was broken, his pomposity gone; all that remained was a blown eggshell.

"I swear, Petrosino, I will do whatever is necessary and use all my fortune to bring this criminal to justice and clear Francesca's and Dante's names."

"Why should anyone believe you've changed?"

"I know if I were in your place I would not, but now I only wish to unite my granddaughter with her mother. You see, I believe in life after death. I hope to see my son someday, and it's the only way Giulio might ever forgive me."

"But if they're cleared, Francesca may never allow you to see your granddaughter again."

Emilio looked down at his empty hands, opening them and closing them spasmodically. "I don't want to lose her, but . . . I must act to restore Francesca's reputation and save her. I was wrong about her . . . completely wrong. When I went to the jail Signor Caruso was there. He offered to have Commissioner Bingham intervene, but Francesca begged him not to." His voice once again was choked with emotion. "You see, after hearing my story, she is willing to risk her reputation, her career, and her fortune rather than take a small chance that her daughter might be arrested and harmed. Can I do less for my only living blood?"

Petrosino nodded understandingly.

"Do you know, she laughed at my dismay, insisting that all the scandalous news will be good for her career."

Petrosino chuckled at Francesca's bravado and Emilio made a noise that sounded like a cross between a laugh and a sob. "When I explained that Kathleen had blackmailed me and how much I feared for my granddaughter's life, she forgave me. Such generosity . . . I don't deserve it. She says she now understands how much I must have suffered when I lost Giulio. She asks only that I protect Filomina, but I have no idea where she is."

"Mina's at her apartment on Mulberry Street," Petrosino said. "Signor Caruso took her there early this afternoon."

"She's safe?"

Petrosino nodded again. "Mina's asked me to find you; she and I have come up with a plan to trick Kathleen and hopefully clear Francesca and Dante."

Emilio's eyes sparkled through his tears. He couldn't believe Petrosino's words. "She asked for me?"

"You're part of the plan," Petrosino said. The coach lurched to a stop. Petrosino grabbed the leather strap to steady himself.

"Where are we?" Emilio asked.

"We're at the coroner's office. Antonio's body has been autopsied. They've found something important I must see. Let's go in."

Emilio put a restraining hand on Petrosino's arm. "The coroner will only back up her corrupt police friends," Emilio said fearfully.

"Not this time. I put Antonio's body in the hands of a special coroner, a medical examiner."

"You're sure the man can be trusted?"

"He was arranged through Enrico Caruso's friend Commissioner Bingham. The Fourth Ward will have no influence over this part of the investigation."

"Thank God!" Emilio said, gesturing toward heaven. "I know Kathleen killed Antonio and planted that evidence. I'll testify to my involvement regardless of the consequences to—"

Petrosino cut him off. "We must prove it. We need evidence, not accusations. After the match last night, Mario searched the Cocked Hat and found all the proof we needed, but unfortunately it's tainted."

"Tainted?" Emilio asked. "But if Mario found evidence, why can't we use it?"

Petrosino rubbed his chin ruefully. "Mario picked the lock. A trick Dante taught him. He searched without a warrant. That kind of evidence is referred to as 'fruit of the poisonous tree.' " Emilio looked thoroughly confused. "You see, Kathleen and her lawyer can say we planted the evidence. It'll be inadmissible in a court of law."

"*Gesù*, what can we do?"

"First, let's go inside and see the results of the autopsy. After that we'll head over to Mulberry Street. If what the medical examiner has found is as good as he claims, Mina and I will piece everything together and Kathleen will convict herself."

Chapter Forty-Five

"OH, CARA, YOU CAN'T BELIEVE how happy I am you're safe," Teresa said, releasing Mina from a long embrace. "We all heard such terrible rumors."

Teresa stepped back to take another look at Mina. She *did* seem like another woman.

Moments before, two strangers had knocked on Teresa's door, asking for the spare key to Mina's apartment. She'd drawn back warily, unable to recognize the man and woman in the shadowy hallway. Short dark hair framed the woman's face and she was dressed in elegant clothing, giving her an aristocratic manner.

It took several minutes for Teresa to digest the transformation. It was Mina, but a new Mina, who seemed to have finally set down the heavy burden she'd been carrying for the last six months. Her friend was no longer shadowy and indistinct, but shiny and bright like a newly minted penny.

"Unfortunately," Errico said, breaking into Teresa's thoughts, "my singing engagement makes it impossible for me to stay, but I'll come again tomorrow."

Teresa forgot the change in Mina for a moment in the presence of "the great Caruso." He'd been the strange man on Mina's arm in the hallway. Mina had introduced him, but Teresa had been so startled to see Mina that, without a word, she'd gone to fetch the spare key and climbed the stairway behind them.

"Please, signora," Caruso said, bowing like a courtier, "I ask you personally, take good care of Mina. I will return to visit you both tomorrow."

Teresa was flabbergasted when the famous tenor kissed her hand. "*Ma, certo!* But of course," she managed to squeeze out breathlessly. She couldn't believe her good fortune, and before he could slip out the door, her natural loquaciousness took hold. "Tomorrow!" Teresa cried. "Tomorrow, I'll make lasagna. You like lasagna, don't you, Signor Caruso?"

"I'm the duke of lasagna," Caruso joked. "Lasagna *mobile . . .*" he sang, mocking the famous aria from *Rigoletto*.

"Of course you are!" Teresa replied, beaming. "Do you like sausage or beef? Should I use cheese like the Sicilians? Or béchamel?" She didn't wait for him to answer, but rather continued on as she always did. "Tomorrow you'll eat supper with me," she announced. "And tell me all about Tetrazzini! Tetrazzini's my favorite singer, besides you of course! She's a scandal! So naughty, isn't she?" She laughed heartily, shaking her bulk. "Is it true," she asked conspiratorially, "a chef really named a special dish after her? You know, I heard that when she was young she—"

Caruso hugged Mina good-bye as Teresa continued her barrage. "Don't worry," he whispered. "I'll come tomorrow to rescue you and you can visit with Dante and Cesca. My lawyer says they'll be released in the morning on bail no matter how your plan works out. Have faith in God. Their names will eventually be cleared and everything will work out for the best."

Teresa followed him into the hallway, still chattering. At the top of the staircase he bowed low, then rose with both hands over his head in surrender. "*Domani, signora!*" he sang dramatically. "*Lasagna!*" He turned and bounded down the stairs.

The abrupt end didn't offend Teresa; she pushed back her untidy gray hair and rushed back into Mina's apartment grinning. "*Dio! Cara, che onore!* Caruso, the golden voice of Naples, in your home!" She clicked her tongue and made a sign against the *mal'occhio*. "*Madonna,* how your life has changed."

Now that Mina was back in her old apartment, the gravity of her situation struck. She glanced around the grimy room as Teresa bustled about lighting the stove and putting on a kettle. Everything was in its place. The rickety table, the mended stove pipe, the saints in the corner on the shelf . . . She may have changed in a few short weeks, but this world had stayed the same.

After living in elegant surroundings uptown she saw her home for what it was—a hovel. She couldn't raise her child here. Well, at least I have my coffee can money for a ticket back to Italy, she thought. She put her hands on her stomach. Oh, my poor baby, all our hopes shattered.

Once I help clear the Signorina and Dante and tell them the truth, I'll most likely be deported. The Signorina won't want anything more to do with me, she thought, and Dante . . . Dante will never marry me now. Even if he doesn't care about the rest, how can he marry a liar? Her hands shook as she attempted to unfasten the buttons on her coat. After she told her story she was certain that she would never see him again.

"Here, *cara*, let me do that," Teresa said.

Teresa removed Mina's hat and coat as though she were a child. Mina didn't protest. She had a distant look in her eye and sat stiffly looking out the window. Teresa bit her tongue as she checked the kettle and put the cups on the table. She glanced at Mina and thought how terrible the death of a husband was for a woman. A woman's world revolved around the man in her life, even a vile man like Antonio. What would happen now that he was gone?

She's still young, Teresa thought, she can easily marry again if she chooses. Will she go back to Italy or stay? Will she continue to work for the Signorina or return to the costume shop? Teresa had a hundred questions, but on occasions such as this, it was customary for the grieving person to speak. It seemed to take forever for the water to boil in the silent room.

A few minutes later when they both had a strong cup of tea in front of them and the room was warming a little, Teresa reached across the table and squeezed Mina's hand. She was just about to fill the uneasy silence with one of her many questions when Mina's eyes moved from the window to her face.

"Antonio's body is at the morgue. I must bring it here to lay out and arrange for a funeral."

Mina's voice was confident, but her eyes were like those of a fish in a market basket. She shouldn't let the death of such a horrible man destroy her, Teresa thought. No, just bury his body and forget him. Now was the time to begin a new life. Teresa knew the correct thing to say was "I'm sorry," but she didn't feel sorry. She'd listened to too many beatings to feel sorry for Antonio.

"I know it must be difficult for you," Teresa finally managed to say, then added, "Roberto can go with you when he gets home."

"Thank you, Teresa."

Mina got up suddenly and went to her *letto matrimoniale*. She drew her battered wicker trunk from under the bed frame. Teresa watched as she opened the lid and lifted a white wedding dress and veil out of the tissue. Teresa smelled the faint scent of lavender as Mina pressed the dress against her face.

"It's beautiful, isn't it?" Mina asked. A tear streaked down her cheek.

"Very. I never understood why you let those two bitches talk you into wearing a suit."

Mina came back to the table with the gown and sat down, spreading the satin over her lap. "Haven't you noticed it doesn't have lace?" she whispered conspiratorially. "All my dresses have lace."

Teresa wondered why not having lace on her wedding dress would make Mina cry. She wanted to ask, but she jiggled her foot and held back her curiosity, feeling as though she were choking from unasked questions. She hoped Mina would tell her everything quickly.

"My whole life is a lie, Teresa. I had no right to marry Antonio."

"That's behind you now," Teresa said, patting her hand.

"I cheated Mario and he died because of my lies."

"Two men dead," Teresa said, making the sign of the cross and kissing her bunched fingers. "*Gesù! Maria!* Protect us from a third." Teresa gestured to the heavens, invoking the aid of all the saints.

"They can't help me now," Mina said. "Now I've got to be strong on my own. I can't rely on God to save the Signorina or Dante or me. I've got to help set them free and prove Antonio was murdered by his mistress."

Teresa struck the table with her fist, rattling the cups. "It's ridiculous! Why would the police think they killed Antonio?"

Mina smoothed the oilcloth tabletop over and over with her fingertips. She didn't look at Teresa. "The Signorina thinks she's my mother. Antonio's mistress convinced the police the Signorina killed him to protect me from his beatings."

"She thinks she's your mother?" Teresa asked in shock. "Your mother's dead."

Mina lifted her head and met Teresa's troubled eyes. "It's my fault. I lied and she took the bait." Mina felt the tears start to grow, but she cut them back. She had no right to feel sorry for herself. Everyone took the bait, she thought. Not even Teresa realizes I've deceived her. And now because of me Antonio's mistress and her corrupt police friends are going to destroy the Signorina and Dante. "Everyone I've met since coming to America has been ruined. Mario, Antonio . . . if only Simonetta hadn't sent me to the Signorina's dressing room with the shawl, none of this would have happened."

Teresa shook her head sadly. "*Destino!* Mario's death is a grave loss, but Antonio got what he deserved. He was an evil man with many enemies."

"No man is truly evil. Destiny falls on him and makes him so," Mina replied, shivering.

Teresa got up and stoked the fire, putting on several pieces of wood. She took her shawl off and wrapped it around Mina's shoulders. "Destiny is destiny," Teresa said, trying to comfort her. "No woman can change it. No matter how she tries."

"I was the destiny that befell him," Mina insisted. "Don't you see? Without me, Mario, Antonio, and even his mistress would have had different lives. Without me the Signorina and Dante wouldn't be in jail. Antonio wouldn't be dead."

"Nonsense! Antonio was a festering sore waiting to break open. He beat other women before you came. I know; I heard the abuse. Someone was bound to kill him. And his mistress was no better. The capacity for evil was in their souls like fire is in wood. That part of them could never be different."

"But I was the tinder that released the flame," Mina said. She rose, clutching the dress. The filmy veil fell around her feet as she pressed the sleeves and bodice against her body. She remembered the day she'd first seen the gown. "I just wanted to find love," she said. "It was all I ever wanted. Is it so much to ask? Would God deny me a husband and a family because of my past?"

"Of course not," Teresa soothed.

Mina felt her chin tremble. She didn't want to start crying. Tears were of no use, and once she began, she was sure she'd break into a million pieces and never collect herself.

"I will listen," Teresa said softly. "There isn't much a fat old woman can do, but if I can help you, I will."

It was quiet for a long time. Mina heard the children playing in the hall, the logs snapping in the fire, the jangle of a bell belonging to the man who ground dull tools for the housewives. Her shoulders dropped slowly with resignation and she lowered the wedding gown.

"I'm not who you think I am. My name isn't Filomina Rossi—"

"I know that," Teresa said. "You changed your name when you moved from your village so no one would know—"

"I changed my name, yes, but that was after . . . You see, the crossing took almost two weeks. It was so foul below I couldn't work on my lace. The motion and the smells made me sick, so I went up on deck and walked. I walked and walked. I didn't know what to do, but other women gave me advice. I had a lot of time to think and plan. . . ."

Teresa was confused. She watched Mina stroke the sleeve of the wedding gown over and over. What was she trying to say? What had she planned?

"You must have been afraid," Teresa offered.

"Yes, I was, but I prayed to *Sant'Anna.* I thought my prayers were answered when she gave me a new friend: a woman who came from the mountains, not far from where I grew up. The woman believed in *destino* and assured me everything would work out. And I believed her because she understood my anxiety about the future, because she too was going to America—to get married.

"I had a shameful life in Italy. I told her all about my past and she wanted me to have respect. You see, she made me promise, promise—"

There was a sharp rap on the door.

"*Madonna!*" Teresa cried, jumping up from the table and crossing herself.

"Signora DiGianni?" a man's voice inquired.

Mina hurried to the door, dragging the gown behind. "Signor Petrosino, is that you?" Mina asked.

"I've brought Don Emilio as you asked, signora," Petrosino said.

Mina quickly turned the key and was ready to slip the bolt when Teresa put her hand over the catch. "Wait!" Teresa whispered. "Perhaps it's a trick. Signor Caruso said to be careful."

Mina nodded thoughtfully. Teresa was right. Antonio's mistress might try anything.

"How do I know it's you, Signor Petrosino?"

"Because," a familiar voice said, "I came along to reassure you, Signora Di—"

Disbelief coursed though Mina as she pushed Teresa's hand aside. It couldn't be! She threw open the door. "Mario!" she cried, rushing into the hall to embrace him. "Mario! I thought you were dead!"

The forgotten wedding gown was crushed between them as relief and gratitude washed over her and tears of joy erupted from her eyes. Now she could cry, now she had a good reason.

"*Grazie, Sant'Anna!*" she whispered. "*Grazie Dio!*"

For a moment it seemed as though Mario had risen from the depths of the Hudson River like Lazarus from his tomb—the light of the Holy Spirit seemed to show around his head in the gloomy hall. But Mina caught hold of her wild imaginings—it was only a gas jet glowing behind his head. She clutched his hand and pulled him into the apartment.

"*Gesù, Maria!*" Teresa cried. "It's a miracle."

Petrosino and Don Emilio followed Mario and Mina into the apartment.

Teresa felt light-headed from all the activity, but her faintness didn't stop her curiosity. "Mario, what happened? Why couldn't they find you?" Teresa asked. "No, I know! Don't tell me. You killed Antonio. That's why you're in hiding! That's why no one—"

Mina hushed Teresa and offered the men chairs. Petrosino and Don Emilio sat while Mario stood. He was dressed like a gentleman in a new suit, shyly holding his bowler hat before him. Teresa and Mina supported each other, alternately sobbing and laughing as Mario told of his exploits over the last few days.

"So you and Dante searched for me after the kidnapping?" Mina asked.

"Of course. We searched the city," Mario said.

Mina was pleased that they had tried to find her, but she worried about the trouble she'd caused everyone. "Please," Mina said, "tell me everything that's happened since I disappeared."

Mario explained Dante's double role, his disguise as Vittorio, and how he'd tried unsuccessfully to extract information from Antonio's mistress about her hiding place after the kidnapping. He told Mina about the brutal boxing match on the river and how the barrel she'd been hidden in had gone overboard.

"Yes, I know that part," Mina said. "Thank you again for saving me, Signor Catanzaro."

Mario brushed off her gratitude while Petrosino fiddled with his monocle, looking uncomfortable. "I'm sorry to say," Petrosino said, "that one of my own detectives turned traitor for money." He didn't look at Don

Lampone or implicate him in any way because he didn't want to stir Mina's memories of the kidnapping or her displeasure with him.

"Please tell me what happened to Dante after the fight," Mina said.

"We found Tonio's body floating at Catherine's Slip," Mario said. "It was wedged between our cutter and a piling. Dante had to get into the water and pull Tonio's body to a place where we could pull it out. That's when Kathleen's police friends arrived."

"We were forced to flee or be arrested with Dante," Petrosino said. "I immediately contacted a special coroner to investigate. I knew there'd be trouble."

"I doubled back to the Cocked Hat," Mario said. "It was locked up, but Dante had taught me how to pick locks. I searched the bar, hoping to discover what had happened to Tonio while Kathleen was away. In a bean sack in the locked pantry I found Tonio's medallion, wedding ring, identification, and loose papers—everything he'd been carrying in his pockets when he was killed. She'd taken them all to make it look like a robbery. They were all wrapped together. I thought my discovery would convict Kathleen of murdering him, but I made a stupid mistake. I ruined—"

Petrosino put his hand up to stop Mario's apology. "As I explained to you before, Mario didn't realize that without a warrant the evidence he found is tainted and useless," Petrosino said.

"But we've found something at the morgue that will prove Francesca and Dante didn't kill him," Don Emilio interjected.

Mina looked at Don Emilio. She'd been aware of him sitting silently at the table staring at her. Now when her gaze fell upon him he looked acutely uncomfortable. She was surprised that he chose to speak because he knew she was upset with him. He'd come to the Signorina's brownstone to tell her that he was her grandfather and she'd sent him away quite abruptly.

"You've found something that will *prove* it?" Mina asked.

"Please forgive me for interrupting," Don Emilio said, softly. He lowered his eyes with shame. "But I want . . . I want to help in any way I can. I'm so sorry for my part in this tragedy. I never realized that my bitterness and pain would cause you or Mario—or anyone—such . . . such harm."

Mina wasn't afraid of Don Emilio anymore. He'd withered to half the man who'd tried to defend her at the saloon. With Petrosino's help and the stories the Signorina had shared she'd come to understand why he considered her his granddaughter. Don Emilio was the landowner *Mammina* had worked for. He thought she was his blood, the only child of his dead son, Giulio, and Francesca Frascatti. She understood the pain he must have felt over his loss and his desire to get revenge. Like her, he'd made a bad decision he hadn't realized would end in tragedy.

She pitied him, for when he learned the truth about her he would suffer terribly. But the stab of pity she felt was quickly offset by anger. Don Emilio was almost as responsible for everything that had happened as she was. If he hadn't sworn revenge on the Signorina and tempted Antonio and Kathleen with his money, none of this would have happened.

"You have every right to be angry with me," Don Emilio began when he saw her eyes flash, "but please, use me in any way you wish to help your plan. Perhaps I can make up for the evil I've wrought."

"Perhaps you can, Don Emilio," she said, remembering her own complicity and feeling compassion. "Antonio and his mistress both lusted after your money. It cost Antonio his life. I'm hoping her greed will put her behind bars."

Don Emilio nodded eagerly. "She's demanded I deliver an additional five thousand dollars to her new saloon by this afternoon at four. It was money meant to purchase you, and if I don't give it to her she'll have you arrested and charged as well."

Mina smiled. "I've suggested an idea to Signor Petrosino, and *if* you agree to help us," Mina said, "and *if* we clear the Signorina and Dante, I will forgive you. For in the end you will find I'm as responsible for this tragedy as you are."

"I promise to do what I can," Don Emilio said solemnly. Petrosino nodded and signaled to her with his eyes that she should trust Don Emilio's word. She sighed. The players were in place. Now it was time for her to take charge and save the people she loved.

"Very well," Mina began confidently. "Hopefully, when we add what you gentleman have learned to what Signor Petrosino and I discussed earlier, we will drive Antonio's mistress to act foolishly. I've been thinking that a new technique Dante told me about—a new science that proves we're all unique—might be used to trap her. You see . . ." Mina hesitated. Perhaps, she thought, I should leave the technical explanation to the experts. "I'll explain my role in a moment," she said, putting her hand on Petrosino's arm. "Signor Petrosino, would you be kind enough to explain about fingerprinting?"

Petrosino took off his jacket and rolled up his sleeves eagerly. "Well, the new science of fingerprinting, along with a startling piece of evidence discovered this morning at the morgue by the medical examiner, will be added to Mina's idea to bravely confront Kathleen Shaunessey. . . ."

Teresa only half listened to Petrosino's words as she collected the discarded wedding dress from the floor. She was still too preoccupied by the apparent change that had overcome Mina since last week. Mina seemed to Teresa a different woman, with a different soul.

Chapter Forty-Six

KATHLEEN'S TOE WAS TAPPING as she filled glasses and blissfully watched the dancers spin. The two fiddlers she'd hired for her *Céilí* were sawing away at a jig and the room was packed. There'd be dancing, drinking, eating, and card playing all day in honor of the opening of her new saloon, Flynn's.

Tonio crossed her mind for an instant as she pushed a schooner of ale across the bar to a blue-eyed stranger. His eyes were near the same color and they would've been twinkling with the same mischief. Tonio would've enjoyed the sport today. Her victory over poverty would've been his victory too. She ripped him from her thoughts before his memory could toss a pall over the day. He was dead. The jug had cracked, the liquor run out.

She filled the next schooner, feeling stiff in her new duds and baubles, a bit too aware of herself. But she was getting used to them. When she occasioned to glance in the mirror, she admired the striking lady reflected back. She breathed on her new emerald ring, rubbed it against the sleeve of her dress to enhance the sparkle, and held it out to admire. A beauty!

Just that morning, after checking on preparations for the opening and setting the charwomen to work, she'd bought all the items she'd coveted for the past year. She still smiled at the memory of the shocked faces the shop owners had pulled when she'd taken the new bills Don Lampone had given her from her purse and counted them out, easy as you please. The cash changed their snooty tunes right enough. They'd hustled about, bundled everything up, and seen her to the door with cards for next time, all smiles and compliments.

She glanced in the mirror again at the dark green silk caressing her tightly corseted figure. She'd taken scissors to the high lace neck, making the dress lower in the bosom, but it was still ladylike, edged with tiny pleated ruffles, ample in the skirt, and finished with three-quarter-length sleeves. A wee bit of cotton batting had been stuffed in the bodice, in lieu of alterations, but no one could tell she didn't fill it out naturally.

Her hair was held up by two carved tortoiseshell combs and topped with a braided switch of false French hair. Around her neck she'd knotted a double strand of pearls that swayed rhythmically at her waist. On her ears she wore gold pendant earrings. As she leaned forward they brushed her neck, reminding her of the earrings Tonio had given her not three weeks before. Once again she forced him from her mind and focused instead on two thick bangles of gold pushed up on her forearms and the square-cut stone on her index finger. She couldn't help but admire the twinkle of success.

Outside the window, the tricolor was wafting in the raw wind, calling her countrymen to her side. She'd survived the worst, and just as she'd planned, her destiny had arrived before she was thirty. In spite of everything she felt as though she'd been borne to heaven on angels' wings. She topped off a pint, delivered it with a grin, then turned the operation over to her new man.

"Go ahead now, Colm, and don't be so timid. Just remember, no jawboning and call everyone Sir and Ma'am. This is a class operation. Ya ain't on the same deck with these blokes, so keep it genteel. I'm going to make the rounds. The taps are yer province. Keep yer apron clean and an eye on Tommy."

In a few minutes she was taking a spin on the boards with Charlie Murphy, one of Jack's old friends from Tammany. God bless him, he'd started her off right by handing her an Irish pound note to pay for his whiskey and she'd put it back of the bar for good luck. Charlie was the most powerful man at the hall, but a shy, darling man just the same. He swung her around smartly to the tune of "Kitty of Coleraine" while she sopped up the cheers and applause of the crowd.

Flynn's was only a few blocks from Union Square and Tammany Hall, so anyone wishing to oil the works—politicians and their upper-class constituents—was sure to turn up. These boys had climbed up from the muck themselves, so she'd be stepping up the board rapidly, for they hadn't forgotten where they'd come from or the helping hands given them.

After a dance or two she stopped, fanning her hand in front of her face. Her corset laces were close to busting. "I want to make a toast," she called when the fiddlers stopped to resin their bows. Colm poured her a shot of Hennessy's VSOP, the only liquor she was going to drink from now on, and she held the pony glass up to the murmuring crowd. "Quit now! All of ya! On the occasion of Flynn's first day and all ya fine gentlemen being here . . . I want to say . . ." She felt awkward in her new gear and her face reddened as she got up her nerve. "Here's to you, as good as you are. Here's to me, as bad as I am. As good as you are and as bad as I am, I'm as good as you are, as bad as I am." She tossed the shot down to roaring approval. It was an old spud but a good one, considering. Let no man doubt that she knew who she was or where she'd come from.

Biaggio pressed through the crowd toward her carrying a bouquet of roses. Trailing behind him were a group of Tonio's pals from the Cocked Hat. It was a gallant gesture for the men to bring her flowers for her opening. But then again, she'd been with Tonio five years. Biaggio kissed her cheek and offered her condolences for Tonio's death and good wishes for her opening.

"Colm!" she called. "Give the lads whatever they'd like. The drinks are on me, in honor of Tonio." The men settled in at the bar while she spoke to Biaggio. "Did ya say the Hat was busy?" she asked him, taking an egg from the tiered rack on the bar and tapping it. She was about to brush the shells to the floor, but caught herself. She was a lady now. She reached for a saltshaker.

"Jimmy's behind the bar," Biaggio said, "and the five-cent lunch is winding down."

"That's fine. Perfect. Ya know we got Scotch eggs if ya've a mind."

"Thanks."

She ordered him a sausaged egg with mustard. "Ain't it grand? I knew when I was a wee girl that I was made for better things than working the stick in a pub. I just wish Tonio could be here to share it with me."

Biaggio smiled at her and nodded his head sadly. "I almost forgot to tell you, Kathleen. There were some men down at the Hat poking around."

"Who were they and what did they want?" She banged the saltshaker down on the bar and forced her last bite of hard-boiled egg down a suddenly dry throat.

"Police from *uptown*. They came to search for evidence," Biaggio said.

"About Tonio's murder or about Mario?"

"Both. They wanted to get into the pantry, but Jimmy stopped them. They didn't have a warrant but they said they'd be back."

She'd been gripping the pearls at her waist, but she tried to relax and forced a laugh. She hadn't realized she was so nervous. She hoped it didn't show. "That's my man Jimmy. Well, let them look. They ain't going to find nothing. That guinea broad probably sent them to—" She saw Biaggio's face darken and caught herself. She put a hand on his arm. "Sorry Biaggio, I didn't mean that against ya. Tonio was an *eye-tal* like you, but yer different from those snobs, ain't ya?"

"It don't bother me. Those snobs ain't my kind," Biaggio said. "They're more like your people." He gestured at the swells hanging around the bar. "They got money," he continued, "and fancy lawyers to help them out."

Biaggio pulled her onto the boards for a waltz, but she didn't much feel like dancing. The men showing up to reminisce about Tonio and Mario had darkened her mood, and Biaggio's remark about the coppers had taken the head off her ale. "Those two won't be charged," Biaggio whispered in her ear. "They'll walk away from Tonio's murder."

"Yer right there," Kathleen said. "Did ya know that high-gloss bitch is noising it about that I killed him?"

Biaggio gave her a serious look and smiled. "But you did kill him," he said lightly.

She pulled back sharply, examining his eyes. What was he saying? Was he teasing her? "Biaggio, ya shouldn't joke about something like that."

"I say, good riddance. He was a brutal bastard. He was responsible for Mario's misery and he deserved to die."

She put her hand over his mouth and glanced around. She didn't want to be overheard. "Ya mustn't speak ill of the dead."

"How did it happen?" Biaggio asked conspiratorially. "Did he hit you? Was it self-defense?"

She gave a weak laugh, feeling a pang of caution. "I'm as dry as an old lady's cunt. Let's get a drink."

Biaggio wouldn't release her. He had to keep her busy and help get her worked up before the others arrived. So he guided her into another tune and continued. "I figure Tonio backed out of the deal for the money and you stabbed him. You didn't mean to, but it happened."

Charlie Murphy raised his glass in her direction; she winked and faked a smile. How did Biaggio know about the deal for the money? Maybe Mario told him before he drowned, she thought. The two of them were always thick as thieves. "That's enough now, I don't want to think of Tonio's death today."

"Don't be a hypocrite," Biaggio laughed. "You aren't mourning him."

It looked true enough. She should be sitting by the body weeping and wailing like a banshee, and toasting his honor here at Flynn's. But she wanted to separate herself from the old life and not draw attention to her past. She'd made sure there were wreaths and plenty of white ribbons at the Hat. "His wife can mourn openly," Kathleen said. "I can't get mixed up in that, not with the stench of murder hanging over the whole kit and caboodle. I'll have the rest of my life to mourn Tonio and honor his memory. Now hush. Ya don't know what yer saying."

Biaggio's observations prickled her with fear for a moment and the waltz was suddenly heavy and complicated. She stumbled over her feet. He's fishing for the truth, she thought, but he can't prove nothing. Mario and Tonio are dead, but most important, there ain't no evidence to link me to the crime. She searched her friends' faces as she circled the room. Were they all wondering why she wasn't mourning Tonio? Stop it! Brighten up, Kathleen, she told herself, ya got the world by the tit. She steadied her pasted-on smile and reminded herself that she needed to keep her nerves under control and her wits about her today.

One of the Tammany boys tapped Biaggio's shoulder when a jig started. Biaggio gave her up to her new partner and went to the bar to join his men. She lifted her skirts and flashed her assets, doing her best to show she was gay, but her heart was heavy with unease. She clamped her jaw stubbornly. This is my day! I'm gonna enjoy it, she thought, trying to get her nerve back. She wished Tonio's friends had stayed downtown.

A reel was in progress, and as she reached out her hand to switch partners, she spotted Don Lampone at the edge of the crowd with his leather case. She faltered, treading on the heels of the woman in front of her. She watched as Don Lampone made his way through the crowd and stood at the bar near Biaggio. He put the case between his feet and ordered a drink. After a moment she caught his eye and he nodded to her over the rim of his snifter.

She was waiting for a break in the music to go to him, her mouth as dry as a clod of turf. Biaggio broke in on her partner and continued the reel.

"There's a man over there looking for you," he said, tilting his head in Don Lampone's direction. "He said something about delivering money."

Like the strings under the fiddlers' thumbs her legs were suddenly quivering with nervous tension at the notion of collecting the other five thousand dollars. She stepped in a shaky circle, back to back with Biaggio, her eyes raking the crowd for fear of thieves, her tongue wetting her lips with anticipation. No one knew what was inside the old man's case, but she'd have to get it into a safe directly or die from anxiety.

"Is that the old man who wanted to buy Tonio's wife?" Biaggio asked.

"Yeah, it's him," she said without thinking. She broke off from the reel and started toward Don Lampone, but Biaggio pulled her back.

"Let him wait!" he whispered in her ear. "Don't make yourself so obvious. Go to him after the reel." He picked her up and spun her around.

She suddenly realized that she was very, very rich. When she put the five in the case with the other money, she'd have close to ten thousand dollars. She forgot her fears and screamed with glee as Biaggio whirled her around. Oh, it was grand! It was glorious! She had everything she'd ever wanted: a successful uptown saloon, fine clothes and jewels, almost five grand in her pocket, and five more in the satchel waiting for her. Her time had come! She was on top of the mountain, on top of her dream!

Biaggio plunked her down. A blur of black rushed toward her.

"*Assassina!*" Mina cried. The crack of Mina's hand on her cheek stopped the fiddles while the strength of the impact sent Kathleen flying into the crowd. Don Emilio rushed forward with his case to grab Mina's arm. "Filomina!" Don Emilio cried in a shocked voice.

Mina felt Don Emilio's rebuke vibrate in her breast. The room was silent. This is what Biaggio, Mario, Petrosino, and Don Emilio had rehearsed at her apartment: the confrontation. Everyone had a part to play. It was her turn, but Mina didn't feel like she was in her own body. She was watching herself, as if she'd wandered onto the opera stage and stood alone in the spotlight. The moment reminded her of when Scarpia suddenly realizes Tosca has stabbed him. She looked at the faces around her; the audience was waiting for her next move.

"What are you doing here?" Don Emilio coaxed in English. "You were supposed to stay at the hotel. This display does you no credit."

The words sounded stretched out like rubber. Mina's mouth wouldn't work. She saw the worry on Don Emilio's face. Across from her Biaggio stood waiting to act as interpreter. Everyone was in place, but what was it she was supposed to do? Say? She bit down on her lip, drawing blood, petrified of making a mistake. The players were depending on her; she had to remember her lines and act.

"Mrs. DiGianni," Antonio's mistress said tightly, "I was going to call on ya this afternoon." Everyone was staring at them. Mina saw his mistress's eyes dart around the room. The imprint of Mina's hand was red on her face; she was obviously trying to hold in her temper when she said, "I was very sorry to hear about yer husband's death."

Don Emilio tried to pull Mina away, but as rehearsed she shook him off. "You murdered my husband," Mina announced carefully in English.

There was a stir and a murmur. Kathleen glanced around, feeling the shift in mood of her bar crowd. "I think yer very upset and don't know what yer saying. Colm! Tommy! The lady needs a hand. Please take her out of here." Mina saw two men step from behind the bar and push forward.

"Filomina. Let's go now," Don Emilio urged as he pretended to lead her away. "Don't make a scene."

"No! Don't touch me," she said, throwing up her hands as dramatically as Francesca did when she was acting the diva on stage. Her gesture stopped the advancing barmen. "This woman," she said slowly in English, addressing the crowd as though she were a politician on a stump. "was my husband's mistress. She killed him when he tried to return to me."

Mina heard the immediate undercurrent of whispering as everyone now focused on Antonio's mistress. His mistress's forehead glistened with sweat and her eyes darted fearfully around the room. Mina experienced a shiver of satisfaction. Now his mistress knew what it was like to fear for her freedom.

"Mrs. DiGianni, come to the back room, we can talk there," his mistress said through her teeth.

"*Questa donna,*" Mina announced, switching to Italian. "*E un'assassina. L' ha detto il pretore!*"

Biaggio translated loudly: "She says the coroner told her you murdered him."

"Sssh! Are ya crazy?" Kathleen hissed, pulling Biaggio away from the crowd. "Help the boys get her into the back room."

Biaggio pretended to be on Kathleen's side as he took Mina by the arm. "Please, signora," Biaggio soothed in Italian. "Come to the back and we'll talk. I'll translate for you."

Biaggio had no intention of taking Mina away from the crowd. Mina's plan was to confront Kathleen in front of her friends and respected guests and rattle her enough to make her act recklessly. Biaggio tugged a little as Mina refused to move. Then Mina whirled away from him into the middle of the crowd. "What I say, I say to everyone! This woman killed Antonio with a liquor bottle." Biaggio translated again for the onlookers' benefit.

"Shut her up!" Kathleen hissed to Don Lampone. "Get her out of here or there ain't going to be enough money in the world to keep her out of jail."

"But that can't be, signora," Biaggio said to Mina. "The police say they have the murder weapon, your mother's knife."

The room was hushed as everyone tried to follow the details.

"It's a lie!" Mina said, turning back to her target. "There was a spear of glass in his side." Mina held her index and middle finger together and made an underhanded stabbing motion with them. "The spear of glass came from a liquor bottle, and when you stabbed him, it broke off in his side."

"A spear of glass?" Emilio echoed with the crowd.

"The coroner can match the edges of the piece he found inside Antonio to a bottle taken from your bar. He can prove you murdered him," Mina said.

"Yer crazy," Kathleen said. "There are thousands of bottles in the city. Maybe he *was* stabbed with a bottle. But ya can't pin the murder on me. Plenty of people have liquor bottles." The crowd murmured in agreement.

"But they're numbered for tax purposes, Mrs. Shaunessey," Colm blurted out.

"Shut up, Colm," Kathleen snapped.

"It won't matter," Mina said. "The numbers won't convict her. This will." This time Mina held up just her index finger and turned in a circle to show it to the crowd. "It will only take this," Mina said, "to expose this woman as Antonio's killer."

Kathleen looked at Mina's extended finger with scorn. "Yer loony. Ya'll end by being locked in a padded room."

"Our fingers are etched by God," Mina continued passionately. "Not even twins have the same pattern. Anything we touch leaves behind our mark—a little stamp that says, I passed this way, me, and no other."

The men whispered doubtfully as each man examined his fingertips. "It's true," Biaggio assured them. "Mario read about it in the papers, it's a new technique being used by the police in France to identify criminals."

"Yeah?" Kathleen said. "Well, this ain't France."

"A special coroner has been called to read the marks," Mina said. "He's already read the ones on the glass spear taken from Antonio's side and will read the ones on the bottle left behind. When they match he'll have the killer."

Biaggio continued to translate. He knew Mina was stretching the truth, but the crowd didn't. The crowd shifted to examine Kathleen's reaction to this news.

"Even the beast in the Bible has a mark that's his alone," Mina said. "When the police return to your bar with a warrant, they'll find the bottle you used with your fingerprints on it. The two pieces of glass will fit perfectly together along the broken edge, and the tips of your own fingers will lock you in jail."

The crowd erupted in speculation. Everyone was watching Kathleen. She saw them sizing up the possibilities. It seemed to her that in just moments, most of her countrymen had already found her guilty. The bitch had created quite a hullabaloo. Kathleen lost her tightly leashed temper and lunged at Tonio's wife, but Biaggio caught her arms and held her back. It surprised Kathleen that Tonio's wife didn't flinch.

"Ya think it's yer turn to have me in a barrel, to get yer revenge, don't ya?" Kathleen snarled. "Well, I ain't scared. Spin all the fancies ya like, I didn't have nothing to do with Tonio's murder."

"If there's no proof, you have nothing to worry about," Tonio's wife said, challenging her.

"Get out of here!" Kathleen shouted, pulling hard against Biaggio. "I got no time to listen to twaddle about fingers and marks. I got a business to run."

Mina regarded Kathleen sadly. "I thought I came today to confront Antonio's murderer, but part of me came for revenge," Mina confessed. "I felt you stole Antonio away from me—"

"Come away, Filomina," Don Emilio said, fearing that she would say the wrong thing. This wasn't part of the scene they had rehearsed.

"You would have sold me to this man," Mina said, pointing to Don Emilio, "a man you thought a pervert, to make yourself a fortune and seal your relationship with my husband."

"Tonio was never *your husband*," Kathleen said, glaring at her. "He belonged to me."

Mina was silent for a moment, then replied, "You're right. Antonio wasn't mine. I should have known, but I was desperate for love. As desperate as you for money. He was your man, but he was taken from you as he was taken from me. I'm sorry for you, but it's your own hand that will lock you in a cell and set those you accuse free. Remember my words when *destino* comes for you."

The room buzzed like bees trapped in a bottle as Mina turned and walked gracefully out of the circle. With her hand on the doorknob, she hesitated, trying to decide if she was satisfied. She hadn't screamed or spit the way she'd thought she might. And she hadn't pulled his mistress's hair or torn her dress. It surprised her that she didn't seek physical retribution for all the suffering she'd gone through.

She'd only slapped Antonio's mistress because Mario had suggested it would infuriate her and draw the crowd's attention. It hadn't been out of a need to be requited for her pain. It seemed that with one slap the anger that had been building inside her for six months drained away, leaving pity in its place. It was true; Mina knew how it felt to be desperate for respectability and love. Hadn't she nearly destroyed her life in the hope of obtaining it? Faintly, she heard the fiddles start up, scratching out a jarringly merry tune, and then she heard the murmur of voices.

She glanced around. People were examining her, their eyes filled with contempt . . . or pity . . . or something else. In a handful of faces a strange admiration gleamed. In the past she would have timidly put her head down and hurried away, embarrassed by the turmoil she'd caused, but now she returned their stares, proud of her strength.

She remembered the day the girl had pulled Antonio off Gaetano, allowing God to exact his vengeance. Vengeance was the Lord's after all; but today she'd helped prepare the ground for God's seeds by standing up for herself. If she'd learned anything from the horror of the kidnapping and from Dante's gentle encouragement, it was that she deserved respect and love.

Chapter Forty-Seven

$\mathcal{A}$S SOON AS ANTONIO'S WIFE
had left Flynn's, Kathleen grabbed the case from Don Emilio and scurried to double lock the five thousand in the back office. She rushed back to buy everyone a round and settle them down. Laughing and joking, she made her way through the room soft selling the incident: ". . . a hysterical widow, blaming others in her shock and fear. Obviously, she hopes to shift blame away from her own mother's crimes. . . ."

A few praised her for the dignified way she'd handled herself in raw circumstances, but she could see their ardor had cooled. Charlie Murphy and his crew left abruptly. Those that stayed were strangers to her and pushed into her new dining room for supper. They'd heard she'd hired a fancy French chef like the joints uptown and they weren't about to pass up a free feed.

For a few tense minutes she oversaw the waiters, then she left the dining room to check on the kitchen staff. She grabbed the case and blew out the back door. Rushing along the icy walk she frantically searched for an empty hack. She had to get to the Hat before the coppers . . . but the hacks were all full. Two blocks west of Flynn's, on Union Square, she flagged down one of the new "taxicabs" that had invaded the city the year before. "Cherry Street and make it snappy."

The meter clicked furiously until the cab jolted to a halt. "Be careful, ma'am, this neighborhood's dangerous," the driver warned her.

She slid across the seat dragging the case behind. "Thanks, but I'll be fine. Wait here. I'll be back before ya know it." She handed him a fiver and yanked the case out with both hands. "There'll be another one of those for ya when I get back, plus yer fare. I need to get back uptown lickety-split."

The driver tipped his hat. He'd never been offered that much cash for the few blocks he'd traveled in his career. "I'll be right here waiting, ma'am."

She cut through the garbage-choked alley with her heart banging against her ribs. With her fancy combs and gold earrings swinging, she had the look of an easy mark, but she made it to the back door without incident. She slipped inside, finding the kitchen a shadowy still life of scattered debris. Same old Jimmy, she thought, setting the case down. Even though he was going to be part owner now that she had the place uptown, things hadn't changed—he was still lax. She locked the door.

Her throat felt as tight as a compressed bedspring and she feared she might vomit from nerves. The sound of an energetic bar filtered through the closed barroom door, so to ensure privacy, she slipped the lock and turned the gaslight key up full. She peeled off her coat and pulled a busted crate of empties out from under the sink, shaking her head with disbelief. She couldn't believe she'd been so stupid as to bring evidence back to her bar, but then again she'd wrapped everything up in her skirts when she pushed his body in.

Rummaging through the bottles she found the amber one she'd been looking for and wrapped it in a wet bar towel. Carefully she rubbed down what was left, then, using the cast-iron skillet she'd threatened Tonio's wife with, she smashed the glass inside the cloth until she was satisfied with the pulverized remains. She dumped the pieces into the crate, cracking a few other bottles on top for effect, and shoved the container back under the sink.

Again she listened at the barroom door. Satisfied, she popped the padlock on the pantry and pulled aside a new flour sack. Crouching, she untied the jute bag hidden behind it and plunged her hands into cranberry beans; it took several tries until her fingers found the rough corner of a towel. She pulled the bundle out, sat back on her heels, and lay it atop her knees. The towel was fouled with dried blood and stuck together. Her stomach convulsed as she remembered wiping Tonio's blood off her hands. She peeled apart the cloth.

Inside it lay what was left of Tonio's pockets. A few loose greenbacks sat on top, bloodied and stiff. Underneath, a worn collection of cards and loose coins, a wedding ring, and a gold medallion with an attached chain.

Satisfied that all the evidence was still there, she refolded the towel and got up. She needed to dispose of everything that might incriminate her as quickly as possible. I'll keep the cash, she thought, backing out of the pantry and locking the door. The rest I'll tie to a brick and toss in the

Hudson. If they ever find it or if Mario's body ever turns up they'll think—

The cellar door creaked.

She whirled toward the sound, grabbing a knife from the side of the wooden chopping block for protection. She heard her own voice squeal out like a pig caught under a fence.

"Hello, Kathleen."

She thrust the knife at a shadowy figure in the cellar doorway. She thought for an instant it was Tonio, but she knew that was impossible. Almost as impossible as the man who stood before her holding his grape knife. Mario? She looked more closely. It *was* Mario, but he wasn't holding a knife, he was holding a pocket watch. "Jesus Christ, Mario! Yer alive! I can't believe it. Oh, Lord! What a shock! Ya scared the blood out of my veins! Mother of God!" She clutched her heart as her legs buckled and braced herself against the wooden block for support. "What the hell are ya doing here?"

He focused on the knife in her hand and shifted his body to the right. "I was waiting for you to arrive," he said with a strange smile. "It didn't take you long." She glared at him, the adrenaline running through her like fire through dry grass. She was so muddled, she wasn't sure she'd heard him right, but his next words drove the dark confusion from her mind.

"I came to give you the money," he said. "The money Tonio gave me to hold."

That steadied her nerves. The missing four thousand dollars. That would come in handy to pay everyone off without touching her budding fortune. The annoyance and fear drained from her in a flash as her greed for the lost money took hold. "That's awful good of ya, Mario."

"Well, it's not mine," Mario said simply. "Tonio promised me a piece for helping, but he got it from the old man for agreeing to sell his wife, so I figure it belongs to you now that Tonio's dead." He took a packet of money from the inside of his jacket and reached out to hand it to her.

"Not many would return four thousand dollars," she said, putting the towel with the evidence down on the chopping block with the knife. She put her hand out to take the money, but he didn't let go.

"You were partners, weren't you?" Mario insisted. "I mean, I'm not being stupid giving it to you, am I? I helped him a little, but you planned it."

"Of course I planned it," she bragged, prying the money from Mario's fingers and riffling the bills. "Didn't I club the old man and hide Tonio's wife in a barrel to deliver? Didn't I blackmail the old man for another five? There'll be a cut of money for ya, just like Tonio wanted. But right now I've got to go—" She turned to take the evidence from the chopping block, but in her haste to leave, her dress brushed the folded towel. It fell to the floor, spilling open.

"What's this?" Mario asked, stooping.

"Don't touch it!"

He rose, holding the bloodied towel. On his extended finger was a gold chain with a medallion. "This is Tonio's medallion," he said, pretending surprise.

"Yeah," she said, snatching the evidence back and wrapping the four thousand dollars inside the towel. "Ah . . . the police gave it to me . . . from off his body. Didn't ya hear how it happened, Mario?"

"I read in the papers that the opera people Tonio's wife worked for, that gigolo Dante Romano and the diva Frascatti, killed him."

Something smelled shitty. Mario was the educated one in the group; he read morning, noon, and night. Now Mario ought to know every detail of the murder, she thought, including the supposed robbery. The dailies had reported over and over that there hadn't been a thing left on Tonio's body or in his pockets when he was found at the dock. What was Mario up to? She gripped the towel in her suddenly sweaty hand.

"How did ya get into the cellar?" she asked suspiciously. "Jimmy let ya in?"

"I picked the lock," Mario said. He pulled a little tool from his pocket and showed it to her. "Dante Romano taught me how."

"That so?" she said with an unbelieving laugh.

"He's a master of disguises, but I heard you've already met him. He's the dandy boxer you got so friendly with." Mario turned and called into the cellar through the open door. "Vittorio Fusco? Come up here."

Nothing happened. Kathleen darted a look at the cellar, then looked back at Mario, relief washing over her. The bastard was playing with her. "Ya had me going there for a minute," she laughed grimly.

"It's no joke, Kathleen. I'm going to see you hang for stabbing Tonio."

The smile left her face and cold contempt took its place. "Me hang? It'll be you swinging when they find out yer alive. Everybody knows you hated Tonio for taking yer fiancée. Everyone knows ya carry a knife strapped to yer calf."

"But they found a spear of amber glass in his side. They can match the glass with the bottle. The coroner will easily prove my knife didn't kill Tonio. How are you going to explain your prints on the bottle?"

"You can thank Tonio's cocky wife for tipping me off," Kathleen said. "I'm in the clear now." She put on her coat.

"You think you got rid of your fingerprints by smashing it?"

"Smashing what, Mario? There was never any bottle, leastways not here." She picked up Don Lampone's case with her free hand. "Ya should have been smarter if ya wanted to catch me. Ya should have kept that bitch away from me. But she clued me in, and I got here before the cops could and I took care of all the evidence." She shook her head as though she were supremely sorry for Mario. "Ya dumb wop, I've known ever since he took her from ya that you'd have liked to kill him. Well, ya lost yer chance for revenge and ya lost the four thousand that could've been yers for helping me with the kidnapping and keeping quiet about Tonio. I'll keep the money for myself." She shook the wrapped towel at him. "It don't exist, just like the bottle don't."

"Assassina!" Mina cried, coming up the cellar steps. Kathleen jumped and whirled toward the stair. Tonio's wife came into the light, holding a stick with a broken amber bottle threaded through the neck.

"As you can see, the bottle does exist," Mario said. "We got here before you."

Kathleen looked at Tonio's wife, then at Mario. She clutched the case of money to her breast and backed toward the alley door.

"Yer after the money, ain't ya, Mario?" Kathleen asked.

Mario translated for Mina. Mina couldn't believe Antonio's mistress could be so coldheartedly greedy and think Mario the same.

"Once the police check the serial numbers on the money against the list at Don Emilio's bank," Mina said, "and match the edges of this bottle to the piece they took from Antonio's side, they'll put you in jail. I told you your own fingers would lock you away."

Mario translated. Antonio's mistress smirked. "No one's ever going to believe ya, ya guinea bitch. I'll say ya broke in here and planted everything."

Antonio's mistress tossed the bloody towel with the evidence and money on the floor between them. "Mario took that money off Tonio's body when he dumped it at the pier. I ain't never seen it."

"What about my earring?" Mina asked. "The one you planted on Antonio. I spoke to the old woman at the market. She'll testify that you told her my husband was selling me back to Italy and that you assaulted me."

"That batty old lady's testimony won't stand up in court. Ya got a keen mind, darling, but ya forget one thing, I've got the police and the politicians in my pocket. It's going to be yer word against mine. And it'll be me that comes out on top."

There was a creak on the beer cellar stairs. The mistress's eyes darted toward the sound.

"I'm happy to say you haven't got all the police in your pocket, Mrs. Shaunessey," Petrosino corrected her, coming up from the gloom. Two men in blue uniforms stood behind Petrosino. It was clear the three men had been watching and listening on the stairs. Antonio's mistress jerked toward the alley door, but Mina stepped in front of it.

"I'd like to introduce you," Mina said, "to the Police Commissioner of New York City, Theodore Bingham."

The mistress's jaw flapped for a moment. Then she clamped it shut.

Commissioner Bingham came forward and cocked his head. "Pleased to meet you, Mrs. Shaunessey. I'll take that case, if you please."

Antonio's mistress seemed more distressed over giving up the money than being caught and possibly heading to a hangman's noose.

"Gentlemen," Petrosino asked, "are you prepared to testify to all you've seen and heard this evening?"

"I am," Commissioner Bingham said. The others nodded. "Oh, by the way, Mrs. Shaunessey, I have a sworn affidavit here," Commissioner Bingham said, drawing a paper from his pocket and looking it over. "It implicates you in blackmail, kidnapping, and murder. It's signed by one of our officers, someone I believe you know well: Sergeant Patrick Sullivan."

With that statement Mina watched the last of Kathleen's defiance flee like a rabbit before the dogs.

Chapter Forty-Eight

CELEBRANTS PACKED INTO the High Mass for Antonio DiGianni at the Church of the Transfiguration near Mulberry Bend Park. The priest peeked at the overflowing chapel and gasped. Even if he broke the hosts into quarters he wouldn't have enough. As he put on his vestments, his altar boys hastily filled him in on the life of the boxer, ditchdigger, and all-around Lower East Side legend: "One of the toughest wop boxers ya ever like to see, Father." "My Pa said he had a head like a brick and a right fist like a sledgehammer."

The priest had planned brief, nonspecific comments for a man who'd only appeared in his church once, to be married, but he cobbled together a eulogy out of the boys' comments. He kissed his stole and slipped it over his head, thinking this Mass one of the most unusual he'd ever celebrated.

The great Caruso was up in the loft with the organist. In the front pew, Francesca Frascatti, the "diabolical diva," with her flaming tresses and elaborate costume, supported a demurely clad widow on one side while a whale of a woman in threadbare garments and a black woolen kerchief supported the widow on the other.

Behind these three, an old rooster with silver hair leaned on a cane and the arm of a nubile blond woman dressed to the nines. The altar boys pointed out the mayor and the police commissioner surrounded by a phalanx of blue-suited police officers. On the fringes of this group the priest recognized a sprinkling of political and social luminaries he'd seen pictures of in the dailies.

Biaggio looked around at the ragtag mob that filled the rest of the church—curiosity seekers, mostly, from the Lower East Side. Biaggio stood with Tonio's work crew: Salvatore, Paolo, and the rest. Sale blew his nose into a bandanna and wiped his eyes, while his fat cousin Pepe patted him on the back. Biaggio held his hat over his chest and fingered his rosary beads. He was proud of the role he'd played in exposing Tonio's real killer, but he mumbled Hail Marys over and over, doing his best to tamp down the guilty satisfaction he felt now that Tonio was dead and Mario revenged.

Biaggio nodded to Mario and Petrosino, who stood with Dante in the first pew on the other side of Tonio's casket. Petrosino's men flanked them, and a cadre of Pinkertons who had worked the case for the past month filled the pews behind. Roberto and Peppina were present, as were Sean Catagan and his mates. The only person missing from the gathering was Kathleen Shaunessey.

After her careless disclosures she'd been booked, but she'd still had enough pull to make bail. Sergeant Patrick Sullivan had indeed turned on her. He'd let her sink to save himself from prosecution once he'd discovered that Police Commissioner Bingham was involved in the case. And when word of her involvement in murder reached the former owners of Flynn's, it was sealed up tighter than a coffin lid. The down payment had been confiscated. Serial numbers were being checked. The Hat was all she had, and after legal fees she probably wouldn't be able to keep it. She remained behind its locked doors, drunk as a lord.

After Mass the cortege wound its way to Calvary Cemetery. Dry-eyed, Mina placed a small bouquet of white mums on the casket before it was lowered. It was her duty to toss the first handful of soil, but she knew sprinkling dirt on a casket wasn't going to erase the memory of the past seven months. Antonio might be dead and buried, but his memory and his child would live on.

On the way to Mulberry Street Mina was silent, staring out the window of the coach. Dante and Cesca didn't press her to share her thoughts. They were pleased that she wasn't morose or tearful, and there'd be time enough in the days ahead to talk about the events of the last few weeks.

Cesca had arranged for catering from Delmonico's to be waiting at Mina's apartment for the mourners, if they could be called that. Teresa helped by setting out the trays. They left the door to Mina's apartment open and most of the people stood in the hallway and on the landing, chatting as though at a cocktail party. As the mourners came through the building's wreathed door, Peppina took coats and piled them on her mother's bed in the downstairs apartment, then the mourners climbed the stairs. Anyone with any connection to the case wanted firsthand gossip.

"It was kind of Signorina Frascatti to arrange such a beautiful funeral," Simonetta said.

"Well, he was her daughter's husband."

"Some husband, planning to sell her into sexual slavery," Lilli sniped.

"Hush, Lilli! When will you learn not to listen to gossip?" Simonetta asked. "That's an obvious falsehood. How could a husband sell a wife?"

Lilli shook her head and whispered to the group: "Frascatti did it for respect. For the baby. A baby's not to blame for its father's crimes." The women nodded, taking cookies from a tray being passed in the crush.

"Who'd have believed that she'd be a diva's daughter?" Lilli said to no one in particular as she examined the cracked plaster and helped herself to a tiny roast beef sandwich. "And heir to a fortune?"

"Or that the man posing as the diva's lover was a detective searching for her daughter?" another whispered back. They all glanced at Dante, who stood conversing with Oscar Hammerstein near the window. "I wonder if he's available?" one of the girls giggled.

"Let's go offer our condolences before Hammerstein orders us back to the grindstone," Lilli said.

Mina greeted everyone graciously, even though most of the women commented on her clothing and her good fortune rather than on the death of her husband. She kept her hand over her heart, the place where her baby's soul dwelled, to remind herself this was a serious moment that demanded dignity even if others treated it like a carnival.

For Mina, time seemed to unfold as stiffly as a new bolt of cloth. Friends and strangers filed by one after the other. She felt numb and empty when they took her hand or pressed kisses to her cheek. She had little to say. Yes, she was sorry Antonio was dead, but she felt little connection to him. Her sorrow was for her unborn baby and what might have been, not for the reality of the last six months or the mockery that had passed for her marriage.

Finally it was over. Teresa and Peppina came over to express their sympathy as they prepared to leave. Mina remained seated, her heart swollen with dread. It felt enormous, as though it might plunge through her stomach and crash at her feet. She'd found bravery and a new spirit during her recent struggle, but she feared the coming confrontation more than anything she'd faced in the past six months. When Teresa and Peppina left, she'd be alone with the Signorina and Dante.

Teresa stooped to press a kiss to her cheek. "It's a wonderful thing that's happened, Mina," she whispered in her ear. "Not to be blasphemous, but it's a miracle. You've found your *Mammina*. You were led to each other by *Gesù*'s hand and I know you'll find the words to forgive her and make things right."

"But you don't understand," Mina said, clinging to her hand. "I was trying to explain the other day—"

"Yes, yes, the girls from the shop explained it all," Teresa said sotto voce. "You're Francesca Frascatti's daughter and the granddaughter of a rich *padrone*. It's better than hitting the numbers! Now you have the whole world to offer your child. Finally *Sant'Anna* has answered your prayers. You've been blessed."

"Good night, Signora DiGianni," Peppina said, stepping out into the hall. "*Buona fortuna*."

Mina got up and followed Teresa to the door. "Lean on your *Mammina*," Teresa said. "Saint Paul says, 'Love is the greatest gift.' Forgive her and start again." Embracing Mina she added, "I hope you'll see me again, before you go back to Italy." Teresa patted her cheek; tears sparkled on her lashes. "I've come to love you, Mina. I'll miss you."

Mina's heart raced, but she steadied herself with a deep breath. She could make it. She was strong now. She kissed Teresa good-bye.

"Good night, dear friend," Teresa said. "I'll pray for you."

Mina closed the door. She didn't know what to do or where to start. In the kerosene lamp's light her wedding band glistened on her finger. Antonio's wife, no more. She looked at the ring for a moment, not seeing it, but remembering the day that Antonio had put it on her finger. How happy she'd been.

She twisted the ring off and turned it slowly around the tip of her index finger. It had promised a new beginning, a life of eternal love, but it had been a lie from the start. She set it on her palm. So light. Who would have thought her bargain would bring such a heavy burden of grief?

Her thoughts turned to the Signorina and Dante, who were waiting. She knew they were watching her, wondering what she'd say. She'd told them she wanted to speak with them right after the funeral. Her fingers closed over the rings as she smiled at them weakly. It crossed her mind to snatch her coat and rush down the stairs, never to return, but she knew she would have to face them sooner or later.

She slipped the band onto a chipped blue saucer resting on the table. She didn't feel free of its burden, but chained down by regret and her fear of the coming repercussions.

Dante stood beside the mended window; she couldn't see his face. The setting sun cast him in silhouette, as though he were cut from black paper. Behind her Mina heard the springs protest as the Signorina collapsed onto her *letto matrimoniale*. The Signorina gave a dramatic groan of fatigue and tossed her shoes to the floor.

"I need to speak with you both," Mina said. "It's important."

To her own ears, her voice sounded as empty and fragile as a soap bubble.

"*Cara,*" the Signorina said, "let's talk later. Come sit by me."

Dante came toward her, away from the window, and the light moved over his face, bringing his features into focus. Mina thought of the first passages of the Bible when God separated the light from the darkness. Dante seemed to her one of God's most beautiful creations. *Sant'Anna,* what will I do without him? she thought.

"Now may not be the best time for a heart-to-heart talk," Dante said.

"Yes, let's pack the things you'll need and go back uptown," Cesca agreed.

Mina pulled out a chair and sat. Crossing her arms over her chest, she rocked forward, unable to meet their eyes.

"What is it?" the Signorina asked. "Are you worried about the baby?"

"No," Mina said, biting her lip. She examined the faded roses on the linoleum and remembered her life before the Signorina had appeared. It seemed so far away. She heard Dante come to sit at the table. He said her name, but she wouldn't look up and meet his eyes. The air seemed thick and viscous. Her throat felt constricted and her chest hurt. She began cautiously, "I started to tell Teresa the other day. I guess I was trying to find the words so that I could tell you—"

"*Cara,* you needn't speak now," the Signorina said. "Let's leave these awful memories behind. There's a great deal I'd like to explain. Why I left—"

"No, I must say my part here. In my world. First, I have something for you." Mina went to her bureau and drew out a carved wooden box. At the bottom, tied with a bit of faded pink ribbon, was a lock of plain brown hair. "Here," she said to the Signorina. "This is for you."

Puzzled, the Signorina took it from her. "What is this?"

Mina could feel Dante's eyes on her—examining her, weighing her reactions. "It's something I've treasured. I was saving it. I just didn't realize I was saving it for you."

"Maria," the Signorina said, "I don't understand."

"Please, don't call me Maria." Mina felt a stab of pain in her chest, and turned away sharply. She could tell that the Signorina sensed something important coming. Something she too didn't want to face.

The Signorina caught Mina's hand. "I'm sorry," she said. "In my heart I think of you as Maria. Please don't reject me, Mina; give me a chance to explain."

"I'm not your daughter, signorina," Mina said softly. As gently as she could, Mina disentangled her fingers. From her dresser drawer she took a cloth envelope—the one she'd worn pinned inside her corset when she arrived in America. She gave it to the Signorina, who opened it and withdrew a grease-stained letter. The letter was folded so that just a penciled address, carefully printed by Mario months before, was showing.

"Dante, do you understand what she's trying to say?" The Signorina held the slip out to him uncomprehendingly, her arm as stiff as carved marble. Mina felt the pain in the Signorina's voice.

"I believe it's something from the ship," Dante said. "Something from Maria. Filomina Rossi has something to tell us."

"I don't understand what you're saying!" the Signorina said through clenched teeth. The Signorina's arm remained extended; her hand still offered the letter.

Mina focused her eyes on her statue of *Sant'Anna*, in the corner, above the Signorina's head. Oh, patron saint of mothers, please make her understand, Mina prayed.

"It's Mario's address," Mina began. "He and Maria should have been married six . . . seven months ago, but . . . that letter was inside the cloth envelope I'd pinned inside my dress when I got off the boat. In case I couldn't find him in the crowd. In my hand I carried a carpetbag, and inside that, wrapped in a pillowcase, a lock of hair, a gold watch, and red stone earrings. As I searched the crowd, my heart was hammering so hard I was sure Mario would find me just from its noise. I wanted to run away, but I couldn't. You see . . . I had her papers. The sweat from my hands had made the tag for her luggage soggy and the inked numbers had run. The clerk made me describe the wedding dress and the veil folded in tissue, before they let me claim the trunk."

Cesca was worried that the strain of the past few weeks had affected her daughter's mind. "What are you trying to say? Dante, do you understand what she's trying to say?" Cesca's eyes flickered fearfully to Dante for an explanation, but he only shook his head and motioned for her to remain silent.

"I wish I were Maria, signorina. I wish I could lie to you and pretend . . . but I can't. I'm an impostor. A liar and a cheat. I don't deserve to be your servant."

"That's nonsense! Why, you—" Cesca started to say.

Dante held his hand up to silence her. "Go on, Mina," he said.

"On the ship, coming over, there was a woman who came from a village not far from Naples. She was about my age, only taller and fuller-figured. She told me she was coming here to marry a man she'd never met. When I asked her why, she told me about her shameful *Mammina*. Over the week we had together she told me everything about her life. All the stories about her past, her hopes and dreams for her future . . ."

Mina turned her face toward the one pane of glass that wasn't mended, with its view of a gray sky. She felt closed in and trapped by their staring eyes. She yearned to soar into the sky and escape, but the clouds of pain kept stacking up.

"She told me beautiful, elaborate tales . . . some happy, some sad, but all recounted with such passion and detail that I felt I'd met the characters and understood their feelings. We talked all day and half the night for over a week. We were inseparable, sleeping in each other's arms so we could whisper our hopes throughout the night. She needed to share her life with me and I listened; for truthfully I had little to tell and would have been ashamed to tell it."

Mina faltered. The silent questions in the Signorina's eyes felt like a millstone pressing the life from her body. No one spoke, and after a moment she forced herself to go on.

"Her illness began to show itself when we slipped past Gibraltar. She'd been hiding her pain, even from me, because she was afraid they would put her off the ship. First it was only a fever. I asked for the doctor, but in steerage it takes time for him to come. I thought she was sea-sick and I bathed her forehead with cold water. She bore it all without a cross word. But as she got sicker . . . she got melancholy.

"She didn't want to lose her beautiful dream, her *destino*. So she begged me to do something for her. I promised I would do anything I could. She told me she'd always wished for a sister and she thought of me as one. She hoped I would wear her gown and veil. . . . You see, she knew I was going to an uncertain future and she wanted me to be happy. So she unpinned the envelope with the address inside and she handed it to me. 'Go,' she said, 'marry my fiancé and be happy. If you are happy, then I will be also. Complete my dream for me . . . find love and let me rest in peace.' "

The Signorina shook her head fearfully from side to side and tried to pull away from Dante's supporting arm. "No," the Signorina said. "She doesn't know what she's saying."

Dante folded the Signorina against his chest. "Hush," he said. "Listen."

"She didn't just give me the dress . . . the earrings . . ."—Mina swallowed hard—"she gave me her destiny."

The Signorina moaned. She sprang away from Dante, thrusting her hands out, palms flat, as though to ward off Mina's words. She stumbled over her shoes, and Dante reached out swiftly to steady her. She was visibly trembling. "No, no, I don't want to hear this. I don't want to listen."

"You remember the story of the stoning, signorina. Antonio was like a god to her. He'd saved her that day, and she loved him with such child-like devotion, she thought him so good, you cannot imagine. She believed it was God's hand that had brought them together again. That it was fated. She'd worked it all out. How she would win him back to her . . . how they would marry and be happy. She told me what I must do and say. She explained that I was to tell Mario I feared him . . . that I felt safer with his best friend from my village. . . ."

"Antonio was not—he never knew?" Dante asked.

"He hadn't seen her for seven years. We were from the same region, the same age, had the same coloring, but most importantly, I knew all the stories. I remembered the names."

Her explanation answered some nagging questions in Dante's mind, the little inconsistencies, why the names and villages didn't fit with the records they'd checked, her insistence on trusting *destino*. But most importantly, it explained why the immigration records Petrosino had shown him listed Filomina Rossi as having died on board the ship. "You switched papers with her," Dante said, "and ever since you stepped off the ship you've been—"

"Lying, yes."

Cesca swayed in Dante's arms. He sat her down on a chair. It isn't true, Cesca thought, it can't be true. My daughter's making up a tale to punish me. To retaliate for the pain, for all the years she thought I was dead. She wants me to see how it feels to think the one you love is dead . . . that's all. Please, God, don't let what she's saying be true. But in her heart she knew by Mina's resigned tone that she was speaking the truth.

"I only thought to steal a little happiness for myself," Mina said. "How could it matter to anyone when they didn't know her? *Mammina* was just a dim memory, a remnant of a dead girl's past. . . . I could make myself happy and fulfill a dying wish. It seemed like such a good plan, but every day it got worse. I thought at first that it was God's will that Antonio beat me—"

"Nonsense!" Dante interjected. "No man has a right to lift his hand against a woman."

"I was not a virgin, he knew." Mina put her head down, fighting back the tears that threatened to flood her throat. Now Dante would despise her just as Antonio had.

"It's God's place, not ours, to judge your choices," Dante said.

Mina looked up and met the Signorina's eyes. "Signorina Frascatti . . . I've come to love you and I don't wish to see you hurt, but your daughter, Maria Grazia, is dead."

The Signorina shook her head slowly and closed her eyes. "That cannot be true."

"She died on board the ship. The doctor said he thought it might have been appendicitis. There was a small service for her, and then, because there was not enough ice, they put her in the sea."

It remained silent in the room after Mina finished. It was almost as if by not speaking Cesca could extend the fantasy a little longer. Her mind felt as confused and challenged as when she learned a new aria. How could such a thing happen?

" 'Not enough ice?' " Cesca asked, her voice strangled by emotion. She couldn't believe it. To have come so far, only to find death? Cesca's eyes searched Dante's face for a way out of this dilemma.

"I am sorry," Mina said softly.

"Dante, you would know if what she's saying is true, wouldn't you? You could check the ship's records?"

"Cesca, I was waiting to tell you. Petrosino's man found records confirming that Filomina Rossi was buried at sea. Mina switched papers with Maria Grazia and got tangled up in lies when we appeared at the opera house."

Cesca turned to Mina, disbelief mixing with frantic hope. "You lied about yourself before—" Cesca started desperately. "I forgive you for that, but tell me the truth. Tell me what really happened. Are you my daughter? Are you trying to punish me? I understand that you would be angry with me. It's normal to feel anger for a mother who deserted you." Mina shook her head and put her hands over her eyes. "Did you steal her things? I won't be upset. If you stole her belongings, just tell me what happened. Where was she going after the ship? Tell me where she went."

Mina uncovered her eyes, pressing her hands together as though in prayer. Her whole body expressed shame and regret. "I am not lying, signorina, she *gave* me her things and made me promise to fulfill her contract."

Cesca began to sob. Dante moved to support her.

"She loved you so very much. She told me, many times. She said that when she was little she was angry with you for dying . . . because she always hoped that you'd return and take her to Naples to live, but she confessed that later she found contentment with her adopted family. How could I know that Maria's *Mammina* was still alive and a famous opera singer? Or that she would come to the place where I worked? When you insisted we tell our life stories, I told the stories that Maria had told me." Mina turned away from them, her voice becoming almost inaudible. "I couldn't tell you about my own life."

"Who are you?" Dante asked.

"Who I am is not important, Signor Dante. As you see, I am nobody. My own mother died when I was a little girl, and then my grandmother. I had no living family and made my way in Naples as best I could. I wished only to escape the life I'd come to know there. I wanted a change. I was determined to go to America, and then I met Maria on board the ship and was reborn." She took a breath. "At the price of her own life, Maria offered me a new beginning . . . so I took it. Our switch wasn't supposed to hurt anyone. Maria believed *destino* was being served. She convinced me that by marrying Antonio, I'd ensure happiness for both of us," Mina finished.

"*Destino,*" Dante said, chuckling ruefully.

"Yes," Mina said. "I understand you won't want to see me any longer. That's why I didn't want to have this . . . this meeting uptown. I've created enough turmoil in your lives. I want you to have Maria's things. I didn't wear the gown or veil and of course you now have the earrings. I'm so sorry to have caused you so much pain."

Cesca said nothing. She couldn't accept the dreadful words Mina had spoken: "Your daughter, Maria Grazia, is dead."

"It can't be, Dante. It can't! Buried in the sea? Taken from me completely?" Cesca realized she didn't even have a grave to visit. Oh, God, she thought, what a terrible payment you've demanded for my ambition.

"Signorina, in those last moments Maria was peaceful and . . . yes, I think happy. She said she was free of the burdens of this life and that she was yearning to join you. It was a joyous, sacred moment. I felt as though she were resting on our Lord's palm."

"Maria's not dead," Dante said with authority. He took Mina's hand and held it firmly.

"I'm sorry, Signor Dante, but I'm certain of it. You checked the ship's records yourself."

Cesca thought of gray waves, laced with foam, closing over her daughter's body. Gone forever, she thought. I'll never hold her sweet body in my arms again. "What a horrible way to end, Dante," Cesca said. "Alone, without love."

Dante knew that Cesca wasn't just referring to Maria, she was thinking of her own hope.

"You're only without love if you forget her and her wishes," Dante said. "She made Mina promise to find happiness and love. She's found it with us. Cesca, Maria Grazia's right here before you, don't you see? You need only open your heart to find that Maria's been given back to you by the grace of God."

"I don't understand what you mean."

"Madame Zavoya, that old witch, said it: 'You will be found and so will she.' Mina doesn't have your blood running through her veins, and it's not the destiny you planned, but it is just and perfect in its symmetry. You 'died' so that Maria might find love, and now, through Maria's death and the promise she extracted from Mina, she's returned the hope of love to you." He placed Mina's hand in Cesca's. "Your daughter's here. She's the flesh and blood woman before you."

Cesca lifted Mina's chin. She brushed aside the wisps of hair as she'd done that first day in the dressing room and stared into Mina's warm brown eyes. Dante had spoken the truth. This could just as easily be Maria as any other woman. Her daughter would have been a stranger to her. . . . But Cesca's stubborn heart insisted, This woman is an impostor, only a substitute for your own flesh and blood. *Sangue è sangue è mai acqua*: blood is blood and never water.

"This is the truth you are speaking?" Cesca asked, squeezing Mina's hand. "Total and complete? There's nothing more you want to say to me?"

"Forgive me, signorina. Forgive me, I—"

"Sssh! Let's not speak of forgiving. There's much in my life that needs the same."

Dante felt the struggle in Cesca's soul. He saw her doubt and fear and said, "I learned to love this woman, Cesca, just as you have. Does it really matter if she's called Antonio's wife, Maria Grazia, or Filomina?"

Dante was right; she'd come to love Mina without the tie of blood. The coloring, the age, the disposition were the same as her daughter's would have been. Maria Grazia's dying wish had given Cesca another chance to find love. Could she toss aside her daughter's gift so easily?

Love was the missing ingredient in her empty, jaded existence. She needed it more than any fantasy or dream of what might have been. Here was a worthy role for her to tackle, greater than Tosca or Madama Butterfly. To come to love another human being without the selfish desire to gain something for herself would be a true challenge to her spirit.

She folded Mina into her arms and pressed her lips against Mina's cheek. Thank you, Maria Grazia, Cesca said silently, thank you for this chance to love you again and honor your life. She cannot take your place in my heart, but I will love her like your sister and cherish your gift to me for all my life. "Maria has found a way to give me the love I've longed for," Cesca said, "and to allow me to make up for the mistakes of my past."

Mina met Dante's eyes and smiled.

"The past is illusion," Mina said, hugging Cesca tightly. "There's only this moment. This reality."

Epilogue

❦

FEBRUARY 9, 1950

Naples, Italy

❧

THE LACE

*T*HE SHIP LEFT NEW YORK HARBOR in the morning, when the sun was a handful of golden coins tossed upon the bobbing waves and the clouds were streaked with lavender and rose. Our little company stood at the railing huddled against the chill, for I wished to catch a glimpse of Lady Liberty and her torch of hope. I believed that seeing her would be a good omen for the new lives we were undertaking. I waved good-bye and turned my face to my future, my time upon her shore behind me.

Healing is a journey that is long and arduous and we had already made our first tentative steps upon its rocky path. I tried to practice the wisdom my fiancé had taught me: there is no past, there is only this moment. His words are true and they have set us free. For the past is only memories, figments of moments lost forever, and the future only fantasies and hopes, which may never be. We only have the breath we take and the present moment in which to live and to create love.

Teresa and Peppina, my dear friends, stayed behind and moved to Brook-a-lyn. I'd pressed my little coffee can savings upon them and they put it together with their own money to make a down payment on a small house and garden. They would grow their own vegetables and live in a rat hole no longer. One day, not too distant, they would own a grocery store.

Mario continued working as a detective under Giuseppe Petrosino for another year. In December 1909, Petrosino, that wonderful master of disguises, was assassinated in Palermo, where he'd gone to uncover the roots of the Mafia and the Black Hand criminals who were giving our countrymen a black eye. Mario stayed with law enforcement for a few years, though he could have done anything he pleased.

After the evidence was processed by the police, Don Emilio gave Mario back the money he'd had in his pockets the night he dove into the Hudson River to save me. I was pleased that such a good man would never want for anything. A few years after we left for Italy, I received a letter telling of his marriage. A newspaper clipping fluttered out. His bride looked lovely and it was obvious that he'd married well. His occupation was listed in the clipping as alderman and he would go forward with a political career.

Oscar Hammerstein's Manhattan Opera House and his dreams of glory ended happily when the "old lion" bought him out for over a million dollars and received a promise from Hammerstein that he would not produce opera for ten years in New York, Philadelphia, Boston, or Chicago. After that the Metropolitan Opera House reigned supreme.

The age of the tenor was upon the world of opera and Errico was its king. Such a golden voice, they said, would never come again, and when he died in 1921, we mourned with the whole world. But before then we were to see him many times and he would be godfather to my first child, Maria Grazia.

Maria was born on May 5, 1909, on my grandfather's estate on the slopes of Vesuvius. No one considered it unusual that she arrived two hours and twenty minutes before the anniversary of Maria's death. We took it as a good omen, a sign that Maria had found peace and was watching over us still.

Dante and *Mammina* convinced me that it wasn't in Don Emilio's best interest to know the truth about my birth. He wasn't in good health and hadn't been for years. His desire for revenge had kept him alive, but his regret had changed him and now he was living for love. Since he'd drawn up papers in New York City turning his estate over to his son's legal wife, Francesca Frascatti, what would be accomplished, they asked, by breaking the old man's fragile heart?

I don't regret my decision to remain silent, for when I saw the joy he felt holding Maria Grazia or playing with her, I realized they were right. He had been transformed. Without question he was still proud of his bloodline, but he'd softened and learned to love.

Whenever he lost his temper and declared that Maria Grazia had Giulio's stubbornness or resembled the Lampones more than Francesca's side of the family, we drifted out of the room with laughter. When he died a few years later, he died happily believing that a part of himself went forward. And it was true, for his influence was stamped upon Maria Grazia as surely as my own.

Mammina gave up the opera stage and took over the estate after my grandfather's death. It was good for her. She loved working in the shadow of the vines where she'd first made love to Giulio and conceived her child. The winery expanded under her guidance, becoming a world-famous label that has been on most American tables at one time or another.

When the wars came she was firm as a wine stake against the invaders, though she was smart enough to beguile them with good wine, arias, and her unique charm. We held on to the estate when many others lost theirs and hid our old bottles first from the Fascists, then from the Nazis. Lately the winery has expanded in land and production, adding grappa and other distilled spirits. It's *Mammina's* way of honoring Giulio's love of winemaking.

My husband, Dante, and I are happy. Maria Grazia, our other children, and our grandchildren keep us busy. Dante has given up detecting for pay, though he still loves poking around to uncover how things fit together and why they work as they do. His latest passion is reading the theories of a man named Freud. "It's the ultimate challenge," he claims, "unlocking the mind of man."

He still likes to tramp through the countryside in the morning hours. He picks wildflowers to paint in the afternoons when the light is right. Now that *Mammina*'s slowing down, he does his best to help with the estate and plays with the idea of expanding the winery to California someday.

Antonio's murderer went to jail, though her fingerprints on the amber bottle that I held up that day at the Cocked Hat did not put her there. The new forensic technique of fingerprinting wasn't used successfully in America to convict a criminal until 1911. It was the contents of Antonio's pockets found in the pantry, along with the serial numbers, and Patrick Sullivan's testimony, that forced a confession of sorts.

Kathleen Shaunessey broke down and entered a plea of self-defense. With Antonio's reputation and her political connections, it was enough to cheat the hangman. She received a ten-year sentence. No one knows what happened to her after she served her term, but I know she's bound to turn up one day dressed in silk and pearls.

Time flows on, like pins pressed into pricking, one pin at a time. The making of lace cannot be hurried, and there is a concealed wisdom in its twisted knots and threads, for only the Maker knows the pattern. The lace is an elaborate work that no mortal hand can unfashion. For knots have been tied and threads cut and even the Maker cannot redress creation.

As the seasons pass, bobbins cross and come together for a time. The Hand works a flower or a figure, then those bobbins are set aside while others take up their place. The threads twist and turn, loop and whorl. Although it may not be clear to us from where they come or where they're going, the Maker knows.

Only His hand knows when those motifs reappear or in what guise. *Destino,* the gimp thread, flows strong and steady through the work, drawing attention to its most important aspects. It is *Sant'Anna* whose hand does the network that allows me to admire the wisdom of the pattern and the cleverness of His design. She is the patron saint of mothers and honors me with her patience and grace.

In the moments when I knead the bread or listen to the magic of Errico's voice spinning out to me from vinyl or hold my grandchildren in my arms or hear the steady breathing of my beloved husband beside me, I smile, knowing I finally understand *destino*'s path. Another Hand guides us as we cross our threads, place the pins, and tie the knots—a Master Maker of lace who knows the how . . . and the why.

Author's Note

$\mathcal{W}$HILE I WAS GROWING UP, my fa
ther and mother told me numerous stories about my grandmother
Filomina and my great-grandmother Anna. Filomina did indeed grow up
in Rocca San Felice with an adopted family, and her scandalous mother
Anna periodically came from Naples to visit. Filomina was eight years
old when she and her mother last saw each other.

Filomina later heard rumors from friends that Anna had been seen on
the streets of Brooklyn in 1912 and that she was living there with her
husband and family. I believe my grandmother came to America as a
mail-order bride—perhaps, as some say, to reunite with her "real"
mother. Although she hoped to find her after settling in America, she
was newly married and living upstate. Her husband refused to let her to
go to the city to search.

Details of exactly what happened next have been lost and confused,
but the depth of my grandmother's longing for her mother survived her
death. It was that longing, and the unsolved mystery of what became of
Anna, that worked on my imagination and became the basis for

Antonio's Wife. My parents had communicated so much love and respect for these women that I couldn't resist the promptings I continually felt to put a form of their story down on paper.

Now I'm compelled to take *destino's* urging a little further. If you know of an Anna who may have come from Sant'Angelo di Lombardi, Lioni, or Rocca San Felice in Avellino around 1900 and was raising a family in Brooklyn around 1912, please contact me. It would be a fitting epilogue to find half sisters and brothers and share her story with new family members.

Destino works in mysterious ways . . . perhaps this book and you will be the crossed threads that finally tie Filomina and Anna together. It would be a fitting ending to an intricate lacework honoring my grandmother's enduring love for her *Mammina*.

Please contact me through my publisher, ReganBooks/HarperCollins.